DOG EAT DOG

By Charlot King

The Cambridge Murder Mysteries Series:

Book 1: POISON

Book 2: CURSED

Book 3: BLOOD MOON

Book 4: A CHRISTMAS MYSTERY

Book 5: VALENTINE'S DAY – KISS OF DEATH

Book 6: HOLIDAY MYSTERY

Book 7: DOG EAT DOG

Book 8: Coming Soon!

Copyright

First published 2025
Published by: Beautiful Day Cambridge Ltd
ISBN: 978-1-8384781-6-2

Illustration: Robin Howlett

DEDICATION AND THANKS

I thank all the dogs I have met while walking with Moobear over the past eight years for their waggy tails, kisses and pure joy. I dedicate this novel to Moobear, who is almost always by my side, and for that, I am eternally grateful. She has changed my life for the better and will forever be in my heart. Finally, an enormous thank you to all my readers – I am so grateful for your support and encouragement. I really hope you enjoy this as much as I've enjoyed writing it. Cxx

PROLOGUE

Dogs are man's best friend, woman's, child's. Always so pleased to see us when we come home. Love us unconditionally. They are loyal, are our protectors, sleep on our beds when we are sick, jump and run beside us when we are excited, sit quietly with us when we are tired, and never leave us – even when others do. Dogs forgive everything. Dogs don't ask for much. Forgive us when we forget to fill their water bowl or have enough money for their favourite food. Dogs are unequivocally kind. There is a reason why when you spell dog backwards, you get...

So why are there so many dogs in kill shelters right now? This story is for all the dogs...

1 IT'S ALL HOT AIR

"Hold the Puppy. C'mon. Open your arms," Terrence Montagner's PR is insistent her boss does as he is told. She sweetly cajoles. "Look at her. She's so gorgeous! A little darling sweetie-pie poppseechord." A tiny mixed breed puppy, which looks like a living teddy bear, tries to lick Terrence Montagner's chin by reaching across from the PR's arms, their little tail wagging furiously, but Terrence is having none of it.

"That's not even a word?" Terrence Montagner opens his eyes wide at his helpful assistant. "Look, I've a Saville Row suit. I can smell dog from here," Terrence Montagner pulls a face, brushes the arm of his jacket, then looks around the rescue centre as if there is a bad smell under his nose. "Remind me why we agreed to do this?" Well known for his ability to eviscerate his rivals with his acerbic tongue, Terrence Montagner is a backbench Member of Parliament. With more frenemies than true friends, he's on a charm offensive for votes today.

"Just hold this little cutie pie. Remember why we're here, darling," The PR pleads with her most persuasive, cheeky tone, nodding towards the camera. They look at the little ball of fluff wriggling in the PR's arms, both with very different expressions on their faces. "Her name is Rosie," the PR continues, now whispering, "Did you read the stats I sent you? You're trailing in the polls. Think of this as an opportunity to win back a few hearts. You're in Cambridge for the next couple of days. It won't hurt to have you associated with some cuddly puppies. Everyone loves puppies. This will make the Thursday night news. Of course." The PR looks down at the puppy. "Yes, you will. Yes, you will," kissing the puppy, who is furiously wagging her tail.

"Tell me I have space in the schedule for a stiff drink and to be left completely alone after this for the rest of Thursday," Terrence scowls, knowing he probably has other things in the diary.

The PR woman smirks, pleased about what she will say next to Terrence. "What d'you call a dog magician?" Then she waits for a few seconds, knowing he is clearly not in the mood, frowning at the puppy. "No? A labracadabrador." The PR woman laughs brazenly as she plonks the puppy into Terrence's arms and notices him visibly wince.

Seventy-one-year-old Eadie, a little grey-haired bird of a lady, who part-owns and runs the 'Rescue Me' animal rescue centre, spots the puppy in a mild amount of peril, being held like a dirty pair of football boots. She walks towards Terrence, happy to take Rosie back into the safety of her arms and delve into the pocket of her linen smock full of treats.

"Leave it!" The PR brushes Eadie's arms away, reassuring her, "It's fine. We've come to highlight your centre and all its tremendous work so that everyone on the news will see how they can help," the PR nods to the camera. "We need a puppy for that, don't we." The PR woman rolls her eyes at Eadie, acknowledging what she has to work with. She looks at Terrence's scowling face, which is, in turn, staring at the dog. She waves to grab Terrence's attention and, with her two fingers, draws up the corners of her mouth, indicating that Terrence should turn that frown upside down, noticing the camera is about to start rolling. She whispers to Terrence Montagner, "Try to be paw-lite."

"Does he have a dog of his own?" Muriel, the other co-owner of the 'Rescue Me' rescue centre, in her eighties, with skin like parchment and hair pulled back neatly into a bun, standing behind Eadie, asks worriedly. "Rosie is only fourteen weeks old. He cannot take Rosie away today. We need her back after this interview. She's not properly weaned," Muriel exaggerates to the PR, thinking how inappropriate an owner Terrence seems, devoid of any warmth towards Rosie.

"What breed is she?" The PR, completely uninterested, asks, again stopping Muriel this time from going back to rescue Rosie.

"We don't know—a mix. Maybe a bit of Pomeranian, and we think a bit of Jack Russell? But it could be something else. The puppies were handed in, not born here."

"How sweet." The PR tries to imagine the moment when two different breeds might have met in the park or woods. But her thoughts are interrupted by the reporter, who is walking over to stand near Terrence Montagner, having looked at her questions and now holding the mic up to Terrence. The boom is raised, and the light on top of the camera is switched on as the operator lifts it onto his shoulders and hits record.

What follows for the next few minutes is a white, privileged, snooty sixty-something-year-old – overly educated with a clipped upper-class voice –mansplaining the socio-economic situation in the city of Cambridge and stating how he and his party are the only option to put things back on track, even though they've already had over a decade to try. There are a few nods from the reporter, who looks jaded, seeing this bullshit for what it is, a pack of lies. The camera operator smirks, noticing that Rosie, the puppy, has started to wee while Terrence Montagner continues his brawling waffle. The PR woman shakes her head and hopes that this makes him more relatable but doubts it, having already spent what feels like more than a lifetime with this unredeemable man. Then, out of nowhere, in the concluding remarks of the interview, Terrence says to camera, "I think I'm going to adopt a couple of fish today. I've always wanted some fish."

"Fish?" The PR woman frowns, confused. "Could he not have chosen a more adorable pet? One that people don't associate with chips?" She says quietly to herself as Terrence, who has now finished the interview, chucking Rosie into Eadie's welcoming arms, takes off the microphone and makes sure that the camera has been lowered and there is no red button on the side before he speaks, remembering his last but one interview where he forgot, went to the loo, and trash talked the place to high heaven. He spent a month explaining that he was going through andropause and how men of a certain age have hormonal imbalances, too. It's not just women. But then had to suffer the backlash from women genuinely going through the menopause. What a debacle.

"Can you direct me to the fish?" Terrence ignores his PR and looks at Eadie expectantly, exuding an air of impatience and entitlement.

"You didn't mention our fundraiser when you spoke just now," Eadie replies, extremely disappointed. "That's why we agreed to this in the first place?" She looks confused and questioning at the PR woman.

"Sorry, you know what these things are like? The reporter just wanted to hear about all the problems in the party. Never even let Terrence get a word in. We'll come back, I promise," the PR woman lies through her teeth.

"Oh, well, I suppose nothing changes," Eadie relents from any attempt to show how cross she is with them. What is the point? "Okay, well, we have some fish actually. There have been quite a lot of people having to hand over their animals recently because they cannot afford to look after them anymore, what with the cost of living crisis," Eadie glances at Muriel, who has sat down behind the counter, now holding Rosie.

"Madam, the cost of living is neither my nor my party's fault." Terrence looks at Eadie and smiles, waiting to be taken to the fish. So Eadie, who really cannot be bothered arguing with this man, agrees she will take him. At this point, the PR woman can see the reporter leaving with her crew and wants to catch them.

"Catch you at the constituency!" She shouts back at Terrence, who has started to follow Eadie towards some fish tanks along a corridor, completely ignoring his PR.

"We will have to inspect your home and check you have a heated fish tank. These fish are tropical and need a lot of care. Cleaning the tanks, the right temperature," Eadie explains as they walk along the corridor.

"Oh yes, I have all that," Terrence brushes away her concerns. "State of the art."

Eadie follows Terrence, who has increased his pace and marched off in the wrong direction. He stops by the locked door to the cat shelter. "Can you open this door?" He looks at his watch and sighs, frustrated.

"We cannot let you in there. That's where the cats are. You want fish," Eadie hurries, trying to catch up.

"Might as well browse. Maybe I'll find the cat of my dreams," he laughs to himself, folding his arms.

"I'm sorry, Mr Montagner, but we don't like to disturb the animals at this time of day. There are special viewing times. And you'd not mentioned cats. Animals are not creatures we can pick and choose on a whim. We need to know that you're serious. Now, you said that you'd like to see the fish. I can take you there briefly, but we're just closing for lunch. We will need you to fill out the forms and check your home. You cannot take any animals home with you today."

"What? How do you expect people to rescue animals when you don't even let them look at them? This is ridiculous!" Terrence

Montagner's face begins to turn red.

"You don't really rescue them. They rescue you. You can look at the fish now, but you've gone the wrong way down this corridor to the cats, like I say. We need to turn back to the entrance and take the direction of Shelter C Wing."

"I haven't got time for this. Just let me in here now. I've changed my mind. I definitely want a cat." Terrence Montagner is not used to people saying no to him and feels in the mood for a fight. He has no intention of adopting a cat, but he was displeased with having to come to this smelly centre in the first place. He's sure as hell not going to be bossed about by some old biddy.

"I'm sorry, but we don't want you frightening the cats," Eadie replies calmly but firmly. "Perhaps the interview was a little much? Maybe come back another day. You're welcome to make an appointment to see the cats. We just don't like people who, you know, just want to be a voyeur and don't have any intention of rehoming. You understand, I'm sure."

"Not really, no? I don't understand at all. I've said I'd like to look at the cats with a view to adopting," Terrence Montagner says, using his most irritated voice and almost stamping his feet.

"I'm sorry. But maybe you're not in the right frame of mind." Eadie now feels a little nervous about this tall man, who looks quite strong. She wonders whether she should just walk away, back to reception, and let him calm down alone.

"Right frame of mind? Oh, stuff it! I don't have time for this. I'll buy an expensive Persian and feed the fish to him one by one!" Terrence Montagner storms off, leaving Eadie in some state of upset.

"What an utterly unpleasant man." Eadie says, having followed Terrence Montagner back towards the exit, leaving some distance between them, and watching him storm out towards the entrance of the 'Rescue Me' rescue centre. Eadie catches up with Muriel. The two women make a fuss of Rosie before putting her back into her pen and try to forget all about the nasty man and the unwanted fuss from the TV crew. Muriel takes great pleasure in turning over the 'closed for lunch' sign.

"I'm glad we didn't give him any fish if all he wanted to do was feed them to cats," Muriel replies, her eyes wide open, shaking her head. They watch Terrence storm away, his neck, and they presume his face, still blood red with rage.

2 LAVENHAM

Inspector Bob Abley has driven to Lavenham countless times for business and pleasure. A seasoned copper, crinkled and tanned like a walnut, fifty-something with a kind demeanour, he has certainly done the rounds. Having shut out and long forgotten most of the murders and crimes that have pulled him away from the city to help on local cases here, he most remembers a more recent romantic weekend visit, perhaps only a few years ago, with his now ex-wife Maureen. As he drives along the High Street, he is transported back to the smells, feels and comfort of a trip they took together. Staying at The Swan Inn, a splendid building with a black and white Tudor exterior. The kind of place where they put chocolates on the pillows and leave bathing products that smell of tangerines and spice in the bathrooms. He remembers mooching, arm in arm, enjoying finding independent shops in the tiny alleys and streets, buying Maureen a pretty scarf covered in blue butterflies, walking past the medieval homes which lean precariously over pavements with their crooked walls, and how they both sat for afternoon tea behind the impressive Guildhall, within its National Trust garden where birds sing and children run around holding their etchings and brass rubbings.

This Saturday morning, those fond rose-tinted memories are now long gone as he pulls into the carpark of a small gothic church, down a quiet street on the edge of this village, where his next thought is of the weddings this church must have seen over the hundreds of years. All those dreams. He bets the happy couples would not have gotten divorced so quickly in times gone by, where vows meant something, not to be thrown away so casually, not after all that love and effort had been placed into building their meaningful relationships with each other. He bet those people would not have tossed out their marriages for some dickhead neighbour next door. No, he is confident that other couples could not have been so cruel. Nor would they have stamped on one another's hearts so callously or thoughtlessly and left the other broken, unable to function or appreciate sunshine, rainbows, or moonbeams anymore. No, but that is precisely what happened to Bob Abley, who was left in a state where everything was slightly more grey than before. Well, not a little, a vast amount more. Huge amount. No, those people in the past would have stuck together through all the tough times because it was in their ruddy vows. Part of the bloody deal! And their other half would have at least shown them some warning that things were not good before they chose to abandon them, just like that. Yes, those who married in this church would have protected their marriages and held them sacred and special.

From inside his parked car, Bob Abley turns off the engine. He pulls down his windscreen visor to restrict the view for anyone looking into the front of the car from where he stares back out at the church door. Out of the corner of his eye, he spots a limousine pulling up outside. The shiny black menacing vehicle, somehow out of kilter with the hollyhocks and gladioli framing the church walls, pulls to a standstill. He watches as it crunches over gravel, then realises that it is a bride's car, causing him to sink further into his seat and, for some reason unknown to him, activate central locking (perhaps deep down stopping him from jumping out and doing something he might regret). An old man steps out of the limo and walks around to open the far side door. At that moment, Abley's breath is stolen. Maureen.

Maureen is wearing white. He thought only brides getting married for the first time could do that. Also, he did not know you could marry in a church if divorced, especially if the ink is not even dry. The vision of this bride, whom he knows all too well, delivers a punch to his stomach, but his eyes are glued and refuse to blink. Not thirty feet away, he watches her holding flowers that trail down at least three feet in an elaborate posy as she smiles at her father. He remembers how when they married, she was happy with some wildflowers from the back of her mother's wall in the fields that ran onto Fen Ditton. She looked a picture back then. He does not recognise this woman with all her fancy bride paraphernalia, a tiara, and a veil. When did she start wearing four-inch heels? He looks down at what he is wearing today. His golf moccasins, a pair of chinos, and a baby blue Harrington jacket covering his white T. Hardly dressed for the occasion. His mind is in conflict with his heart and feet. Abley leaves about thirty seconds for Maureen to enter the church, holding her father's arm, then checks his messy brown mop of hair in the car mirror and tries to tidy it with his fingers, along with his unruly eyebrows, before following them.

Sergeant Lemon pulls into the church car park just in time to see his Inspector open the heavy wooden door and disappear inside. What the... Lemon is finding this whole episode unsurprisingly sad. Having returned from his two-week leadership course, he is trying to remember how the skills might help him cope with rescuing his boss from witnessing the marriage of his boss's former wife to his boss's former next-door neighbour. Lemon sighs and looks down at the sandwiches and tins of pop he bought to console Abley in case he had not been too late. Lemon had best laid plans to pull his Inspector away before he made a fool of himself. But with that gone out the window, Lemon knows there is no time to avert a crisis and jumps out to follow his Inspector inside, glad he is in plain clothes today, as the church door bangs behind him.

Stepping inside, Lemon's eyes need a few seconds to acclimatise to the gloom, his feet creeping across the stone floor which seems intent on picking up every squeak from his running shoes. His lanky frame crouching, so as not to be noticed, he spots Abley sitting in a pew near the back, so slips in behind. As Lemon gets his bearing, he becomes acutely aware that the vicar, speaking from the chancel, with bride and groom on either side, is already into the meat of the ceremony. Oh no. He is perhaps only a foot away from his boss and can hear Abley sigh and fidget through the words, and then it comes to the part, "Should anyone here present know of any reason that this couple should not be joined in holy matrimony, speak now or forever hold your peace," and he watches his Inspector begin to stand up. Lemon instinctively reacts and roughly pulls Abley's collar and drags him out of the church. Both are unaware that the congregation, on hearing the kerfuffle, has temporarily turned around, but when the door at the back of the church swings shut, turn back towards the vicar, who continues. The groom breathes a sigh of relief that it might just have been a trapped pigeon.

Outside, the two men stand alone in the glaring sunshine, a little in shock at what just happened and what could have just happened.

"What were you thinking?" Lemon finally lets go of Abley, glad, at this moment, that he is taller and perhaps a little stronger.

Abley shakes his head, his tanned face creased and exuding warmth and sadness. In truth, he wasn't thinking. He was just acting, following his feet to find the woman he has spent most of his adult life with.

"You followed me?" Abley looks at Lemon's car on the far side of the church car park.

"I'm glad I did. You nearly made a complete –"

"Yes, alright, alright." Abley shakes his head and momentarily frowns. It is unclear whether he is angry with Lemon or with himself. Tipping his head back, he looks up at the clouds. There are very few in the sky today. Abley fights back the tears and an uncontrollable urge to scream, instead awkwardly joking, "All in all, a perfect day to get married, don't you think?"

"Oh, I don't know. It might rain," Lemon replies, his smile a little crooked, aware this is a beautiful warm English summer's day, worried for the fragile situation they are both now in, having one eye on the door in case Abley decides to bolt back inside.

"A bit of thunder and lightning wouldn't go a miss." Abley walks over to the churchyard wall and jumps up to sit while he attempts to recover from what nearly happened. Lemon follows Abley but remains standing. Although temporarily relieved, he hopes they can leave soon before the bride comes out with her groom. Leaning against the wall, Lemon offers his boss a peanut butter sandwich from his pocket.

"Hungry?"

Abley looks at the sandwiches, then at Lemon, then gestures for a sandwich. Lemon unwraps the silver foil and takes one himself. As they munch on the half-white half-brown bread, Abley shakes his head.

"What did I nearly do in there?" he clocks Lemon, giving him a look that confirms he thinks Abley's an idiot. "Did you see Maureen all in white? What was that?"

"She looked like a meringue," Lemon replies immediately.

"They say love is blind, but marriage is definitely an eye opener." Abley pops more sandwich in his mouth. The two friends say nothing for a while, the silence deafening.

"Why d'you think I'm not married?" Lemon finally comments, opening a can of cola for Abley, which shoots out from the pressure of being shaken in his pocket during the altercation.

"There are only two times of the day when I'm stressed at the moment," Abley says, taking a glug of the cola. In the day and at night," Abley looks contemplatively back at the church door, imagining what is happening inside now: the photographs, the smiles, the coos, the air of happiness.

"Don't take this the wrong way, and I might be out of place–" Lemon begins.

"Why do people always say that? I'm immediately going to take it the wrong way and think you're out of place." Then Abley munches on his sandwich. "I do prefer crunchy. Something to get your teeth into. And, what is with the half white, half brown bread situation?"

"Just that, have you thought about getting some help?" Lemon pauses, then continues looking directly at Abley. "See a therapist or something?" Lemon scrunches up his eyes, making a face to show Abley that he means well but is serious about the suggestion.

"I've already spent hundreds on a therapist. You know, all they did was listen." Abley pops in the last of the bread.

"I know we're in Lavenham, but it's pretty medieval for her to send you a wedding invite." Lemon waits for Abley to agree, but there is silence for at least a minute.

"She didn't," Abley finally admits.

"How are you... I mean, how did you find out?" Lemon thinks this is worse than he originally thought.

"Stalked her online," Abley replies flatly. "Like a weirdo. I also know that her flowers are from 'One and Floral' and that she bought her dress from 'Marry-Go-Round Bridal Boutique.' Did you know women sell their wedding dresses when they divorce so other women can buy them? Nothing lasts. And all the photographs and preparations. All the excitement. Did she need to be so blatant?" Abley pauses. "Was it to rub it in my face? I mean, my kids were tagged. What did she expect?" Abley is quiet again, the reality of her cruelty sinking in. "Though I did notice that they haven't liked anything she posted."

"Well, you know that's all sorts of wrong. I mean stalking, not the posting," Lemon hates to remind Abley that they are coppers. But coppers they are. "And I'm sure the last thing she's doing is thinking of you." Lemon realises how hurtful that could seem as soon as the words escape his mouth. "I mean, her photos were not meant to hurt you. Of course, they weren't."

"You think?" Abley wonders. It all just does not sit well in his mind. "I feel like Pooh Bear, you know? When he got stuck in that hole. I can see Maureen, but I can't reach her."

Lemon looks at a broken man in his boss, sitting, lifeless on the wall, looking more pale than he has ever seen him. So, he tries to lighten the mood. A latecomer to the wedding, wearing a bright mauve dress and matching hat, walks across the car park towards the church door.

"When I saw you in there, for a minute, I thought I'd entered the mad hatter's tea party," Lemon nods at the hat disappearing on the head of the woman into the church. "I half expected a giant rabbit to run in for a very important date. What is it about weddings and hats? Really. Who thinks they look good in a hat?" Lemon thinks how much he hated his old constable's custodian hat and shivers. He thinks it is unfair that they can now just wear the bump caps.

"Well, good luck to them. He'll be the one now to appreciate her extensive collection of porcelain unicorns." Abley looks bitterly at the church door, then down at Lemon's silver foil parcel, now balancing on the wall, and sees another round of peanut butter sandwiches and points. Lemon nods, so Abley picks one up and takes a large bite.

"It wasn't a waste," Lemon says thoughtfully.

"No, I really like them. Thank you," Abley chews his peanut butter sandwich.

"I mean your marriage," Lemon sips his cola and nudges his boss's arm. "You have two beautiful children and were happy for a long time. I saw it."

"What has that leadership course done to

you? Turned you into a wise owl." Abley pauses, then jokes, "Did you see that dirty scoundrel's beard? He could hide snacks in it." Abley sighs, realising he is being bitter about the groom, then finally acknowledges Lemon's words. "I know. Was I too busy?"

"Probably. The sin of a copper," Lemon replies lightly. "But she knew who you were when she married you. What does the dirty scoundrel do?"

"Sells windows. I mean, if we're talking competition?" Abley notices the church windows, which are really ornate and multi-paned with bright colours. "Not like those. More like bathrooms, backdoors, conservatories. Really naff ones, you know? Cheap." Abley does his best to muster a sneer, but it is replaced by munching.

"Best to forget both of them. Neither are worth your energy or thoughts now," Lemon says kindly, taking the last peanut butter sandwich.

"Is that what they teach now on leadership training? You know, I expect you to address the Super now starting every conversation with 'As a leader...'"

"Deal. And, as your leader right now, I say we split before they all come out," Lemon picks up the silver foil and nods towards the cars.

"D'you think anyone saw me?" Abley suddenly has a moment of sheer panic at what he just did.

"No, you're good," Lemon replies reassuringly. "We were a blur."

"Thank you," Abley looks at Lemon, takes a big sigh, his face full of gratitude.

"S'ok. I was rightly steered to save you by our own true guru, the one and only Prof. She told me the locale," Lemon raises an eyebrow at Abley. "Have you called her since she's been back from Italy?" They both think of Professor Elizabeth Green.

"I think she's still mad at me about that," Abley shakes his head.

"On holiday with her grandson and being made to get involved in a murder case while she was just trying to enjoy the sights. Hmm, I wonder why?"

It wasn't me. It was Raynott. You know that. And anyway, she could have said no."

"She did say no. Multiple times. To the Super, to you, to me. Godric told me in no uncertain terms. Actually, his language was more 'eff off, old chap, or I'll stick it to you'," Lemon tries to mimic Godric's accent.

"It got messy," Abley acknowledges, "But I didn't drag her into it. You know who's really to blame." Abley channels his anger of the day towards his boss.

"The annoying little tarsier," Lemon agrees. They both think of Superintendent Raynott.

"Precisely. Causing all the damage. He's why I'll have to work hard to rebuild my relationship with Elizabeth. She's a ruddy good consultant. I need her." Then Abley looks at Lemon's tall, thin stature and, changing the subject, asks, "Have you grown while you were away on this course?"

"Groan," Lemon replies, shaking his head. Then thinks about his Inspector's close relationship with Elizabeth and how she helps him on most murder cases these days and tends to solve everything before either of them has found their bearings. "Maybe don't leave it too late." Changing the subject, Lemon pulls Abley off the wall. "Come on. Or this cunning plan to maintain your dignity will have all been for nothing. Eating peanut butter sandwiches outside your ex-wife's new wedding is hardly the place to be seen. And, surely, you're wasting precious time when you could be on the golf course. It's Saturday. I hear your course rating is two at the moment."

"Where did you hear that?" Abley asks innocently.

Abley follows Lemon to their respective cars. As he slumps into the driver's seat of his car, he looks down at his phone. Seven missed calls from Superintendent Raynott.

3 CAMBRIDGE POLICE STATION

After a swift pint on the outskirts of Lavenham, Inspector Bob Abley and Sergeant Lemon arrive back at the Cambridge Police Station HQ on Parker's Piece. The large windows in the Inspector's office afford a view through the trees across the Piece to see people playing frisbee and enjoying picnics on the grass this warm summer afternoon.

"Where have you been?" Superintendent Raynott frowns at the Inspector, talking to him like Abley's a child. "Did Lemon have to retrieve you from the nineteenth again? Clearly, you're not answering your ruddy phone!" At five feet tall and no more, Raynott's eyes, like large plates, dart about the room as if being spun at the circus.

"There's no need for that," Abley smiles and tries not to react, popping a mint into his mouth. "I'm actually on my day off, but came in with Lemon as we bumped into one another. He's just back from his leadership skills training course. Two weeks in sunny Manchester. I thought I'd introduce him to the new Constable so we can all hit the ground running on Monday."

"I take it you've heard about Terrence Montagner's disappearance, have you? Not been seen since Thursday," Raynott replies, completely uninterested in whether Abley is supposed to be at work. "Press have picked it up. His own office tipped us off as to his disappearance."

"Yes, exactly," Abley replies, lying through his teeth, glancing at an open newspaper on the desk with a two-page spread about a missing MP. "Not much to go on at the moment." Abley picks up the paper and hurriedly reads the news. Mr Terrence Montagner, Member of Parliament for Cambridge South West, disappeared midweek. "His PR has not heard of him since she was expecting him to return to the constituency," he quickly reads aloud.

"We were speaking about it just now, Super. The Inspector has been thinking of nothing else," Lemon lies to the Superintendent to protect his boss.

"Quite," Raynott replies, now aware Abley is not technically at work. "Well, it was called in yesterday evening to the station. It does look like he might really be missing. A Westminster member. Missing! We need to get onto this straight away." Raynott looks at Abley like a small, angry marsupial about to nip at his ankles.

"News reports intimate Montagner was being investigated for hiding money, not paying taxes, and inferring he's absconded," Lemon suggests to the Superintendent, having read the news this morning but decided not to burden Abley with it today and now covering madly.

"No speculation, please. Just results," Raynott replies with a clipped tone, then realises he hasn't asked Lemon about his training. "Good, was it?" He asks, as an afterthought.

"As a new leader, I can say the leadership skills course was very instructive. Now I have an insight into the challenges you're dealing with daily, Sir," Lemon replies vaguely.

"Right, right. Yes," Raynott answers, disinterested.

"Well, I'm here. Might has well chip in. We can take this," Abley nods to Lemon that he will help.

"Right, let's all get on with it. Chop, chop. The last thing I want is a call from Westminster, or worse," Raynott adds. "I know his ruddy whip. He's like a pterodactylus. One swoop, and I've lost my head." Raynott winks at the junior Constable he hasn't even bothered to introduce to Lemon, who is sitting in the corner of Inspector Abley's room and whom Lemon can't stop glancing at. The Constable nods and beams, watching

Raynott leave.

"Would that be so bad?" Lemon says quietly to himself, thinking about a Superintendent with just a body, his bloody head floating below the claws of a dinosaur, eyes still blinking in surprise.

"Where are my manners?" Abley looks at Lemon to explain the presence of the new Constable. "Meet junior Constable Jack Love. Jack, meet Sergeant Lemon." Abley watches as the two police officers eye each other up and can only guess that Lemon is judging Love's stocky appearance, with muscles bulging through his shirt and a smile revealing super white veneers.

"Constable Love has come from the Met for a week as part of his summer work experience. All high stakes, high action to sleepy Cambridge." Abley thinks back to when he spent a few months himself, when young, on the streets of London as a bobby, dealing with drug crime, theft and murder. And how happy he is to live in this beautiful city now, where the pace of life is altogether more respectable, and even if still dealing with drug crime, theft and murder, it is with an altogether far prettier backdrop and close to the best golf club. Abley notices both men are now staring at him. "The Super thought it wise for me to mentor the Constable while he is here, and we're getting on like a house on fire, aren't we, Jacky boy," Abley smiles, and Constable Love beams at Lemon like an eight-week-old puppy, the muscles in his cheeks pulsating with expectation that they will both be best of friends. Love does not take his eyes off Lemon, as he pulls open a desk drawer and starts to rattle items in it, looking for something. "Pay no attention," Abley whispers to Lemon. "I met his father, who came up for a day trip. Completely the same expression. I thought I was about to be squeezed with love. Ah, Love, love. That makes sense."

"Good to meet you, Constable," Lemon says, holding out a hand to shake in his best leadership skills learnt way.

"I can't find my vape," Love replies, taking Lemon's hand to shake, then putting his hands on his head endearingly and looking around, his arm muscles bulging as he keeps looking lovingly at Lemon.

"Right, Constable. I don't suppose you've done anything on the missing MP? While you've been here this morning, and I've, well, been out of the office?" Abley asks.

Constable Love switches his gaze back to Abley and then turns his computer screen to face the room.

"The MP, Terrence Montagner, did a TV interview, Sir," Constable Love explains, stroking his chin. "I'm sorry, I haven't downloaded the file yet for you. Would it be okay to look here? Sorry."

"Great, where?" Abley asks. Love presses play and gets up to leave the room.

"I've seen it five times now. You have some

peace to watch it. I'll be back in a minute," he says apologetically before heading out to charm the overweight officer on reception with gym tips in order to raid his snack drawer.

"Who's that?" Lemon is flabbergasted by Constable Love's sweet nature. "So Raynott's sent in a spy with charm?"

They both start to watch Terrence Montagner's interview at the 'Rescue Me' rescue centre in Cambridge. They notice how the MP squirms with the puppy in his hands. "And I intend to adopt some fish. I've always wanted to bring a bit of wildlife into my home and help animals who need rescuing," Terrence signs off his interview in a wholly unbelievable fashion.

"Fish?" Lemon looks down and spots Constable Love's notebook. "Looks like Sergeant Love has already been making notes on the case." Lemon starts to read them to Abley. "Apparently, Mr Montagner has two ex-wives, and neither has had anything to do with him in years. Looks like Jacky boy here has already called them. One in America and one in South Africa," Lemon turns the page in the notebook. "Looks like the one in America was cross at being woken up. And it looks like the MP's PR gave in his phone, and Jack has it from this," Lemon pulls out the police phone docket then searches the Constable's desk and draws for Terrence Montagner's phone. Love comes back in, realising what they are looking for. He takes back his notebook, smiling at

Lemon.

"I've sent the MP's mobile to tech. They're unlocking it," Love explains helpfully.

"The wives?" Abley asks.

"Both have alibis, Sir," the Constable replies.

"No need to call me Sir. Inspector will do," Abley tells Love. Love nods, then opens a big bag of crisps from reception and starts munching loudly. Smells of bacon or prawn cocktail or cheese, it is hard to tell, waft over towards Lemon and Abley. Love holds out the crisps to share. Lemon shakes his head, but Abley takes a handful. "You know, these have forty-five different chemicals to make this flavour?" Abley reads the packet.

"Really?" the Constable's eyes light up. "Cool. How do you know that, Sir?"

Now it is Lemon's turn to roll his eyes at Love's seeming naivety.

"His PR said he had a meeting with a think tank in Cambridge about democracy later that day but didn't turn up to that either," Love opens his notebook wide to show Abley.

"Do you have the PR phone number?" Lemon asks, still leaning over the Constable's desk.

"I've got all the details. I can share them," the Constable replies, then starts to leave the room again, "Going for a break. I'll bring back sticky buns," he announces and has gone.

"What the hell? What's he doing in your room? Raynott can't take your putting green away?" Lemon looks at the floor and notices Abley's long fake putting green, metal hole and putters that have been in his office for years have all been tidied away into the corner.

"Raynott would like to crush my dreams and sip on my tears," Abley shakes his head, then chuckles. "Good job he can't reach, isn't it."

"And Love. A bit much?" Lemon says, not enjoying his encounter with Love, perhaps a little jealous that he is so nice, then guilty that he is jealous, especially after his leadership course.

"Well, all his emails have two kisses, so he has a certain something. He'll go places," Abley replies.

"Yes, but will they be legal places?" Lemon narrows his eyes. "I mean, he's left his post to buy sticky buns?"

"Let's be kind and lead by example to young Jacky boy and be the best versions of ourselves. That's all we can do," Abley smiles.

"You think he's just missing? Or," Lemon pulls his finger across his throat to indicate deceased.

"A politician is missing, Lemon. Missing."

"Yes, but–"

"Let's keep our opinions to ourselves. Quite frankly, the way I feel today, the last thing I need is a murdered MP." Abley breathes in deeply.

"If anyone can find him, you can," Lemon

tries to buoy his Inspector, but at the same time feels quite concerned about whether this time he is up to the task. All things considered.

4 SUPPER AT ST ANDREW'S COLLEGE

Professor Elizabeth Green is already wearing her gown for tonight's formal supper at St Andrew's College, Cambridge. Her thick brown curls are a little unruly, her linen green sundress peeping out underneath, a little muddy from earlier gardening, not that she cares. She is delaying the inevitable on this balmy summer's evening, taking a moment beside the pond on a back lawn, enjoying the rare ducks of this beautiful College on St Andrew's Street, and avoiding entering the dark, heavy, thick-set wooden panelled Dining Hall. Not to be pipped in the beauty stakes by her own College, Granta, St Andrew's is, nevertheless, one of her favourites, not least because it is home to esteemed Fellow and Professor of Classics Emily Masters, a woman who always looks like she could have walked straight off the cover of Vogue, but most importantly is Elizabeth's best friend.

"The mandarins are doing well this year," Emily points to little ducklings at the pond's edge as she walks over to hug her friend, "their plumage will begin to change, of course."

Elizabeth observes Emily's nails, which glisten vermilion against the grass, raising a thought. "Where are the teals this summer? I haven't seen them." Elizabeth receives Emily's hug and pats her friend's back.

"Oh, they're about. They like to wander. Exotic and contrary. Rather greedy in their grasp of all the specialness, I think." Emily replies, looking up at the blue summer sky, "Such a beautiful evening. I sometimes wish it was summer every day."

"You're looking well," Elizabeth stands back and observes her friend, having picked up the dogs when she returned from Italy but not properly spent time in Emily's company since. She notices Emily's suntan and soft white silk shirt. "Summer suits you."

"One cannot give England the credit for that. Rather, two weeks on the Amalfi coast, thank you very much, Cuthbert. Literally, as soon as you took the dogs back, we jumped on a plane," Emily pauses to adjust her jewellery. "He has his uses, you know."

"Ah, new trinkets," Elizabeth acknowledges Emily's expensive bracelet. "No murders while you were there, I bet," Elizabeth sighs, happy for her friend but missing Italy more than she thought she would.

"None, other than murdering the food every evening," Emily holds her stomach. "We had a chef in our hotel. I'd have smuggled him back in my suitcase if he'd have let me. I would have done things for him, just for his food." Emily pulls a suggestive face.

"I presume you wouldn't do the same for the chef here," Elizabeth says, looking at the door leading into the Dining Hall at St Andrew's, where graduates and undergrads have started filing through in their robes.

"Robert is good, but that level of intimacy has to be earned," Emily replies.

"I noticed the seating plan has Atticus Stamp suppering tonight. Enough to put anyone off their food. Why didn't you warn me?" Elizabeth frowns at her friend.

"You wouldn't have come," Emily raises her eyebrows while watching a pair of mallards waddling towards the pond.

"They've sat me right beside him. Do they not know me by now?" Elizabeth thinks about the Head of Kitchen at St Andrew's and her past conversations with him, trying to get him to introduce a more expansive vegan menu. "He's just punishing me, I know it. Swap places, else I'll throttle him." Elizabeth bends down and places some seeds from her pocket on a stone by the pond. She watches as the mallards rush over and start to peck.

"If I do, you'll be seated next to Logan Lax," Emily admits more detail about the evening.

"Oh, this just gets better and better." Elizabeth's forehead furrows further.

"He likes to make an entrance. Off the seating plan. A surprise. The Master is simply in love with him," Emily reminds Elizabeth.

"With his billions, I suppose any Master would be. What will it be this time, another wing? New tennis courts? An extension on the library?" The two best friends look at each other, anticipating the lively discussions that will ensue and whether they have the stomach for it. They stand together, pleased to be in each other's company but a little glued to the grass.

"Remind me why we're here?" Elizabeth watches ducks eat the seed.

"I thought you could share the burden of my duty. Without your company, it's really dreary, stuck at top table. I wouldn't mind if we could mix with the freshers. Most intelligent bunch this year," Emily mulls her responsibilities.

"Some evenings, supper really should be brought out onto the lawn, don't you think? It would all be so lovely out here. I'd be happy to carry my chair." Elizabeth is about to detail the merits of carrying all the tables and chairs out, but her thoughts are interrupted by the Master, who skips up to them and pulls them along into the Dining Hall.

"Chop, chop. Yes, before you ask, we have a vegan menu," the Master specifically looks at Elizabeth, waiting for a thank you that never comes.

"About time, too," is all that Elizabeth can muster. She is unsure about this evening or spending too much time around people from whom she would ordinarily run a mile. Having returned from Italy, where despite initially going on holiday, she spent much of the time working on a case for the Cambridge Police, she is now taking time away from work, College life, and everything else to recharge. Things were going well so far. She has spent time in her beloved garden with her wonderful animals. And up until Godric, her grandson, decided to go back to Italy for the summer, she had spent a couple of idyllic months sharing suppers with him at home. Everything was beginning to settle and starting to feel just about okay. And she really hopes that tonight will not rock all that. More than anything in the world, Elizabeth wants peace and quiet.

*

White linen and silverware cover the high

table, adorned with posies of wildflowers from the meadow on the front Court. Serving staff are already fussing, pouring wine, bringing bread, and adjusting little bowls of olives and nuts to be within closer reach of VIP fingers. A server brings out miniature flans and soups at one end of the table, and the aromas build. Sure enough, Atticus Stamp is already seated, the media mogul, the empire-building newspaper television station, and the radio entertainment man, one of the most powerful in the world. To look at him, you wouldn't know it. With a lazy eye and balding hair, he wears an off-the-peg suit under his creased gown and a bad haircut, perhaps the only tell-tale sign of his immense fortune is his trophy girlfriend (not wife, as he's not doing that again). Daisy, thirty-something, has all the trademarks of having lived a life of luxury. Elizabeth finds it difficult to stop staring. Not at her couture clothing, which must run into the tens of thousands, but at her blue eyes. Like the colour that only children paint the Caribbean sea. Daisy smiles at Elizabeth, and there it is. That winning smile, dimples and all. Atticus certainly did not fall for her scintillating conversation, as Daisy asks loudly, "Do penguins have knees? I've always wondered."

"Yes. Yes, they have knees," Elizabeth replies, ignoring where her nameplate instructs her to sit and instead sitting next to Daisy—girl power.

"Oh, are you a biologist?"

"I study plants," Elizabeth explains.

"Oh, well, that's easier, isn't it?" Daisy replies.

"Why?" Elizabeth is curious about this woman's certainty, to be so sure of facts.

"They don't move. I mean, it's easier to study something that's not always running away or about to eat you, isn't it," Daisy laughs with abandon.

"Plants move," Elizabeth replies kindly, picking up an olive with a cocktail stick and nodding for a 'little stout' to the waiter, who potters off to get her 'off menu' drink of choice.

"Don't be silly," Daisy laughs.

"Seriously, take the Codariocalyx Motorius," Elizabeth raises her eyebrows wide.

"What?" Daisy's smile drops. "What's that when it's at home?" Daisy moves a roll around on her side plate with no intention of eating it.

"The telegraph plant, you can see it move with the naked eye," Elizabeth continues, smiling at Emily.

"Yes, but not along the ground," Daisy frowns, confused. "Maybe waving about in the wind." Daisy waves her hand about, trying to emulate tall grasses bending over.

"Pumpkin, sweet potato, strawberries," Elizabeth continues. "They all move."

"They can't run away or chase you though, can they?" Daisy asks, believing anything

Elizabeth would tell her.

"You win. You've got me," Elizabeth replies, not wanting to make Daisy look bad.

"I mean, I don't want to start getting scared of strawberries," Daisy sounds relieved like a small child and smiles warmly at Elizabeth. Elizabeth feels like she's had a spell cast upon her, so much so that she fails to notice Logan Lax walking towards the top table to take his seat, to sharp intakes of breath around the room. A waiter whispers something to the Master, who then gets up and quickly marches out of the dining hall, looking angry.

"I'm coming back, Logan. Don't go anywhere. We need to talk," the Master winks at Logan, who smiles and then turns to look at his favourite woman.

"Daisy," Logan drools. "Mwah, mwah. You look divine." Unlike Atticus Stamp, Logan is dressed impeccably. His gown looks like it has been hand-stitched by the finest French designers. A dark grey suit underneath is understated and perhaps could itself have an agent. His strong mop of blonde hair and large blue eyes exude cutting-edge sophistication. Logan leans across to a waiter, who then hurries off and brings back a case of expensive champagne, pops a cork and pours.

"Dear boy, are you trying to get my Daisy drunk?" Atticus observes Logan indicating to the waiter that Daisy's glass should be continually topped up with the best champagne. Emily is quite pleased to be offered a glass and shrugs at Elizabeth.

"When in Rome," Emily whispers to her friend.

"I bought vineyards in the north of the Champagne-Ardenne, in La Montagne de Reims, last year," Logan replies proudly to anyone who will listen.

"Aren't you busy enough running a fashion empire?" Emily asks, but Logan turns to speak with Atticus, completely ignoring Emily (who raises her eyebrows at Elizabeth), but clinks her glass at the waiter to keep her topped up.

At that moment, a meek-looking man, Professor Martin Smith, pencil-thin, with a mop of jet-black hair, unibrow, and a fixed expression of kindness, joins the table. Elizabeth is pleased that, having moved seats, he sits beside her on the other side.

"Sorry I'm late," he apologises to the table.

"Hello, Martin," Elizabeth greets this Fellow of St Andrews. "Long time," she says, ironically, seeing him most days on Jesus Green with his dog. "At least I have one good man sitting beside me."

"Yes, quite a delight to have your company," he replies. "Do either of these men pay any taxes in this country?" Martin whispers sweetly to Elizabeth about Atticus Stamp and Logan Lax. "Shall we make a citizen's arrest? You work for the police. I'm sure there's mounting evidence of fraud, deviance, underhandedness and worse." He raises his eyebrows and beams at Elizabeth with the innocent chuckle of a young schoolboy.

"I've been told that if you count in your head for long enough, you can make anything disappear," Elizabeth replies wryly to Martin.

"That would be a dream. I'm starting now. Disappear, moguls," Martin pops a small quiche into his mouth as he sits, having stretched across to get what his stomach could not ignore. He uses his fingers to start counting.

"How lovely is this college?" Daisy addresses Martin sweetly. "We're always in London, which is so loud, or New York, even louder."

"It must be nice, though, dating a billionaire. How many houses does Atticus actually own?" Martin asks, his eyes wide with the expectation of a straight answer.

Daisy starts counting on her fingers, having seen Martin do it. She pauses and then replies,

"Probably too many."

"I'm surprised Atticus said yes to speaking at the Student Union. He's not the most popular figure you know, around these parts," Martin replies, half hoping Atticus overhears. Atticus, however, is engrossed in conversation with Logan.

"Atticus loves the drama," Daisy rolls her eyes.

"There's always a lot of drama in his papers, for sure," Martin admits, then embarrassingly adds, "though I confess, I don't read them."

"It is so depressing he's still printing this drivel and losing precious forest," Elizabeth adds, hoping she has found a persuadable ally in Daisy.

"I think the news is mainly consumed online now, my lovely colleagues. You're rather dating us," Emily smirks to Martin and Elizabeth. "This young woman will think we're only ripe for pasture."

"Have you heard that Terrence Montagner is apparently missing?" Martin asks Elizabeth and Emily, changing the subject. "I'm sure the police have their theories, Elizabeth?" Martin stares at Elizabeth, prodding her to share intelligence, but she won't be drawn.

"I just heard this today. Terrible news," Logan Lax says, engaging with this conversation and popping in an olive.

"Oh, hello." Martin is a little taken aback that Logan, this billionaire at the table, is listening in. "Well, there is talk that he's run away to avoid paying his taxes. Politicians are like bank robbers these days, who give themselves legal pardons. They steal all our money and get away with murder," Martin replies matter-of-factly. "The press loves it, feeds off it."

"All politicians have a shelf life," Atticus Stamp joins in on the conversation. "We publish what we know. We're not holding anything back. And I'm sorry that you don't buy my papers, Professor Smith. Perhaps you should be well-informed before you lecture your students about contemporary British politics. Your area of expertise?"

"You really can't stand Montagner, though, can you?" Logan nods at Atticus, chuckling. "Not sure you've given him a fair fight."

"Are we not sympatico?" Atticus is surprised by Logan's comment, especially in front of intelligent ears. "True, he's like bad Wi-Fi, failing to connect with people right in front of him. Doing the side no favours. But I don't want harm to come to the man." Atticus then pulls out a place card he found in Terrence's gown in the robing room with Martin's name on it. He shows it secretly under the table to Logan. Logan shakes his head. "Was in Terrence's gown," Atticus explains. Both men gaze on Professor Martin Smith, who continues to speculate with Emily and Elizabeth on Terrence Montagner's track record on paying taxes.

"Montagner is so clearly a corrupt man," Martin whispers, "he undermines the rule of law and public trust. His malfeasance is at the expense of us all. The consequences are far-reaching and multi-faceted." Martin sips some of

Logan's expensive champagne with a look that butter wouldn't melt, his eyes innocently wide, his foppish black hair and rosy cheeks belying his age. Daisy, meanwhile, looks up from her soup and beams at Atticus and Logan. Logan holds out his hand to catch the smile and pulls it to his chest.

"She's all mine. Hand's off," Atticus reminds Logan.

"For now, maybe," Logan smiles wryly. Both men gaze upon her as if she were a creature too beautiful to possess. Elizabeth glimpses their fawning and rolls her eyes at their stupidity.

"So, do you study animals?" Daisy turns to Emily, noticing the little flamingoes on her silk skirt under Emily's gown.

"Classics," Emily replies, popping in a piece of sourdough bread and butter.

"Oh, is that like Rome and Egypt and that kinda stuff?"

"Precisely," Emily replies. "At the moment, I'm most interested in women in Rome, particularly Livia."

"Oh, so you know all about the gladiators. They've brought them back, haven't they."

"The gladiators were indeed significant in the period, demonstrating the power to overcome death against the odds."

"Well, I was watching them on Saturday," Daisy agrees. "Very powerful."

"I haven't seen it yet. Was it good?" Logan

steps in to save Daisy. "There's nothing better than having a night off and sitting in your PJs with ice cream in front of the box on a Saturday night."

"No! I agree!" Daisy beams.

"When do you sit in on a Saturday night?" Atticus frowns at Logan in disbelief.

"All the time. All the time," Logan winks at Daisy.

Elizabeth watches the dynamics between Atticus Stamp, Logan Lax, and this beautiful young woman, Daisy. It is completely impossible in her mind for her to work out which older man this woman has chosen to be with. Either way, she feels nervous for her. Does Daisy really know what she is letting herself in for?

*

"Did I miss the memo with the secret handshake to get past the Lodge?" Inspector Bob Abley smiles at the Master of St Andrew's College, having been not let past the Porters this time.

"My soup will be getting cold," the Master replies impatiently.

"Gazpacho. Perfect," smiles Sergeant Lemon. "Fancy." Lemon has arrived with Abley, wanting answers about the missing MP, who happens to be an alumnus of this College and who also happened to have something in his PR diary to visit.

The Master rolls his eyes and looks at the

Inspector and Sergeant wearily.

"Look, if you come in now, you're going to disrupt a perfectly splendid supper. I can't allow it. With no life in immediate danger, I cannot see any reasonable circumstances for you to break up the evening with your questions. We have a number of notable guests. You already have one of your own on the inside. We can leave it at that."

"Who?" Lemon is confused.

"You should give her a bloody medal," the Master rolls his eyes. The penny drops for Lemon, who cannot argue.

"And if we kick up a fuss?" Abley sighs, knowing he has lost this one.

"Really?" the Master looks at them both, knowing that never happens. "Come back in the morning. We can organise something then. I will have a quiet word with our former alumni that you will be requiring an audience."

"First thing, mind," Abley starts to walk backwards to leave.

"Precisely," the Master is irked by the Inspector's last words. He makes a note to forget letting anyone know Abley wants to speak with them, just to be sure to send a message of who is in charge here.

"And, I shall want to speak with you too, Master," Abley adds, reading the Master's thoughts like a book.

"I shall have tea and crumpets ready. I

cannot wait," the Master's words roll off his tongue with disdain.

The three men nod, and Abley looks at Lemon, who shakes his head at this antiquated gentlemen's agreement between the College and police matters.

"They heard I bring the party, so he didn't want to risk it," Abley chuckles, heading for Parker's Piece.

"You know you're giving them additional time to prepare their statements," Lemon reminds him.

"And more time to sweat. They must know something about Montagner's disappearance. Local MPs who happen to also be St Andrew's College alumni don't just spontaneously combust. Nor do powerful people avoid their Colleges. Even if we wish, some of them might. Knowing that I know they've had more time to prepare will put them on edge."

"So you think there is something they should be on edge about?" Lemon replies.

"Don't you?" Abley makes clear that there is something very fishy about St Andrew's College alumni Terrence Montagner MP's disappearance.

Abley and Lemon walk away from St Andrew's College, knowing they will be back soon and having a sinking feeling that the Master knows that too. They all know it might be increasingly likely that the 'missing' bit, in this case, might be something altogether more serious.

5 A POLITICIAN'S PAD

The following morning, Abley thought he'd clock in some overtime and, after a full English Sunday breakfast in the station canteen, decided to pay a visit to the still missing MP Terrence Montagner's bachelor pad in Panton Street. Abley told Lemon he was, of course, free to see him Monday morning, not to work today on his day off. The reality was that Abley had already got up early and played golf and just needed something to take his mind off the shock of the wedding. Still in his running gear after a workout, Lemon thought he'd check in on his boss today, mainly because of the wedding. They both knew it could all be a complete waste of time, as it was still a possibility that this MP would turn up in Monaco or the Cayman Islands. But they both knew that was increasingly unlikely, so found themselves this morning in the city centre on a street of upmarket period homes.

Reading back 'Bachelor pad' on the notes left by Constable Love made the place sound like Terrence Montagner's place was an apartment or maybe a maisonette with large windows overlooking colleges, with dark walls and leather chairs, or hard cold edges and modern steel and industrial warehouse vibe. Instead, both policemen walked into a very grown-up three-storey detached home.

"This is an unusually heavily guarded property. Security links direct back to the station?" Lemon says as he removes the electricity source from the alarm and texts the station to alert them that it is Abley and himself entering the home. "And what is that stench?" Lemon walks through to the kitchen and opens the fridge, his sleeve across his face. "Who spends that much on an alarm system to protect microwave meals?" Lemon observes a stack of expensive-looking pre-prepared food. He reads the label on the top packet. "Yum. Chilli smoked salmon and new potato salad. For the man who lives alone, it seems." Then Lemon realises what he has just said and looks at his boss. "Not that you–"

"Don't start digging. It's unbecoming," Bob

Abley shuts Lemon up and moves on without a grudge to open as many windows as he can find. “Anyway, I don’t have tins of caviar in my cupboard. Or a rack of champagne,” Abley notices a full wine rack. “I clearly need to pop to Sainsbury’s after this. Something smells like it died in here?” Abley then walks over and opens an eye-level cupboard above a granite preparation surface and moves the tins to see if there is anything hiding behind. He covers his nose with his shirt. He then notices the coffee cup with a fresh pot of coffee still on a warming pad. He pulls out a glove and turns off the electricity. They don’t want to have to call on the Scott Polar Research Institute just up the road again for water to put out a fire. That was really embarrassing last time. Abley then opens the back door, and finally, the smell begins to abate.

They wander into the living room, with its table lamps that look like they cost more than Lemon’s monthly salary, and a photograph of the late queen over the fireplace. Lemon walks further into the room.

“What’s that?” Lemon asks. They both look at a strange painting plugged into the mains, which is moving and changing shape.

“Ah, I’ve seen this before. I think it was in the Fitz or maybe Kettle’s Yard. Magnetised ferrofluid art, they call it. I would have thought you’d know that, given your electrician days,” Abley teases.

"A shark. Moving in the tank," Lemon stares at what feels like an exhibit. "This is so cool. A big fish. A great big fish. Moving from the magnetic pull. And that's not water," Lemon cannot stop staring, but Abley grows disinterested.

"Don't stand too close. It might pull out your fillings," Abley chuckles to himself, glad to have Lemon's company. Abley's eyes wander, and he notices a wall of awards Montagner has won – public speaking, lawyer awards, some for fishing.

"Nothing looks touched since yesterday, does it?" Lemon says.

"What?" Abley looks back at Lemon.

"The house. Everything's on. I get the feeling he never returned. I'll go check to see if his bed has been slept in," Lemon suggests, still looking at the shark. "Look at that!" Lemon watches as the shark's tail whips and thrashes, then calms before thrashing again. Abley shakes his head in agreement. They both know no one is likely to have been here since they arrived. But best to check. He could be asleep in his bed. Abley can hear Lemon walking about upstairs for a while, opening doors, airing cupboards and bathrooms, as Abley stands still in the centre of the living room, waiting for any shout from Lemon that he has found something, wondering about the type of person this MP must have been. He has seen it before. Successful and unpopular always equals enemies. But who are Montagner's enemies? Lemon returns, jumping down the stairs two by two.

"Have the SOCO's been here yet?" Abley muses as Lemon stands in the doorway.

"I guess not as still a missing person? Nothing up there. Bed is made." Lemon shrugs.

"I'd like them over," Abley asks. "There's a lot here to go through. We could be here all day. Where to start?" Abley, all of a sudden, feels mildly concerned by the lack of clues.

"On it." Lemon phones the station while looking out the room's back window to the small city garden. The two colleagues then move into the drawing room.

"Has the office got the data from Montagner's phone yet?" Abley asks.

"Yes. Calls but no saved messages or texts. Maybe he wiped them? The politicians' way," Lemon raises his eyebrows. "Tech is looking into retrieving deleted stuff from the cloud. Calls out from PR, Westminster, to his assistant, dry cleaners. Calls in from Atticus Stamp, Logan Lax, all the hot shots, plus a lot of other rich guys. Could be any one of them who've kidnapped him," Lemon reads from his notebook.

"Let's not speculate," Abley reminds his Sergeant.

"He keeps high stakes company, that's for sure," Lemon shakes his head.

"Look at this," Abley says, picking up a newspaper. It has been folded on a story about

Terrence Montagner hiding money offshore in Monaco, exposing his tax dodging and how he was a non-dom.

"What counts as a non-dom again these days?" Lemon asks his boss.

"Non-domiciled. Not allowed in the country for more than 90 days a year, but for that, they can pay tax abroad."

"No tax?" Lemon also puts on gloves then lifts open a box on the coffee table. Inside are just mints. He drops the lid back down.

"Yup, that's right. For years, this has been going on. I didn't think it was allowed if you are an MP. I think you have to be domiciled? I suppose he wasn't happy with Atticus Stamp, who published the piece," Abley stares at the paper.

"You think they had a fight? Atticus Stamp is in Cambridge, after all." Lemon asks, now examining the contents of a drawer from a side table. A pack of cards, a magnifying glass and some cracker toys.

"I don't think, Lemon. I look at the facts." Abley puts on SOCO gloves and then picks up a scrapbook. It has all the critical news stories in Atticus's paper about Montagner. They flick through it together.

"Who keeps bad press?" Lemon ponders. "And cracker toys when you are mega-wealthy?" Lemon holds tiny screwdrivers and a flimsy-looking bottle opener. But Abley is already looking in the corner of the room where he spots a graduation photograph on the wall, where a younger Montagner is seen in the back row of five rows of young men, possibly at Eton or Rugby. Abley is trying to identify the tie.

"Isn't that Atticus Stamp?" Lemon walks up behind his Inspector and examines the photograph.

"Yes, I think you might be right. So, they were at the same school."

"A bunch of rotten apples," Lemon replies.

"Let's not bring our judgement into this, or it will cloud our investigation." Abley continues to look around. "Where are the fish?"

"Fish? It certainly smells of it in here. What a pong!" Lemon pushes a window further open.

"Montagner said he was going to adopt some fish, didn't he? In that news piece at the rescue centre. He was going to adopt fish!" Abley is frustrated with himself. This is getting nowhere.

"Maybe he was lying? You know, to make people feel like he was a decent guy when he's not?" Lemon shrugs.

"Or, maybe where we find a bag of dead fish, we'll know he's not far away," Abley lifts a couple of cushions in case they are behind.

"I don't think you're allowed to transport fish in bags anymore. It's not like when you used to win them at the fair when you were a boy,"

Lemon laughs.

"Well, how do they transport them then?" Abley asks.

"They'd die if you put them in a plastic bag for longer than an hour. They'd run out of oxygen," Lemon replies.

"Is that right?" Abley picks up some paperwork on a desk and sieves through it until he finds something interesting. He drops the rest and holds it so Lemon can see as well. It is an invite to speak at 'The Pond', an exclusive gentlemen's club on the Mill Pond, which has remained a male-only domain. Consequently, the average age is probably in their seventies, given most young men are progressive and wouldn't dream of excluding the fairer sex when, if invited, it will undoubtedly lead to more nookie. Abley shakes his head.

"Our Mr Terrence Montagner was due to give a talk today," Lemon reads on an invitation card amongst some papers Abley has yet to sift.

"What about?" Abley asks, looking.

"Fish," Lemon replies, looking as confused as his boss at the card in front of them.

Both Abley and Lemon stand looking around in this house. Where is this politician, who has seemingly disappeared for no apparent reason, who had appointments in the diary which he failed to turn up to, and who appeared to have a reasonable life which some could only dream of at the very point he vanished? With champagne, caviar, and posh ready meals in the fridge. Instead of choosing to go missing, rather this might be more a case of finding who wanted him missing?

6 FOXES' HAVEN

Professor Elizabeth Green is at home, which to those in the know is Foxes' Haven, a house with a garden which slopes down onto the idyllic River Cam, where ducks quack, swans glide, and the summer's haze floats across the salad days of young minds, intoxicating them with dreams and hope. Overlooking Jesus Green and a punt station which picks up tourists for river trips and steers them along The Backs, it could not be a more romantic location—a place she bought with her now-deceased husband many decades ago.

Elizabeth has been sitting at the bottom of the garden, wondering whether to mooch inside for a cup of tea or to put the paper down and tilt the brim of her hat for a snooze. Instead, she wanders to join Bertie, a cat who shares his home with her. He has completely chosen to cook himself through the glass of her futuristic summerhouse 'pod', which rotates to follow the sun, and much sun there has been this summer. It feels like a heatwave might be building. Elizabeth strokes Bertie, who is stretched out across a book about growing lavender – something on which Elizabeth is already an expert but reads up on in the hope of finding new varieties.

"Can't you find somewhere more comfortable? Oh, Bertie, you're almost on fire," Elizabeth feels his toasting fur. "I'll be accused of animal cruelty if you bake yourself." But she knows that Bertie prefers to be out of reach of Elizabeth's many dogs and has retreated for peace and quiet. She ponders whether she is doing the same thing. No College, no lectures, and positively no helping the Cambridge Police. "We are like two peas, Bertie. Two peas."

Dogs of all kinds – two Afghan Hounds, an Old English Sheepdog, and a very scruffy-looking Bolognese – are stretched out in the wild summer meadow lawn, which undulates down to the river's edge. It pains her that she is yet to succumb to rewilding her entire garden, although anyone who comes to visit congratulates her on the triumph that exists thus far. Elizabeth recently paid craft carpenters to build her an excellent boathouse, and bought herself a rather lovely wooden craft to potter up and down on the river, where she spends much time rescuing ducklings and untangling swans from fishing tackle. Emily, her best friend, told her it was clear Elizabeth dreams of living inside the books of Kenneth Grahame, and she cannot disagree. On a fine Sunday like today, with the sun high in the sky and not a cloud in sight, Elizabeth feels happier than she has in years. Her academic sabbatical stretches out until at least September, and with nothing to do and Bertie having had enough of her stroking and backchat, she decides to stand up and walk out onto the lawn.

"I suppose I can make a fuss of all of you today," she says as she lies down next to Clive, the recently groomed Old English Sheepdog, who has been shaved short for summer. Now lying on her back and smelling fresh daisies which surround from all sides, Elizabeth watches the puffy white clouds in an almost clear blue sky.

What could be more relaxing? She thinks back to her holiday in Italy earlier this summer. It had been so stressful, yet it had also been so magical. Florence, Pisa, San Gimignano, Portofino, Siena. And then there were all the French places they fell in love with along the way. As she remembers, a tear falls onto her cheek and towards an ear. She misses Godric, her grandson. All the cafes they sat in and laughed about this or that. The evenings walking in the balmy Italian air, stopping to look in an art gallery window, or for a hot chocolate. Walks among the poppies, and just sitting together looking out across the beautiful Tuscan views.

They had become so close while together abroad. Godric has grown up into a fine young man since he came to stay that first term of his first year as a fresher. His gambling and drinking had slipped away, and he had been the perfect travelling companion.

Elizabeth hated to admit it, but just having that company from a family member confirmed that she was alive and not entirely alone in this world. She went to Italy to at least try to find a way to cope with the death of her husband, Gerald. But somehow, all it had done was put distance between them, making it harder to picture his face or remember all the small details and hear his laughter. She wonders if that is what really happens. The mind just forgets the little things. Even his jumpers she has kept, which remain folded in the wardrobe, smell a little less of him and a little more of her every month that goes by. The clouds pass slowly above her head. She is painfully aware of the beauty surrounding her and can hear the bumble bees feeding in the flowers amongst the long grass. Clive is snoring and has found a comfortable position with his legs in the air. So why can't she just be happy?

That is when she hears the front doorbell. Ugh. Elizabeth decides to ignore it. She just is not strong enough to listen or speak to anyone. The dogs bark, and everything stops her from getting up. Everything else can wait. However, it isn't long before she hears the barks change to excitement and the back gate swinging open. An intruder? Everything is an intrusion right now. She sits up and then sees Emily walking down the lawn, followed by a number of waggy tails.

"I come bearing a profuse apology brunch." Emily holds a basket with delicatessen goodies. "What was I thinking suggesting we dine in Hall last night? Atticus Stamp is unbearable and trying to wind up Martin no end. What an impossible man. Time for us to catch up in nicer circumstances." Emily has already started talking nine to the dozen. "You know who I saw this morning? His lady friend. Daisy. Out early on Christ's Pieces. She seems nice, you know, if a bit –" Emily doesn't finish the description as she refrains from being mean. But the pause is damning in itself.

"I was just about to put the kettle on, but I couldn't quite reach," Elizabeth stretches her arms out towards the kitchen dramatically, clearly not moving her legs.

"You stay there, I'll do it," Emily smiles. Emily walks off towards the house as Elizabeth stretches back into the grass. The dogs, now all awake, treading all over her and the flowers. If there had to be an uninvited guest, then Elizabeth thinks how happy she is that it is Emily. It isn't long before the two friends sit at an old oak table under a large parasol beside the river and talk of Italy.

"So, Godric's gone back?" Emily checks she

heard right last night. "Have you heard from him?"

"He left straight after his final exam." Elizabeth shakes her head. "He was lucky to finish early. He tells me he's in heaven."

"Where is he, exactly?" Emily asks fondly, thinking of her last trip with Cuthbert.

"Florence."

"Ah, Tuscany. The wine, the pasta, the pizza, and, let's not forget, the Renaissance masterpieces. Michelangelo's David, the Duomo." Emily closes her eyes and smiles. "Is it love?"

"I think it might be, of a kind." Elizabeth sips her tea. "You know, while we were there, there was so much pain. The murders, the investigations. But, through it all, it really is one of the most beautiful cities. I can still see the vistas, hear the mopeds, smell the pasta sauces. The history, the valleys, it was impossible not to unwind. And, of course, this little one, Patty, found us and decided to join us on our adventures." Elizabeth looks down at the little Bolognese, begging for some of the snacks Emily has set out on a tray. "She holds her own with Hector, Monty and Clive. I'm quite relieved. In fact, I'd say she's the boss." Elizabeth looks at the dogs, all crowded around, particularly interested in the breadsticks spilling over the edge of the table. "But I have to stop. Enough now, or I will be accused of being a hoarder."

"Technically, you're only looking after

Hector and Monty for family. And this little one, rescued in Italy. How could you leave her behind?" Emily makes excuses for her friend. Elizabeth smiles, and Emily continues, "Did you finally get all that murder and investigation out of your system? I mean, crumbs, Lizzie, does it follow you around, or does it follow you around?"

"You know, I'm intending to do as little as possible for the foreseeable. I've not been into the department once since I got back. Are you jealous?" Elizabeth asks.

"And what about the police consulting? Has Bob been rat-a-tat-tatting on your door yet? He's insatiable. Can't the man do his own dirty work?" Emily pours tea, which has been brewing in a pot on the table.

"Bob has yet to call, no. Strange really. I'm sure there must have been happenings since my return. And he might see things differently. He does work very hard," Elizabeth pulls her cup closer and starts to pour some oat milk into her tea.

"Hmm," Emily sips her tea, firmly not in agreement. "If you want time to recuperate, don't answer the door or pick up the phone."

"You managed to find your way in, not that I'm not very grateful for your company. I was a little lonely today. There, I admit it." Elizabeth cannot look at her friend in the eye. "With all this time, I'm also at a bit of a loss on how to fill it. I've re-read my Wodehouse collection, repotted everything, and even brushed up on my La Campanella." Elizabeth is a little flushed, uncomfortable admitting her emotional state, and ready to close the window immediately and talk about something else. Emily can sense this and decides to pick up the cue about music.

"Ah, Liszt. I challenge you to Chopin's Étude Op.10 No.4 before you open the door to the Inspector!"

"Don't be ridiculous. I need my fingers to be able to still open sachets of pet food." Elizabeth pops a sugar cube from a dish into her mouth, pleased that Emily has not probed about her possible loneliness, how she is coping without Gerald, and whether the holiday helped. "Bob must be feeling the heat."

"A missing MP on his hands. It's all over the news. Won't be long before he implores you to assist the Cambridge constabulary once again," Emily replies, observing her friend more closely.

"Exactly, currently missing, not poisoned. Reportedly, Terrence Montagner, Member of Parliament, has absconded due to owing an inordinate amount of tax to Inland Revenue," Elizabeth replies, having read the paper this morning.

"You think he's run away without his phone and wallet?" Emily looks at her friend, wondering if she recognises the woman in front of her, the woman who never misses a clue. A group of tourists in a punt pass by, taking photographs of everything.

"Of course not. He's definitely dead." Elizabeth picks up a knife from a tray. Now, are we going to eat this carrot cake you brought with all the other goodies, or what?" Elizabeth slices into the gooey cake.

"So, you're not going to work on this case, are you?" Emily eyeballs her friend.

"Yes." Elizabeth lifts her slice of cake and takes a bite.

"Yes, you are? I know you like being a consultant for your favourite Inspector."

"Yes, I'm not. And, anyway, what are you not telling me? All this missing people drama is linked to your College, not mine," Elizabeth reminds her friend, popping in another piece of cake.

"Well, they're hardly a feature of St Andrew's day-to-day." Emily feels herself being dragged into a conversation she'd prefer not to have.

"These powerful men control much of our lives, our news, our politics, our business. I read Logan Lax has his fingers in so many businesses outside of fashion. How well do they know each other?" Elizabeth probes.

"I believe Logan Lax was the best man at Atticus Stamp's first wedding. There are photographs of them fencing together in the JCR.

Why do they subject that to freshers? Goodness only knows," Emily raises an eyebrow, pleased to see Elizabeth eating so heartily.

"What cads. Rite of passage traditions. Where would we be without them?" Elizabeth replies, deadpan.

"But as for Mr Montagner, he has popped in perhaps a little more frequently, always alone. I suspect that when he's visited Cambridge from his London digs, he's been at a loose end. From my small experience of witnessing his behaviour in College, I fear I have absolutely nothing nice to say about that man. Acerbic conversation, utterly cruel to students. If someone told me they'd seen his horns stick from his hair or his tail swing from his tailcoat, I would not be surprised." Then Emily pauses and adds, "I once sat near him when he was dining with the Master. Montagner was telling the Master about a hunt he'd been on, in Europe somewhere, shooting wild boar, and how he had accidentally shot one of the flushers and had to pay him a tidy sum so there were no complaints."

"What an abhorrent man," Elizabeth drops her cake on the plate.

"No, that wasn't it. Montagner went on. He told the Master that he got a feeling in his veins when he shot the flusher, and for a split second, that shot was more enjoyable than the boar he shot later. It gave him a buzz, and he wondered if anyone organises such hunts anywhere."

Elizabeth and Emily look at each other and then at the river. Did Emily just say that a man enjoyed shooting a man and desired to do it again for fun?

"You must tell Bob," Elizabeth says solemnly. Emily nods. She knows this is important information and wonders why she did not say anything before. Elizabeth observes Emily's face, quite disturbed by her own thoughts, and so decides to change the subject. The last thing Elizabeth needs on this glorious day is to waste any time on a nasty politician.

"You know, I have some of my biscuits, too. Let me go and get those. I baked them yesterday." Elizabeth puts down her cake fork.

"But we have the cake. That should do me, honestly." Emily tries to stop Elizabeth from bringing back some of her homemade cookies, knowing that she loves her friend but that she is also probably the worst baker in the world.

"No, no. I insist. They have apricots in them, which I soaked in tea."

Emily's face turns to dread as she watches Elizabeth disappear and reappear with a tin.

"They have a unique homemade charm to them," Emily tries hard not to show how she really feels. "So Mrs Cloud kept all the cats alive then?" Emily points to Soot the cat, now walking across the lawn to distract Elizabeth's gaze, so she can throw the biscuit over her shoulder and pretend to munch.

"She knitted them all costumes. Bertie has full pyjamas. And I know we were gone three weeks, but she somehow found time to knit covers for the lampshade stands, the bannisters, and a toilet seat cover which says, 'Now wash your hands'. Very intricate."

"You know I'm here, Elizabeth," Emily takes Elizabeth's hand. "You're never, ever alone. I'd much rather be nattering with you than listening to Cuthbert talk about his five-iron." Emily looks at her friend to see if her words have sunk in.

"I'd hoped it would get easier." Elizabeth stares at Emily blankly and shrugs. "But it never goes away. Here." Elizabeth holds her hand to her heart, the heartache for her deceased husband feels as strong as it ever did. She cannot think of reentering her life just yet.

7 AN INSPECTOR CALLS

Emily and Elizabeth have sat for a while, watching activity on the river, until Emily admits that she must go to College to check emails and do some work!

"On such a beautiful day, I cannot think of anything worse," Elizabeth says as she gets up to walk Emily out, feeling in an entirely different frame of mind than before her friend's arrival. "Thank you for popping in. Just the tonic."

As Emily and Elizabeth stand by the front door, they are surprised to see Inspector Abley walking up the drive. Or, at least Emily is disappointed that it is happening so soon after the missing MP. However, Abley's chinos and pink shirt do not convey an Inspector at work this Sunday. His eyes crinkle around the edges as he smiles warmly to Emily.

"Spaghetti junction," Emily suggests and kisses Elizabeth goodbye, reminding her of standing firm and whispering, "Remember what you said."

"What did she say?" Abley asks, having heard and toying with Emily, who shakes her head.

"That you should try some of her biscuits!" Emily replies.

"Tell him what you told me about the boar hunting," Elizabeth tells Emily, nodding. "Go, go and talk to Emily as she unlocks her bicycle. I'll put the kettle on," Elizabeth instructs Abley. She watches as her friends talk, then goes inside.

"Blimey. He's in a lot of trouble when we find him," Abley replies about Montagner as he joins Elizabeth inside, having heard all about the boar shooting and more.

"Quite. Now, where were we? Emily loved my biscuits. Do try one. I'm rather proud of them." Elizabeth suggests, happy to have secured Bob Abley's tastebuds to a riotous time with her baked goods. Abley pauses in the hallway, and Elizabeth knows full well that he has come with an agenda. "Come in, then spit it out." Elizabeth shuts the front door and nods at Bob. "I'm in the garden. Too lovely for indoors."

"You look really well. You've caught the sun," Abley tries to bridge the conversation in an attempt to defuse any hostility that he knows his friend might throw back in his face.

"How's the golf, my favourite walnut?" Elizabeth picks up a cup and saucer for Abley and hands them for him to carry.

"Not much golf at the moment. I don't look like a walnut, do I?"

"Your tan," Elizabeth explains her comment, adding, "And whatever would put a halt to teeing off?" Elizabeth replies, knowing full well what is on his mind.

"C'mon. It must have been a topic at supper last night. By the way, a supper that the Master took it upon himself to ban me from, and none of the VIP guests this morning are returning our calls." Abley watches Elizabeth pour hot water into a fresh teapot.

"You would have improved the conversation tenfold. It was utterly painful, with the exception of a rather charming young woman by the name of Daisy. Complete fish out of water. Thoroughly refreshing," Elizabeth and Abley wander out into the garden and sit at the table by the river. Elizabeth pours the fresh pot of tea.

"Only tenfold?" Abley smirks, then stares at Elizabeth knowingly, adding, "Terrence Montagner was last seen doing a TV interview at the 'Rescue Me' rescue centre. He was then due to give a talk at The Pond Club, seconded by Logan Lax. About fish? He did have a fishing award up on his wall. Still no idea what that's all about." Abley tastes one of Elizabeth's biscuits, and while she is looking down at one of the dogs and rubbing their head, he throws it into the river. "Why is it that so many awful people win awards?" Abley asks, adding, "Anyway, he didn't turn up to that on Thursday, then was a no-show all day Friday, so his PR reported him missing, and you know the rest on Saturday when the news broke more widely. It's suspicious as he left his mobile devices and wallet. And apparently, his aid said you'd have to prize his phone out of his dying hands."

"Because awful people crave power, and when they get it, they give out awards to people like themselves," Elizabeth frowns, still thinking about the fishing award Abley mentioned. Then, she changes the subject. "Lemon told me you went to Lavenham." Elizabeth waits to see if Abley is ready to admit his feelings about his marriage ending yet or if he is still in denial. Abley knows exactly what Elizabeth is doing, changing the subject. She clearly does not wish to talk about the missing MP.

"Yes, well, Lemon has been great. He saved me from making a fool of myself. It's been hard to give him the slip since. I told him earlier I was going back to the club to play a few holes. Not sure if he believed me."

"He's a good young man. You're very lucky to have him," Elizabeth reminds Abley of his Sergeant. Abley nods thoughtfully.

"I just had to see if Reenie was really going

through with it, I suppose. I do wish her all the happiness in the world," Abley lies, feeling the pain in his stomach and adrenaline rush just thinking about how awful it was to see his Maureen dressed as a bride.

"That's good. Chapter over," Elizabeth replies, not believing a word of it.

"I just hope he drops dead, the tosser," Abley blurts out, throwing his arms around and then stroking Hector vigorously. Abley wipes the corners of his eyes.

"Maybe he will. None of us are spring chickens. Maybe she'll regret it, decide the grass was not greener and beg for you back."

"She won't though, will she?" Abley wipes his eyes again.

"I don't know, Bob. But I do know that you will torture yourself all in the name of hope. Look for the smallest glimmer until she returns, or grow tired and fed up." Elizabeth tries one of her own biscuits and enjoys the apricot taste.

"Why can't I just forget about either possibility and just get on with my life?" Abley's voice breaks. "It's like, it's like I have a self-destruct button. I mean, what's she doing with that guttersnipe?" Then Abley notices Elizabeth's garden pod. "What is that?" He walks over to it, enters the ball shaped glass summerhouse, and then lies down on the cushions.

"You'll bake," Elizabeth shouts.

"I don't care." Abley shuts his eyes. Bertie

hasn't even opened an eye and is still cooking on the lavender book.

"Come on, both of you, out." Elizabeth walks over, picks up Bertie and takes him up to the patio to find a shady garden seat. Then she walks back down to her friend, who still has his eyes shut. She opens a large parasol above the pod, which casts shade over Abley, and then goes inside the kitchen to give all the dogs treats.

By the time Elizabeth comes out into the garden, she can hear Abley snoring. She reflects on what a sorry pair they are. Both heartbroken, albeit for different reasons. The old Elizabeth would have kicked his shoe to wake him up, but she allows him to sleep. She finds that sleep takes away the pain and offers a glimmer of hope and the chance to start again each day. Elizabeth sits and ponders, then catches herself. Godric told her to abide by a new rule, not to think about the future but to live in the now. She smiles and knows full well what Godric will be doing. She looks down at Clive, who has not left her side, has followed her back down to the river, and is currently nudging at her knees.

"Good boy, Clive. Love you lots, jelly tots." Elizabeth puts her hands into Clive's hair. It feels soft. She rests her hand there for a moment until Clive nudges her for the apple that is precariously balanced on the side of the table. "Okay, okay. Let's share." Elizabeth feels the unconditional love from Clive and leans into it.

She buries her head in that love, knowing that it is the best feeling, bar one, in the world.

8 VANISHING MAN

After Abley woke up an hour later, still in Elizabeth's garden pod, he found that he had no stomach to ask Elizabeth for her help. Not after Italy. Not after she had changed the subject. He sensed that even if she might seem relaxed to a stranger, he noticed how, around the edges, she was a little frayed. He immediately felt guilty for even thinking about getting her involved. It's nothing to do with poisons. That's her bag. That's why she's a police consultant. Not to help him find missing politicians. He does not know why he had come over to see her in the first place. It was a bad idea. There was just something he felt that was missing. More than her insight, more than the glaring talent – even though he loved and respected Lemon. He knew that with Elizabeth, yes, he would find this missing MP. But more than anything, it was having someone around him who knew him from years ago as a young copper and married man. Being with Elizabeth enabled him to feel like he was still that man, that his younger self still existed and was not just a dream.

Abley was pleased that Elizabeth stayed in the garden during his departure. Had she been present, she might have followed him out of her drive and onto the street, where she would have been surprised to see Abley's shiny new purchase of an electric bike he had hidden from her. She would have been pleased to hear him have to eat his own words. For never had a man been so set against a two-wheel mode of transport than this Inspector. Often ruthlessly berating Elizabeth for not stopping at red lights or for mounting the pavement at times, moaning about how bicycles made the roads of Cambridge unsafe. But something had changed his mind. It could be summed up in one word. Traffic. Over the past three decades, Bob had seen Cambridge increasingly choked in it, gridlocked, steamed up, and going nowhere. Worse in recent years, when the twice-a-day peak times had spread so much that it was hard to distinguish rush hour from brunch or afternoon tea traffic. The last straw came when Bob missed three teeing-off times in one week. That finally swayed this saloon car-loving, driving-glove-wearing, BBC

Radio 2 listening, comforting car-snack-eating habits. Now, he had to concentrate on the road not to get killed by cars, vans, motorbikes, buses, you name it. But he was nippy, flexible, on time, and didn't even have to pedal if he didn't want to. This was important more than ever, as Superintendent Raynott intensified the pressure to find the missing MP. This Sunday morning, Abley had put it upon himself to use his trusty new two-wheeler to retrace the politician's last steps and look for missing clues.

It turns out that Terrence Montagner liked a drink and that he had been imbibing the very morning that he went missing. Abley had been tipped off by a Constable working on another case who had spotted him in the Panton Arms. It was no surprise, come to think of it, as it was only a stone's throw from his Cambridge property, where they had left the fishy smell to be investigated by the SOCOs.

"Yes, he comes in here, often in the mornings. I'd sometimes wonder why he wasn't working as our MP. But I guess it's not for me to judge. I'd be out of work if I did, wouldn't I, eh? But that day, Mr Montagner was here as soon as we opened," the landlord explains.

"What time was that?" Abley asked, lifting his orange juice.

"Midday. We abide by our licence, don't you worry about that." The landlord reminded Abley that they did not sell alcohol before the law allowed it. "He seemed happy enough. He was in his working suit, you know, looking the part for shaking hands and kissing babies. I didn't think anything of it. Maybe he used us to keep away from the crowds of constituents who wanted to complain to him. Let's face it, he's done bugger all for the working man now, has he? Like the rest of them, a waste of bleedin' space." The landlord rolls his eyes and shakes his head. "Anyway, we're a little secret down here. Don't get the tourists. I think the students like that, as do some academics. Terrible in the summer, ain't it? I mean, I shouldn't complain, but you can't walk on the pavements from April to October, can yer?"

"Was there anything that seemed, you know, a little off with him?" Abley asks, ignoring the landlord's commentary. "I mean, coming in first thing. How many people do that?"

"I dunno. I was busy running a pub. It doesn't run itself you know. Talking to the chef about the specials, washing glasses, changing barrels, it's not all just laughs and drinking. I can't say I was really concentrating. I think he was talking to someone at the bar, but I don't know who. It was all pretty friendly. Quiet. Come to think of it, I think he was reading the paper at one point. Maybe. Could have been someone else."

"Right, thank you. Well, if you think of anything, will you call me?" Abley hands the landlord his card.

"Sure." The landlord follows Abley outside to pick up some empties on a table in the courtyard that had been there since last night. "Hey! An Aventon! I've heard about these." The landlord looks adoringly at Abley's electric bike and notices the large size of the carrying capacity on the back rack. "You could have two kids on the back of that."

"Just for the clubs," Abley swings with his arm to illustrate his golfing passion. But the landlord is still staring at the bicycle, making Abley feel proud of his purchase enough to stroke the seat. "She's a good little runner," Abley adds, pleased with the adoration he appears to be getting for it. He smiles but then remembers Maureen, shuts his eyes for a moment and sighs as he departs, heading up Panton Street towards Lensfield Road. His heart now heavy with the memory of yesterday at the church.

*

Next, Abley visits The Pond Club on Mill Pond by Silver Street to find out more about Terrence Montagner's invitation to give a talk at the club, whether he turned up at all the day he went missing, and if they have any news.

"Did you hear from Mr Montagner at all that day?"

"No Sir," A butler explains before the maître d' arrives and further shares that the MP was indeed supposed to give a talk on fishing, but it had to be cancelled after the sad news of his missing status. That many were quite disappointed, and they hope they can rearrange in the future when this all blows over, as it is a very popular topic within club membership. Abley is quite pleased not to have to stay long in the antiquated toffy-nosed establishment, where everyone's head is so far tipped back with disdain that he can see up all their nostrils. He jumps back on his bike to continue his investigations, leaving Mill Pond and heading south of the city centre towards the Botanic Gardens. Before getting too far down Trumpington Road, he turns right into a leafy avenue and arrives at the 'Rescue Me' rescue centre for dogs, cats and other small companion animals who have fallen on hard times, where Mr Montagner paid a visit the day he went missing.

"I don't really know why he came?" Eadie says, answering Abley's question.

"No, the publicity lady told us he was interested in helping us highlight our fundraising efforts," Muriel adds, disappointedly. "But he didn't. He didn't even mention them."

"We're low on resources, you see, Inspector. It costs so much to run a place like this, and we don't get anything from the government, you know," Eadie explains worriedly. "And times are tough. In all my years, it has not been this tight. The energy bills are just making it almost impossible to continue, plus the cost of living crisis."

Abley looks at Muriel and Eadie, these two old ladies who must have a combined age of one hundred and fifty. Then he looks at the faces of rescued dogs in the photographs on a wall behind reception, showing good news rescue stories and sighs. The rescue centre feels so warm. He can see two women's tireless efforts to create a haven of healing and hope written all over their faces.

"Here, let me get that," Abley takes a heavy bucket of food out of Muriel's hands to carry for her as the women go about their chores. "I'm away all the time in the day. My job is busy, or I would take one home," he explains, then asks, "Do you have any fish?" as he follows the women along a corridor towards where they keep the cats, tripping on the old uneven flooring and spilling some of the food. "Oh, let me grab that. Sorry," Abley bends, picks up all the food, and puts it back into the bucket. "This actually doesn't smell too bad?" Abley says, immediately feeling the kindness in this place, compared to The Pond Club.

"This is the last stop for some of these animals, Inspector. They have nowhere else to go. Yes, we have fish, rabbits, guinea pigs, not just dogs and cats. People have to let go of all kinds of animals all the time. Then, the abandoned ones are brought in from the street. And then the lifers. The ones no one wants. They stay with us forever, always dreaming of happiness. Black cats, mainly. We don't put any animal down," Eadie explains. Abley follows them through a door, then another, until they reach what looks like a cat hotel–lines of white walls with white doors and windows. Everything is light but also cool. It must be air-conditioned, he thinks.

"Was he a street cat?" Abley peers into the first cat enclosure and sees this old cat. "He looks like a real character." Abley can see the cat has a bit of ear missing and is quite scruffy.

"No, he's just grumpy," Eadie smiles.

"Grumpy?"

"Yes, we shouldn't really tell you, but he hates men with beards," Muriel explains. "He leaps at them. At their beards. So, no one wants him. He keeps leaping at the glass when they walk past. He's been rejected because men have to grow beards. Why do they do that, Inspector? Poor little thing. Locked up here. What's to become of him? A lovely lady adopted him, then brought him back when she started dating."

Abley tries but fails not to take Muriel's words to heart.

"So, you don't rate his chances?"

"What he really needs is a quiet village home, out of the city, away from people. With open fields. Where he can chase mice and be a cat. Be happy with his cat hobbies," Muriel brushes Arnold.

"What's his name?" Abley says, unable not to be drawn into the plight of this poor old male cat.

"Arnold," Muriel repeats.

"Arnold, you say? Is that Arnold Palmer?" Abley asks under his breath, but Eadie hears.

"Oh, Arnold Palmer. Yes, I think maybe that's his name." Muriel looks at Eadie, and they can see that Arnold has got under Abley's skin.

"Yes, Arnold likes the golf," Eadie smiles. "Loves it."

"Right, Arnold. Let's go home." Abley immediately thinks of Arnold Palmer and his old next-door neighbour from his married home, who stole his wife and has a beard.

"Really? We'll need to come and inspect your home." Eadie looks at Arnold and then up at Abley's warm eyes, looking at Arnold as he strokes him. "Usually, we do it first. But, given your job and Arnold's circumstances, we feel you're trustworthy and have Arnold's best interests in mind. But we'd still like to come and visit your home at some point." Eadie tells the Inspector. "Would you be happy to foster him until we can head up to see you? Or, take some photographs of your home and send them through?"

"Perfect." Abley looks at Arnold.

"He just likes to sleep, mainly. I think that's

why no one has chosen him. He gets overlooked for kittens."

"Do you have a carrying basket I can purchase," Abley asks, almost forgetting why he came in to talk to Eadie and Muriel.

"Of course." Muriel walks away to fetch a basket while Abley strokes Arnold, and Eadie puts the bucket of food in a fridge in the cattery for later. Muriel returns, placing Arnold into a wicker basket, while Abley asks Eadie a few questions.

"Would you say there was anything out of the ordinary that day with Mr Terrence Montagner?"

"He wasn't very pleasant, but then I've never met him before, so maybe he's always like that? Politicians are a different breed if you ask me. He was so cross that we wouldn't let him view the cats, even though he wanted to take a fish home. Then he stormed off," Eadie replies.

"Ah, that explains it," Abley nods and smiles.

"What?" Eadie asks.

"Oh, the fish. It's okay. Never mind." Inspector Abley takes hold of the basket. "So, there was nothing out of the ordinary?"

"Muriel, what about that paper you found in the car park?" Eadie looks at Muriel, who then remembers.

"Oh yes. I completely forgot. I kept it at reception." The three walk back, Abley tripping again in the corridor, this time holding Arnold in a basket, the two old ladies wondering if they've made the right decision letting the Inspector go home with a rescue cat. When they get to the front desk, Muriel pulls open a drawer behind the counter. She takes out a crumpled piece of paper and hands it to Abley. "He must have dropped it in the car park on his way out. Or maybe his promotion lady did? It looks like an itinerary?" Muriel peers at the paper now in Abley's hands. Abley studies it. It is indeed a list of times and events that are against them. He spots the talk at The Pond Club, but can also clearly see that Mr Montagner was due to have supper with Atticus Stamp that very evening when he went missing.

"Hmm, interesting. Thank you." Abley waves the piece of paper and then pops it in an evidence bag and into his pocket. There does seem to be a lot of overlap with Mr Stamp, as one thing Abley already knew is that Atticus was a member of The Pond Club. Abley's heart sinks a little. Is this going to be an impossible case to crack? Billionaires are not in the habit of making themselves or their activities traceable or transparent and tend to hide everything offshore!

*

Abley puts the cat basket into his front carrying tray on his new electric bike, and can see that Arnold looks completely fine about it all, perhaps pleased to have had the opportunity for an escape route. Abley wonders if he should go straight back to Grantchester with him, but then, noticing Arnold's demeanour, which seems relatively calm, he decides to make one more stop. To St Andrew's College. He had threatened the Master with a visit and was damn well promised crumpets.

The Porters at St Andrew's know and like Abley and are more than happy to look after his bike, secretly pleased that Abley appears to be carrying a scraggy-looking cat to the Master's rooms, fleas and all. Anything to bring the Master, who is known for his snobby ways, down a peg or two. But unfortunately, Abley's visit is all too brief, as the Master's promise of crumpets is interrupted by a groundskeeper who has to explain, in front of the Inspector, that someone has graffitied 'RIP OFF HIS SKIN AND SEE HOW HE LIKES IT' in large letters in white paint across a College court lawn. Both the Master and the Inspector know full well this is about Logan Lax's use of fur in his fashion empire, something that the press has written about in the past. The Inspector has no desire to be involved, hoping the Master can sort this out internally, but knows that won't work given that a man is missing and the two things might be related. Both the Inspector and Master follow the groundskeeper to take a closer look at the grass. Abley observes

Porters start throwing water at a corner, perhaps hoping it will wash away. Another walks to get the lawn mower to shave down the grass.

"Leave it, please!" Abley shouts to stop them. "I'll send some officers over to look for evidence. They'll need to interview people if there are any witnesses. Presume there's CCTV. If you can keep people off the grass for now, you will need to close the College." The Master sighs and nods – relieved the undergraduates have finished their exams – and has to leave, but not before he has a word or two to share with Abley privately.

"Your Sergeant asked us to look back over the dining room bookings for the past year. We found three occasions when Terrence Montagner had eaten in College. Yes, it looks like he dined with Atticus Stamp. I'm not sure what that tells you. Alumni dine in College." The Master then looks at Arnold, the cat. "Please tell me you are removing that bird killer from my College immediately."

"Someone's got to keep them in shape for long flights south for the winter." Abley smirks, but the Master has already walked off without a goodbye or any excuse for the lack of crumpets.

Before Abley leaves, he wanders with Arnold in the cat basket towards the historic dining room where the supper took place the night before. He looks at the alumni photographs each year for the past twenty years lining the corridor, wearing their gowns and hats. He spots from the corner of his eye that someone has drawn graffiti over a few of the faces. As Abley's eyes peer in more closely, he can see Logan Lax's young, fresh face with an angel's halo drawn above. Then, as Abley scans the photo further, he notices another young man with devil's horns. And if Abley had to hazard a guess, he'd say the horned young man was none over than Atticus Stamp.

As Abley leaves St Andrew's and is picking up his bike from the Porter's Lodge, who should walk into College but Atticus Stamp.

"Mr Stamp. Inspector Abley. I have a few questions I'd like to ask you when convenient," Abley pulls out his notepad.

"I'm afraid I cannot speak now. I have an appointment with the Master about making a donation," Atticus Stamp walks straight past.

"Okay, well, if you wouldn't mind coming into the station on Parker's Piece at your earliest convenience. In the meantime, can I just ask how well you knew Mr Montagner?"

"Only what I read in the papers. We didn't know each other that well. He wasn't a friend," Atticus Stamp shouts back as he walks away.

"They're your papers, though." Abley raises his eyebrows. "Are you holding any news back? What are you not publishing today?"

"What we will publish tomorrow," Atticus replies, disappearing around the corner of the Court and out of view. Abley narrows his eyes, watching him go. The dinner the Master mentioned Atticus had with Terrence Montagner in College contradict the words uttered from Atticus's own mouth. He decides not to chase after Atticus Stamp and instead to get Arnold to his new home, where they can both have a well-earned break and watch the golf on the television. Just for a bit. But as he looks back, he feels increasingly uneasy about Atticus Stamp and his involvement in the disappearance of Terrence Montagner. It would not be the first time a very rich news magnate wanted an MP to be 'silenced'. But what kind of silence? Abley could not bring himself to go there. Yet.

9 THE INFLUENCER AND THE MEDIA MOGUL

An hour or so later, Daisy is standing outside St Andrew's College talking to the love of her life, her Saluki, who shows equal disinterest in her owner. "Don't tell Atticus, but I love you the most, Lady Woof Woof, you're my favourite in the universe. Soon, we will go on a secret squirrel surveillance and sniffing expedition." Atticus walks out the College gates and takes Daisy by surprise. "Ooh, I didn't see you coming," Daisy kisses Atticus on the cheek, towering over his frame as only a leggy model could. At the same time, Lady Woof Woof shows not one ounce of friendliness towards this man, particularly because of his smell of cigars.

"Well, if I must come on a walk with you, let's include liquid refreshment along the way, please," Atticus says, taking her arm, pleased to see his girlfriend.

"Okay, let's take Lady Woof Woof to Parker's Piece first." Atticus and Daisy wander down St Andrew's Street, past the University Arms Hotel and onto the expanse of grass. Soon, Lady Woof Woof is allowed off the lead and takes it upon herself to inspect the cricket green, squatting by the batting crease to relieve herself.

"Daisy," Atticus smiles but also lightly chastises. "Can't you stop her from doing that?"

"Don't be silly. She's a dog. Now, come on, let's talk about something nice. Your talk thingy you're giving. Are you excited?" Daisy's warm voice disarms Atticus.

"Hmm, less excited, but I do feel like I will be doing my duty. I owe this University for a damn fine education. It's my way of paying it back, along with large donations," Atticus nods, then pulls at Daisy's arm. "Can't we go back to London afterwards, though? Or Monaco, or Milan, or–"

"Most certainly not. You promised. I had to sit through that dullest of suppers last night, and in return, you agreed we'd do a week here, amongst the lovely spires." Daisy takes a deep breath and looks to the sky.

"You run rings around me," Atticus looks at Lady Woof Woof, wondering what her secret is, and observes as she glides over to a bin and puts in a lot of effort to pull out its contents. Atticus claps his hands, and Lady Woof Woof trots back, mildly annoyed.

"I don't want a ring, darling, just some quality time." Daisy holds out her camera and takes a photo of herself and Lady Woof Woof in the background, and the Cambridge summer atmosphere of this expanse of green in the centre of it all. She posts it so quickly and, with one hand, writes 'hanging with the LWW' adding, #summervibes #cambridge #doggydays.

Atticus heads towards Melbourne Place. As they walk down the alley, with million-pound homes on one side and a small, friendly-looking local secondary school on the other, Daisy sees a property up for sale.

"Darling, can we just take a peep?" She tugs at Atticus's sleeve. He looks up at the Georgian terrace, with its symmetrical sash windows and a huge vase of flowers in full view on a table inside. The brass door knocker in the shape of a bumble bee, and the pretty old fashioned front garden with lavender bursting out along an old low brick wall.

"What for?" Atticus looked confused.

"Ooh, just imagine what it would be like just to hide out in. No one would know we'd be here. They couldn't find us," Daisy strides into the front garden and peeks in the window.

"But we have the place in Barrow Road. This is a postage stamp. Be careful, people could be at home," Atticus remains on the pavement in protest.

"It's such a dear little thing," Daisy sighs. Atticus rolls his eyes and pulls out his phone. He walks out of earshot for a few minutes as Daisy continues to look inside the window, then returns, ending a call.

"Yes, buy it—Daisy's name. See what deal you can get. Today, I want it today."

Daisy kisses Atticus and gives him the biggest hug.

"You spoil me."

"You were born to be spoiled. I love spoiling you, but you will never be spoilt. That's what's so wonderful about you," Atticus kisses Daisy back, and they walk arm in arm, turning into Prospect Row, with its white homes, then stop at the 'Free Press' public house for a whisky and a glass of champagne. A newspaper has been left open on the bar inside, revealing a story about the missing MP.

"D'you think he's dead?" Daisy asks Atticus.

"How the hell should I know?" Atticus replies, shrugging.

"What d'you think, though? I mean, if you had to guess?" Then Daisy pauses and takes a large gulp of champagne.

"I've no idea, really. I mean, I don't go out of my way to hang out with politicians unless you've failed to notice. There are much nicer people in this world to spend my time with," Atticus replies, kissing Daisy's cheek.

"You know, I met him once at a dinner party. He was all over me. There were photos. He acted like I was into him. You can see me leaning away. His hands were everywhere." Daisy shudders at the thought.

"I know. I know everything about you, Daisy. We have those photos," Atticus replies.

"You do?" Daisy is surprised.

"Well, look, I have all the photos in the world. I run numerous newspapers. What do you think we fill them with?" Then Atticus jokes, "And I still wanted to date you. And, buy you houses." Atticus shows Daisy his phone, and the text from his broker confirms that the house is hers. "In your name, sweetheart."

Daisy looks at Atticus. Did he really just buy her a house in less than a few minutes? Who does that? She kisses him on the cheek but also feels a little nervous of such a powerful man.

*

Not long after their drink, and following another selfie in the Free Press tiny snug, where Daisy has photographed her champagne and Lady Woof Woof standing on the table drinking what looks like beer, they say their goodbyes.

Daisy disappears up Eden Street on her way to Midsummer Common, protesting that she simply must see the rowers today as they look so athletic. Atticus Stamp has other ideas and heads back towards the Piece but doesn't get quite that far before taking a hard left and finding himself in the reception of the Cambridge Police HQ.

"Your empire is so vast. Were you thinking of taking over the internet?" The station receptionist, who has been chatting to Sergeant Lemon, asks Atticus, who has come in without an appointment, insisting he will talk to Inspector Abley and no one else.

"The man who can turn a cat video into breaking news," Lemon says quietly to the receptionist about Atticus, who snubs them both as he walks towards the Inspector's office.

Once up the stairs, Atticus spots Constable Love and shakes his head at Abley, who is sitting at his desk putting the phone down, having just had a heads up from the receptionist that Atticus is on his way. Abley then quietly asks Love to leave as Atticus walks over to the window to look out at Parker's Piece.

"Not a bad spot you have here," Atticus says, seemingly impressed.

"I like it. Thank you for coming. I wanted to ask you what you know about the missing politician, Terr–"

"Yes, I know who Terrence Montagner's is now. He's headline news. Like I told you, I hardly knew him personally, though."

"Supper together in College?" Abley reveals that he knows they've met, having heard it from the Master himself.

"Oh, well, if we did, it would have been purely him asking me for funds of support. Party politics. They all do it. I have a habit of attracting people in need."

"More than one supper?" Abley presses, moving out from behind his desk to walk over to the window to stand beside Atticus.

"What?" Atticus does not turn to look at Abley.

"Dining with Terrence Montagner?"

"Listen, I only had supper with him once. It's coming back to me. I might have seen him about College even. But definitely not much. He was a complete bore."

"His PR said he had an appointment to see you the day he went missing," Abley says, staring at Atticus. "And I've seen an itinerary that he might have dropped outside a television interview he gave the day he went missing, which appears to back that up."

"Nope. Don't you think I'd remember that? It sounds like he was going to try to come and find me, maybe. Maybe at the Club or College? I've no idea." Then, Atticus reaches into his pocket. "I did have something," Atticus turns and hands over a small piece of white card folded in half. On closer inspection, Abley realises it is a place card from a dinner or formal supper, likely from College.

"I found this in the College robing room in Terrence Montagner's robes. Thought I was putting on my robe, a simple mistake. I thought you might need to see it, given the circumstances."

"It says 'Professor Martin Smith' on the place card?" Abley shakes his head.

"Yes, precisely. And look at the date," Atticus taps the card. "The day this Terrence Montagner chap went missing when you say he was supposed to be meeting me."

"You think Professor Smith had arranged to meet Terrance Montagner? Just from this card in Mr Montagner's pocket?" Abley asks just what Atticus is implying and wonders if he wrote this himself.

"What other explanation is there?" Atticus now turns to stare at Abley. "Smith was at our table at College Supper yesterday. Marxist." Atticus grows a little tired of this intrusion on his day and starts to look around. "It has a phone number on it. I suppose it will depend on who that belongs to. I've not tried it," Atticus replies.

"How do you know it was Terrence Montagner's robe and not Martin Smith's?"

"It had his name on the label." Atticus now looks at Abley with disdain.

"So why did you put it on?" Abley asks.

"Because I was late for supper, and Daisy

was already cross that I was making her dine in College. Doing too much, as always." Atticus is overly dramatic about the unnecessary need to give this level of detail. "Right, well, there you are. I hope Montagner reappears soon. I'm just trying to help!"

"We hope so, too." But before Abley finishes his last word, Atticus glides out of the room, hurls himself down the police stairs two at a time and sweeps out of reception, past Lemon and the receptionist, who are still chatting.

Abley watches Atticus stride out across Parker's Piece, presumably heading for the University Arms Hotel and his car or perhaps to buy caviar or whatever men like that do with their afternoons. Abley is busy with his thoughts and scratching his head about what to make of what has just happened when he is tapped on the shoulder. He looks around and then down at Superintendent Raynott.

"I have had an irate call from the Master at St Andrew's. You've been giving him grief. How many times? Leave the Colleges alone unless absolutely necessary. This is just a missing person!" Raynott is fuming because he has had to deal with College again. He huffs out. Standing outside Abley's office, Lemon has heard Raynott's tirade.

"The best leaders inspire greatness in others. They listen, and are kind," Lemon smiles sarcastically, walking into Abley's office like a breath of fresh air.

"Don't worry. I can look after myself. We both know what he's like," Abley reassures his Sergeant. "What I don't know is why Atticus Stamp is lying about knowing Terrance Montagner? And why is he now trying to throw a Professor under the bus?"

10 JESUS GREEN

"He's got the zoomies. Been eating his greens!" Professor Martin Smith arrives in the middle of Jesus Green, greeting Professor Elizabeth Green with his rescue greyhound, Kropotkin, as she stands with a dozen other dog parents. Clive, the Old English Sheepdog, stands by Elizabeth's side, wagging his tail, while Hector and Monty, Elizabeth's Afghan Hounds, race about like the wind with the latest addition to the family, Patty the Bolognese.

"He's straight out the gate this afternoon, that's for sure," Elizabeth replies, stroking Emily's dog, Pepper, at the same time.

"So, he didn't mention the fundraiser?" Professor Emily Masters responds to a worried-looking Eadie standing beside her, who has brought out a couple of the rescue centre's longer-serving dogs for a run around this afternoon.

"We would not have agreed to the filming disturbance at Rescue Me if Mr Montagner had said he wasn't going to help us. Television is always so noisy. The lights, the people with their cables. All the black boxes. It upsets the animals." Eadie shakes her head.

"Typical politician, false promises." Elizabeth is disgusted. "I bet there were no redeeming qualities."

"He was very short with us when we said we would have to inspect his home before he could adopt any fish. He stormed off, looking like he wanted to hit someone. It was a little frightening." Eadie pauses. "And now he's gone missing, or so the news says?" Eadie looks at Elizabeth, concerned.

"It's obvious that he owes the British public millions of pounds," Martin chips in before throwing a ball for Kropotkin.

"Maybe," Elizabeth replies, not wanting to be dragged any further into things. Instead, her attention is drawn towards another dog parent, Mikayla, whom they all know well, walking towards the group, wearing the same matching sunflower outfit as her dog, Luna the cockapoo. With green legs and a large yellowy-orange head, she struts into the middle of the group, flicks her fingers, and wobbles her head to announce her arrival. Elizabeth looks at Emily, who is already smiling at the joyful display. Elizabeth, however, is not happy one jot.

"Hello, beautiful people!" Mikayla beams, a woman perhaps in her forties, though it is hard to tell from under the gorgeous, sizeable yellow hat and her friendly and enthusiastic American accent. "My summer creation." Mikayla gives the group a twirl and then lets her pup, Luna, off the lead to run around, glowing all things sunflower.

"It must be like looking in the mirror. Such a strong resemblance. Like two peas in a pod," Martin says kindly. "You look fantastic."

"It's too cruel, Mikayla. Far too hot to dress a dog up like this and make fun of them as if they're entertainment." Elizabeth says what is on her mind, adding quietly, "You need to remember that one of you barks, has four legs, and is not a doll." Elizabeth walks towards Luna to try to rescue her from her costume, which has slipped a little.

"Don't you be calling me cruel. My Mama was born on Aoshima in Japan, and–"

"Cat Island," Martin interrupts. "I watched a documentary about it. There are more cats than people—such a fascinating place. I'd love to go," Martin smiles directly at Mikayla. "She must be a very interesting mother."

"Thank you, Martin. She's pretty formidable. And I'm proud of my heritage. As a proud Japanese American, God bless America, I've pets running through my veins. My veins, honey."

Elizabeth looks at Mikayla and does not

have the energy to argue that animals are not pets—they share our homes and are our family. Deep down, she also knows that Mikayla is a good woman and cares about Luna. So, what's the point of splitting hairs? Mikayla has already moved on and is trying again to persuade Eadie about her fashion ventures.

"Well, I was thinking I can bring a range of my clothing line to Rescue Me," Mikayla winks again, "just to brighten the place up a bit? Might encourage a few more adoptions?" Mikayla beams at Eadie, completely ignoring Elizabeth's barbed comments.

"You're offering to donate the clothing for the fundraiser?" Elizabeth asks wryly.

"These are worth a lot of money, honey. Hand stitched and all. I am looking for a business partner to help speed up the process. I hear Logan Lax is in town. I need to find a way to collar him. Ahem." Mikayla touches her neck.

"I think they might be a bit too distracting for the potential adopters at the moment," Eadie does her best not to hurt Mikayla's feelings. "But thank you anyway."

"Nonsense, sweetie pie. They'd buy a suit, even matching, and think to themselves, 'I need to rescue a dog!'" Mikayla is determined.

"They really are statement pieces," Emily squints at the bright colours, adding, "Maybe I can see Eadie's point. In a reception, one might require sunglasses to view them. And that's not a good choice when looking around a rescue centre. Quite off-putting if the animals see humans with bug eyes."

Elizabeth catches Luna and removes the outfit, causing Mikayla to shout back gruffly.

"Hey! Leave my dog alone!"

"Only when you stop torturing her!" Elizabeth replies.

Daisy turns up on Jesus Green to find a group of dog parents and their dogs standing around. Lady Woof Woof, Daisy's Saluki, starts to play with one of Elizabeth's Afghans, Hector. They start racing around the Green, covering hundreds of metres at terrifying speed.

"Hello again," Elizabeth says, "We met at the College supper. Do penguins have knees?"

"Excuse me?" Daisy cannot remember at first and pops Lady Woof Woof's lead around her neck.

"Do penguins have knees," Elizabeth repeats.

"Oh, yes!" Daisy beams as the penny drops. "I remember you! It's a pawsome party here. Lady Woof Woof would like to contribute some balls." Daisy pulls out expensive tennis balls, drops them on the grass, whips out her phone, takes a selfie of herself with the group, then posts it before anyone can cough.

"Did anyone give you permission to do that?" Elizabeth asks.

"Sorry?" Daisy does not understand.

"GDPR," Elizabeth explains.

"Oh, this isn't data. It's just a photograph, sweetie," Daisy misunderstands. Emily smirks at Elizabeth. Elizabeth rolls her eyes, too bored with it to argue. Daisy's phone pings. It is an invite from Logan Lax for tea at his house. She smiles, then throws a ball for Lady Woof Woof, who completely ignores the ball, now too busy sniffing Monty's bottom.

"I understand you're staying on the other side of the city, Daisy. What brings you over here?" Emily asks.

"A taxi," Daisy answers helpfully.

"No, I mean, why did you decide to come to Jesus Green today?"

"Because I'm visiting all the places I can, so I can post." She shakes her phone. "Atticus won't let me stay long. He can be so mean sometimes. I love this place. He knows that." Daisy takes another snap of the Green and the avenue of London Plane trees. "Sometimes, I think I'd just like to be a free spirit, blowing in the breeze, in control of my own destiny," Daisy adds lightly, as if speaking to herself. Elizabeth looks at Daisy, trying hard not to wonder what she is talking about. Not to engage, not to get involved. Daisy picks a daisy from the grass beneath her feet and twirls it in her hands, looking at Elizabeth. "I'm wild. That's my nature, my purpose."

"Hmm, well," Elizabeth looks away, too curious about this woman, desperate to keep out of the way of anyone who might be close by association to the missing person case.

"He's gorgeous," Martin strokes Elizabeth's new dog, Patty the Bolognese, picking up Elizabeth's unease. "I'm happy to help you with walkies if you like, now I've taken semi-retirement."

"Oh, that's so kind," Elizabeth replies.

"Have you really taken part retirement?" Emily asks Martin. "From seeing you around College, you seem busier than ever. What is happening with everyone?" Emily thinks of Elizabeth's sabbatical.

"I just go into College to show my face, really, so I'm not completely forgotten," Martin replies, throwing one of the balls for Elizabeth's dog, Patty.

Elizabeth watches Martin, who she has known for a long time. He has such a friendly demeanour, and she knows how popular he is with all his students, a fact not to be underestimated, particularly with such high undergraduate fees equaling understandably even higher expectations. But Martin has always been seen as kind by the undergraduates. He exudes kindness. So, something does not sit well with Elizabeth about his seeming overt dislike last night at dinner of the missing Terrence Montagner MP. One might think it more suitable to keep one's opinions to oneself when confronted with 'disappearance' news–at least until said person is found. Could this meek Professor know something he is not sharing? Is that why he seems so chirpy?

*

As the dogs run, play, and sniff, the dog parents all chatter about the best dog food, how they lost a favourite dog toy, and good walk location tips. Daisy takes more photographs, Emily and Martin chatter about College and Elizabeth finds herself feeling more distant from everything. The final straw is hearing Mikayla happily discuss pet costumes again.

"How about selling my clothes at the Dog Festival? I hear you're having one on Parker's Piece, and everyone loves a display of sparkles and joy. They could be the pièce de résistance, ha ha, the cherry on the top." Mikayla beams at Eadie, trying another tactic.

Eadie looks cornered, unsure how to say no to this upbeat enthusiasm and laughter, especially to a sunflower.

"We're really looking for contributions, Mikayla. You know, donations. Not for profit. So, I'm afraid we cannot accommodate you, dear. I'm very sorry, costumes are also not in keeping with the Festival."

Mikayla droops her head like a sunflower without water, then finally lifts her head again and looks for Luna. "Where's my doodlekins?" Mikayla spots Luna without her costume, running around and playing with Kropotkin, Martin's dog. "What have you done with your sunshine, Luney? Where's it at?" Mikayla looks around for her dog Luna's costume, which she is no longer wearing.

Elizabeth begins to wander home, without saying goodbye, to spend Sunday evening alone. There is too much noise from the loud dog clothing designer, the soon-to-be-retired maths lecturer, and the rich online influencer. Although she has a fond spot for Martin, she does not care one hoot for any of the others or their stories. What she does care about is the sunflower dog coat that she has surreptitiously taken from Luna and is now placing well and truly into a bin where no hands can stretch in to retrieve it. The dog poop bin! Elizabeth is relieved that Abley will not be using her services to find the missing MP, as it already feels like it will be a much harder nut to crack than usual.

11 A LITTLE LOST

Inspector Bob Abley is back home in his garden this Sunday evening after having rushed about today with no real results. The MP is still missing, Superintendent Raynott is on his back, and he wasn't even supposed to be on duty this weekend. He has decided to make the most of the last of the sun before either going to the pub for tea or taking something out of the freezer. Wearing headphones while practising his golfing putts on the lawn means that it is his neighbour, Sid, who hears someone knocking at Abley's front door. Abley's two adult children come back through Sid's garden, step over the small white picket fence that separates the two properties, and pull out their father's earbuds.

"Dad! We've been knocking ages," Penny, his daughter, complains kindly.

"They say the early bird catches the worm, but I think your father prefers the Sunday afternoon tee time to catch the perfect shot. He's like the golf whisperer, guiding his balls into the hole," Sid chuckles as he waves goodbye to Abley's family, then walks back up to his vegetable patch.

"Oof," Bob Abley looks up from his putting green after missing. The ball heads towards the back of his summerhouse. "You put me off. That would have made it," Abley chuckles, beaming, so happy to see his children. He spots that Penny has a hamper of food and his son, Clive, is carrying beer. After they have all hugged and looked around the garden, they take a tour of the tiny house, tiny bedrooms, and tiny bathroom, to see what their father has done to it since the divorce. It felt like ages before he had been ready to sell the family home, so though this feels a little sad to see him like this, they know it is a step forward for their dad in his acceptance.

"We thought you might be in for tea. We took a risk," Clive explains. It is clear to all of them that they have dropped in to support their dad after their mother's wedding yesterday. Just to show they have not taken sides and to create some false sense of normalcy.

"Living here is a bit like playing Tetris every day," Abley moves a pile of papers off the kitchen table so Penny can put down her hamper, then looks for somewhere to put the beers Clive brought, choosing the floor as there is nowhere else. "You know when you live in a small house when you accidentally vacuum the ceiling instead of the carpet? I have to go outside to change my mind," Abley says. Clive shakes his head at his dad's bad jokes.

"You have a vacuum?" Penny asks wryly, looking about at the dust, then glances at her father, knowing how much he must be hurting from her mother's wedding, having spotted him leaving and causing the commotion after all but not wanting to raise it. "You can still have parties, I'm sure," Penny suggests encouragingly.

"Forget parties. Just me now," Abley replies thoughtfully.

"At least you can open the fridge while you take a shower." Clive laughs, having thought of a funny thing, trying to lighten the weight of the situation. Penny gives her brother a look to stop.

They all sit in the living room for a while and talk about the missing politician. Clive, himself a police investigator in London, says he will do some digging. They finally run out of things to say for a moment, and the silence hangs heavy.

"I can't believe yesterday." Penny comes out with what she is thinking, "I also can't believe Mum has dyed her hair red and did you see the length of her eyelashes?"

"What was that? Weird, right?" Clive echoes his sister. Both really just trying to support their father, who they can see is still heartbroken. "I love Mum to bits, but she's completely lost her mind." Clive pauses and looks deeply into his father's eyes. "You know when your parents split, and you're not supposed to take sides, instead, accept and even embrace your parent's new partners? Well, I'm one hundred per cent not going to do that. She's married a dick!"

"She's lost the plot," Penny adds. "We give it six months, Daddy."

"Stop. Don't say all that for me. It's okay to be happy about things. It's not your fault," Abley shakes his head, looking at both his children and loving them so much he wants to cry.

"We love Mum, Dad. We do. But we don't love him, and we never will. We won't be going round for family dinners and things. We said we'd go to the wedding, but he really is, well, what Clive said," Penny stresses to her father.

"This is the last thing I want. Just because it hasn't worked out for your Mum and me, it doesn't mean you can't continue your relationship with us both. You have to. Honestly. I won't thank you for causing your mother any grief." Abley's voice trembles.

"It's such a mess," Clive says. "It's not your fault. It's his. He's brainwashing her."

Abley cannot think straight. All his children's words are circling his mind, but he just sits in his chair, blaming himself for everything, talking quietly to himself. "I tried to keep the flame alive, but it was like rubbing two sticks together in the rain." Just at that moment, when things feel melancholy, Arnold the cat wanders into the living room like he's been living there for years, lifting the mood. He stops in the centre of the rug, beside the coffee table, and starts to clean his belly.

"What the –" Penny laughs. "Who's this?" Penny and Clive are taken aback and also really pleased to see their dad has some company.

"Arnold," Abley looks down at the raggedy cat, who seems completely settled in, even though he's been there only hours. "I got him from the rescue centre this morning. It's like he's lived here all his life already?" Abley scratches his head, then smiles and shrugs. "I think we are going to be very happy together." Abley puts his hand out for Arnold, and the old cat walks towards Abley and rubs his face against his hand.

"You hate cats?" Clive chips in.

"Aren't you supposed to keep them inside for a week so they don't run away?" Penny asks.

"I've told him not to crap on my putting lawn, and he respects that. I don't think he's going anywhere, love," Abley replies to his children.

"Wait, this is now your cat? You have an actual cat?" Clive scratches his head.

"He was overlooked for nearly a year because he's old and a little grumpy." Abley waits for his children to nod and show support. "Don't dare compare us," Abley fake scowls at his children.

"He's adorable, Dad. I'm coming to see you more often." Penny climbs down to sit on the floor next to Arnold and gives him a stroke, which he seems to like enormously. He starts purring and then throws himself over to reveal his belly.

"You just have to make sure you shave. Don't come with a beard. He hates men with beards," Abley tells his son. "Apparently, he flies at men with them. That's what they said this morning. Why he hasn't been adopted. I thought I'd help him out."

"Ah," both children click immediately to what is going on. "Good choice," they both add together, knowing their mother just married someone with the biggest beard in all of East Anglia. Penny tries her best not to smirk. Clive feels his chin and eyes Arnold carefully.

*

When Abley's children have gone, the house is quiet again, and he is left in painful silence. He sits with Arnold in a chair by the television and spots the family photo on the shelf above of his ex-wife and now adult kids that he put there when he first moved in, perhaps in the hope that things might not get this far. He gets up and takes the photo out of the frame, searches for a pen, then colours Maureen's hair red, and adds in unnaturally long eyelashes, then puts it back into the frame and onto the shelf. "Look at my gorgeous wife, Arnold?"

12 THE GENTLEMEN

Mill Pond, an area on the River Cam not far from Granta College, filled with punts, pubs, milling tourists, and ice cream kiosks, also hides an unnoticeable back street, lined with cobbles and bins, four single backdoors and little else. One is the backdoor of a sandwich shop on the corner, another to a pub, where only staff enter and exit, and the third to a bicycle repair shop with little foot traffic, specialising in high-spec racing bikes. The fourth is a grey door with no signage. The grey door is the front door to the most exclusive gentlemen's Club for alumni in all of Cambridge, 'The Pond'.

To get inside The Pond, you need to know a secret code which can be tapped into a bright, shiny keypad. Once inside, up a flight of stairs, you are greeted by a butler with a silver tray, always holding a fresh gin thin. Huge Georgian windows overlooking Mill Pond, high back chairs, real fires even in June, ironed newspapers, billiards and a whiff whaff table. In the far corner, Atticus Stamp and Logan Lax are sharing champagne and a charcuterie board, discussing art, Swiss gold vaults, and who they are currently employing in their Family Office–their clipped accents absorbed by the drapes and carpets.

Another younger man approaches and introduces himself, asking if Atticus is looking forward to speaking at the Union debate and if Logan is planning to be at the opening of a new wing at St Andrew's College.

"I mean, a whole new building named after you? Should they just call you God now?" When the man leaves, they raise their eyebrows. How rude, and how did that gentleman get into their exclusive Club? Logan lifts a finger, and a butler comes over. He whispers and instruction. Atticus smiles. It is a 'non-renewal' for that chap. They both know it. Etiquette is everything at The Pond.

"Where d'you think Terrence's hiding?" Logan asks Atticus, looking at one of Atticus's newspapers.

"Because we write about the corrupt activities of politicians in my papers, my editors don't call me to check their headlines before publication. I've no idea. We move in very different circles." Atticus sips his champagne and straightens his silk tie.

"Hmm, news and politics are much closer than politics and fashion. You must know something," Logan presses.

"Fashion is a big dirty business, and you know it. Everything's political." Atticus eyeballs Logan.

"My people tell me Montagner doesn't back your Freedom of the Press Bill. In fact, they say he has been campaigning heavily against it and you're doing everything you can to persuade him to change his mind," Logan is enjoying baiting Atticus like this, like a fish on a hook.

"That isn't my bill," Atticus replies, looking at his nails.

"The heck it isn't. You've been lobbying for that for years," Logan laughs aloud.

"Look, I don't know who is backing the bill from the Commons and who isn't. D'you think I've got time for that?" Atticus sips champagne, giving nothing away.

"C'mon. You have people for that. Don't tell me you haven't seen interviews with Montagner voicing his opposition, or that there isn't a list of MPs that backed the bill and MPs that don't. You've printed it on the front page of your paper!" Logan laughs, rebutting Atticus and finding the whole thing quite amusing.

"I doubt Montagner supports tax relief on high street shops you're so keen on," Atticus replies, finding Logan's amusement irritating.

"Maybe you have him in your sights, on your lists!"

"So, I'm going to knock off an MP who doesn't lower lease rates on high-street fashion shops?" Logan smiles and opens his eyes wide.

"Knock off, eh? Has he been knocked off then? Maybe," Atticus raises his eyebrows, catching Logan out for speaking about Montagner in the past tense.

"It would appear that neither of us have the faintest clue to the whereabouts of one Terrence Montagner, or nothing either would care to admit to one another," Logan remarks and watches Atticus nod. The two men run out of energy. Neither is interested in this conversation.

Changing the subject, Atticus asks. "Did you buy that boat in Cannes?

"It's a ship, and yes. But it needs gutting completely," Logan replies, a little more excited.

"Of course it does. I heard a Russian rapper owned it," Atticus scoffs.

"What brings you here anyway?" Logan asks, deciding not to get into a maritime argument.

"Er, not to scribble halos on myself and horns on their rivals," Atticus raises his eyebrows.

"Rivals?" Logan laughs, giving it away that it was him who drew on their photos for fun. "(Guilty) as charged."

"I've seen the way you look at Daisy." Atticus glares at Logan. "Look, I've come to talk at the Union, as you well know. What he just said," Atticus shakes his head in the direction of the young member who was with them moments ago. Was Logan really not listening last night at supper, either?

"Oh, yes, yes, I forgot. Public speaking. Your forte. Excellent," Logan beams nonchalantly.

"Daisy always insists we stay a week when I come for the day. I think she'd have me move here. She says it is her spiritual home and has threatened to apply for a natural sciences degree. There are worse places, and I haven't broken it to her that she'd need to get actual A levels first. But I never get enough done," Atticus complains, "What about you, Logan?"

"Did you not listen? I'm opening a building." Logan chuckles. They both have some food from the platter and sit further back in their chairs. Both men, acquaintances, friends of sorts, or might frenemies be closer to the truth. Logan narrows his eyes at Atticus and then smiles as Atticus looks his way. Both men masking their thoughts from one another, just in case.

*

Sometime after they finish their talk, both men decide to go their separate ways. Atticus walks towards King's Parade, while Logan stands at the water's edge at Mill Pond and stares out at the willow trees, which seem to kiss the punts as they glide by on the other side of the river. As soon as Atticus is out of earshot, Logan hits the 'phone' button on his mobile to call a contact called the 'girl of my dreams.'

"Where are you? Yes, by 'The Mill' pub." Logan cuts his call and looks behind him. Walking down Mill Lane towards him is Daisy. He waves coyly as she comes closer. They both step into a punt, sharing the knowledge of the pre-arranged tea-time excursion along The Backs. Daisy loses her footing and nearly falls in, but Logan grabs her, saving her from a watery splash. As they glide away, the punt chauffeur is convinced he is punting new lovers, as Logan sits visibly next to Daisy and puts his arm behind her.

Not long into their trip, three noisy women, laughing and joking, are in a punt, being chauffeured in the other direction as Logan and Daisy. One of them is Mikayla, the doggie clothes designer.

"That's Logan Lax! He's here!" Mikayla screams. She whips out her phone and takes a photograph of the couple, catching Logan frowning down the lens. Mikayla then spots Daisy, whom she met earlier on the dog walk on Jesus Green. She grabs her friend, telling them that she knows that woman. But she can't remember her name, so she shouts, “Hey! You rock that punt, honey! We have some real royalty here, everyone,” drawing the attention of other punters to Logan and Daisy, making Logan even more cross. Daisy, meanwhile, is oblivious and happy to be on the punt with Logan.

“Thank you for suggesting this. I feel better already.” Daisy looks up at King’s Chapel to her right as their chauffeur takes centre stage down the cut. “All Atticus is talking about is the missing politician. He’s obsessed. It’s driving me up the wall. I just want to enjoy Cambridge.”

“You know,” Logan pauses, then faces Daisy head-on. “Forgive me for wondering, but I can’t help but be a bit confused. What are you doing with Atticus? You’re beautiful, you’re smart, funny. Atticus, he’s a dear friend, but a catch he ‘aint.”

“Stop.” Daisy pulls out two children’s lollipops and hands one to Logan. Logan enthusiastically rips open the wrapper and puts it in his mouth dramatically. The chauffeur starts to talk about the history of the colleges, and Logan slips him money to keep quiet.

“Tell me everything about you,” Logan says, looking at Daisy as if she were the best thing in the world.

13 THE CAMBRIDGE UNION

Another day in Cambridge, and people are grabbing coffees, rushing for trains, or photographing the sights. Atticus pays no attention as he steps out of his chauffeur-driven Range Rover. The end of exam season in Cambridge means one thing, not for the students who are either hungover or asleep, but for the more ambitious and politically minded it is the big lunchtime speech at the University Union on Bridge Street. For the eager beavers attending, pushing and shoving through the newly refurbished Cambridge Union Debating Chamber –which holds 300 on the ground floor of the Union building –they share barbed comments about the state of the nation as they take their seats on old leather chairs and padded benches which still stretch back to fill the room. The different College coats of arms adorn the side of the first-floor balcony above their heads.

A house debate has regularly taken place stretching back to 1815. In every debate, there is a motion called 'This House Believes'. But that is not the case for guests. Guests are allowed to speak freely. And Atticus Stamp is now in the chair and pumped, with the building now packed with rowdy and raucous carefree younglings, throwing sweets and chocolate bars at each other across the room, happy that term is over, and pretending that they are at the heart of decision making, rather than the reality of whiling away their salad days with 'let's pretend'.

Inspector Abley and Sergeant Lemon have found a place at the back of the Chamber, waiting for the main event. Abley has brought popcorn, perhaps to entertain himself, possibly because they were selling it outside at the Union bar, and he was actually peckish.

"When I come to things like this, it makes me believe that silence is underrated. I don't know whether to take notes or take cover." Lemon looks around the lively debating Chamber.

"It sounds like they're reading the fine print of the terms and conditions on my new washing machine before they get going. What's the hold-up?" Abley looks at the host, standing at the front, reading a document quietly aloud as everyone around ignores him and continues to chuck things at each other in some kind of public school ritual of dissent.

"Yeah, look at this crowd. They are like misbehaving monkeys jousting each other with cocktail umbrellas." Lemon narrows his eyes at the pasty, privileged faces laughing a little too loudly and a bit too pleased with themselves.

Finally, Atticus Stamp stands up, and a hush descends the room. He starts his speech on 'The Traditional Media in a Post-Modern World,' but only moments in and he is met with 'boos'. Abley can hear someone sniggering behind him and glances around, noticing that it is Professor Martin Smith from the Department of Politics.

"Are you supposed to laugh?" Abley turns and offers him popcorn.

"It was involuntary. You were not supposed to hear." Martin looks a little guilty. "I'm just here in case things turn violent." Martin shakes his phone, which is recording things. "I could do without listening to the propaganda."

"You mean you'd call me? But I'm already here." Abley smiles at Martin, aware of the irony and mistakenly thinking Martin waggled his phone as if he might have called the police.

"Well, I suppose yes." Martin nods and smiles back, guiltily enjoying this crowd's irreverence, which Atticus was surely not expecting. Someone interrupts Atticus's speech, loudly shouting about the role his papers are playing in the news about the MP.

"Is it right to be raking in money from bad press about a man who has gone missing? What if he's in a vulnerable state? You're profiting off his misfortune!" the student shouts.

"My editor has full control of what is printed," Atticus replies, remaining calm, though becomes irritated when he is nearly hit by a marshmallow lobbed at him from the second row. "I don't have time, nor should I interfere. That's what I pay them for," he adds, "What I would say is this. In the public domain, Terrence Montagner has been accused of embezzling tax payer's money and not paying his own taxes. It is common knowledge that Terrence and I do not see eye to eye on many things, but I hope he returns home safe soon." Atticus nods to drive his point home, hoping his words will kill the heckling, but they only worsen things.

"He was a vocal critic of your media empire, repeatedly expressing how you were killing democracy! What do you say to that?" A student roars at Atticus.

"You've been printing stories, Sir, about Terrence Montagner for months now, and yet he is innocent until proven guilty. He has not been found guilty of any embezzling or any tax dodging!" Another shouts.

"You act like you are the court of law! Well, not here, Mr Stamp. Not here!" Another student, further at the back, screams at him. Instead of being ruffled, Atticus Stamp does not raise his voice or show any visual signs of being provoked. Instead, he calmly replies.

"Well, let's get him home safe first, then we can talk politics when he is in the room. I don't think going on with this line for discussion in his absence is fair."

"D'you know why he's absent? Did you have anything to do with it?" another student shouts. After these words, there is a sharp intake of breath in the room, which momentarily falls silent, hanging on Atticus's next move.

"I have come here to talk about media in the twenty-first century. I suggest you let me get on with it."

Finally, the students sit down – having got the sign to behave from Professor Martin Smith with the smallest of glances – now only voicing low rumbles of discontent until the end.

The end, however, proves to be a different matter altogether. As soon as Atticus Stamp leaves the Chamber, he is pelted with eggs, flour, and a milkshake, and someone makes sure that a rival news photographer is there to capture every shutter speeding moment. Martin is standing to one side, smirking from ear to ear.

14 DOG EAT DOG

Daisy is standing in Logan's outlandishly lavish kitchen in his mansion on Chaucer Road, another leafy hidden gem behind a small turning below Vicar's Brook, which at first glance might look like it leads to a back footpath to a random field. Daisy is not used to anything other than breathing such rarefied air, where everything works, is beautiful and full of sparkles and glitter. Something most never even sees let alone experience.

Daisy knows there is an open invitation to Mr Lax's abode and knows how Logan feels about her, particularly after their secret punt yesterday. Daisy also knows she should feel guilty, aware that Logan and Atticus are friendly but clearly rivals. But then, over the past few days, Daisy has found an energy rising inside. Perhaps it is Cambridge or just a feeling that it is time to stand up to the men in her life. Either way, Daisy has a clearer picture of what she wants, and it is becoming less certain that it includes Atticus Stamp and more certainty surrounding Logan.

"I feel ever so naughty for not going to Atticus's Union address this lunchtime." Daisy tries to picture what a lecture hall full of young students and old academics might be like. She cannot see anything other than a deeply dull event with hard seats, musty smells and jeers. Why people find such things a pull she'll never understand.

"Well, you were stung by a wasp on your dog walk earlier. How can you concentrate when you're in pain? I'm glad you took me up on my offer for lunch," Logan touches Daisy's arm gently, then opens a cupboard in the kitchen with many first aid bottles inside.

"It still hurts," Daisy's large eyes water. She watches Logan open a bottle and recoils at the smell.

"Well, this should do the trick. TCP will stop an infection. My mother always used to use this."

"Why do they make it smell so bad?" Daisy pulls back her nose as Logan dabs liquid onto a cotton bud. She winces but then stares into Logan's eyes as if he was her hero.

"If it's stinking, it's working. Hang on, I actually know this, as I looked it up," Logan tries to remember, shutting his eyes and opening them excitedly. "It's the halogenated phenols,"

Logan smiles, placing some cotton wool on the marble kitchen work surface. His staff will quietly make something disappear as soon as he looks away, together with themselves.

"What are halogen fenders?" Daisy is impressed, though she immediately wipes the words from her memory.

"No idea," Logan laughs. "I was trying to be clever, so you'd be impressed."

Logan's point goes over Daisy's head. She is still thinking about the wasp sting and the awful smell.

"So, the wasp doesn't even think about returning because of the smell?" She asks innocently.

"That's exactly it. You're completely safe now," Logan replies reassuringly, brushing a piece of hair away from Daisy's face and looking longingly into her eyes. They stare at each other, lingering on the gaze, and then Daisy breaks focus, maybe feeling guilty.

"Won't Atticus be cross? Did you say you were going?" Daisy asks Logan about missing Atticus's talk.

"I did, but I can say work cropped up. It's okay. It's all about him today, not you, not me. He won't even notice," Logan dismisses Daisy's concern, wrinkling up his nose. He also wipes his forehead jokily to illustrate his relief of not having to listen to Atticus rant on about free speech when he knows full well Atticus only means his own. "I think we swerved a bullet there."

Daisy walks over to Lady Woof Woof, who has decided that the white velvet sofa overlooking the garden is perfect for her muddy paws. She notices the koi carp pond and line of flamingo trees with their pretty pink leaves hanging over a lawn that has been cut within a millimetre of its life.

"I must admit, it's so nice being able to let Lady Woof Woof off the lead inside. Atticus makes me shut her away or keep her like a horse. He even bought her a house for outside. In the cold?" Daisy's eyes are wide open.

"It can be chilly in June sometimes," Logan strokes Lady Woof Woof, "you're so lovely, Lady Woof Woof," and pulls a silly face at the dog. Then Logan has an idea, a way to keep Daisy close, until he can persuade her to fall in love with him and feel the way he feels. "You know, we could take the 'copter to the beach. Norfolk beaches don't have the temperatures of the med, but they're quite empty. I bet Lady Woof likes to run with the sand between her toes." Logan tries to persuade Daisy to leave the city, knowing it will drive Atticus mad, but also increasingly becoming charmed by this pretty young thing.

"It's so rare I get the chance to come here," Daisy replies, uninterested in his offer. "We're always in London, New York, Hong Kong. But here, you know, it's so beautiful, so peaceful. I can hear the quiet. It makes Lady Woof Woof happy. You should have seen her run around on Jesus Green earlier. She doesn't need the beach. There are green spaces everywhere," Daisy smiles. Her thoughts drift back to the punts, Jesus Green trees, the river, tennis courts, and fresh air. Then, her reality pulls back into sharp focus. "I know he'll get back today and want to leave. I'd just like to stay in one place a little longer than five minutes, you know."

"Daisy, I can't stop myself from saying this. You really are wonderful, inside and out." Logan observes Daisy's face, noticing it is beautiful in any light or circumstance.

"I've told you. Stop. I don't think Atticus would like to hear you saying that. He can get quite grumpy," Daisy smiles.

"No, I mean it objectively. I'm just observing a fact. You have a lovely face. I see a lot in the industry," Logan doubles down, pretending he's talking about the fashion business.

"Yeah, I hear it a lot," Daisy shrugs, uninterested, instead looking at Logan's garden and slipping off her sandals to walk on the grass outside. Lady Woof Woof follows her and starts to sniff. Logan stands by the bi-fold doors to stay close.

"Would you be the face of my clothing empire?" He raises his voice, watching Daisy look down at her own bare feet on the lawn and wiggling her toes.

"You don't like Atticus much, do you? He'd be so cross," she replies, not looking up.

"We've always had a friendly rivalry since school days, it's true. But it's a dog eat dog world, baby. And you came to me. I've not kidnapped you." Logan walks away, removes a cooked steak from his fridge, and cuts it up.

"I don't eat–" but before Daisy can finish saying that she does not eat cow, Logan throws chunks of steak to Lady Woof Woof, whose eyes light up with every bite.

"I mean it. I'd like you to be the face of my clothing empire. Think about it. It would give you power and independence. You could do what you wanted to do, for once. You'd be your own boss," now it is Logan's turn to shrug nonchalantly.

"Power and independence?" Daisy asks, holding her phone up to take a pic of herself and Lady Woof Woof as her dog eats steak off the grass. #hungrydog #newbeginnings.

"Complete power and independence," Logan replies.

"I feel like I've found a new friend." Daisy looks at Logan as she puts her phone on the marble counter.

"I was hoping I could be more."

Daisy's phone rings. It is Atticus. She cuts the call.

15 COLLEGE AT MIDNIGHT

Since his address to the Union, Atticus had felt adrift, wanting to leave this place and all its pomp. He does not need it. Is already successful. They need him more. At least the volume of requests for College donations would confirm this. Immediately after being pelted with eggs, Atticus called Daisy. To plead for them to run away, maybe to a desert island, back to New York, away from judgemental England, anywhere. He does not really know what it is about Cambridge, but it had always made him feel small, and today, it was in plain sight. Despite amassing a fortune and a large media empire, he knows what people really think of him when the gloves are off. A bad man, or worse. Blind to the value in anything he has done.

After his driver had handed him wipes to clean off, Atticus had decided to walk to Grantchester but was only greeted with more jeers from young men in their merriment. He had hidden out in The Green Man for a while but began to feel lonely. Meandering back into the city to seek comfort, he had stumbled upon his old alma mater, the sanctuary of his College walls. All evening, Atticus had liberally knocked back whisky in the Senior Common Room. Now, with only two other Fellows left, who, like him, are seeking solace and have no motive for discourse, he decides to take a sojourn around the buildings, perhaps to be reminded of how far he has come, maybe in the hope there is anything that can pick him up out of his fug.

Instead, when he reaches the library, he cannot help but be taunted by a shelf stack carrying Terrence Montagner's latest book, a motivational memoir entitled, 'Serving My Country'. No doubt College thought it might be useful as inspiration for their undergraduates, given that they carry four copies, no less! It is enough to turn the whites of Atticus's eyes red with rage. Overcome with anger fuelled by the College's best single malt, Atticus pulls the stacks off their hinges, causing a thunderous domino effect, leaving books strewn everywhere on the library floor. He has had enough! This man is wrecking his Freedom of the Press bill. Atticus is glad Terrence Montagner is not around anymore.

Not around to disrupt his business, not around to question his empire! Atticus picks up one of the copies of Montagner's memoirs, pulling off the front cover and ripping it into tiny pieces, then tearing up each book and jumping on the pages. He hears a noise in the corridor and rushes out a secret exit only members know, through a wall which takes him to the back of the College, where he can leave from a side gate.

"Saving My Country? What a wxxxxr," Atticus slurs as he staggers out into the night.

16 THE GARDEN PARTY

Once a year, every June, the Vice Chancellor holds a garden brunch at their private residence on Latham Road. Private being the operative word, as for this occasion, unlike the many other duties which the University requires of a VC, this time they may pick and choose their guests without any excuse or apology, so it comes as no surprise that Logan Lax and Atticus Stamp's names are on the list, among other wealthy notables. What might be a little more surprising is that Inspector Bob Abley made the cut for the first time. But then perhaps it is for a different reason, what with a VIP going missing in the city, and in broad daylight at that. Abley is on the phone as he walks in, then sighs as he cuts a call from Raynott, giving him grief for not arresting those who pelted Atticus Stamp yesterday.

"Inspector, is the Vice Chancellor expecting trouble?" Martin Smith is one of the first to arrive and greets Abley in the drawing room, happy to see a friendly face amongst the sour and pinched expressions of the other stressed fellow academics.

"You tell me," Abley gratefully accepts a non-alcoholic beer Martin has retrieved from an ice bucket. Abley takes a sip and looks at the bottle. It is, in fact, non-alcoholic 'cherries and berries' cider, not beer, and he is quite enjoying the sugar kick. "This is rather nice," Abley says to himself as he looks around the place, then back at Martin again. "It's all a bit Caesar's Palace, isn't it? Will someone soon appear to feed me grapes?" Abley chuckles to himself, observing the ornate ceiling and light fittings, then asking Martin, "You seemed to know quite a few of the troublemakers at Atticus Stamp's Union speech yesterday. Can you give me a heads-up? Are they expected here later, too?"

"I cannot control students, nor would I want to," Martin replies, momentarily ignoring Abley's comments about wealth and privilege. "You see, the difference between Atticus and myself, well, one of the many, is that I believe in the freedom of speech and movement. He believes in the freedom of the press. Seemingly subtle but highly different perspectives, you see, Inspector," Martin nods, then looks at Abley seriously to drive home his point.

"Yes, I know the difference, thank you." Abley raises his eyebrows, hoping to avoid any pretension from academics today but knowing he won't be so lucky. "So, you didn't know the students concerned?"

"Yes, of course, I know them. They're mostly in my classes. They're great kids. In fact, I have to leave shortly to give a lecture on media relations, would you believe. Quite timely, don't you think? In the circumstances," Martin gives off all the air of an Oxbridge professor –detached, pleasant, kind, but with precision in his carefully chosen words.

"Circumstances?" Abley asks, knowing full well but hoping Martin will tell him more.

"You know exactly what I'm talking about. Having the largest media owner in the world gracing our presence in Cambridge for a few days has done my lecture numbers no end of good. Might even need to hold a Q&A afterwards. I've never been so popular ahead of retirement," Martin leans in, quite happy with the situation, his warm smile making it impossible not to like him.

Abley wonders, however, if this Professor seems a little too pleased with the situation about a man he clearly detests and who has also disappeared. Why isn't he concerned that the spotlight might be thrown on him?

"D'you know anything about where

Terrence Montagner might be?" Abley asks Martin.

"Why would you ask that? Honestly. We move in completely different circles," Martin laughs, his face moving but no noise being emitted.

"Not so different. Same College. Same University. It's clear you know him better than you're letting on," Abley thinks about the name on the card and the phone number that Atticus shared with him, clearly marking Martin as a man of interest.

"I cannot help it that I'm at my alma mater. The University prides itself on being a centre of excellence, open to all ideas. Unfortunately, the consequences can sometimes lead to the oddest of guest speakers being invited, just to keep us on our toes."

"Can you explain why Atticus Stamp came into the police station since Mr Montagner went missing and gave me a place card from Terrence Montagner's gown, which was your place card from dinner with a phone number and a date to meet him? Is this your handwriting?"

Martin is caught out unexpectedly. His eyes dart around the room. "He was thinking about taking up an academic position, part-time, on the side, in the politics department. I suppose he was sounding me out? He never would have won the approval of the Fellows. He was only ever interested in the legitimacy it would have given him. I gave him my number to get rid of him. It's the number on the University system. Anyone can find it. You can check. Not my mobile, you'll notice."

"Why do you say you would not have supported him if that had been his desire?" Abley asks, curious to hear more.

"Because Terrance Montagner knows nothing about politics. Nothing whatsoever." Martin replies matter-of-factly, looking at Abley through his boyish fringe with piercing eyes, then smiling kindly.

"But he's an MP?" Abley is confused.

"Precisely," Martin replies without missing a beat.

Abley shakes his head at Martin's comment but is distracted by noticing Daisy's arrival with Lady Woof Woof, which feels far more interesting than disappearing down another wormhole with the Professor. Abley watches as Daisy swishes past him, through the drawing room and out into the garden. She heads straight for Logan and sits on a lounger under the shade of some trees, Logan next to her. Noticing Lady Woof Woof beside Daisy being fed treats, Abley feels a bump against his shoulder. He looks at Atticus Stamp, wearing dark glasses, pushing past Abley and anyone else in his way. Atticus has spotted Daisy and is walking down the lawn, grabbing two champagnes from a waiter's tray. Abley follows him down the garden but hangs back, hiding in a milling crowd, close enough to hear what they are all saying.

"Oh, I thought you'd gone back to London?" Daisy sits up, unsure how she feels about seeing Atticus. "You completely disappeared?" It is clear that Daisy is not pleased to see Atticus. "I waited up for you as long as I could."

"I came back for you, Darling," Atticus replies coldly. "Let's go back to Belgravia together straight after this. To the land of civilisation."

"No, I've told you. I want to stay here," Daisy comes as close as she can to a frown.

"You said you'd come to my speech but weren't there?" Atticus replies accusingly. "I was very disappointed. Then I called, but you didn't reply?"

Daisy looks at Logan, unable to find the words, so Logan intervenes on her behalf.

"Look, old chap, don't give her grief. There's a dear boy. Daisy was stung yesterday by a wasp. It was quite swollen. By the time we found some meds, it was too late to join. But I heard you went down a storm!" Logan laughs, having heard how the address was interrupted countless times by protesting students and having seen the egging photographs in all the papers today. Atticus notices something between Daisy and Logan, and he does not like it.

*

Abley has heard enough and decides to walk over to the Vice Chancellor, who is grateful to see him. The Vice Chancellor is standing with Professor Elizabeth Green, the main reason Abley has joined them.

"I half expected to find that Mr Montagner might turn up today. We extended an invitation to him some time ago," The Vice Chancellor explains, hopefully.

"I think that might be wishful thinking," Elizabeth replies.

"Do you have any leads, Inspector?" The Vice Chancellor asks.

"We're investigating Mr Montagner's seeming disappearance and following a number of leads of enquiry. But you know that I cannot talk about that. Did you know him?" Abley asks the Vice Chancellor, sipping his cherries and berries non-alcoholic cider and picking up a mushroom pastry canape from a tray.

"No, no. I never met him," the Vice Chancellor sounds disappointed. "Funny that our paths never crossed. Perhaps there is enough politics in the university for the need to rub noses with the locals, as it were."

"Why was he invited then?" Elizabeth asks.

"Because he's our MP, of course. Would be impolite not to. You'll see the Mayor is over there." The Vice Chancellor smiles, "We have to show that we care about the town," the Vice

Chancellor explains superciliously.

Well, anyway–" but Abley's phone rings just as he is going to ask more questions to try to engage Elizabeth and glean her thoughts. It is Abley's son, Clive. "Oh, sorry, will you excuse me?" Abley walks through a gate into the front drive so he is not overheard. What Clive says is rather alarming. "Slow down. What information?" It is clear to Abley that his son has been digging, as he promised, from his London offices. "Atticus Stamp was blackmailing Terrence Montagner?" Abley repeats his son's words. "Are you sure?"

Elizabeth spots Abley through a chink in the gate, standing in the driveway through a crack in the back gate, looking a little perturbed.

"Is everything alright?" She asks Abley as she wanders through to check on him. Abley is still listening to his son on the other end of the phone. He puts his hand over his phone to fill Elizabeth in while he continues to listen.

"According to Met Police files, Atticus Stamp was blackmailing Terrence Montagner," Abley exhales.

"Why?" Elizabeth asks, now standing with Abley by the hedge, away from the guests. Both of them look at Atticus, who is still with Daisy and Logan, in clear view down the end of the garden. But Abley is still listening to his son, Clive, who continues to explain. Abley puts his son on speakerphone for Elizabeth to listen in.

"There is uncorroborated evidence that Montagner has been insider trading with his contacts and amassed some small fortune on the side. That Stamp found this out through newspaper investigations. It has been suggested by contacts that Atticus Stamp has been blackmailing Montagner in return to promise to support his Freedom of the Press bill," Clive explains.

"Do you have any concrete evidence?" Abley asks his son.

"We're still digging," Clive replies.

"We have the texts back from tech on Montagner's mobile phone from the cloud. We did find some where Stamp up until quite recently was sending increasingly threatening messages to Montagner." Then Abley pauses and looks around before he speaks, making sure again that they are not being overheard. "And, the SOCOs found a dead salmon sewn into the bottom of the curtains in the living room in Terrence Montagner's home," Abley adds.

"Who could be so cruel? Using animals for their own entertainment," Elizabeth chips in.

"I don't think it was for entertainment. It came with a warning of a kind. From Atticus Stamp. He left a note: 'You're welcome, Atticus. p.s. Don't rest easy'," Abley points out.

"You prosecute the hell out of that man!" Elizabeth looks over at Atticus Stamp through the crack in the gate. "Promise me."

"I was half hoping..." Abley looks to Elizabeth to see if she has a stomach to help him. But, to his surprise, she turns on her heels and walks through the gate to meet Emily on the lawn.

"You still there, Clive? Thanks for the intel. Will be in touch. It was good to see you Sunday. Hope to see you soon, okay?"

"Bye, Dad, see you soon."

Abley watches Elizabeth stand with her back to him, then looks again across at Atticus. What game is that man playing, and what does he know about Terrence Montagner's disappearance?

*

Daisy is looking restless while Atticus and Logan are locked in one-upmanship to try to impress her, so she decides to wander over to smell a display of cut flowers instead.

"How tiresome is it to hear men waving their egos about," Elizabeth says quietly to Daisy, rescuing her from staring at flowers as she and Emily stand nearby. "Come with and we can peruse the raffle gifts. I bought some seedlings that people can take home to plant," Elizabeth looks at Emily and nods as she says goodbye and then back at Daisy to see if Daisy is interested in her suggestion.

"I love English brunches in the summer!" Daisy takes out her phone and snaps herself with the tables behind her, covered in white linen and a charity raffle, and the caption: 'Loving life. So cute!' #smallwins #summerparties #Englandnostalgia. Before Elizabeth can even wonder what Daisy is doing, Daisy's phone is back in her purse.

"Who needs a moral compass when you have influencers to show you the way," Elizabeth says ironically.

"Aww, thank you," Daisy replies, making a heart symbol with her hands.

"You have a rather lovely dog," Elizabeth tells Daisy. They both look at Lady Woof Woof, who has found the BBQ and appears to be 'helping' a man working behind it, testing pieces of meat.

"When I was at Jesus Green with Lady Woof Woof and saw all your dogs, I thought that's what I want to be when I'm older. An old lady with lots of cats and dogs. Just living alone, leaving men and all their drama behind." Daisy looks at Atticus and Logan having quite a tense conversation out of earshot.

"Well, these are some sunflower seedlings I brought from my mad old lady home earlier. Amazingly, I managed to ensure all the cats hadn't played with them." Elizabeth raises her eyebrows, but Daisy does not even realise that her words might have been taken as anything less than a compliment.

"Ooh, what treats." Daisy buys a book of

raffle tickets. Then she spots a tombola, enters, and wins a small teddy bear. Then there is a 'guess the weight' of a jar of marbles, for which Daisy buys a turn and writes down a terrible guess.

"Are you married?" Daisy asks.

"I did not leave men behind, as you say. Mine actually left me. As for my age, it has some advantages. I'm practically invisible. I could probably rob a bank, and no one would suspect me." Elizabeth says quietly to herself. But Daisy was not listening properly, so Elizabeth speaks more loudly. "I could even murder someone, and no one would notice."

"Murder someone, and no one would notice? Huh, my Followers love me so much that I could commit murder, and they would think I was innocent even if I confessed," Daisy replies nonchalantly.

"Who would you murder?" Elizabeth asks lightly.

"Oh, I was only joking. I can't even kill a fly. Everything has a right to life. Who am I to take it away?" Daisy replies, then spots a group of guests playing 'bat and trap'. "What's 'bat and trap'?"

"The Vice-Chancellor's wife is from Kent. It's an old English bat and ball pub game," Elizabeth explains as they walk closer, Daisy's words lingering in her thoughts. Her Followers would think she was innocent, even if guilty of murder and confessed to it. Perhaps she had underestimated Daisy. What does she really know about her? What does anyone know? She wonders how the Inspector is getting along with the case, then shakes her head to stop herself. What is she thinking?

*

"I lost it," Atticus rubs his face, thinking of what he did in College. How stupid and childish he is being.

"What do you mean, lost it?" Logan asks, looking concerned, his eyes darting around the garden party, wondering if they should go somewhere quieter. "What have you done?"

"I hate him. Hate him," Atticus starts to sweat. "He's probably out somewhere chasing the Blue Marlin or some salmon in Scotland," Atticus quickly adds, then hangs his head, not really sure why he is talking like this to Logan, who he would not trust with his least treasured possession.

"Do you really believe that?" Logan replies, trying to read Atticus's face for clues to what he really thinks.

"No, no, I don't believe that for a minute. Of course not," Atticus shakes his head.

"Then, what have you done?" Logan gives Atticus the side eye, but before he can extract an answer, Atticus storms out of the party.

"Atty! Atty!" Daisy waves after Atticus but sees he has not stopped.

"Shall we play?" Logan replies to Daisy, dismissing Atticus's departure as nothing. "He'll be back shortly. Apparently, he thinks he can get hold of Terrence Montagner. He just needs to put in a call or something," Logan says, with a bare-faced lie.

Elizabeth looks around to mention this to Abley but cannot see the Inspector anywhere.

*

Abley has been called away from the Vice Chancellor's garden party to attend an incident at St Andrew's College. He stands in the library doorway, looking at all the library books strewn across the floor.

"We thought we shouldn't move anything. It happened last night, but because College term is over, and this is the undergrad library, we only noticed it this morning," the Master explains, standing with his hands on his hips and a little nonplussed.

"Is this not a simple College matter? Frustrated student?" Abley asks the Master, standing behind him, knowing that most of the time, College would deal with minor misdemeanours and damage internally so as not to draw attention to or sully the reputation of the esteemed establishment.

"Look at this." Constable Jack Love appears from behind the remaining stacks, wearing scene-of-crime gloves and shoe covers, and hands part of what is left of a book authored by Terrence Montagner to Abley. "I spoke to the Head Porter, and nothing has been touched after nine o'clock this morning once he found this mess on his patrols."

"Thank you, Constable," Abley takes out a plastic glove and then takes the book from Jack, surprised to see him here.

"I was on St Andrew's Street in Coffee Plus when the call came in," Constable Love flicks his fringe full of product, his white T-shirt and tight jeans making him look anything but a police Constable. "Always keep my phone on, just in case. Part of the job, Sir?"

"You have a keen one here, Inspector. Banging on my door just at the right decibel to dislodge the coatrack. Stepped over my duffel coat and fedoras like a rottweiler out of the gate," the Head Porter explains. "Pressed his badge right up into my face."

"You keep those–" Abley does not get to finish his question about how Constsable Love made it to the crime scene before he did.

"Yeah, I keep them in my pocket," Love replies, waving his hands in SOCO gloves. "Can't take a break in Soho when you hear shots in Holborn, Sir," Love refers to his downtime off shift in London being often disturbed by crime he would have to return to work for.

Abley holds what is left of a book in his

hands and spots that on one page, most of the words have been blacked out – as if being censored – by someone. Abley reads the words left on the page that have not been blacked out.

"I dated a girl who used to do that to magazines and local newspapers for fun. It's a blackout poem," Love smiles.

"Yes, thank you, Constable," Abley says. But Love ignores continues.

"You are an abhorrent person. I will find you and end things for you for good," Constable Love reads out loud. "Oof."

Abley reads it himself and then nods and sighs to the Master. "Let's keep this room locked. I'll send a SOCO over shortly. At least the students have gone down, only post grads now. That narrows it down a little."

"I hope you're not suggesting this destruction was undertaken by one of our own? Why do you think we called you?" The Master is affronted.

Abley's phone goes again. It is Lemon. "Excuse me, Master." Abley starts to walk out of the College library. "Great, Lemon. Hi. Can we get the SOCOs to St Andrew's College pronto? Tell them to go to the library." Abley stops in his tracks and listens to Lemon. "What do you mean?" Abley replies as he hears Lemon explain that he is at Terrence Montagner's constituency offices.

"I'm standing here in absolute

devastation. Everything's turned over. Like someone was looking for something. SOCOs are already here, given he's missing," Lemon explains down the phone.

"Right," Abley looks back at the Master talking to Constable Love, or rather at the Master not listening to the Constable but frowning at him instead.

"Seems like one constituent really made their voice heard, in the form of overturned furniture, emptied out filing cabinets and a message on the wall," Lemon explains, then reads the message to Abley down the phone, "It says 'Now have I got your attention?', written in what looks like masonry paint." Lemon waits to hear what his Inspector makes of it all.

"I'd say it's been done by someone who has strong connections to St Andrew's College," Abley replies. "Meet you back at the station?"

"Right ho, guv."

Constable Love walks up to Abley. "I'm going back to Coffee Plus unless anything else's happening?" Love looks straight at Abley and waits for a reply. Then, when nothing immediately comes back, he knocks his sunglasses off the top of his head onto his nose and shakes his shoulders. He walks away, "Sir, just say the word, and I'll come back on shift."

Abley watches Constable Love leave the scene. He admires his confidence and is somewhat jealous of his current upbeat mood.

One of Abley's least favourite things in the world is when a case encroaches into College and University business. And his very least favourite case of all is when it is so immersed it is hard to see where Town and Gown can be separated. This is turning into such a case.

17 DON'T LECTURE ME

Professor Martin Smith left the Vice Chancellor's brunch party to deliver his lecture about the importance of democracy and how the media is eroding it along with big business. He talked about what happened at the Union Chamber and about Atticus Stamp. He knew he went too far and was inappropriate, but he felt pretty angry in the moment. Not like him at all. He felt his face growing flushed at the level of corruption in today's society, perhaps at having just left a privileged gathering with so many wealthy individuals and being faced with some students in front of him who clearly had very little to rub together. Martin gave an example of how the media hounded Mr Terrence Montagner, perhaps to do something silly, or run from the country, no one knows. He told his students that this would be his last year of lecturing and that he would be pursuing early retirement and taking more of a back seat in the department. There was a rush of 'oh no's' and heavy sighs around the theatre.

At the end of the lecture, Professor Martin Smith walked out of the hall to a round of applause, as he is much beloved. Students patted him on the back and said things like 'well said, Sir', 'democracy is slipping away', and 'thank you for giving me hope'. Martin had been their favourite lecturer and would be sadly missed.

Martin now sighs, unsure and uneasy about what is coming in his life. He knows that AI will change everything, with fake news, rigged results, and the rise of the oligarch. The truth will be hard to keep hold of. He wonders if this generation is ready to tackle it. He knows he is running out of steam to fight the good fight and is very happy to be bowing out. He brushes his black hair out of his eyes and wanders up to his office in the department. His phone starts to vibrate in his pocket, and as he pulls it out, it is the Porters' Lodge at St Andrew's College, and he recognises the Head Porter's voice. "No, I didn't write 'Rip off his Skin' on the lawn. Yes, of course. Lots of people wear jackets and hoodies like mine," he replies. "No, I'm sure."

18 DUMPED DOG

Atticus walks back into the party, looking worse for wear. He has just returned to pick up Daisy and take her home. It only takes a couple of minutes to drive in the car from Latham Road to Barrow Road, and if the neighbours had lived closer on either side, they would have heard their shouting, or rather Atticus shouting at Daisy, but the lawns are wide, and the drives are even more expansive on this most exclusive and private road in all of Cambridge where even satellite images are not allowed to display this location. So, no one hears the car doors slam or the front door bang. Nor do they hear Daisy throw Lady Woof Woof's lead at Atticus, nor Atticus bellow at her about being scatty, ditsy and flakey.

Wisely, Lady Woof Woof runs into the garden, away from this screaming match. A beautiful Saluki that she is, she does not do tension or fights. She has to maintain her poise.

She knows when to jump up on the expensive patio seats and lounge her best life.

"I saw the way you were looking at him!" Atticus spits. "Don't you think I have to put up with enough? You're always seeking attention elsewhere. I don't ever seem to be enough! Why do you need the admiration from Lax, for crying out loud? He's into young women. The younger, the better. He'd ditch you in a heartbeat. But you flirt and give him your best alluring eyes. Don't you have bloody everything already? I see what you're doing. You're going to trade me in, aren't you, eh? Eh?!"

"I'm surprised you can see anything through that hangover? Look at you! You're a mess. If I'd have known what I know now when I first met you, I would not have had anything to do with you!" Daisy screams at Atticus, who has removed his sunglasses to bloodshot eyes. She picks up a bowl of popcorn from the counter and throws it all over him.

"Oh, that's mature! So, you are seeing him. I knew it!" Atticus lunges at Daisy, trying to grab her.

"Argh! You don't even trust me." Daisy jumps out of reach. "You never take me anywhere. You never do anything with me. You're always working. Logan was just spending one whole hour doing what I wanted to do for a change. You should try it!" Daisy is so fired up that she runs upstairs and locks herself in the bedroom. Atticus follows her up and bangs on the door. Their shouting continues for five minutes, and then Daisy hears things go quiet outside.

At first, she breathes a sigh of relief. She tells herself Atticus must have calmed down, maybe gone into his office and shut himself in to fester and work. After ten minutes of stillness, however, she opens the bedroom door a crack. Nothing. So, she bravely ventures out onto the landing and then walks downstairs. The house is silent. Daisy walks through the kitchen to check on Lady Woof Woof. But she's not there. She walks into the garden. No Lady Woof Woof. Daisy opens Atticus's office, but it is empty. Then she hears the car engine start outside. She rushes to the front door, her sixth sense worrying for Lady Woof Woof. Her worst nightmare is a reality. Atticus is reversing out of the driveway with Lady Woof Woof inside sitting on the back seat. He sticks his middle finger up at Daisy and shouts an expletive. Daisy screams a guttural scream. She feels sick to the pit of her stomach.

"Lady Woof Woof!" Daisy screams as Atticus drives away, the dog looking out of the back window. Daisy tries to chase the car, but it is no use. She wastes no time in doing what she does best. She pulls out her phone and starts to post how Atticus has taken Lady Woof Woof, asking her Followers to let her know if they are spotted, uploaded along with a cute photo of the

Saluki. She also then creates a second post and adds a photograph, this time of Atticus on the plains of Africa, holding the head of a dead male lion and a gun in the other hand. Her words are, 'Get this trophy hunting mother fxxxxr'. She posts it and then turns on alerts on her phone. She has to find them. "Don't mess with me, you dog thief!"

19 IT'S ALL POLITICAL

After the Vice Chancellor's Brunch and the commotion at the constituency offices and College library, Abley was hoping to at least get nine holes in at the Gogs and some time to think. It was a perfect June day. Swifts overhead, trees with their fullest greenery, and the sweet smell of summer flowers. But this missing person case hung heavy over him, like the solitary cloud covering the sun in an almost complete blue sky. This was a case where he could do with speaking to Elizabeth about it properly. He felt like he was working on this with one hand tied behind his back.

So far, the SOCOs at Terrence Montagner's house had only turned up an out-of-date fish, which, let's face it, did seem to suggest that Atticus Stamp might have something to do with Terrence Montagner's disappearance. Then again, it was still possible that this slimy politician had faked his own death to avoid prosecution for unpaid taxes or even for shooting a flusher on a hunt – something Constable Love had not yet been able to corroborate. There were so many uncertainties, and what made it harder was the lack of access to the people who were naturally covered in suspicion.

Abley's conscience got the better of him. Golf would have to wait. He remembered Professor Martin Smith mentioning that he was about to deliver his last lecture on media relations before his retirement. Abley was well aware of what had happened at the Union and had noticed a few nods and smiles between the student troublemakers at Professor Smith, both in the Chamber and outside on the steps, as Atticus Stamp was being egged after his speech. Something made Abley wonder if the Professor knew there was going to be trouble and if there was something he could share about Atticus Stamp's involvement in the missing politician case. At the very least, Abley thought it best to turn up and listen. After all, it had been Atticus Stamp who had pointed the finger at Professor Smith, so it would be good to dig more into Martin's explanation about how he came to know Terrence Montagner.

"They told me where I'd find you," Abley

peeks around Martin Smith's department office door in Human, Social and Political Sciences on Free School Lane. A medium-sized room with a small window. Quite drab compared to the lush College offices the Inspector is used to visiting. But then, this was a faculty building. Abley is glad he had his electric bike, or he would have had to park a mile away from this nook behind King's Parade. "Is this your office? Quite central."

"I've been blessed these past years. A jump and a skip, and I can pop into St Bene't's and hear evensong. Quite splendid," Martin warms at the thought, grateful for living in the bubble of College, Department and Don's life. Abley bends down to stroke Kropotkin, Martin's greyhound, who puts his head up from slumber in his overly large dog bed, which looks as soft as a marshmallow.

"I'm quite surprised. Seems a little small for a Professor?" Abley remarks.

"You have a larger office, Inspector?" Martin smiles. "You most definitely deserve it. Catching criminals outweighs all the nonsense that goes on around here." Martin gestures an apology for the mess of papers and books strewn around. "It all amounts to nothing, really. A life's work." Martin opens his eyes wide and looks at his desk and the notebook he was writing in. "Amounts to nothing," he nods.

"You don't like him much, do you, Atticus Stamp." Abley ignores Martin's self-deprecating words, knowing that most academics believe they are the centre of the universe, whatever they outwardly convey. Abley glances around the walls, crammed with bookshelves stuffed with paperbacks, textbooks and papers. There is a teddy bear. Martin notices Abley looking at it.

"Student gave it to me for pulling them out of the Cam after they'd fallen in drunk. And a bottle of Merlot, but I drank that already." Martin offers Abley some coffee from a pot. Abley shakes his head and puts out a hand to decline.

"Atticus Stamp? The billionaire media mogul?" Abley repeats his question a little more forcefully, squinting his eyes at Martin. "You don't like him."

"Is that a rhetorical question?" Martin sits in his desk chair, wiping his forehead with a handkerchief as the sun streams into the little room without air conditioning. Martin opens his large window. "Do sit, Inspector," Martin gestures to a seat for Abley, then looks wistfully out the window. "I do love that Japanese acacia. You should see the sun shine through the leaves in the Autumn. Positively aflame. You know, a blackbird often sings. Such an overlooked bird, don't you think? Taken for granted."

"I'm not in the habit of asking rhetorical questions, Professor. I think that is more your department." Abley stares at Martin, reminding him he is not there for social reasons.

"Yes, alright, I'll admit it. I don't

like the corrupt, evil, contemptible, nihilistic, controlling, undemocratic son of a gun Atticus Stamp. I wish him not one jot of wellness." Then Professor Smith looks into Abley's eyes. "Hang on, is this a formal interview? Do I need a solicitor?"

"I'm just making enquiries." Abley pulls out his notebook and looks for a page to write on. "I'd just learnt that your specialism is 'the British media and big business, and their impact on democracy.' Is that right?"

"A brutal simplification, but if it makes it easier, yes, partly," Martin stirs milk into his coffee and clinks the spoon. "Funny to hear one's life's work reduced into a sentence like that. Pretty genius."

"I must say, I find it hard to disagree with your comments on the media earlier at the Vice Chancellor's Brunch." Abley picks up one of Martin's books. "Newspapers make my job harder. Always giving too much away, or printing dead alleys, riling up the public when we need calm."

"Power, influence, yacht parties collide with fake news and clickbait. Who needs democracy when you can buy airtime." Martin pauses, again aware that he is looking at a police Inspector. "Forgive me. I care less about these things as I grow closer to the soil. Simple pleasures are more important these days. Kropotkin. Good coffee."

"You see, Mr Stamp tried his best to connect you to Terrence Montagner. As we spoke about at the Brunch at the Vice Chancellor's just now, the place card. You remember. So, I have to ask again, can you shed any light on Terrence Montagner's whereabouts? Have you heard anything?" Abley fishes, hoping perhaps Martin will slip up or tell him something he has not already heard—anything to move this case forward.

"Is it a crime to speak out against power?" Martin says. Abley's heart sinks. The last thing he needs is another lecture about power. But Martin continues, "Even at a university? We have been over this already. He had my number and a date for lunch on my nameplate because he wanted to meet up to talk about a position in the politics department. We only sat together by chance that evening at supper when I gave him my details anyway. Not many people were attending supper, as the Formal Hall was the same week," Martin shakes his head and sips his coffee. He opens a packet of biscuits.

"Squashed fly, Inspector? Garibaldi. I cannot eat Bourbon. I'm not a royalist, for goodness sake." Martin passes the packet of biscuits to Abley. Abley decides a biscuit won't get him into trouble for accepting bribes, so takes a couple. He rather likes them, and if he has to listen to talk about academia, they might sweeten the pill.

"Thanks," Abley munches. "College supper?"

"Yes, yes. But you're speaking to the wrong person. That night at supper, Terrence told me he was worried about a certain person."

"Who? Atticus Stamp?" Abley writes in his notepad.

"Who else?" Martin dunks another biscuit into his coffee.

Abley decides not to share that Terrence Montagner's constituency office has been ransacked nor that his books have been defaced in the College library. Nor about the possible blackmailing of Montagner by Atticus Stamp. He is pretty sure that Atticus was just trying to throw shade on Martin at this point using the place card, but still has a feeling that there is something Martin is not telling him. However, he is less inclined to believe that any more sharing will take place in this tiny office today.

*

After the Inspector has left, Martin picks up something from his desk. It is a brochure for a new wing of St Andrew's College. It looks all futuristic and out of place in Cambridge. Attached with a paper clip is an invitation to attend the grand opening, telling the reader about a champagne reception and that Logan Lax will cut the ribbon. Martin pulls the invitation off the brochure, rips it in two, and chucks it in the bin. Then he chucks the brochure in, too.

"Good riddance, I say." Martin looks at Kropotkin, who is looking back at him with big brown eyes. Martin opens a tin on his desk and gives his dog a canine biscuit from it. "Who needs wealth when you share your life with a dog?" He smiles at Kropotkin, stroking him softly, then leans down to kiss his head.

20 THE MONSTER

"This is the young lady I met walking the dogs on Sunday," Eadie tells Muriel. "She's very kind to animals. I'm glad she's come." They both watch Daisy walking up the drive to the 'Rescue Me' rescue centre, then through the automatic glass doors of the entrance. "Hello, Dear." Eadie smiles at Daisy. Daisy is far too preoccupied for pleasantries, having been frantically looking for Lady Woof Woof for hours, and now completely out of breath, having run here from Trumpington Road after someone posted a sighting online of her dog in the area.

"I live with a monster! He's the worst human being on the planet. We all know it. Let's face it. Who was I kidding?" Daisy looks at Eadie and Muriel. "Well, this is the last straw!" Then

Daisy brushes her hair out of her eyes and calms a little. "Is it true? Do you have Lady Woof Woof? Thank you for calling me."

"Yes, yes. We scanned Lady Woof Woof's chip in the back of her neck and found your phone number. It's always such a good idea to have the latest number with the chip, so well done. But I do remember you from Jesus Green anyway, so we would have found you somehow," Eadie tells Daisy. Muriel, looking a little tired, nods and then opens the office door, letting Lady Woof Woof out and back to her rightful owner.

"I'm so grateful to you for taking her in. Poor darling," Daisy cries, kissing Lady Woof Woof, clearly very upset and emotional. "I'm not going back to him. That's for sure. He's done it this time!" Daisy squeezes Lady Woof Woof, who has actually enjoyed the peace and quiet of the centre compared to being shouted at by Atticus Stamp in the back of the car. But the Saluki knows which side her bread is buttered and wags her tail and licks Daisy, happy to be back in the arms of the one who spoils her the most. "I bet he wasn't even sorry?" Daisy asks them.

"Oh, he didn't come in to hand over your dog. He tied her up outside, attached her to our railings then walked off down the avenue," Muriel explains, tired of people who treat animals like objects. "We really don't like it when people do that, as it's hot outside, and we are not always looking at what's happening out there.

We have put up a notice explaining that people must check in their animals if they wish to leave them."

"What the hell?! You're kidding." Daisy pets Lady Woof Woof and looks upset.

"Don't worry, she drank water and ate some food we just gave her."

"He took her a couple of hours ago. I've been looking everywhere. He didn't answer his phone. When I see him, I'll kill him!" Daisy screws up her face, Eadie not having seen this side of Daisy before and is a little taken aback.

"Oh, I wouldn't do that, dear," Eadie replies, looking at the anger in Daisy's face. "A nice cup of tea, that's what you need." Muriel holds out the teapot, and Daisy nods okay. "We are happy to keep hold of Lady Woof Woof for a little while if you need time to calm down."

"Oh, don't worry about that, I'm fine. I'm leaving Atticus, and I know exactly where to go," Daisy replies, narrowing her eyes.

*

Less than an hour later, Daisy is knocking at Logan's house. His butler opens the front door and looks at her small bag. Logan shouts from the house to ask who it is.

"I've nowhere to go and nothing to wear!" Daisy shouts back. Logan bounds into the hall.

"You have come to the right place. You can stay here for as long as you like. And in case you've forgotten, I'm a billionaire, honey, and have the wealth to make your dreams come true." Logan picks up Daisy's small shoulder bag, strokes Lady Woof Woof and invites them inside the house. He whispers to the butler to tell the chef to get some refreshments straight away. Nothing will stop him from convincing Daisy to be his girlfriend now.

21 PUTTING PRACTICE

Abley turns up at the police station to find that someone has set out his putting green in his office again after Raynott had it cleared away earlier – the metal hole, the fake grass, and two of his favourite putters. Lemon is there, talking to Constable Love who looks less than happy about it.

"Forget boardroom meetings. We're all about the greenside chats now," Lemon kindly explains to Constable Love, making it clear it was Lemon who reestablished the game.

"Who needs a thinking cap when you've got a golf cap," Abley winks at Love as he puts on his cap, which he notices is waiting for him on his desk.

"Oh, my stuff has gone?" Love asks Lemon, a little teary. Then he lifts his muscular arms and throws them down by his sides so hard that Lemon and Abley are shocked by the strength they hear in the slap of skin on skin.

"You'll do well with the other Constables in the main open-plan office. I've set you up there, as that is where you should have been originally. There was a mistake in my absence," Lemon explains, smiling. "Near the reception. I'm not sure why the Super thought this was a spare space. It's not." Lemon sits down at the desk where Love was seated and pushes a box of the Constable's belongings across the desk for him to pick up.

"The Superintendent put me here as he said I'd learn from you, Sir," Love replies heartbroken, looking at Abley, then at the putting green, and finally shuffling out of the room with the box.

"He might be super sweet, but that Constable's not lazy." Lemon turns Love's screen towards Abley. They both see a story about how Daisy knew Terrence Montagner. The story runs a photograph of the two of them at what looks like a posh London event. "I bet her phone's contact list is like a VIP lounge. Full of tycoons and the powerful."

"Have you just ousted Constable Love, Sergeant?" Abley smirks at Lemon. "I like your leadership skills. Please continue."

"We'll get this desk out shortly to make more space for your practice swings." Lemon then looks at his own phone and searches for Daisy's personal posts. "Oof." Lemon shows Abley the photograph Daisy has loaded onto her profile of Atticus Stamp kneeling beside a dead male lion, him holding up the head proudly, having just shot the lion in so-called 'trophy hunting' style. "Throwing some serious shade right there on her boyfriend." Lemon then clicks on the local news site to see if they have picked it up, and the image is right there for all to see.

Abley tries hard to think of the facts, pacing and fidgeting with his golf cap, picking up a putter and ball, "So, this is what we know. MP, Terrence Montagner, is missing. Billionaire media mogul Atticus Stamp came to Cambridge to give a talk to the Union. Logan Lax, fashion billionaire, has paid for and is here to open a new wing of his College, St Andrew's. Both arrived the day before Terrence Montagner disappeared. There are uncorroborated stories that Atticus Stamp was blackmailing Terrence Montagner over some insider trading in order to gain votes for the Freedom of the Press bill. But we have no proof. We also know that both Atticus Stamp and Professor Martin Smith have both lied so far about knowing each other and Terrence Montagner, even though they all went to school together." Abley putts a ball, then watches his ball narrowly miss the metal hole. "We also now know that Atticus's girlfriend, Daisy, also knew Terrence Montagner. Fact."

"Doesn't this all point towards Stamp having something to do with Montagner's disappearance? Jealousy? Money?" Lemon suggests, adding, "The blackmailing, which, as you say, is still being investigated? Didn't you say you thought Daisy was also getting cosy with Logan Lax at that posh garden thing you went to? So, she knows them all. Is she the missing link?" Lemon asks.

Abley moves his head from side to side, mulling. "No evidence."

"So do we think none of them are involved, and Montagner has just done a runner because of his taxes, and or worried that news will break that he shot a man while boar hunting?" Lemon asks.

"Ah, the flusher during the hunt. How are we getting on with corroborating that?"

"Nope, nothing yet. Nothing either from Emily's conversations. The Master cannot remember. Convenient that." Lemon reads from his notebook.

"So, what we know is that Terrence Montagner left his phone and wallet, but more significantly, none of this staff has any record of him making contact since." Abley picks up his ball.

"He could have orchestrated the whole thing. And, there's no evidence to suggest foul play yet." Lemon reminds Abley of the evidence. "You're always saying follow the evidence."

"True. But there have been no CCTV sightings of Montagner since he went missing—no visitors to his home. The calls to his phone have been from other MPs, Westminster staff, plus Atticus Stamp's angry threats." Abley takes another swing at the putting hole. "Don't forget the break-ins and vandalism at his constituency offices, and in St Andrew's College library," Abley adds.

"And what about the fish? Montagner said he was going to adopt some fish, and he was going to give a talk about fish at The Pond Gentleman's Club. And, it is likely that Stamp either himself or had someone else place a dead fish in the lining of Terrence Montagner's curtains. Is that just a red herring?" Lemon chuckles to himself, watching Abley's ball enter the hole. "You've still got it!"

Abley smiles, picks up another ball from a basket of golf balls on his desk and lifts a putter to aim at the hole again but misses. Then he leans on his putter and looks at Lemon directly in the eye. "We don't have enough evidence."

"Atticus Stamp, Logan Lax, Professor Martin Smith and Terrence Montagner all know each other. Like you say, Stamp and Lax arrived the day before Montagner went missing?" Lemon reminds Abley.

"I think they know more than they're letting on. But I don't know if that is significant to his disappearance," Abley puts his putter down for a moment against his desk and walks over to the window. The two men stand in silence for a while, both thinking.

"What about Daisy?" Lemon asks. "We've skirted over that."

"What about Daisy?" Abley turns, shrugging, not quite seeing any evidence.

"Well, there's the photo of her with Terrence Montagner here, as we see. Could Montagner have something on her, and Atticus has got rid of him to protect her?" Lemon suggests.

"I don't know. But from everything I know, she seems to care mostly about her dog." Abley pauses and then adds, "You know, people who like animals are usually good."

"Eh? You've never said that." Lemon crumples up his face, surprised by his boss's comment.

"Well, maybe I've mellowed, and of course, there are exceptions," Abley pauses, then feels the need to explain his comment. "Look, I've adopted a cat. Arnold." Abley watches the surprise spread across Lemon's face, then adds. "He's such a clever cat."

"What, he's trained you to open cans of tuna?" Lemon smirks.

"Yes!" Abley sighs, then thinks of the case. "We need to make some headway, and fast."

"We have cancelled non-essential staff leave for the next few days. We've searches down by Lammas Land, also up at Wandlebury, Fen Ditton, along the river. We've looked at the CCTV from the train station, bus station, spoken the taxi firms. We're expanding into private doorbell footage," Lemon reassures his boss that everyone is working hard on the case.

"Tell them to keep at it. It's still on the news, which is actually working in our favour. It might smoke out the clue we need to make sense of this all. He could be anywhere in the world right now. But the chances are, he's still here, somewhere. I wish–" Abley stops himself. In his gut, he knows he is searching not for a missing person but instead a dead body. He wonders why Elizabeth seems completely uninterested in helping him solve this one.

22 WATCHING YOU

Professor Martin Smith stands on the pavement beneath a beautiful lime tree, vibrant in the full sun. Finely cut lawns tumble down towards the leafy road, and borders lined with hollyhocks, buddleia bushes, roses, and lavender flow up to thick hedgerows. Martin is not in the city centre, crammed with its lines of Victorian terraces, or further out towards the more modern cereal box constructions. This road, off-grid, is only reserved for multi-millionaires. Barrow Road. Usually, nothing of note happens. But, tonight, Professor Smith has plans.

For Martin has read what Atticus Stamp's newspaper has just published about himself today. He has it in his hands. Accusing Martin of all kinds of bias and being a risk to students.

The paper even dug up Martin's old communist card, which he had from joining the party as an undergrad all those years ago. There are quotes saying Martin is calling for revolution, that he is an extremist, has a bunker where he is plotting the end of democracy, and lots of other made-up stories. This is a deliberate piece to discredit Martin, just as he is about to retire, perhaps even to get him sacked, thereby causing him to lose his pension.

Martin pulls up a hood over his face and walks up the drive. He glances left and right and bends down next to what looks like Atticus's car. He pulls out his keys, and opens a keyring which has a little knife. It is enough to stab the tyres and deflate each one, then he keys the sides of the car. He looks inside and spots Atticus's car keys still in the car ignition. Eh? His eyes dart about, in case Atticus is about to come back. The vandalism makes Martin feel slightly better, but not much.

23 INSPECTOR AT THE GOGS

Abley has come to the Gog Magog Golf course in Cambridge, four miles south of the city centre, up on a range of low chalk hills on an otherwise flat land with big skies. Now, with his trustee electric bike, it only takes him fifteen minutes from the Police Station. Abley is in the frame of mind to take the little wins where he can. It gives Abley time to think, precious moments away from phone calls and the pressure growing around him to find the missing MP. And anything to take his mind off the wedding and his ex-wife's glowing face at the altar still seared into his memory. Maureen told him he was the only person in the world who could make her feel happy. Are her feelings so fake that she can just switch men like they were tins of beans in the supermarket? How could he have been so stupid? He had been hoping all this time she'd come to her senses, tell him she'd made a big mistake, and beg him to take her back. Isn't that what is supposed to happen? What is she doing? Married?

He looks up at the green grass, trees and fairways. The fresh air hits him, and his first few holes on the old course would usually immediately transport him away to a calmer place – the club allowing him to head out without a partner these days, especially on a late afternoon midweek. Today, however, the open space and quiet cannot quite lift his despair. He can hear the crickets in the long grass. He spots a couple of red kites fly above the rough and notices a vapour trail in the sky from a commercial flight, carrying passengers off on their holidays, no doubt. There are yet to be any players behind or in front of him, a rare treat. After doing well on three holes, he swings and lands his ball on the green. Everything is going right for him today in his game. Abley's phone rings. He sighs.

"But I've just come from there?" He replies, walking back to the nineteenth at the clubhouse, where golfers come to drown their sorrows or exaggerate their victories. That is when Abley notices Lemon sitting at the bar.

"Hey! I was just–" Abley is pleased to see his colleague.

"Sixth sense?" Lemon slides a stiff drink

along the bar to Abley, who makes no argument and downs it in one.

"His exact words were 'tell him to stop thinking and get back here immediately and do something.'" Lemon sighs. "I've been ordered to find you. He's had a call from No.10. I'm presuming he's not trusted me to get you back and is hounding you on your phone." Lemon knows Superintendent Raynott well. Abley nods, and then, from somewhere, this well of anger rises inside.

"He makes it worse. He makes me want to dig in my heels and be disobedient." Abley notices a golfer frowning at Abley, so he adds, "Metaphorically speaking. Not actually digging heels on the putting greens. I'm speaking about a person, don't worry," Abley explains, but the other golfer is a little suspicious and tuts as he walks away. Abley shakes his head, then turns back to Lemon. "Raynott has not one iota of respect for my methods, my policing. It's his way or the highway."

"Yes, well, don't daydream about hitting him with your electric bike," Lemon replies.

"He just barks orders or yaps. Yap, yap, yap" Abley moves his hand like a mouth, chatting away.

"Where shall we go?" Lemon. "If we are not going back?"

"Doesn't a leader make suggestions rather than ask questions?" Abley reminds Lemon of his new training.

"Out to finish your round, then. I can walk with you," Lemon says. He picks up his drink and knocks it back. Unlike Abley's stiff one, his is a pineapple juice.

"You're getting good at this leadership malarkey." Abley pats Lemon on the back, and they wander back into the sunshine. Abley has missed his turn at the tee, as they wait for a slot. "We have time," Abley looks at his watch. "I'm two under par. I'm not stopping now." Abley looks up at the kind golfers who wave him through. One woman, perhaps ten years his junior, with a tan, pink shirt and white skirt, smiles coyly from under her visor. It leaves Abley cold. He remembers Maureen giving him that same look at the start of their relationship as she walked the course with him, and look where that got him.

The two friends quickly march around the fifteen holes, taking just over an hour and a half. By then, they are able to get on their bikes and head back to the station.

"It's strange how the angrier Raynott is with me, the better my golf gets. Did you notice that?" Abley shrugs.

"I think your golf is going to be good for a while then," Lemon suggests.

24 THE NO SHOW

Following the Vice Chancellor's Brunch, it is customary for there to be supper in their private home the same evening. This is another opportunity for the Vice-Chancellor to invite whomever they so choose. Historically, these occasions are packed with high donors and notables, and tonight there is no departure from tradition. Accompanied by Daisy, Logan Lax takes pride of place at top table. Perhaps more unusually, Inspector Bob Abley has also been invited over again, or rather, is taking the place tonight of Superintendent Raynott, who was as keen as mustard to rub shoulders but could not turn down an invite from the Commissioner of Police, which happened to clash with this evening. Abley hopes he can talk through the case with Elizabeth, also in attendance, but unfortunately, Emily has plonked herself between them and, so far, has succeeded in steering all conversation towards dogs, the classics, or even golf to keep Abley from speaking about anything remotely related to work.

"So, I hear from Cuthbert that your course rating is now two?" Emily asks Abley. "That's pretty impressive."

"I played off one today," Abley replies, correcting his handicap.

"Really?" Emily is impressed.

Professor Martin Smith walks in a little late, dishevelled, and sits opposite Elizabeth.

"Well, I guess the phrase 'go big or go home' takes on a whole new meaning when 'home' looks like a small country." Martin opens his eyes wide at the banquet before him, the silver service and tables dressed with huge displays of orchids and candles.

"You were just here for the brunch," Elizabeth greets Martin with a smile. "Surely the swank comes as no surprise."

"I don't even remember this room. Does this place come with a map?" Martin looks around at the forty-plus guests. "I feel completely underdressed." Martin is still wearing a hoodie under his jacket.

Elizabeth's eyes are drawn towards Daisy. She notices Logan's arm behind the back of Daisy's chair and Daisy fawning into his shoulder as he cracks some witticism. "It's like witnessing a silent dance, where every step is choreographed to mask the undeniable chemistry bubbling underneath." Elizabeth notices the empty chair with a name card for Atticus on the other side of Daisy.

"You know you're in posh food territory when the garnish on your plate costs more than your own watch. Is this gold?" Martin ignores Elizabeth's comment about Logan's love life and instead uses his fork to pull off some edible gold leaf. "Is that safe to eat? Is it actually gold?" Martin shakes his head in disbelief, looking at Emily.

"Yes, I believe so," Emily replies. "A symphony of flavours orchestrated by a culinary maestro. Michelin, apparently," she nods towards what must be the kitchen as a flurry of waiters appear and disappear through some wide double doors at the end of the room.

"So, Liz, do you have any thoughts on what happened to Terrence Montagner?" Abley asks.

"More wine?" Emily leans across Elizabeth to stop her from seeing Abley's face.

"No, none at all," Elizabeth shakes her head, replying to Abley as she studies the gold leaf Martin is now holding up into the light.

"We continue to pursue every lead and have more feet on this case now. We're still putting a call out for Mr Montagner to come forward." Abley tries again to entice Elizabeth into a conversation.

"Who are your suspects?" Elizabeth cannot help herself and asks as she moves her own gold leaf to the side of her plate, frowning.

"None formally, as yet," Abley replies. Martin can feel Abley's eyes on him, but then thankfully notices Abley looks towards Logan Lax and Daisy.

"And what about Daisy?" Elizabeth asks quietly.

"There's a photograph, actually," Abley whispers to Elizabeth, "where she was snapped having supper with Terrence Montagner. But rather like this here tonight. She could have just been sitting next to him in a crowd."

"Hmm," Elizabeth replies. Emily is unhappy with this conversation and drops her fork loudly on her plate.

"What do you think, Liz?" Abley asks, ignoring Emily.

"I heard Daisy say that sometimes she wants to be a free spirit on her own," Elizabeth says, leaning away from Martin so he cannot hear her speak. "She told me she could murder someone, and her Followers would believe her to be innocent." Elizabeth raises her eyebrows at Abley.

"These mushrooms really are special. Chestnut. Scrummy." Emily leans to block Elizabeth and Abley's conversation.

Abley looks across at Daisy. It becomes clear that Atticus Stamp is a 'no show'.

"Atticus. What are you doing? Why aren't you here?" They all hear Daisy and see her holding her phone to her ear. It is as if Daisy has heard Abley and Elizabeth talking.

"Where's Atticus?" Elizabeth shouts along the long top table to Daisy.

"I don't know. We had a fight," Daisy openly admits. Logan can see Elizabeth's brain whirring and steps in to defend Daisy.

"Atticus is allergic to Daisy's dog, so I offered Daisy rooms until they return to London," Logan explains. Daisy is a little confused by this response, as surely they are together now. Or, at least, that is how it seemed to her when they spent the afternoon together in quite intimate positions. Logan scrunches his eyebrows as if to make it clear to Daisy not to pay attention to his words. Of course, he is into her.

"So, you've left Atticus?" Elizabeth asks Daisy, raising her voice again. Abley listens closely.

"I need to speak with him. If you see him, can you say I'm trying to get in touch? He's not answering his phone. The staff don't know where he is. Maybe they're lying, and he just doesn't want to speak to me," Daisy says, not wanting to share her private life with all and sundry and aware there are many eyes on her now.

"I do like shouting, can we all just talk about the food?" Emily says to Elizabeth, worried this is pulling Elizabeth into a stressful situation that she knows her friend can do without. Daisy decides to get up and walk along to speak to the women rather than continuing to shout up the line of diners. She leans over Elizabeth's chair and smiles at Martin.

"Was he allergic?" Elizabeth asks Daisy, not skipping a beat.

"No. He didn't grow up with dogs. He's a bit of a travel-light type of person. Dogs leave hairs." Daisy shrugs, looking at Emily and shaking her head at Atticus's attitude towards canines.

"Do you know where he is?" Elizabeth asks again.

"I've honestly no idea. I went back for some things, and he wasn't there. I wish I knew. I need to speak with him."

"You went back?" Elizabeth doesn't understand what Daisy means.

"To his home, for some of my things. I've come over to ask you, Inspector, if you've heard anything. I'm a bit worried," Daisy opens her eyes wide at Abley, waiting for a response.

"Here, here," Martin applauds Daisy's decision, ignoring her concerns. "You've seen the light. Bravo, I say. Dump the bugger." Martin takes a large gulp of red wine. "Would you like some gold?" He looks down at the gold on everyone's plates, a little relieved that he can forget about slashing Atticus's tyres. Daisy leaving Atticus trumps that, for sure.

"When was the last time you saw him?" Abley asks Daisy, a little surprised to hear that another person might be missing.

"This morning. He's probably just punishing me," Daisy shrugs. "But, like I say, his staff don't know where he's gone. I mean, they don't always know, or they're lying, like I say. Well, listen, it's not my problem. So–" and Daisy shuts up.

"Bravo! Dumped and missing!" Martin takes another gulp of wine.

"And you're a communist propagandist apparently," Elizabeth replies to Martin, aware Atticus Stamp's rag mag had slandered Martin Smith in his newspapers.

"Red under the bed. That's me," Martin smiles, shaking his head. "How can he get away with this utter character assassination?"

"You must, still, be pleased that two of the country's biggest capitalists seem to have vanished," Elizabeth replies to Martin, now ignoring Daisy.

"Cheers," Martin nods, taking another large gulp of wine. "If I thought these disappearances would make any dent in the greed of big business, yes, I think I would be happy." Martin fidgets in his chair. Elizabeth notices this but decides not to say anything. Abley also notices and narrows his eyes.

"That's not very nice of you," Daisy says to Martin, still listening and offering the smallest of frowns.

"No, no, it isn't. I'm not feeling very charitable today," Martin thinks about the paper. "I don't even read it. You know, I've had what seems like hundreds of people contact me today on my phone. I've had to turn it off." Martin removes his mobile from his pocket and waves it about, which is turned off. It becomes more apparent that perhaps Martin is already a little drunk.

"D'you think Atticus knows where Terrence Montagner is? Did he say anything about it? You leave him, and he disappears? Are you sure you didn't know Terrence?" Abley leans over to ask Daisy. But this causes Daisy to run out the front door, clearly upset.

"Who invited the police? I thought this was supposed to be a polite occasion?" Logan looks directly at the Vice Chancellor, who cannot quite hear what is happening. Logan gets up and follows Daisy. Abley feels frustrated that he is getting nowhere fast.

"So, does this mean you'll help me?" Abley asks Elizabeth quietly.

"Not on your nelly. I'm not ready to deal with dead bodies," she replies, looking at Abley and then Emily, who nods back at her, indicating that it is the right decision.

25 A NEW WING

The following morning, Abley and Lemon enter St Andrew's College just in time for the opening of the new multi-million-pound wing from the generous benefactor, Logan Lax. Cordons and signposts usher them towards the very back of the College, where lawns undulate between large oak trees and rose borders and meet the second duck pond within College walls, a pond almost large enough to launch a small dinghy. Before the grounds end, a rather unusual building, which looks more like a spaceship than anything suited for study, gleams in the sun, all white, glossy and brutalist.

"Beam me up, Scotty," Abley smiles at Lemon.

"It's like a spaceship crash landed in the wrong century, and that bit looks like it melted in the rain?" Lemon scrunches his forehead, trying not to stare and be dazzled by the sun bouncing off the gleaming monstrosity.

"Oh, I'm sure this is the architect's signature pièce de résistance!" Abley chuckles as they wander closer.

"That must be him." Lemon points at a man wearing a bright yellow jacket that matches his bleached blonde hair and, with checked green and white trousers, looks like something out of Alice Through the Looking Glass. The tell-tale sign is that he is pointing at the melted section, standing next to Logan Lax, and being applauded by a group of sycophants and Fellows who have left their rooms mainly for the early alcohol fix to cope with their supervisions later.

Abley and Lemon notice Daisy arrive with Lady Woof Woof. They both half expect Atticus Stamp to turn up late, but it becomes more interesting when they watch Logan put his hand around Daisy's back a few times as they talk to adoring guests. After a while, Daisy spots the Inspector and walks towards him, Lady Woof Woof bounding ahead. Lady Woof Woof begins to lick Abley's face, having jumped up, his paws on Abley's chest.

"Alright there, doggie. I can smell anchovies mixed with dirty socks," Abley says quietly to Lemon about Lady Woof Woof's breath. "Does she jump up like this normally? Abley asks.

"It's a sign she's missed you. All those vol-au-vents you gave her at the Vice Chancellor's garden party. Maybe she smells something. Have you been eating gravy? That's her favourite," Daisy beams, pleased to be talking about anything other than buildings.

"You had Marmite on toast this morning," Lemon laughs at his Inspector.

"Lady Woof Woof loves Marmite," Daisy smiles, her teeth almost as white as the building behind.

"Yes, well. Ahem. So, you're here on behalf of Atticus?" Abley asks, wondering where Atticus might be.

"No, I'm here to support Logan. He's been so kind to me," Daisy does not go into again the fact that she has moved out of Atticus's home and into Logan's – albeit temporarily. She said enough last night at dinner. Undoubtedly, the Inspector can put two and two together for himself. "Logan's dreamt of this building for a while now. It's helping to save the planet."

"Eh?" Lemon frowns. "By using up all the plastic?"

"No, it's supporting research into sustainable clothing," Daisy explains, pleased with herself having grasped the point of the morning.

"Nothing says saving the planet like a twenty-thousand-pound organic cotton suit, does it," Lemon replies, looking at the expensively dressed Logan Lax.

"Atticus not interested?" Abley asks Daisy? "Another no-show?"

"I don't know. I need to talk to him. I still haven't seen him at all. Logan thinks he's probably on a trip to buy up more publications around the world. Building his empire," Daisy sighs, adding, "This feels more meaningful. Doesn't it? Here, I mean." Daisy looks at the white melting building. "People need clothes."

"Hmm," Abley looks down at the programme in his hand, promoting the opening. "'Sustainability and Ethical Fashion Research. Materials Science.' Sounds very–" Abley decides not to finish his sentence, rather, he notices Logan walk towards a television news crew, the same crew that interviewed Terrance Montagner at the 'Rescue Me' rescue centre. Daisy nods goodbye, puts Lady Woof Woof on the lead and heads back to stand nearer the interview. Abley and Lemon listen to him talk about the future of fashion, how materials will change, more will be recycled, more natural products. Then, out of the blue, Logan announces, looking straight into the camera filming a live insert into the morning news bulletin, "Atticus, if you're watching, you're worrying people. Just get in touch. Tell everyone that you're okay. Stop playing silly buggers."

Abley glances at Daisy and notices that she is crying. What? So, Atticus really is missing, too, now? Only moments after the live broadcast does Abley's phone start ringing. He shows Lemon, it reads 'Tarsier Supremo'. Abley hits the answer button. "Hello, Super. Yes, yes, I'm here.

No, I didn't know. Yes, yes that will be our next steps. Exactly. Well, I'm currently talking with you. No, I'm not being facetious. Yes, right away." Abley cuts the call, "Three bags full."

"So, we have two 'missing' persons?" Lemon states, making air quotes with his fingers.

"Looking like it," Abley replies. "Atticus's staff just called it in half an hour ago. He never returned home to any of his residencies. They cannot get hold of him. Love took the call and chose to tell Raynott first."

"Even if Atticus Stamp is blackmailing Terrance Montagner about some Freedom of the Press bill, what would that have to do with his disappearance? Why disappear? All these things are not helping," Lemon states.

"Hmm. That's not been confirmed yet either." Abley hears a noise in the sky. "We need to speak with Mr Lax and Daisy." But as soon as Abley opens his mouth, a helicopter noisily lands on the lawn and swoops both Logan and Daisy away.

"That's one way to avoid the traffic," Lemon suggests.

"And our questions," Abley replies, now completely convinced he needs to speak to them both urgently. But how is he going to achieve that?

26 A CLOTHES EMPIRE

Mikayla hops into the 'Rescue Me' rescue centre this morning wearing a bunny rabbit costume, carrying a suitcase full of her designer doggie clothes, just as Eadie and Muriel are giving a rescue dog to new parents for his forever home and helping with some friendly advice.

"Just remember that he might cry tonight, but he'll soon settle. Cuddles always work," Eadie kindly suggests.

"A treat often will do the trick, too," Muriel reassures the new dog parents. "Nothing too rich for the first few days. Just the ones we've given you and the food you're taking home. Important to keep them on the same food for a while, then if you want to change their diet, do it gradually," Muriel explains.

"Of course," The dog parents reply, looking at each other and smiling excitedly about the new adventure.

"Here," Eadie hands the child, who has come with the family to adopt the dog, a blanket.

"Put this in their dog bed. It will make their new home smell familiar. Soon, you will smell like home, and they will relax and feel safe. This will help them for now. Also, keep talking in quiet and calm tones," Eadie explains.

The little child beams up at Eadie and takes the blanket as the dog, tail curled up underneath his body, nervously tries to determine if the family is friend or foe. They stroke the dog, now named Jasper, and speak in hushed tones, having a really intimate and special moment with their new family member. Mikayla interrupts, drops her suitcase on the floor and starts to try to flog the family some outfits. She holds a strawberry hat and red coat against the terrified rescue dog. Mikayla ruffles the dog's hair on his head and then kisses it. "You are the cutest, most gorgeous little thing."

"Er, please, what are you doing?" Muriel asks as Eadie grabs the outfit, smiles, and waves to the confused family, who decide to take their leave. "Thank you very much, and do stay in touch. We're here if you have any questions!" Eadie shouts across Mikayla. Mikayla then grabs her clothing back from Eadie.

"I was about to make a sale there," Mikayla

beams. “It was a perfect size. They could see what a stylish garment this is.” Mikayla kisses her fingertips and shuts her eyes.

“Not in here, you weren’t. We’ve not granted you permission,” Eadie replies grumpily, being well aware of Mikayla’s pushy nature when she meets her in the dog group on Jesus Green.

“Look, I’ll make you a deal. You stock them here,” Mikayla looks at the merchandise around the reception area, “and it looks like this place needs a bit of magic, and I’ll cut you in for ten per cent of the sales. I can’t play nicer than that now, can I?” Mikala starts to spread her clothes across a display stand.

“These are actually cruel, Mikayla.” Muriel looks at the strawberry hat. “They’ll cause the dogs to seriously overheat. And no dog should be wearing a coat in summer. It’s an absolute no, no.” Muriel hands the dog costume back.

“Are you kidding? This isn’t cruel. This shows our pups that we care and makes dogs much more appealing,” Mikayla replies, not listening to a word Muriel says.

“To whom?” Eadie asks. “I think you should leave if this is all you’ve come for,” Eadie glares at Mikayla but is also a little bit frightened of her refusal to take no for an answer. This is the third or more time that Mikayla has come in.

“Alright, twenty per cent, and I’m practically giving them away.” Mikayla removes a line of dog toys from a vertical stand and replaces them with some more of her handmade robot-silver body suits for dachshunds.

“Have you considered making children’s clothes rather than dressing animals up as humans?” Muriel asks, ushering Mikayla out of the reception and encouraging her to pick up her suitcase of samples. Eadie follows, lifting off the garments already hung up on the stands and removing them to take with her to the exit.

“You’ll be sorry when Logan Lax picks up my line of doggie designer outfits.” Mikayla winks. “Aww, no, I couldn’t do that to you. I’ll still sell you some at discount. Because you’re both gorgeous.”

Eadie hands the outfits to Mikayla and waves her to leave, then says to Muriel, “I just don’t have the energy this morning,” Eadie tells Muriel as they watch as Mikayla turns her back on them and bends over to reveal a bunny pom-pom tail on her bottom, then turns again to bow before walking off. “Charming. I can never tell if she’s joking or not.”

“I think that woman has a darker side,” Muriel replies. “How can anyone be that happy all the time? And, she’ll be lucky if she gets Logan to even listen to her say hello, let alone pitch her business proposition.”

27 LAIR OR LIAR

Daisy and Logan have returned home after the Wing opening in College. Daisy throws herself onto a couch that overlooks the large garden. It is clear to the chef, busily preparing brunch, that this young lady is the new feature in Logan's life. He overheard Logan telling the butler to arrange for all of Daisy's favourite things to be placed around the home–flowers, music, drink. It helped the chef assess how to adjust his menu, as he could search online for her most-loved dishes, so he is making shakshuka, a low-carb option for a slim lady. The chef listens and watches but tries to remain invisible as he sprinkles fresh coriander and rosemary leaves into a pot.

"I thought the opening went rather well, don't you?" Logan walks over to join Daisy, kissing her on the top of her head. He can tell there is something on Daisy's mind as she looks pained. "Hey, what's the matter," Logan asks warmly, reaching out for her. For a while, Daisy stares out into the garden and says nothing but then looks at Logan, shaking her head in disbelief.

"I can't believe Atticus is actually missing. Maybe I should go back and wait for him there?" Daisy looks into Logan's eyes. It is the last thing she wants to do. "I mean, missing? What's going on?" Daisy looks frightened.

"Don't you dare. Your home is here now," Logan kisses her on the lips and then stares into her eyes.

"What if he comes back and is mad at us? What if he does something crazy?" Daisy's eyes begin to water.

"He won't get past Dozer if he comes here." Logan casually points at his bodyguard, who has been standing behind the door and looks like he can lift a truck in the air with one hand – Dozer's earpiece connected to three other bodyguards dotted around the property. Daisy looks at Dozer, realises he could crush Atticus with one little finger, and breathes a sigh of relief.

"Thank you," she replies.

"I won't let him bother you ever again. Promise. When he comes back, that's his affair, not yours. He was beastly to you." Logan leans in to give Daisy a proper kiss. Lady Woof Woof sits down on the edge of the room and the garden and lets out a sigh of contentment. Logan pulls back and smiles, all while holding eye contact with Daisy. He takes her hand and pulls her up, then gently coaxes her towards the stairs and bedroom. The chef looks at Lady Woof Woof and realises he will be eating this brunch with the dog.

28 RING TONE

A group of dog parents have congregated in the nineteenth-century Mill Road Cemetery for lunchtime walkies. An historic landmark, not an active place of burial, it is known by locals as a wildlife haven, with its mixed trees, wildflowers and many blackberry bushes already showing signs of fruit. In the area known as St 'Mary the Less', around twelve dogs are sniffing each other's bottoms, wagging their tails and chasing balls in varying order. Elizabeth is standing beside Eadie from the 'Rescue Me' rescue centre, who has popped home for lunch and brought a long-termer rescue dog with her for a longer stretch of their legs, and Martin, who still has Kropotkin on the lead, is nearby chatting to another dog owner about how to keep dogs cool in summer using frozen ice-cube snacks. Mikayla comes skipping towards the group, her dog dressed as a strawberry in one of her outfits.

"No! It's too hot, Mikayla!" Elizabeth

shouts.

"Not again. She's only just left the rescue centre this morning trying to flog us those outfits. I told her no so many times," Eadie explains to Elizabeth. "I hope she doesn't try to sell them this afternoon at our event on Parker's Piece. We need things to go smoothly. I'm going there as soon as I leave here. So much to do." Eadie frets.

"Calm your pants, ladies," Mikayla responds to the complaints about her costumes. "Logan Lax is in town. I saw him with my own eyes two days ago, and he was literally on the news just now. He's still here. He'll lap these up. It's a no brainer," Mikayla beams.

But Elizabeth pulls off the jacket from Mikayla's dog and offers Luna some water, which they lap up. Mikayla stretches out her hands for Elizabeth to give her back the outfit, but just as there is about to be a tense exchange of words, they all hear a mobile phone ring. At one point, someone says, 'Answer your phone, will you?', but they soon realise that the phone ringing does not belong to any of them. Mikayla lets go of Luna's strawberry costume and walks into the bushes, following the sound of the ringtone.

"Perhaps whoever lost their phone is ringing it? You know, to find it," Mikayla suggests thoughtfully. She picks up the phone and answers it. "Hello?" But the phone goes dead on hearing her voice. "No one," she shrugs. Then she notices the image on the screen saver. "Hey, isn't that Daisy?" All the dog parents crowd around Mikayla to peer in at the screen, Martin placing his hand on Mikayla's shoulder and moving closer. It is indeed a photograph of Daisy. "Is it Daisy's phone?" Mikayla asks, knowing Daisy has been in here before with Lady Woof Woof. "You know, when I saw Logan Lax a couple of days ago when I was with my friends, she was there. They were both on a punt together. Looking really cosy. Isn't it a small world?" Mikayla opens her eyes wide and covers her mouth.

"Who has a screen saver of themselves on their own phone?" Elizabeth ponders.

"An influencer, that's who," Mikayla beams, holding up the phone.

"Or, it could be Atticus's phone?" Martin looks around to see if the group agrees.

"I saw Logan Lax on the news just now too. He was telling Atticus Stamp to come home? As if he was missing," Elizabeth ponders.

"No, that's the politician," Martin replies, shaking his head. "Terrence Montagner is missing."

"No one has seen Atticus now either. He has failed to attend two functions he was invited to. You were at one of them, Martin. Last night." Elizabeth reminds Martin.

"Ah, Stamp'll probably turn up. What are the chances of two missing rich men, eh? The world isn't that lucky," Martin replies.

"He must get invited to so many functions," Mikayla replies thoughtfully. "I bet he's spoiled for choice and can't go to them all?"

"Well, the phone has your fingerprints all over it now, Mikayla." Martin looks worried for Mikayla. Mikayla stops laughing, realising that she does not want that, wipes her prints with her jumper, and then places the phone on a gravestone.

"Now you look guilty, wiping your prints off it. What were you afraid of?" Martin asks quietly, trying to avoid anyone hearing but failing.

"You weren't trying to cover anything up, were you?" Eadie asks innocently.

"I'm beautiful. I don't have a bad bone in my body, guys. You are freaking this baby dog Moma out! C'mon," Mikayla now has the creeps about the phone, which rings again. She squeals and dances about in her strawberry outfit. They all peer in to see who is ringing and see that it is Logan Lax. Mikayla so desperately wants to pick it up to answer but is freaked by the fact that just maybe this is too serious, even though the temptation is excruciating with the opportunity to pitch her business to the richest fashion mogul in the world.

"You not going to get that?" Eadie asks. "Your potential new buyer?"

"Leave it, Mikayla. Let the police deal with it. Don't get involved," Martin says kindly, holding Mikayla's arm to keep her from doing anything she'll regret. Mikayla smiles gratefully at Martin.

"Thank you, honey. You're right. I'm not going near that thing." She looks around behind them and across the cemetery. "Maybe that Atticus man is buried in one of the tombs in here," Mikayla says out loud, horrified. "Maybe you're right, Martin? Maybe it is Atticus Stamp's phone."

"So, now two are missing, like you say, and this is the phone of one of them, and it is possibly Atticus Stamp's," Martin looks at Elizabeth.

"Mr Stamp dumped Daisy's dog outside our shelter. She turned up when we phoned after the chip gave her number," Eadie tells Elizabeth.

"What?" Elizabeth is quite surprised.

"Lady Woof Woof, that beautiful dog. I mean, I'd seen Daisy with the dog on Jesus Green, but I wasn't completely sure. We watched back our CCTV, and there was Mr Stamp, tying the dog up to the railings outside, right where we found her," Eadie explains.

"That must have made Daisy really mad?" Elizabeth suggests.

"She wasn't best pleased with him, no. She said she was going to kill him," Eadie opens her eyes wide.

*

Inspector Abley and Sergeant Lemon turn

up, along with a few SOCOs who put up a cordon around where Mikayla found the mobile phone – interested clearly on hearing that Logan Lax had called and it has a photograph of Daisy as the screensaver.

"Holy Moly. This is serious! Why are you doing that?" Mikayla asks Sergeant Lemon.

"If you can move aside, Madam," Lemon replies, helping the SOCOs with the cordon, trying not to be drawn into the fact that Mikayla is dressed as a strawberry.

"Who found the phone?" Abley asks the group.

"It was ringing. We all heard it, didn't we?" Mikayla looks for backup from the group, who nod.

"Maybe if it is Mr Stamp's mobile he put it there deliberately," Eadie wonders.

"Please keep away from this line," Lemon kindly ushers Eadie away.

"What if he was the one who knows where that MP is and is pretending to disappear to frame Montagner," Martin moots the rather muddy idea.

"You mean he knocked off Terrence Montagner and is now pretending to be knocked off himself?" Elizabeth asks Martin wryly. "Bit of a stretch."

"Maybe we need Ghostbusters!" Mikayla suggests.

"This is no joking matter," Abley raises

his eyebrows, then turns to Martin. “D’you know anything about the whereabouts of Atticus Stamp?”

“What? No, of course I don’t. I’ve not seen him and don’t want to,” Martin frowns, then scratches his head, looking at Mikayla, who nods at him.

“Maybe that Daisy, you know, the influencer, might know something. She’s his girlfriend, after all, isn’t she? Like I said, I saw her getting all cosy in a punt with Logan Lax. Where was her man? Has she got space for two men? That’s just greedy,” Mikayla nods, hoping perhaps to have Logan for herself in some mad dream in the recesses of her mind.

“You’re very quiet, Elizabeth,” Abley says to his friend out of the ears of the others.

“This is your case, Bob, your case. I’m just walking my dogs here. Wrong place, wrong time.”

Abley looks at Elizabeth. She is giving nothing away and clearly will not be dragged into things, even though it is clear to both that he’d like that more than anything as he is struggling to find any hard evidence.

29 BACK ANY MINUTE

Daisy stands in Atticus Stamp's home. She has come to pick up a few things she left behind after her rapid exit yesterday afternoon. She knows that none of his staff have heard from him, so now might be a good time to slip in and out without a fuss. Daisy was quite taken aback by Logan's plea for Atticus's return on television. It felt over the top and too early to make such a noise. Perhaps Logan knows more than he is letting on, as Daisy is beginning to realise that he always has an agenda.

Daisy notices a gardener at the far end of the lawn. Otherwise, the house is silent, all but for Lady Woof Woof's paws, exploring the kitchen for any dropped food. It is just when she thinks the house is empty and begins to relax that in walks Atticus's chef with some fresh produce. He is surprised to see Daisy there.

"Hello Roberto, it's okay, I'm not staying," she explains. "Would you mind telling Atticus just to let us know that he is okay? Everyone's so worried." Daisy corrects herself. "I'm worried."

"Miss?" chef Roberto cocks his head to one side.

"Let him know," Daisy explains, "to call me or text. Or something. Send a message by pigeon. Just tell me he's alright." Daisy rubs her forehead.

"I'm sorry, Miss, but I've not seen him since yesterday," Chef Roberto shakes his head, placing a large brown paper sack on the kitchen surface, which is bursting with colourful vegetables and healthy-looking food. "But he pays me to be here, so here I am until I hear otherwise. You understand I've to cook food, in case he walks in hungry. Food is so important, Miss. Got a nice bit of Dover sole today. If he doesn't make it, can I cook it for you? You always liked my sole."

"No, thank you. I'm not (staying). But thanks so much, Roberto," Daisy looks around at the masculine space, a space Atticus never let her put any of her own personality or stamp on. "I'm not staying."

"Oh, it is a tragedy," the chef is surprised, as he has been cooking for her many times before. "Well, I'll take it home for the missus later if it doesn't look like he's about. I'll stick about, in case," Roberto explains.

Daisy nods, glad that the chef's words make everything on the surface seem normal, as if Atticus is about to walk in and eat some lunch. But she knows in her heart that this is anything but normal. The chef looks at Daisy, and she wonders if he can tell what she is thinking. At that moment, the front doorbell rings. A butler appears from nowhere. Perhaps he might know where Atticus Stamp is.

"Hello, may we come in?" Abley asks the butler, Lemon standing behind him. They both notice Daisy. "Ah, hello. Still no sign?"

"No. No one has seen him here since, well, I think, yesterday afternoon. I suppose he could have gone back to London? But it doesn't feel right. He usually has his assistant tell his staff. I thought I'd come over to check. I'm concerned." Daisy looks around.

"We spoke to his assistant. She has not seen him since yesterday afternoon either," Lemon explains, hoping it will prompt Daisy to share more intelligence.

"We planned on returning to London soon. I wanted to stay longer," Daisy explains as her phone pings. Daisy receives a message from a journalist asking for comment as he has had reports that Atticus Stamp's mobile has just been found in a graveyard. Daisy shows Abley and Lemon her phone and the message.

"Would you know anything about that?" Abley asks, irked that the media already has news about this clue, which he would have preferred to keep quiet about for now.

"What's going on?" Daisy stares at Abley.

"Yes, a mobile phone was found hours ago in the Mill Road Cemetery in Cambridge. I can confirm that it was Atticus's," Abley explains, deciding to share limited information." Still charged, so we're guessing he dropped it within the last twenty-four hours. More I cannot say."

"I've literally just rung it. Probably twenty minutes ago," Daisy explains, now starting to pace. "Oh, something is up. Something bad. I can tell. I should never have fought with him. It's all my fault."

"Are you still with Atticus Stamp? Are you still partners?" Lemon asks.

"I told the Inspector already. No. We had a fight over my dog," Daisy replies, continuing to pace.

"A fight?" Lemon asks.

"Over Lady Woof Woof. He was being mean. Then, he stole her and gave her to the shelter! That was the last straw." Daisy looks concerned about hearing Atticus is without his phone. "Atticus is never without his mobile? Never. He takes it to the toilet. Do you think he's been attacked?" Daisy asks, visibly upset.

"What else did you fight about? Did you fight about Terrence Montagner?" Abley asks.

"Who?" then Daisy remembers. "The MP? No, I don't remember?" Daisy tries to think, then adds, "I get papped with all sorts." Daisy shakes her head and watches the chef give Lady Woof Woof some fish.

"Hmm," Abley remembers the photograph in London both he and Lemon saw of Daisy with Terrence with his arm around her. "We saw a photo of the two of you together. So, you must have known him a little," Abley replies.

"Everyone wants to be photographed with me, Inspector. I don't remember them all. Politicians are the worst. They think they're rock stars and try to hang out with the young and beautiful. They're really not."

"At a party?" Abley presses, hoping Daisy will share more details.

"Exactly. I don't know him from Aran." Daisy replies.

"Adam." Lemon corrects Daisy.

"Who?" Daisy doesn't know what Lemon means. She watches Lady Woof Woof catch more fish from Roberto.

"Can you think of anything out of the ordinary before yesterday? Anything at all?" Abley says kindly.

Daisy thinks and pulls a face. "I wish there was something I might have noticed. I honestly can't. We came up here because he wanted to give his Union address. That's why we were here, really. Or, at least, nothing he admitted to me. D'you think there was another reason?" Daisy waits for Abley to say something, but he doesn't, so she continues, “You know, he bought me a house the other day. It’s so cute, small, attached, tiny, and old. It’s off Parker’s and not far from your offices. In Melbourne Alley.” She holds up the keys. “I saw this on the side just now, with a note. Well, I say note. Just a kiss. Maybe he really does love me,” Daisy looks thoughtful.

“Melbourne Place,” Lemon corrects Daisy, irked by her comments of what he would call such a gentrified line of homes, adding, “They’re really sought after along there. It’s a terrific location. Close to all the amenities, the city centre. Not that small.” Lemon tries not to glare at Daisy, who decides to stop jingling the keys in front of Lemon, and instead puts them in her pocket.

“Atticus’s been himself while we’ve been here. We’ve gone for walks, drinks, dinner. He wasn’t behaving oddly or anything. It’s just weird. He didn’t meet anyone out of the ordinary that I know of? He spent a bit of time at the club with Logan.”

“So, nothing at all?” Abley asks.

Daisy walks to the window and watches the gardener pulling up weeds. “What if I’m next? What if I’m disappeared by tomorrow?” Then she turns dramatically. “Where is he?” Her eyes open with confusion, staring straight at Abley, pleading for answers. “Where is he?!”

*

A short while later, after Abley and Lemon have spoken to all the remaining staff at Atticus Stamp's home and no new information has been obtained, Abley is outside unlocking his electric bike in the driveway. He spots two slashed tyres on what looks like Atticus Stamp's car parked furthest from the front door. He stops what he is doing and walks over to take a closer inspection. All four have been slashed. Peering in he can see the keys are still in the car. Abley looks around and wonders if he missed this on the way in or if it is fresh and happened while he was speaking with Daisy. He has a terrible sense of foreboding. Unless Atticus Stamp has intentionally disappeared, it sure looks like something terrible might have happened to two very powerful men, both while visiting his city.

"Come on, race you back." Lemon says as he speeds away.

"I'll catch you up!" Abley shouts at the back of Lemon's head.

Abley has tried to look for leads, but as yet nothing. He glances back at Atticus's house and thinks of Daisy. He was a little surprised to find her there when she clearly seemed to be with Logan Lax. Did she know he would not be there? And still be missing? She seems so lovely, like she wouldn't say boo to a goose. How could she have harmed two fully grown men? He is glad for some time on his bike before he heads back to the station, where he knows he will be met with Superintendent Raynott's questions. If only he had answers. Perhaps now, he should really start to focus more attention on the beautiful woman whose ex-boyfriend has just gone missing.

30 SABBATICAL

Elizabeth is sitting in her garden. Punts sweep past on the river, carrying tourists loaded with blankets and champagne picnics while people stroll in the park on the opposite bank on Jesus Green. Patty sleeps beneath her feet. She contemplates whether to close her eyes and rest or do a bit of weeding when she hears a cycle bell cha-ching from the other side of the river on the footpath by the pizzeria. A cycle slows down to a stop, and the man waves. It is Martin, looking happy, his hair a little scruffy from his ride, his satchel across his shoulder. He points to Jesus Lock and the cycle path across the river as if to indicate that he is up for coming to say hello, and she nods. Elizabeth feels strong-armed into the nod, not having any excuse for being busy. She ribs herself for it. Why could she not think of something to stave off the intrusion? She used to be better at keeping people at bay. Huh, if it is just for a few minutes, she supposes she will cope. And Martin is one of the loveliest men she knows.

It is not long before he pushes his cycle up her gravel driveway, and Elizabeth opens her back gate to let him through. Martin can see that she is already enjoying a quintessentially English afternoon of tea and scones, an old-fashioned parasol shading the table with a vase of delicate summer flowers and surrounded by comfortable wicker chairs like something from a stately home. They both wander into the kitchen to fill up the teapot. The smell of dogs in the home hits Martin's nose. She notices and smiles.

"Take a deep breath. That's the smell of unconditional love," Elizabeth suggests.

"I adore the smell of muddy paws. Same in my home." Martin sighs and smiles again. "You know, this is serendipitous. Long time no see," he says ironically. "I was just thinking what a lovely day, and now to share a cup of tea with one of my favourite Professors. And look what I have in my satchel." Martin pulls out some chocolate fondants with lavender and rose fillings. "I made a point to get some for you, and well, now I can give them to you."

Elizabeth, who has been pouring hot water into a fresh pot, is taken aback for a moment. She has known Martin for a long time, walked their dogs together in the same places, grown fond of each other.

"You had them in Hall once. Told me

how Gerald used to buy them for you," Martin explains. The penny drops. "Best put them in the fridge for later."

Elizabeth is handed the box, which is a pretty lilac colour and bow-adorned. She pulls at the ribbon and opens the top, immediately popping in a chocolate and offering Martin one.

"Chocolates need to be eaten, whatever the temperature," Elizabeth smiles at such a thoughtful gift. Martin nods and takes the closest, smiling at the small gesture.

"Have you come to talk Atticus Stamp and missing phones?" Elizabeth asks.

"Most definitely not. Although, that was rather an unlikely coincidence, don't you think? Finding his phone like that? I always knew the cemetery was spooky but not dangerous?" Martin replies, seemingly a little bothered by Atticus's vanishing. "Have you been asked to work on the case?"

"Not this time, no thank you," Elizabeth replies bluntly.

"I don't understand. How can Stamp and Montagner just vanish?" Martin ignores Elizabeth's desire not to speak on the matter.

"They're very rich men. They can vanish if they want to. I thought you understood money?" Elizabeth replies, a little irked that Martin is ignoring all the signals that she would do anything to change the subject. She offers him another chocolate, and when he declines, she pops another in herself and puts the rest in the fridge for later.

"I don't know what to think. Someone would have spotted them surely if they'd decided to retire to a Greek island," Martin replies, watching Elizabeth picking up the teapot and walking out into the garden.

"Coming outside?" Elizabeth asks, looking back. Martin follows, and they are both hit with the heat of summer. "It's true, Atticus could have dropped his phone on purpose to make it look like something sinister." Elizabeth looks back at Martin, hoping her next question might shut him up. "You think they're dead?"

"Don't you?" Martin looks surprised.

"If they're both dead, then you know you must be a prime suspect," Elizabeth looks at Martin straight in the eye, running out of patience.

"Wait, what?" Martin is shocked as he watches Elizabeth place the fresh pot of tea on the garden table. "A prime what?"

"You detested both of them. Everybody knows that. You spent your entire academic life trying to prove we'd all be better off if the rich and powerful were overthrown," Elizabeth stirs the water in the teapot.

"Peacefully. I've never recommended the tactics of the French Revolution," Martin opens his eyes wide, not waiting to be asked, and takes a scone in his hands to eat. "Mm, these look delicious!"

"Okay, Martin, you know I love you, but my grandson told me that you paid students to ask Atticus Stamp tough questions at the Union debate and to egg him outside. Waste poor chicken's offspring in an act of violence," Elizabeth frowns at Martin.

"It was not a debate. It was a speech, and I bought them pints. Not guns. I wouldn't ever wish harm on anyone, Elizabeth." Martin watches a group of young girls try to punt, going around in circles. "You know, Terrence Montagner had something he wanted to tell me. I don't know what. What if it was important, and he knew he was in trouble? I try to rack my brains about any connection I ever had with him. I only told the Inspector that he wanted to have a post in our department, which was ludicrous. But what if it was something else?"

"Didn't you go to school with him?" Elizabeth remembers noticing a photograph of the pair and other 'notables' on the College wall.

"I'm close to retirement. I cannot remember anything about school," Martin replies sweetly, then sighing, "Other than the relentless violence, intolerable loneliness and longing for home, oh and extremely uncomfortable beds."

"Well, were there any clubs you were in together? Debate club? Chess? Spelling bee?"

"So, you don't see me in the rugby,

lacrosse, or swimming clubs?" Martin looks at Elizabeth. "There has to be something more recent that he has done. That they have both done to piss someone off? It can't all be pinned on me from school days," Martin half laughs.

"They must have upset a lot of people. You don't get to be that powerful and not step on a large number of toes, it's true," Elizabeth grows tired of the conversation, watching the wasps who have found the scone jam. Martin notices, puts a dollop of jam on a plate, allows the wasps to find it, then moves it a few yards from their table on a branch in a tree, then puts some jam on Elizabeth's plate and passes the plate of scones for her.

"Has the Inspector shared anything with you? Like I said, you're the police consultant. There must be emails from Abley, updates?" he asks.

"All unopened, I'm afraid. I'm not sure I'll go back." Elizabeth replies, trying to convince herself as she takes a bite of a scone. "I need to take my time. I–" Elizabeth stops herself before she explains the level of burnout that she feels. She looks at the sky. She sighs. The day is so beautiful. She wishes she could find peace and inner calm. She is aware Martin knows she lost her husband. "I'm just getting used to living with the grief, like holding a heavy rock every day and carrying it everywhere. I've even privately named it Sebastian. I know I have to make friends with it, as he is not going anywhere. He is part of the furniture."

'Elizabeth?" Martin calls out, "Are you okay?" All Martin could hear was Elizabeth mumbling the word 'rock' repeatedly as she got lost in her thoughts. "Elizabeth?" Martin touches her arm, which snaps her out of it. She shakes her head. What just happened? Elizabeth tries to paper over her moment with a question, perhaps going in too forcefully, given that her friend has been so kind.

"Godric also told me that you've written an article about Atticus Stamp. My grandson might be in Florence, but we do speak, and he has his friends everywhere."

"How on earth did he hear about that? Yes, I did. That was years ago, though, and I didn't write it. I was interviewed for a magazine called Politiks Rocks. I remember as I have been misquoted from it all the time. I was young and stupid." Martin thinks back to when he was young and stupid. "It feels like such a long time ago. We all say things when we are young."

"'Revolution is the only way', that's what it was called. Where you talk about knocking powerful people in politics and right-wing media off their pedestals and worse. Isn't it great that our library here contains a copy of everything published? Well, partly shared with the British Library, the Bodleian, and so on. Godric retrieved it for me yesterday. I have an email of it somewhere," Elizabeth admits.

"We were all radical then, weren't we?" Martin spreads some vegan cream on top of some jam, then pops in a piece of scone. "Is it cream on jam? Or jam on cream? These really are yummy. Thank you." Martin's black fringe hangs like weeping willow branches over his eyes.

Elizabeth looks at him carefully. Such a kind face. She notices a chip in one of Martin's front teeth. He glances at her, his eyes look like pools of tranquility. Elizabeth is aware she has hit a nerve. But before she allows the thought to fester, she spreads jam on a scone and then gives a bit to all the dogs. They have been at her feet, waiting patiently for crumbs for quite a while. Yes, she will take them out soon and meet Emily. The shade of a cherry tree and the tea by the river is soothing. She cannot be bothered to interrogate Martin today.

"Thank you for the chocolates. It was a thoughtful gift," she says, now aware that their meeting was not a coincidence. He must have been aiming to pop by all along, perhaps Emily had suggested she be 'checked up on'. Martin nods and picks up his cup to 'cheers' Elizabeth with. She picks up hers and clinks it with Martin.

"You know, Elizabeth. I think a sabbatical is such a good idea. And, when you're ready, you'll go back to the department with such gusto. Well, all others will be blown away. In the meantime, a little self-preservation now and then is essential. Or, well, we'd explode with the unwarranted pressure of it all. I know I cannot wait for my retirement."

"What will you do?" Elizabeth wipes her hands on a napkin, frowning a little at Martin.

"I've been thinking about it. I think I'll adopt another dog. And then, well, I might buy a little boat like yours over there and just potter about. Yes, I shall maybe write some bad poetry. Perhaps try my hand at making pickle. But just enjoy this magical ride we are all on. Isn't it just the most beautiful thing?" Martin looks at the day. The bees, the flowers, the river, the tea in front of him.

"Yes." Elizabeth agrees and thinks about why he just popped in like this. Was he just a thoroughly lovely man, or did he need an alibi, to win her over, to find out what she knew, or all of it?

31 WATCH THE DOGS AT THE DOG FESTIVAL

From June to August, it is not uncommon to find something happening on Parker's Piece in Cambridge every day, whether it's the big wheel, comedy tent, or a market produce fair with a myriad of stalls selling organic this and real natural that. The Piece is the most central point in the city, not far from the train station, a checkpoint between town and gown, used by the local school for cricket, running track and games, and by locals for frisbee and five-a-side.

Despite very important and wealthy white men having gone missing, nothing would stop the merriment and joy that would ensue with the yearly Charity Dog Festival this afternoon.

Although small, it has attracted quite a few to help raise money for dogs locally. A police dog display is always a winner, with the Police Station on the Piece nearby. Then there is the scruffy dog show, dog ice cream vans, a dog massage and chill-out tent, the ball-fetch-game field, temporary doggie water fountains to cool down in – all things dog are taking place on Parker's Piece this afternoon, apart from dressing up shows. Eadie and Muriel, the organisers of this long-running cute little event, put a stop to any costume wearing a few years ago. It is a firm no. They needed no lobbying from Elizabeth either. Dogs are not to be exploited at this Dog Festival. Only happy experiences for all who attend.

"I've not seen so much tail chasing, zoomies, ball fetching or rolling in what looks like smelly things for a long time," Elizabeth smiles, chatting to Emily as she watches a bunch of dogs off the lead in a large cordoned off play area, with lots of hay and dog toys, and a few dog parents standing around the edge, throwing in a ball or five.

"Why do I want to eat those treats in the dog bakery? They smell so good," Emily replies. Elizabeth has brought Patty who is excitedly sniffing the grass for pee-mail, while Emily is holding Pepper back from stealing some buns on display. Both women prowl for new ideas to keep their pooches happy and occupied.

"Okay, the paw print art is genius, and I shall visit the photo booth. But Poochy Massage. Really?" Elizabeth peers into a small marquee with cushions on the floor. "I must take back treats for Clive, Hector and Monty too."

"They'll be okay. They had a good run on the Green just now," Emily replies to Elizabeth reassuringly.

They both wander a bit further and spot the auction table, with Muriel standing behind it and Daisy handing over what looks like a very expensive watch. Elizabeth and Emily approach. On the table, there are vases and baskets of fruit, a pair of expensive-looking shoes, and Emily has her eyes on a rather nice box of dog chews all up for auction at the end of the afternoon.

"You can have it. Auction it off. You should get quite a bit for it. Those are real diamonds," Daisy points to the diamonds on the watch she no longer wants.

"Well," Muriel's eyes open as she looks at the watch. This is clearly expensive. "Are you sure?" Muriel stumbles back at the shock of knowing that this single watch is probably enough money to keep the rescue centre going right through winter.

Daisy presses the watch even further into Muriel's hand and replies firmly, "Yes, I'm sure."

Elizabeth notices Muriel's shock, glides around the stall, quickly finds a chair for Muriel to sit, and offers her some water.

"Do you need to be here?" Elizabeth quietly asks Muriel? "I can stay and help Eadie. Where is she?"

"Stage four. Where else am I going to go? To bed to curl up?" Muriel and Elizabeth see Eadie coming over, worried about how pale she is. Muriel hands Eadie the watch. "This young lady might just have solved all our troubles," Muriel explains to Eadie. Eadie gives Muriel an understanding look, pats her on the shoulder, and then picks up the conversation with Daisy.

"Thank you so much. We have the auction today and our online auction that we're running over the next week on our website. I'd like to suggest we put this in that rather than here today, just to get the best price for it," Eadie explains, now holding the watch while also stroking a little Chihuahua that she is holding in her arms, which she has brought from the rescue centre for some time out of the kennels.

"Oh, no, don't do that. Please send it to Christie's or a large auction room. You'll get far more," Emily interrupts, unable to see the two older women not getting the true value for it.

"Really?" Eadie replies, not knowing anything about auctions other than the silent ones with dried flowers and bowls of fruit.

"She's right," Elizabeth agrees. "Let the professionals sell it for you. They'll get you a fair price."

Eadie and Muriel look at Daisy to see what

she thinks.

"I suppose I hadn't thought. Yes, sure, whatever you see fit. Get the best price for it," Daisy nods, then smiles. She doesn't really mind and is just pleased to get it off her hands.

"If that is Atticus's watch, can you technically give it away?" Elizabeth asks Daisy quietly, not wanting to worry Muriel and Eadie, but they can hear anyway.

"Actually, it is. But I bought it for him, and he threw it at me the other day and gave it back." Daisy shrugs. "So let the dogs benefit from it, as I don't want it."

"Well, thank you. We'll take it and keep it safe until we get a good bid for it. Could you suggest a reserve?" Eadie asks Daisy tentatively while Elizabeth and Emily listen intently.

"D'you know, I can't remember exactly. It must have been a hundred or hundred and fifty."

"Pounds?"

"Thousand. I think I still have the receipt." Daisy digs into her bag. She pulls out an old fashion filo-fax. "Atticus taught me to keep my receipts for the tax man. Which is a bit ironic."

"Ironic?" Elizabeth asks.

"With his main residence being in Monaco," Daisy laughs bitterly.

"Right." Eadie is staring at the receipt. The watch is worth two hundred and fourteen thousand pounds.

"We might contact an auction house about

this item today, Emily. Thank you, Daisy. Thank you so much." Eadie then asks Daisy. "Might you agree to write us a short note, just to say that you are handing this over willingly, so there is no confusion. And, may I keep the receipt?" Eadie looks at Daisy guiltily. "Just in case the auction house asks to see it?"

"Sure. Of course, don't worry," Daisy rubs Eadie's arm. "So long as it helps your rescue centre. I don't know what I would have done if you hadn't taken in Lady Woof Woof," Daisy starts to write a note on a clean piece of file-o-fax paper, then hands a signed declaration of the gift.

"It must be upsetting, with Atticus missing," Emily asks Daisy, watching Daisy's dog eat a treat out of Daisy's hand.

"Well, I must say, we weren't speaking before he left anyway, so," Daisy admits, shrugging again. "I really don't like him at the moment. He's a total nightmare, giving my dog away was the last straw. But I wish he would contact me, you know, to let me know he's okay." Daisy's eyes water, and she looks away to pat Lady Woof Woof. "You don't miss him, do you, Lady. No, you don't," Daisy says to Lady Woof Woof.

"You know the police have found his phone though, don't you?" Eadie mentions tentatively to Daisy, now rocking the little dog in her arms.

"Yes, I've spoken to Inspector Abley already about it." Daisy pauses, and then her face turns to anger. "They don't seem to know anything or be doing much. Still completely in the dark." Daisy frowns. "They've even no idea why it was in the cemetery?"

"They're not magicians. What do you expect?" Elizabeth defends her friend, Bob Abley, a little irked by this young woman accusing the police of not doing enough. She is pretty sure Daisy has not told the police that she is handing Atticus's belongings to a festival, though privately pleased that she has. The charity needs all the help it can get right now.

"I don't know," Daisy admits. "It's a mystery. I mean, how can he just vanish? Surely his staff somewhere would know something" Daisy bends her knees to stroke Pepper. "I'm just not sure what we should be doing to help find him. I've gone over and over it in my mind. What can I do?" Daisy looks up at the women, but no one speaks. "D'you think it has anything to do with that MP?"

"Terrence Montagner?" Eadie asks.

"Yes. I mean, what do you think?" Daisy looks at Eadie for answers. But Eadie just shrugs her shoulders too.

"Well," Elizabeth pauses, watching Daisy's face look so anxious. "Atticus's newspapers seemed to have run negative press on Terrence Montagner for months. Saying how he hid his money abroad."

"Hiding money, and we struggle to get the food. The world is topsy turvy. But this watch. It will get a lot of food and keep the lights on this winter. You're an angel, Daisy. An angel." Eadie strokes Daisy's arm. Daisy reacts calmly to the gratitude, used to hearing it by now, having lived in a world of extreme privilege, but then catches sight of Eadie's eyes watering a little, in shock from Daisy's generosity.

"Here, have this too. Atticus bought it for me. I don't have the receipt this time, but you could check online. I'll write I gave it to you." Daisy takes off her own watch. It is dainty and much more delicate, perhaps with fewer jewels, but still looks super expensive.

"Are you sure?" Muriel says from her chair, flabbergasted.

"Yes, absolutely. You'll be doing me a favour. The sooner I can get rid of all memories of Atticus, the quicker I will feel better." Daisy realises what she has just said. "I wish him well, of course, just, well, he's a mean man. Not for me." Daisy starts to write another note for Eadie and Muriel.

"Yes, I saw the news this week which picked up your post on him, about the trophy hunting. They carried your photograph on the local news last night." Eadie replies. "He does not appear to be a nice man at all." Eadie focuses on the watches in her hand.

"Wow! Look at this afternoon! It's doggie paradise!" Mikayla walks over with her dog, Luna, this time they are both dressed as monkeys.

"I just don't understand your desire to 'match-match' all the time," Elizabeth tries to restrain her thoughts. It is too hot to wear this," she starts to take off Luna's outfit again. "There is a reason this is banned from the festival."

"Look, you're getting up in my face, and I'm telling you now, I don't like it," Mikayla rolls her eyes at Elizabeth, then uncharacteristically scorns Muriel, "Good job you've got people helping you, or where would you be, you tell me? There's no fun here. My costumes would bring it, but you can't see it." Mikayla then looks at Eadie directly and raises her eyebrows.

"Well, that's a nice thing to say!" Eadie replies, then speaks firmly, "Please either leave or remove the clothing from your dog now."

"Ouch," Mikayla huffs off with Luna, shaking her head and strutting over to look at a doggie treats stall, ignoring the instruction to leave. Elizabeth watches her go, a little surprised to see this other side of Mikayla, willing to upset an old lady and be rather unpleasant.

*

Given that the Dog Festival is more or less opposite the Cambridge Police Station on Parker's Piece, it is not hard for Abley and Lemon to observe the goings on, especially when they notice out the window that a smart looking limo has arrived on Parkside and Logan Lax is stepping out. Abley stands at his office window, watching Logan wander through the crowd until he finds Daisy.

"She seems nice, but clearly, she's banging a billionaire now," Constable Jack Love peers through the same window, having come back into Abley's office to pick up some of the papers he left on his desk.

"Don't talk about members of the public like that," Lemon tells Love as he stands behind Abley, looking over his shoulder.

"Well, if they're going at it, then doesn't that make him suspect number one for knocking off Atticus?" Love asks, sipping a coffee.

It is not long before Abley and Lemon leave Love behind – asking him to keep at it on the case and think creatively – and nip over to the festival to mingle. They join Logan by the police dog display, watching a German Shepherd run up and down a frame and then through a hoop.

"No fire?" Logan asks.

"We don't make our dogs jump through fire unless it is really necessary," Abley has heard the question so many times before now. "We must think of canine welfare. And speaking of dog welfare, how is it going now that you have taken in a canine and her owner. Lady Woof Woof and Daisy. That's very kind of you, given

Daisy has finished with the now disappeared Atticus Stamp," Abley segues into the real issue of the day.

"I'm a good citizen, what can I say?" Logan replies, continuing to watch the display and noticing Daisy and waving to her. She indicates she will come over to join him.

"Why did you make a call out for Atticus to make himself known during your television interview about your College building opening?" Lemon asks.

"It's driving Daisy around the bend. She's agitated and on edge. She's worried about him. I thought if Atticus heard from me. Well, we're old chums. We go way back."

"And yet, Atticus's girlfriend seems to be your girlfriend now?" Lemon replies.

"That's nothing to do with anything, and he's not here. I will talk to him when he comes back. Someone has to look after Daisy. She's not–"

"What?" Lemon asks.

"She's fragile. She needs protecting. Quite frankly, I want to keep her safe. No one knows where Atticus is or what's happened to Montagner. That's why I'm here now. Someone needs to keep an eye out for her," Logan says, watching Daisy buying Lady Woof Woof a doggie burger from a stall nearby.

32 UNIVERSITY ARMS HOTEL

After the Dog Festival on Parker's Piece, Daisy and Logan decamp to the University Arms Hotel bar. The peaceful Art Deco environment and quiet ambient music conjure a surprisingly intimate moment for them both. The heat of the day outside and the raucous chaos of the milling festival crowd all dissolving away. Despite the calm atmosphere, Daisy's mind is racing with thoughts of Atticus.

"Everyone thinks I know where Atticus is. They all think I'm either keeping his secrets or worse. I hope he knows all this agony he's causing me. Honestly. Where is he? Why would he do this? It's like he's punishing me." Daisy sips her mocktail, Lady Woof Woof beside her on the sofa – the staff unhappy with this rule breach, but the manager is keeping quiet, due to the gargantuan sized tip Logan has just pressed into their palm.

"Atticus is probably cross that you left him. He's a vindictive bugger. Just enjoying making you sweat, though I'm not sure posting that pic of him with the lion will dissipate his anger. Maybe that type of thing should be kept on the down low."

"So why pose for a photograph with the poor creature?" Daisy replies, lashing out angrily.

"I mean, I don't condone it, but it can't be easy," Logan replies, leaning back into his chair. "It's called a hunt for a reason."

"They drug them," Daisy screws her huge eyes up and is very adamant with her words. "I hate him for it. Hate his bones. Part of me wishes he's dead for some of the things he's done." Daisy stares straight into Logan's eyes. "I don't really, but I also do."

"Yes, of course. I think we're going a little off-tangent here. Let's refocus. Breathe." Logan leans forward again, then takes Daisy's arms and tries to get her to calm down.

"You don't think it has anything to do with that missing politician?" Daisy frets, her eyes now wide open again, looking to Logan for answers.

"Do I heck. Atticus's taken to one of his private islands and told the staff not to tell anyone. It's not hard to disappear if you have oodles of money, Darling. Try not to worry your mind." Logan lets go of Daisy's arms and encourages her to sit back on the huge sofa and relax.

"Thank you, Logie. I don't know what I would've done without you. You've been such a rock." Daisy finishes her mocktail. Logan looks at a server and draws a circle in the air for the same again. The waiter nods.

"Yes, well, you're a special woman. How could I not be here for you? Impossible." Logan beams, with love in his eyes, for Daisy. He can feel his heart beginning to long for her every moment of every day. "You're the type of woman I could fall in love with," he says without realising it.

"What?" Daisy looks at Logan, confused. She is aware of the love bombing but also likes the security Logan brings. She replies, "Thank you," which she can tell is not quite the response Logan was hoping for. They both look at the food menu the waiter has left to avoid the awkward moment, but Daisy cannot stomach the idea of eating right now. She shakes her head.

"You need to eat. You need to keep up your strength, even for Lady Woof Woof. Honestly, he's in the Bahamas."

"Really?" Daisy pauses. "I heard someone say that he might have been harmed. It's weird that someone found his phone in a cemetery?" Daisy cannot get Atticus out of her head.

"Maybe he dropped it elsewhere at the

shops, and a thief tried to break into it and failed, then dumped it there. Come on. We know the types of people who hang out in cemeteries."
The waiter returns with a mocktail for Daisy and a glass of red wine for Logan. He quickly orders four starters to come at the same time, just to get Daisy to eat, then orders a steak for the dog. The waiter's ears cannot believe what he has just heard, but then it is confirmed when Logan tells him to bring it 'medium-rare'.

"I don't go to cemeteries, Logan. Why would I do that?" Daisy takes a big breath. "I don't feel safe, I just don't feel safe anymore."

"Darling, come here." Logan pulls Daisy in for a cuddle. He nods to a server. "Let's have some tea too. Tea with sugar. We're in England. It's what makes everything better."

"Yes, we're in England. Sometimes I wish I could just settle down and blend into the background," Daisy shuts her eyes. "Just to stay still forever."

"I'm not going anywhere," Logan looks at his watch over Daisy's shoulder. "I have all the time in the world."

They sit quietly for a while, and then Daisy asks. "D'you think the police suspect me?"

"Utter nonsense." Logan pulls her up to look into his eyes, then takes something out of his pocket. "Look, I wasn't going to give you this until later. But I saw it and thought you must have it." Logan pulls out a gold necklace shaped like a daisy chain. Each daisy looks like it has a gold diamond on the inside of the flower. Daisy looks at the beautiful necklace and gasps.

"I've never seen anything so beautiful," she gushes.

"Neither have I." Logan looks again into Daisy's eyes. "If I haven't said it clearly enough, then let me say it again. I think I'm falling in love with you, Daisy."

Daisy looks at Logan. She wonders what she feels about him. Here he is, offering to look after her, worship her. And, all she can think is what a mess. The waiter arrives and brings afternoon tea for them both and a cut-up steak for Lady Woof Woof, mixed with peas. Maybe it is the care Logan shows to Lady Woof Woof, or the feeling that something bad has happened to Atticus. Either way, Daisy decides to curl back into Logan's arms and say nothing.

Logan pours the tea, then over her shoulder, he opens his phone and starts to scroll through messages. He reads a text from Atticus to his own phone, sent yesterday. It reads, "Leave my girlfriend alone, or I'll have you killed."

33 BBQ

After the start of the week they have had, Lemon suggests to his Inspector that they go for a pint. But Abley has a better idea. A barbecue in his garden!

"I haven't got it out yet," Abley explains as he fires it up. "This is the first time."

"It's so shiny," Lemon shields his eyes from the silver beast, which the sun hits from every angle. The metal absorbs the rays, emits its own heat, and bounces to the back of his eyes. You could probably not even light that, and it would cook the food for you."

"My daughter bought it for me. Arrived in a van this morning. Isn't it great?" Abley stands next to the barbecue, dancing about like a young boy who has just opened the wrapping paper on a new desired toy, so proud of his gift. The new barbecue is the size of a small kitchen, entirely out of proportion with the tiny terrace garden in which they stand. "It doesn't take long, apparently, to get nice and hot, you know. Top of the line." Abley checks if the charcoal is hot enough to place skewers across the grill plate.

"Actually, you might need to wait a bit longer," Lemon advises, having his own barbecue and being a bit of an expert. "You have to wait for the charcoal to go white."

"It has a pizza oven, too, which you can switch to put on top. Impressive, eh?" Abley points to another large piece of metal and stone which is still in the box to the side, which has a chimney and knobs and is still shiny.

"Maybe pizza next time," Lemon replies encouragingly.

Both men stand in the garden, the warm summer breeze blowing across the row of terrace gardens, birds singing as they perch on fences, trees and chimney stacks, bumble bees humming on the lavender. In the distance, a water cannon sprays a farmer's field of greens. Thankfully, no other neighbours are outside, so the two men feel safe to speak their minds. As it happens, they are happy to stand in silence for a while, savouring this moment of calm. Both feel a little at sea with the case and the pressure weighing down on them directly from the Superintendent's office. All the leads keep running to nowhere, and Raynott has upped his number of emails and increased the number of Constables on the beat. He slowly seems to be taking over, barking orders at Abley and Lemon whenever they come into the office. As far as Raynott knows, they are presently knocking on doors in the vicinity of the Mill Road Cemetery to ask neighbours for doorbell footage. But there are six assigned to that task already. They sure as hell will not solve it by making it eight.

"Constable Love checked. Atticus Stamp has not arrived on any of his three islands," Lemon shakes his head, then takes a sip of his beer, "how can a man have three islands?" Lemon watches his friend put jacket potatoes on the grill. He has to bite his tongue not to tell Abley that it is too soon and the flames will turn the skins black. "Both of Atticus's private jets are grounded, Love said. One at Heathrow and the other at LAX. Neither have been cleared to fly in two weeks." Lemon scrolls through Constable Love's email. "I suppose he could have flown public, but is that likely if you have two jets?" Lemon pauses. But Abley is too preoccupied with moving coals around to hear, so Lemon carries on, lifting a handful of crisps from a bowl and shoving them in his mouth. "Also, there's no CCTV of him leaving via Cambridge rail or bus stations. No helicopter's chartered, nor small planes from Cambridge airport, no public taxis hired." Lemon sighs.

"Hmm," Abley replies, still not engaging in work talk. Lemon stops, looking out across the fields, and then back at his boss. He wonders whether to say anything. Knowing what is really on his boss's mind. It has only been a few days since they both saw Maureen in her wedding dress. He knows nothing he can say that has not already been said. Instead, he looks back at his phone for more on the case.

"We have Atticus's phone, as you know," Lemon continues. "I suppose he could have more than one, and there's no way we could check all his multiple bank accounts to see if he's spending. But there is no evidence of him leaving Cambridge, also his staff haven't seen him and have made formal statements to that effect. And, the day before he goes missing, he finishes things with his girlfriend." Lemon says, adding. "And now we have the texts. He threatened to have Logan Lax killed?" Lemon pauses. "It has to be Logan or Daisy?"

"Atticus threatened Logan, not the other way around, and Daisy left Stamp. She's not married to him," Abley finally speaks quietly, concentrating on trying to stop the potatoes from burning. He pulls out some foil and spreads it across the grill to offer some protection from the smoke and flames.

"True, but Stamp just bought her a house on Melbourne Place? Would he have asked for it back, and Daisy didn't want to give it?" Lemon suggests a motive for Daisy.

"Atticus is a billionaire. She could have got so much more staying with him," Abley replies, nonchalantly adding, "and they're not that great, those homes. They face a school. It's noisy down there and is a complete shortcut for the world and his wife."

"Okay, but Stamp got rid of her dog?" Lemon replies, emphasising the words, as surely this is a big deal. "You said she mostly cares about her dog."

"How anyone can get rid of a family pet," Abley looks at Arnold the cat, who has come out of the house and is now sitting on the step, watching Abley lift fish from a plate and start to wrap it in foil. "I put an extra one on for you, don't worry," Abley says in a cutesy voice, just for Arnold. "Yes, I diddy widdy."

"Arnold, we finally meet." Lemon looks at the old male cat, mangy around the edges, who scowls back at him. "What a handsome fellow you are," he adds, lying through his teeth. Arnold's eyes visibly narrow.

"Did you shave this morning?" Abley notices Arnold's glare at Lemon and looks worried for his colleague.

"Yes, yes. Had no shaving foam. Had to go electric," Lemon replies. Arnold finally looks away from Lemon's four o'clock shadow, and both men are relieved. "Who says older cats aren't full of charm," Lemon opens his eyes wide after the threat of being scratched by a cat has thankfully dissipated. "A second chance at happiness for you both. It's a retirement paradise for Arnold here. I'm gonna buy you matching slippers."

Abley's phone rings, and he cuts the call. From Abley's expression, it is clear to both that it was Raynott. There is a moment of silence before the two switch their attention back to the fish, which Abley is starting to brush with some chilli sauce.

"I think your fish is going to be ready before those potatoes," Lemon says.

"Haven't you heard of starters and mains? Not that posh your side of town after all," Abley replies.

"Having gone on a leadership course, all I can say is I think it had made one thing clear. My boss's boss needs to go on a leadership course." Lemon can't help but dwell on Raynott's bullying of Abley.

"Elizabeth would have found the missing links," Abley admits. "She has dogs. Daisy and Martin have dogs. But she's not returning my calls since I went to see her," Abley sighs, poking at the potatoes.

"A break's a break. She's on one." Lemon shrugs and looks around for anything to eat, wondering what else Abley will be putting on the barbecue and when. His stomach is rumbling. "Got any more nibbles?"

"We hire her to work as a consultant on cases. She's still on the payroll." Abley pulls out some sticks, ready to skewer things. He cuts up a pepper into squares and fishes out some vegetarian sausages. "I thought we could try some vegan." Abley then throws some lentil puffs and hummus from the ice box at Lemon.

"Er, fish isn't vegan?" Lemon replies, adding, "C'mon. She was on holiday in Italy and supposed to be enjoying herself and we called on her in a big way. It must have been crap." Lemon finishes his beer, steps into the kitchen, opens the fridge and takes out another. When he rejoins Abley, he watches Abley turn over the potatoes, the skewered veggie sausage ensembles still on the side with the fish, waiting for the charcoal to stop burning with flames. "Let's focus on motive," Lemon suggests, turning back to the case, opening the hummus tub and dipping in some of the lentil puff crisps. "Daisy has motive. Maybe Atticus Stamp would not let her get away or leave him. Logan Lax has motive. He was rescuing Daisy. And don't forget Professor Martin Smith. He hated them all."

"So, you think either Logan Lax or Martin Smith could have done it? Logan to protect Daisy, Martin for being a communist, I presume?" Abley shakes his head. "We don't have any evidence."

"And Daisy. She could have done it," Lemon reminds Abley.

Abley says nothing, finally deciding to add the sausage skewers onto the grill. "I've never understood barbecues. My kitchen is five feet away," Abley, all of a sudden, feels frustrated with the lack of work surfaces around him.

"Yes, but you're cooking under the stars," Lemon opens his arms wide encouragingly.

"It's five o'clock in the afternoon and summer," Abley frowns.

"Here," Lemon opens another beer from the ice box and hands it to Abley. "I think you need one of these."

"Ah, now it all makes sense." Abley relaxes again. His phone pings, and he starts to read a message. "Apparently, we now have Atticus Stamp's mobile phone messages too. The file has been sent. You should have it, too." Abley looks more serious, opens the messages, and starts to read. Lemon opens his phone and does the same.

"You cook, I'll read." Lemon glances at the barbecue, which could go either way right now. "Yup, here it is. Stuff from Atticus threatening Montagner. Like we saw in the texts on Montagner's phone from Atticus. Looks like the blackmailing by Atticus to get his Press Bill through checks out. Oof," Lemon opens his eyes wide at some of the foul language in the messages, "I'm not surprised Montagner was scared for his life," Lemon looks up, but Abley still doesn't respond. "So, did Stamp finish off Montagner and is now on the run?"

"The peppers are beginning to smell cooked already. I've only just put them on! It is all out of sync," Abley sighs, listening to Lemon but finding himself unable to add anything intelligent. Arnold walks to Abley and rubs himself on Abley's legs. Abley bends down to stroke his cat.

Lemon wonders if Abley is even thinking about the case or if his boss has given up. "I think I might do this more often this summer. Living outside the city has its perks. You're too far away for people to just drop in on you," Lemon smiles. Abley touches his nose, thinking about Raynott. Abley then goes indoors for a short moment and comes back out with a small speaker. He fiddles with his phone and connects the two up, only to start playing his favourite tracks, the first of which is The Boss, by James Brown. Abley shuts his eyes and starts to shuffle his feet. Lemon starts to move his arms about like he is the dude. Then, out of nowhere, Abley says.

"In the absence of evidence, this all points not to kidnap or disappearance."

"Both dead then?" Lemon stands still.

"As doornails," Abley replies, still dancing. The fish starts to sizzle.

34 GWYDIR STREET

Eadie opens her front door to take one of the rescue dogs she is currently fostering out for a walk and immediately bumps into Martin and Kropotkin, walking past her house. Living on Gwydir Street makes it usual for Eadie to see another dog parent, given that the street runs parallel to the Mill Road Cemetery, where dogs and people enjoy walks without fear of being hit by bicycles. Gwydir Street is also one of the longest streets of Victorian terraces in Cambridge, with close to 200 dwellings, and both Eadie and Martin live on the street, making it all the more common to see one another. What is less normal this tea time is the fact that a missing billionaire's mobile phone was found in the cemetery not long ago, that he is still missing, and it is the subject of a police investigation. In fact, both can see uniformed officers still knocking on doors further along their street, carrying out enquiries. Both Eadie and Martin initially exchange pleasantries, but it is not long before the conversation turns to Atticus Stamp, in case either of them has any updates.

"I haven't seen anything in the paper yet," Eadie says, hopeful that Martin will have further news.

"They're both foul people. Utterly malicious, deceitful and cruel," Martin replies, almost sounding pleased that both Terrence Montagner MP and Atticus Stamp have 'disappeared', at least to Eadie.

Eadie strokes the rescue dog, a bit stunned by Martin's outburst. "I hope they find them safe and sound," she replies.

"Hmm, I'm sure they will be sunning themselves on some luxurious yacht, paid for by the taxpayer," Martin replies, though not believing his own words. He pats the rescue dog Eadie has. "This fellow is rather wonderful. What's his name?"

"Barney," Eadie replies about the large mound of hair she is walking, then adds, "I hope so. It's rather worrying, don't you think? As if someone else will go missing next?" Eadie frowns.

"I can't believe anyone hasn't adopted this gorgeous ball of fluff. Bearded Collie?" Martin adds, waiting for Eadie's nod to confirm the breed, then adding, "We can only hope it all ends well," Martin replies enigmatically.

The two walk into the Cemetery and meet with Elizabeth and Mikayla, this time Mikayla is dressed as a Lemon and is carrying a heavy bag.

"Hello. No news?" Eadie asks them both.

"Just checking, I'm allowed in here, am I?" Mikayla pointedly asks Eadie, after Eadie told her to leave the festival earlier.

"The Dog Festival seemed to go well?" Elizabeth comments to Eadie, grabbing Mikayla's dog, Luna, and removing the lemony outfit.

"If I wasn't such a wonderful person," Mikayla says to Elizabeth, grabbing the outfit back off Elizabeth.

"Yes, and with the generous donations, we will have enough food to keep going for the next year. I have literally just left the end of the packing up. Had to give this one a comfort break," Eadie replies, adding, "Muriel was so worried about everything. Daisy's generous donations are going to save the centre. Supplies were so tight. Food, bedding."

"You didn't have enough for food?" Elizabeth asks. "I didn't realise it had got that bad."

"It's always running low, but with the economy the way it is and people abandoning dogs due to the cost of living crisis things are stretched to breaking. Vets bills, food prices,"

Eadie replies, looking a little depressed. She reluctantly admits, "And with Muriel, what with how things are, I didn't know if I could keep it going. But those watches. They're in the safe. I've called an auction house in London. If it means I have to get someone in to help, then I can." Eadie's face shows relief. "What a generous woman Daisy is. So kind. So good." Eadie looks relieved. Elizabeth squeezes her arm.

"The rich get richer and the poor, poorer. That's capitalism." Martin spits out his words, hatred on his face, continuing, "We all work for the man. And the man grows fat. Fat off our backs. Then he chucks us a bone, and we're expected to be grateful." Eadie does not know what to say, listening to Martin as she strokes her rescue dog again. He continues, "She got a kick, I'm sure, out of parting with a miniscule part of her fortune. She'll probably write it off her tax bill if she pays any, that is," Martin's face turns red with anger, which surprises Mikayla and Eadie, who clock this and glance at each other.

"Why don't you come for a drink? Get some shots down your throat. We can take the dogs. The Free Press, Martin," Mikayla suggests, smiling.

"Sounds like a date," Elizabeth nudges Martin, who looks surprised, then grabs the lemon dog costume back out of Mikayla's hands.

"Elizabeth, will you stop stealing my costumes?" Mikayla rolls her eyes, having grown tired of Elizabeth undressing her dog every time they bump into each other.

"No. Don't you have a childhood teddy you could dress up instead if you want to play dolls?" Elizabeth pockets the outfit.

"A lot of people love my creations. People with imaginations and a love of life," Mikayla replies, "I'm always bumping into terriers dressed as clowns or pugs dressed as pilgrims. You confiscating my outfits is theft, and it's gotta' stop, Hun. Give it back."

"No, I won't. Not until you agree to stop this nonsense," Elizabeth is not budging.

"Look, I love you, Elizabeth. You have that dry sense of humour. You're your own woman, you know? And I love that about you—a real rock chick. But, honey, you cannot be stealing from me every single time I see you. As quickly as I make my creations, you take them away. Now, I'm a calm dame. But damn, you don't want to see me angry. And, for the record, I will meet Logan Lax, and he will give me a fashion deal. And all those past outfits you've taken. I hope you keep them because they will be worth a fortune!" Mikayla reminds Elizabeth of a fact about which she is convinced. She twists the outfit out of Elizabeth's pocket but knows better than to put it back on the dog in front of her.

"Good luck with that," Elizabeth replies dryly.

"I don't think that Daisy is as good as

you think, you know," Mikayla replies gently to Eadie's earlier comments. "When I suggested that she feature my outfits on her online profile, what with her being an influencer and all that, she told me to go away, so I asked if Atticus would be interested, and she laughed out loud and said that 'he won't be around much longer.' Won't be around much longer. Hmm."

"Let's go for that drink," Martin pulls Mikayla away before she says anything else. Mikayla is surprised by the strength of Martin's arm and squeezes his muscles.

"Don't mind if I do," she giggles and winks back at Elizabeth. "I've pulled!"

Elizabeth watches them go, wondering whether to believe Mikayla telling everyone Daisy told her that Atticus would not be around much longer, or whether, in fact, Mikayla was actually lying to stir the pot?

35 THE PITCH TO THE BILLIONAIRE

A few hours later, having just left the pub where she drank her supper instead of eating it – Martin hanging on her every word about her designs – the bee in Mikayla's bonnet is buzzing loudly. She is determined to impress her doggie friends, make her aspirations come true, and do something with her life she will be remembered for. A billionaire is in town, and he knows what is what. Logan Lax will see a good thing when it hits him in the face and when she gets to show him her portfolio of work in her bag. Designs which have taken months to make, hand stitched, with cloth from the local stores and some charity shop curtains for fun. They look fabulous! The matching convict outfits have black and white horizontal stripes for pooch and owner. The pretty peacock display opens on both the back of the canine and human costumes with glorious blues and greens like a fan. She particularly loves the skeleton Halloween costume she designed with the forward-thinking trendsetter in mind. If she can impress Logan, she will be able to go back to the Rescue Me centre, as well as the local pet and veterinary centre – who forbade her from adding some of her designs to their wall or even coming in again unless it was explicitly a matter for her dog to see the vet – and tell them all about her success. Even Elizabeth, she thinks. Well, perhaps not her. But life will be full of fairy dust and unicorns, nevertheless.

Mikayla has arrived at this point today after having already written to the fashion billionaire, called in at the reception in his Cambridge offices, and turned up at the HQ of his London fashion retail shop just off Regent Street. She has stood outside a club in Soho Logan Lax is sometimes known to frequent – watching drunk people come and go all evening in case, even though he was a 'no show'. She visited a restaurant he reportedly is known to frequent in Mayfair, only to be told that it is illegal to loiter as they own the pavement and it is private property. So far, all she has to show for her efforts has been a huge fat failure.

But Mikayla is not a woman ready to give

up on her dreams. With a new tactic, perhaps a little controversial, she found out where Logan resides in Cambridge, as this, she expects, is a much-guarded secret. She had followed him and Daisy home in a taxi from the University Arms Hotel after she'd seen them go in together from the Dog Festival. Having bottled it when she first discovered the location, she was now coming back again, straight from the pub and time with Martin had given her the courage she needed. It is just a matter of time to wait until Daisy leaves, and she can then try to corner Logan alone. She slams the cab door shut and stares up at the expensive bricks. Trying to imagine what it will be like when she has a lot of money and lives somewhere like this. She is far from stupid. She guesses there will be staff protecting him. She has to figure out how to break through those lines, as she is convinced that as soon as Logan sees her dog dressed up, he will be amazed, immediately plough large amounts of sterling into her bank account, and she will be rich! No more needing to work as a waitress at that overpriced restaurant where the guests are rude and the chef smacks her hands for eating the leftovers. Once she becomes a world-famous doggie designer, the rich and famous will want to be her friend. They will fight to take her picture and hang on her every word. More importantly, they will say yes to her and believe what she says, not ignore her or tell her that her ideas are stupid. No, she knows that only those who persevere get anywhere these days. You have to be determined. Mikayla notices a side gate which has one of those intercoms on it. She tries her luck. It is now or never. She presses the buzzer.

"Gardener," she speaks into the buzzer as confidently as possible, adding, "Come to prune the lemon trees." The whole improvised lie appears unnecessary when she is let through the gate and around the back of her house. She looks down and realises she is still wearing her lemon costume and her dog, Luna, having got the costume back from Elizabeth, is again dressed the same, with a large leaf embroidered into the doggie hat. She looks up at a CCTV camera watching her and gives it a nod and a wave. She looks down and sees her costume. It must have magic powers.

Mikayla slips around the back, trying to be quiet so as not to draw attention. She wonders how she will be able to enter the back of the house itself. But when she turns the corner, she finds Logan Lax sitting at a large table under a gigantic parasol, and he is all alone. On the glass table in front of him is a solitary drink with lots of ice melting in the tea-time sun. He is reading some papers.

"Argh! I was going to be so cool, and I'm about to lose it right now!" Mikala squeals and then regrets shouting, perhaps leading to her getting kicked out too soon. Logan looks up behind him to see if anyone can get this woman away from him. Mikayla sees his eyes dart around and knows it is only seconds before she will be evacuated from the garden. She picks up Luna and gives them a kiss. "This is Luna, and I wanted to talk to you quickly. It won't take more than a minute, as I think my dog clothes would work well in your stores. Women go shopping, and women with dogs can find matching outfits for their dogs or cats. It would be so good. I would always buy my dog clothes that matched mine if I could."

"You mean like women who buy clothes for their babies that match their own outfits?" Logan asks, knowing that this whole trend didn't catch on and just looked out and out weird in his shops when they tried it.

"Yes, exactly. But for their dogs… or cats." Mikayla puts Luna down, starts pulling out more outfits, and spreads them as neatly as she can across the table. "See, there are pumpkin outfits and bats for Halloween. Then there are Father Christmas costumes." She continues to spread as a man walks out and shakes his head in apology to Logan. He grabs Mikayla's arm and starts to pull her towards the back gate. "D'you like them? They could be for special occasions or for every day."

"Look, I don't know who you are or how you got into my home," Logan realises he is now not physically under threat and starts to relax. "I would say, bravo. You have some nerve breaking in like this, all for your business. I can see that. So, I will let it slide. But you need to quietly follow Dozer out, d'you understand?"

"That's right. It's for my business. You understand. Yes. I love you, Mr Lax."

"But I'm sorry, love, I cannot ever forgive you for the crimes against fashion that you've committed. Did you make these yourself? You won't want to hear this, but they look like a school project. I don't know. What do I know about fashion?" Logan looks at Dozer and shrugs his shoulders. "You might persuade one of those shops on the high street that do deals and knock-down prices, and they might be interested. Maybe leave the designer end of things. Maybe a market stall?" And with that, Logan takes a sip from his expensive-looking crystal glass and waves Dozer to do the rest. Mikayla is swiftly escorted out.

*

Outside, Mikayla stands on Logan Lax's gravel drive. Dozer has gathered her clothes and chucks them at her, then walks back through the gate. Mikayla does not recognise the feeling in her body until she does. It feels new—this feeling of anger. Well, the worm has turned. How dare Logan Lax tell her that her designs are no good. How dare he!

36 A COLLEGE INSPECTION

"Come and have an aperitif. You don't need a warrant for that," the Master of St Andrew's College says as he stands at the Porters' Lodge. The Porters behind the Master are alert and ready to answer any of Abley's questions.

"We won't take up too much of your time," Abley suggests.

"We already had an excellent barbecue," Lemon whispers to his boss.

"A barbecue, how quaint. There's a little bit of our lord and saviour in every burnt offering," the Master hears, amusing himself, "What with carbon being no doubt a little piece of the past," seeing the blank faces and explaining his humour.

"It was nice, but leaving conversation

of food aside, you mention you have CCTV showing that Atticus Stamp entered through the Porters' Lodge the night someone vandalised your library, then he left again soon after," Abley reads his notes, which brought him and Lemon to cut short their afternoon in the sun to do some work, hoping for a breakthrough in the case. "Do you have the same of the lawn being vandalised?"

"We do, but nothing to identify the culprit. They were dressed in black with a balaclava." The Master replies regretfully, holding out a hand to suggest they walk with him towards the main security room of the College. "Unfortunately, the rampager in the library was not so clever."

"Hmm, and he was carrying a pile of books?" Abley is puzzled. "Why vandalise the library but then take some of them away to read?"

"Quite." The Master reluctantly leads Abley and Lemon into the CCTV room. They crowd around a chair where a security officer nods at the Master and hits play from the saved video footage. He explains this is from the night of the break-in. Abley and Lemon watch Atticus Stamp enter the library, stand, and stare for ages. The security guard fast-forwards the digital recording and stops it again just before Atticus pulls books from their shelves and hurls them around. They watch Atticus screaming to the high heavens (silently, as the CCTV footage has no sound), running around the stacks, searching through dropped books, pushing a stack over. When Atticus finally leaves the library, it is clear that he is carrying a number of books away.

"The books were about fishing," the Master says quietly, almost embarrassed this happened on his watch.

"Why would a rich man steal books about fishing?" Lemon asks.

"It is a sorry affair," the Master replies, pausing before continuing. "We do know that Terrence Montagner donated them." The Master hangs his head heavy and then changes gear. "You'll have to excuse me. Davis will show you anything else you need. Hall won't start eating until I arrive, and I'm now two minutes late for supper. There'll be rumbling stomachs and food fights. Are you sure you don't want to join for some charcoal-free nosh?"

"Thank you, we're good," Abley replies, thinking there is nothing less that he'd like to do than sit in a room with a bunch of academics dressed in their gowns, looking down their noses at him. "But I would like to know why both men who have disappeared are St Andrew's alumni. And why did one of them steal books from your library just before he vanished?"

"Quite," the Master mumbles, then heads to the dining hall. Both Abley and Lemon can see the strain of the disappearance of these VIPs, which is no doubt weighing heavily on his shoulders, too. Abley knows full well that when murders occur in the city, they are a police matter. But when likely murders are of College men, the University machine will quickly become involved and be looking for answers, and pronto.

37 MIKAYLA WON'T TAKE NO

"I'm begging you, have another look. They really are super for the dogs. They keep them cosy and make them look like movie stars." Mikayla stands in the Rescue Me rescue centre with her bag of clothes again, having come directly from the rejection and humiliation of Logan Lax, who laughed until she was out of earshot. She had envisioned the success of the meeting and adoring adulation for her best idea ever. But now her face is still red and puffy and not at all her usual demeanour. She can still visualise the look of the security guard who threw her dog clothes at her and unkindly called her a 'weirdo'.

It is obvious to Eadie and Muriel that Mikayla has been crying for some time. It is also clear that she has been using her arm to wipe her tears–her shirt sleeve wet. Beside Mikayla stands Luna, her dog, still dressed as a lemon. Luna looks up at Mikayla, a little concerned. Eadie spots this and bends down to stroke Luna, giving her a special treat from her pocket and pointing her to a fresh bowl of water. Luna devours the treat and then gulps down the water. Afterwards, Eadie slowly removes one part of Luna's clothing while Mikayla isn't watching.

"Look, we have told you, it's nothing personal," Muriel replies kindly, "but we cannot sell fashion clothes for dogs in a rescue centre. We don't think it's in the best interests of the dogs, even if the outfits are lovingly made." Muriel tries to stay firm to close this whole thing down and not give a window of hope to Mikayla, who has returned multiple times now with her wares. Muriel sits back down behind the counter, trying to disengage after she has said her piece.

"But you sell these jackets?" Mikayla pulls at a dog coat patterned in blue and red check, rather like a sofa blanket. "It's rubbish, boring, but you sell it for £27.99!" Mikayla then pulls at jackets roughly the same size and shape in a luminous yellow. "Pff, look at these. Awful." From somewhere inside, Mikayla's tears turn to rage.

"They are plain and functional, not fancy dress. They keep dogs warm or visible at night. They're not fashion items." Muriel sighs, not feeling well enough to tell Mikayla to leave. "We have had this conversation before."

"So, it is just the fashion that you object to. Ah, I see. So dogs are not allowed to look good. We are in a Stalin situation! Maybe I should talk to Martin about this abuse of power." Mikayla throws the luminous jacket she was holding on the floor in protest. "Look, look at this!" Mikayla pulls out of her bag a doggy costume of a carrot, with an orange jacket and green hat with a long green leaf design sticking out the top of the hat. "I really, really need you to understand!"

"Look, Mikayla, we're about to shut. We have both had a very long day," Eadie looks at Muriel, who looks dead on her feet. "We just want to go home. Didn't you say that you were going to show Logan Lax? He's more into fashion. Why don't you try him?" Eadie pleads with Mikayla.

"Oh, I've had second thoughts about him. He wanted to cover my line, but I refused when I found out he sells fur! Can you believe it? He uses fur from fur farms in Europe in his fashion line. That's real exploitation. Look!" Mikayla shows Eadie her phone, and on it is a story with Logan Lax selling mink and baby seal fur. A rehash from an old buried story, the same paper did years ago. "He's going for it, trying to expand the fur industry. I'm disgusted. I told him to his face. Mink, fox, baby seals! He should be taken out of action. I'm half a mind to go back and–" Mikayla is now in a frenzy, lashing out at the world. Luna runs behind the counter, either to say hello to

Muriel or to hide.

"Alright, alright," Muriel wants Mikayla's shouting to stop. She can feel a headache coming on.

"What is this world turning into? I dread to think. Fur is banned, so he can't sell it in the UK?" Eadie looks at the photograph.

"Torturing defenceless animals, what a wa–" Mikayla shouts but is cut off by Muriel.

"I need to go and lie down," Muriel looks at Eadie, who nods.

"Come on, Mikayla. We need to close up shop," Eadie repeats.

"Why are you so short sighted, that you cannot see an excellent idea when it is staring you in the face?!" Mikayla shouts at the top of her lungs.

38 PLAYING A GAME

Daisy arrives at the Gog Magog golf course with Logan. Although she has never played, she is enjoying the sense of security right now from being in Logan's company after Atticus's disappearance, especially after Atticus's mobile phone has been found, his car tyres slashed, and it has been some time now since anyone has heard from him. Daisy is unhappy, however, that the golf club requires Lady Woof Woof to stay in the car, but Logan reassures her that his driver will take good care of the dog, find a nice shady spot, and sit under a tree and snooze. The air up on the Gogs indeed seems cleaner and fresher. Daisy looks out across the old golf course at the sweeping English countryside, the manicured tees and bunkers nestled beside, and all of a sudden feels excited to be doing something different today. Perhaps to take her mind off things.

Daisy holds Logan's hand, which he kisses, and then keeps hold of as they walk towards the golf shop. The door opens with a swish, and the plastic and metallic smells of brand-new golfing equipment, folded tables of shorts, hangers of shirts and rows of shiny leather shoes below all waft into their nostrils. Through floor-to-ceiling windows, the brightly lit space offers panoramic views of the first tee, where a group of four are ready to spend a glorious morning out on the fairway and leave any troubles behind. A young man with a deep tan stands behind a counter. He looks up from a golf club magazine, where he is checking power shot ratios of a pitching iron for a customer, all smiles in their direction. Daisy skips over to the golf club headcovers, which include fluffy gorillas, unicorns and zebras, perhaps meant to encourage the younger golfer. She pulls one from its plastic covering.

"A glove puppet!" Daisy puts her hand up into a male lion cover and purrs at Logan. Logan smiles and then turns to the golf pro, hoping for some help to part with his money.

"I need to buy a set of clubs. Left mine in St. Andrews two weeks ago. I'm quite annoyed as I was playing well with them for a change," Logan smiles warmly. "What can you do to help me continue my winning streak?" Logan's eyes peruse all the golf clubs for sale as he walks towards the tanned pro, who immediately drops the magazine now thinking of his commission. At that exact moment, from behind a stand of bottled green golfing jackets, Inspector Abley appears and continues his own conversation with the golf shop pro about his shorthand swing. "Not bad," Abley says, nodding, holding a pitching iron, then looking up, surprised to see Logan and Daisy.

"Fancy meeting you here," Logan opens the conversation, relaxed and happy, patting Abley on the shoulder.

"Golf helps me think," Abley replies, knowing he is speaking to a fellow golfer, judging by the worn golf shoes Logan is wearing, together with a pair of checked trousers, pink shirt and yellow bucket hat. It reminds Abley that golf is the only game where you can dress like a pimp, and no one bats an eye. "Hello Daisy," Abley adds, spotting her jeans and a loud T-shirt with 'fxxk the patriarchy' on it and holding a golf head cover like it is a toy.

"I need a set of clubs. Left mine at the last course. They're keeping them safe, but that's no use right now, is it? These any good?" Logan points to a glass cabinet displaying some clubs which look like polished trophies.

"Oh, I wouldn't buy a whole set of those," Abley replies, "That'll set you back 60K at least, wouldn't it?" Abley looks at the pro for confirmation. "Just a wood, maybe a nine iron, a three will get you out of the bunker, then all you need is a pitcher. These are pretty good." Abley swings his cheaper pitching iron to show Logan.

"I'll have the set," Logan tells the shop pro of the display set behind the glass. The pro opens his eyes wide and nods, unlocking the cupboard before Logan changes his mind, knowing there will be a nice commission from this. Logan's face then changes from joy about golf to concern, "Have you had any news about Atticus?" Logan looks right at Abley, adding, "I've had my personal security look into it, and they've drawn blanks. It's like he's gone to Mars or the centre of the earth and decided not to leave a note?"

"We have some leads. I have to ask you not to get involved or ask your 'security' to do so." Abley says a little firmly. "We found his phone, which Daisy may well have told you. And, looking at the records, the last person to call his cell was yourself, Mr Lax. What might that have been about?"

"Call me Logan," Logan replies, nodding, then continues, "No, it's okay. It's fine to ask. I did call him." Logan lifts a wood out of the cabinet and swings in the golf shop, remarkably near Abley's head. "We were going to meet at the Pond Club again, just for a game of chess. He beat me last time. I don't like to lose. But he never called me back? He always calls me back, Inspector. Even if it's the next day," Logan replies calmly.

"Yes. We saw a text from Atticus to you

saying he would have you killed if you stole his girlfriend." Abley nods, not appreciating Logan's swing. "And have you been to the Mill Road Cemetery, Mr Lax?"

"If we're going to play golf together," Logan pauses, checks that Daisy is okay – who he notices has gone to look at the sweets and is not listening – and stands up straight to look at Abley in the eye, making it clear that this was an invitation to play golf with him, "then you have to call me Logan. I insist. And yes, of course, I've been to the Gravy. Many an hour of misspent youth reading poetry under the wild cherry tree with blossom like a wedding dress. It's a wonderful place. Overgrown, wild, nostalgic, full of lives from the past, moody." Logan takes the golf clubs. "But not for years. Why would I get down and dirty with muddy boots among the dead when I can walk up high here on the King's grass with the angels?" Then Logan looks at Daisy, smiles, and casually back at the golf pro. "Can we have three buggies as well, please? And coolers." Logan's security and assistant appear out of nowhere to hand the pro his platinum credit card, pick up the clubs, making sure Logan has nothing to carry. Logan pulls the lion off Daisy's hand and signals the golf pro to beep it through the till. Then Logan hands it back to Daisy with a beam.

"I'll be your personal sports commentator. I can rate every shot, but instead of insightful analysis, I can offer 'oohs' and 'ahs'," Daisy says, picking up a bar of chocolate and some Jelly Babies that get beeped through.

"See, I stole nothing," Logan looks at Abley and winks.

Abley watches Daisy and Logan zoom off in their cart, his cart full of Logan's security men following behind. He wonders if he will have the opportunity to discover what these seemingly new love birds know about Montagner or Stamp.

*

Logan and Abley play nine holes on the old course. Logan's security is working to keep him safe, mainly hiding discreetly amongst the trees and the rough when possible. Daisy enjoys watching, doing the occasional handstand and cartwheel, then tires of it all, telling them both that she had heard someone tell her that playing golf is like eating soup with a fork, and now she knows why. Logan has his security take her back to the nineteenth to relax.

Logan and Abley are left alone. Abley had reluctantly agreed at the start of their game to leave the case off the golf course, but as Logan hits his last ball into the final hole, he says something to Abley about Atticus Stamp.

"Make no mistake, there have been times when I've wanted to strangle Atticus. But I'd never have anyone hurt him for me." Logan does that thing again, standing up straight and staring right into Abley's eyes. Abley is mildly unnerved but says nothing, hoping to hear more, and Logan does not disappoint. "Look, if anyone was mad with each other it was Montagner and Atticus. I'm guessing you heard all about this Freedom of the Press bill. It means the world to Atticus. He stands to win or lose big time. Atticus has some hold over Terrence, and Terrence doesn't like it. I don't know what it is, but know it is serious."

Abley and Logan arrive back at the nineteenth bar, and Daisy has clearly raided the golf shop. She has more fluffy friends and a clear yellow golf visor on her head, her hair now in bunches. After all three share some version of mocktails on the terrace for half an hour, Logan breaks up their time together.

"Right, I need to get back to the home office for an hour," Logan says. "Really nice playing with you, Inspector. You're a damn fine golfer. I'll have to keep my eye on you."

Abley smiles, looking jealously at the golf clubs in Logan's bag. "Yes, owning expensive golf clubs is like owning a Ferrari. It doesn't make you a better driver."

"Home?" Daisy feels disappointed, having spent an hour waiting at the nineteenth. An idea comes to her. "Oh, I'm not ready for home yet. It is such a lovely day. Inspector, shall we do something nice? How about a picnic?" Daisy looks pleadingly at Abley.

"A picnic?" Abley is thrown but curious about her suggestion. "I'm working."

"You've just played golf?" Daisy smiles.

"I was thinking," Abley raises his eyebrows.

"Well, we can talk about the case if you need an excuse?" She says persuasively.

"I would need an excuse, Daisy. You've not met my boss," Abley raises his eyebrows.
Daisy twists up on her tippy-toes and whispers. "I can talk about Atticus. There are things I want to say." Daisy opens her eyes wide at Abley.

"Okay, let's have a quick picnic," Abley replies, rather disappointed he could not ask Logan more questions while at the Gogs.

"That's settled. You can look after my Daisy," Logan says, "and I will see to business. Then you can come back straight after." Logan looks at Daisy, hopeful.

"I only have an electric bike," Abley warns. "Where will this picnic be?"

"Ooh, please let me ride on your bike!" Daisy jumps up and down. "I've never been a passenger before. It's such a lovely day!"

"I'll have your clubs delivered back to the station. You can take Daisy. Does it have a back seat? I can look after Lady Woof Woof." Logan suggests, a little disappointed not to be going on the picnic with Daisy. "She will remind me of you and sit at my desk with me."

"Thank you," Daisy kisses Logan. "How

exciting!" Daisy looks for the Inspector's electric bike. Daisy runs towards the car park, looking for Abley's electric bike.

"Might I ask a favour? Can you deliver my clubs to the Blue Ball Inn in Grantchester instead of the station? They know me well there. I live a few doors down. Ask for Simon behind the bar. Otherwise, they'll get nicked if they're left outside. I'm quite attached to my woods."

"Sure, I'll get my staff to sort that for you. No problem," Logan replies, pointing at the clubs, and one of his staff picks them up and makes a note of the pub.

Once out of earshot of Logan, Abley is curious why Daisy has swapped romantic partners, particularly in these circumstances.

"You seem to be growing close to Logan?" Abley asks.

"Whatever or whoever is coming for me, he'll protect me," she replies thoughtfully.

"But he's not here now?" Abley is curious, watching Logan's security leave in dark, black, shiny cars as he unlocks his electric bike.

"No, but I'm with a police Inspector. Some might say that is a grade above." Daisy winks.

39 OOPS!

Logan is happy to return home, having enjoyed the round of golf with the Inspector much more than he expected, and is ready to attend to business. He already misses Daisy and thinks about their whirlwind romance over the past couple of days as his security opens his front door for him, and he walks through to the large living area towards the back of the house. He looks at Daisy's things scattered around the place. Cardigans, hair brushes, some boots. He picks up one of Daisy's scrunchies and smiles, holding it to his nose. He loves Daisy's childlike outlook, optimism and kindness –such a big, innocent heart. No one falls into his arms like Daisy. She is utterly beautiful, and after all those years of admiring her from afar, he will not lose her, not now he finally has her all to himself. All those times watching Atticus take her for granted. How could Stamp mistreat her like that, making her do what he wanted all the time? Logan knows he can make it work if Daisy wants to stay in Cambridge for longer. If she wants more dogs, then she can have a whole pack. A farm in the country. It has been ages since Logan has felt himself. He has all the money in the world and his health, but what is it for without someone to love?

Logan stands, staring out into the garden, the open door letting the summer breeze in to envelope his senses. A warm feeling of gratitude spreads across his mind. He has a successful business, good health, and now his one true love. Logan turns to head for his office, thinking about his life and everything he has worked for. It is only now he has Daisy that he realises it would all be worthless without her. He hopes Daisy enjoys her picnic while he sorts things out for the future and runs through some business deals. Logan enters an office with a huge desk and books surrounding him – all about business – but his mind wanders as soon as he tries to knuckle down to tasks. He starts to wonder whether to take Daisy to one of the Cambridge Shakespeare Company's open-air performances tonight. Or, perhaps supper on the roof terrace in the Varsity. Or, maybe Midsummer House or Restaurant 22. Somewhere lovely for them both to have a romantic time. He has everything a man could need and much more. He catches his reflection in a mirror and looks at his own face. For a moment, he really studies the man looking back. Is he the luckiest bugger in the whole world? Logan smiles again and shakes his head. He realises the house is so quiet, really quiet. Why is it quiet? Hang on, where is Lady Woof Woof? Where is Daisy's dog?

"Lady! Lady!" He steps out into the garden. "Lady!" He points for his security to take a look in the garden and see if they can see the dog while he wanders around the ground floor. Nothing. He runs up the stairs, now his heart pumping. He cannot lose Daisy's beloved dog. It takes him a while to run along the landings and between all the rooms, bathrooms, gyms, and chill-out zones. But Lady Woof Woof is nowhere. When he runs back downstairs, his security guards shake their heads. She can't have disappeared. Then they all see it, the open back gate. Could it still have been unlocked from Mikayla's entry yesterday teatime? Why was it open? Logan swears loudly at his staff. "Find that dog!"

Logan runs out the front and along the middle of the road, calling for the most precious Saluki, leaving his front door open, keys inside, his phone—everything. He keeps running down the road, looking up driveways, into front gardens, calling for Lady Woof Woof.

40 THE HEDGEHOG

Professor Elizabeth Green found a baby hedgehog out in the day in her garden, wandering around on the grass. Anyone who knows anything about hedgehogs knows that this is not a good sign, being nocturnal creatures as they are, at the very most, perhaps venturing out at dusk in the summer, impatient and hungry for the end of daylight hours. Rare as they are these days in England, either squashed like pancakes on roads or skinny and sick after finding it hard to acquire food in built-up areas – with humans determined to place six-foot-high fencing around their gardens with absolutely no exit or entrances – Elizabeth thought the best bet for the little creature's survival would be some kind of intervention. For a moment, she wondered about taking in the animal herself, but with four dogs and three cats already in her home and no spare rooms, the best bet was to take the hoglet elsewhere that could provide a safe hutch, food and care while it recovered from whatever the ailment.

It was no surprise that she found herself with the little creature in a box in her bicycle basket, heading off to the leafy burbs south of the city centre, where the well-to-do lived, and the Rescue Me rescue centre nestled down a cul-de-sac had such facilities. As she peddled, the little hedgehog was scratching about in the box, perhaps unsure about the journey down Sidney Street, along Lensfield Road, and past the Botanic Gardens. Not long before she arrived and lent her bicycle against the railings did, she realise that she had forgotten her bike lock. She looked around to see if it was safe to leave it. Although there was no security camera, it was a very leafy neighbourhood. The bicycle should be okay.

Inside, she stood in front of Eadie and Muriel, and all three peered into the box, observing the small hedgehog sniffing about in the cardboard cell. Elizabeth could see that the rescue centre had a couple of families looking at the dogs, but she was glad that Eadie and Muriel were giving her rescue their full attention. It was more than she expected.

"It's a good sign that they still appear curious," Muriel commented on the prickly creature sniffing about in the enclosed walls. She set about putting down a water bowl and some dried cat food in with the pog. Eadie began to speculate.

"Hmm, it could be flystrike. Too young to be carrying a litter. We can take this little one in and give an antibiotic injection, check for any wounds and monitor for a few hours. We have the air-conditioned cabin with the other rescues, so we can make sure that this hedgie is comfortable. You did the right thing, Elizabeth. You really did. The population of hedgehogs has declined steeply over the last ten years."

"Oh, wonderful. I'll make a donation to help towards expenses. There are so few places I could think of to take the little one." Elizabeth replies. "I feed them outside the back door. I have about three now."

"We'll keep you posted. If we need to call the vet in, we will. I must say, they look how I feel," Muriel smiles, then sits with the box on her lap, waiting for Eadie to speak with one of the families about a dog they like.

Just as Eadie is pulled away, Logan Lax rushes in on foot, clearly sweating and anxious. Like the privileged man he is, he expects everything to stop and his needs to be answered immediately.

"You haven't seen a dog this high," Logan holds his hands up to the middle of his thighs, "blonde, longish, straggly hair. Have you?" He says, interrupting a family about to say they were ready to adopt a dog.

"I'll leave you to it," Elizabeth tells Muriel, not wanting to get involved and feeling the hairs on the back of her neck prickle. A sign she is familiar with. She knows full well that if she stays in the room for another second, she won't be able to help herself. She knows he is talking about Daisy's Saluki. As she walks away, she wonders how Daisy could have lost her pride and joy again and hopes the dog is found soon. Elizabeth hears Muriel telling Logan that they don't have that dog, sorry, and no, he cannot check out back. He will just have to believe them. Maybe he could try the Cambridge dog warden. Elizabeth hears Logan shouting, and then he runs out past Elizabeth, shouting back, "They said it's not there. Wouldn't even let me look to check. I just wanted to be sure! Lady W can't have gone far!" Logan shakes his head in exasperation.

Elizabeth is aware that she is shaking her head, trying to stop the thoughts from creeping in. Why is the dog missing? She looks at the trees surrounding the rescue centre. She looks down at the bricks on the driveway and the little van with the words 'Rescue Me' on the side. She thinks exactly! Rescue me from any more thoughts about what it all means.

41 PUNTING WITH DAISY

Many might wonder why an Inspector has agreed to go on a picnic with a young woman whose billionaire ex-partner has gone missing, especially after having just played golf with her new boyfriend, who appears to be even wealthier, all when he should be working on the case. Abley, however, knows full well that it is nigh on impossible to get an audience with the wealthy, who, more than most, successfully build barriers around their time and space, which can often become impenetrable without a search warrant or a round of discussions with lawyers. Abley is under no illusions. Daisy will have no doubt asked him to go punting to pick his brains about her old flame, Atticus. So, while the cat is friendly, let them play with the mouse for a while, at least allowing the mouse time to work out his next move. But, as Abley steps onto the punt and Daisy begs him to take the pole so they can be chauffeurless, then tells him how strong he is, one cannot help but wonder if Abley's own sense of perspective is a little skewwhiff and whether he is thinking rationally at all today. Especially when he beams at her after she starts complimenting his pole action. He seems to be uncharacteristically letting his guard down by the second.

"I never have time for punting. It's for tourists and posh Johnnies." Abley beams at Daisy, "But this is quite relaxing," he says as he places the pole successfully on the central shelf submerged under the water's surface along The Backs – a local secret making punting ten times easier – and punts along towards the Bridge of Sighs, like a pro.

"I'm just happy you came with me. I knew Logan was going to be busy after this morning, and, well, I don't know anyone in Cambridge," Daisy removes a flimsy cardigan to reveal bare golden tanned shoulders and a pretty little sun top. "And you're such a fabulous golfer, putting Logan to shame, that I knew you'd be an excellent punter, and you are," Daisy smiles back, looking up at Abley with a youthful glow straight from a photographic advert in a magazine. "It's really nice getting to know you." Daisy's voice trembles.

Abley watches Daisy stretched out on the seat like a movie star. Her slight melancholy tone belies her appearance. “It does sound like you travel to some fascinating places, though,” Abley replies, half watching the other punts so he doesn't crash and lose his veneer of expertise and half watching Daisy's smile and trying to stay focused on the case and not her beauty.

“Yes and no. After a while, you get bored of it. It isn't exciting anymore. When you do something every day. And you start to dread getting on another plane,” Daisy says, quite upset that she has not found a place to call home for a long time. “You know, it gets very lonely. Atticus is very busy. That's okay. But when he wants me to accompany him on business, what kind of life is that? Like I say, I don't have any friends. I'm not sure Logan will be any different.” Daisy shrugs.

“What, even having a private jet, private spas, the best chefs?” Abley teases Daisy, perhaps aware that he has gone into rescue mode. Not a mode for professional police Inspectors.

“Even.” Daisy smiles thoughtfully, hoping not to see the inside of a plane cabin for some time. “This is the first time I've listened to anyone talk about anything other than stocks and shares, profits and losses.” Daisy is aware of how she must sound. “I mean, I know I have choices. I could leave. But what could I do?” Daisy pauses. “I want to get back in control of my own life.”

"I have a daughter your age," Abley proffers. "She's a formidable woman. I'm sure you're much stronger than you think."

"You're married?" Daisy is surprised. "I thought you might be a man about town. Solving crimes, playing golf, pub with the guys, befriending the ladies at the bar," Daisy replies, surprised.

"Don't hold back. Tell me what you really think." Abley flicks water from the punt pole towards Daisy in gest. "Don't you think I'm a bit old for that!" Abley laughs, unable to remember the last time he chatted up a woman at a bar, having spent most of his adult life with his ex-wife. "No, I'm divorced."

"Oh, what happened?" Daisy tightens her lips. She knows the drill and is ready to think the less of this Inspector.

"Why do you think it was me?" Abley fakes offence, but thinking about Maureen's affair makes him very sad. He accidentally lets the pole slip through his fingers, making a clanging noise on the side of the punt. "No, she ran off with the next-door neighbour while I was working." Abley takes back control of the punt, a little red in the face.

"Oh," Daisy replies, her eyes wide open, "Her loss." Daisy trails her fingers in the water, then adds, "She needs her eyes tested." Daisy leans her head to one side, holds up her hands, and joins them to create a frame to look through at Abley. Abley shakes his head and smiles. He dips the pole in again and points up at Bene't's Chapel so that Daisy pays attention to the beauty around her. "I'm looking at you, Bob," Daisy adds disarmingly.

For a moment, Abley is flattered and can feel himself go a little red. Then, in the back of his mind, he realises he is almost definitely being played. So why does he feel like a fly caught in her web?

"I beat myself up wondering if it was because of this job," Abley says, half to himself.

"Would you have quit the job if that were true?" Daisy asks pointedly.

They pass Bene't's College and glide parallel to Christina's. Abley looks right at Daisy, attempting to turn the tables. "Forgive me for asking, but how well do you know Logan?" He smiles, knowing this will land hard with Daisy, who seems to be deflecting. "And, you lured me here to say you wanted to tell me things about Atticus Stamp, your former partner. I'm on the clock and interested in what you have to say."

"Ah yes, on the clock," Daisy replies, glancing across at a large weeping willow on the river bank, its leaves kissing the water.

"I'm working, Daisy. I do need to find some excuse for holding a pole mid-summer and drifting along The Backs like someone without a care in the world," Abley lifts the pole, drops it in the water, then pushes against it, propelling them forward again. Daisy looks up at the underneath of Christina Bridge as they pass through, the reflections from the sun bouncing off the water shimmering on the walls.

"We kind of know each other from knocking about on the circuit, Logan and I. You know, same regattas, events, fundraisers, balls. It was odd that we never really spoke before really. I'm beginning to think that Atticus always managed to keep us apart intentionally. Maybe he knew there was an attraction there? Logan is such a great guy," Daisy smiles, then shrugs.

They head past All Saint's College. More willow trees on the banks hide punts parked up, People in their salad days, laughing. A rewilded nature bed on All Saint's College lawns is full of bees and butterflies. Abley breathes in deeply, enjoying the punt as they head towards St James's College and the Bridge of Sorrows.

"I've lived in Cambridge for so many years, but I don't see all this every day. I'm either in the office or–"

"Dealing with murders?" Daisy interrupts as a punt full of tourists passes them around the bend of the Cam by The Bridge of Sorrows, where punts are bunching up in a river traffic jam. Abley spots this in time and pulls in to moor up against the bank.

"Oh, you have to be a student at St James's to dock here, don't you?" Daisy can see a gardener watching them.

"I'll risk it if you will," Abley focuses on locating a safe space on the edge.

"You're the Inspector here, aren't you? That should count for something." Daisy shrugs.

"It counts for nothing along these stretches, let me tell you," Abley replies matter of factly, "But I'm not about to get caught in that tangle." Abley pulls in, his arms getting tired. Perhaps he will use that excuse if they come across a bossy Porter. The two pull up on the banks with a view of the other Colleges and punts going by.

Once stationary and the punt rope wrapped around a small tree, they perch on the bank with the picnic. Daisy encourages Abley to dip his toes in the water, which he does, and just for a moment, he remembers what it feels like to be a young man again. They sit in silence for a while, Abley eating a cucumber sandwich Daisy picked up earlier from the local store, along with scones, strawberries, and some non-alcoholic bubbles.

"Cheers," Daisy says, handing Abley a beaker of bubbles, now very happy they are moored, listening to the clanging of punt poles in what only can be described as spaghetti junction up ahead.

"Cheers." Abley wipes his hand on his shirt and takes the glass from Daisy, popping the rest of the sandwich in.

"I love your sun tan. Have you been

abroad?" Daisy holds her phone high and takes a photograph of them, leaving Abley's face out, just capturing his legs and feet in the water. 'Hanging with a new friend', she posts.

"You'll get me into trouble," Abley spots what she is doing. Daisy shows Abley the photograph on her phone to reassure him of his anonymity. Then she turns and looks him straight in the eye.

"This is hard to ask because I'm scared of the answer, but am I in danger, Inspector?" Daisy's demeanour changes. So, this is why she asked him here.

"Honest answer. There's no evidence to suggest you're at risk, but if it would make you feel more secure, we could offer you a bobby to stay with you." Abley cannot sugar-coat the situation. Two men are missing, one of whom is her ex-boyfriend. But there is nothing pointing to Daisy being the next in line.

"Oh, so I am in danger?" Daisy turns pale. She places her drink on the bank wall's flat edge and stares into the water.

"I'm not saying that at all. As a policeman, I deal with the facts. There are no facts to suggest you're at risk. But you seem to believe you might be. Why is that?" Abley consciously refrains from admitting to Daisy that much of the evidence is pointing towards a likely outcome of Atticus already being fully deceased.

Daisy pulls at her top, mindful. "I

mean, where's Atticus? Did Terrence Montagner disappear just so that he could come back and do something sinister to us both? Logan said Terrence hated Atticus."

"What makes you think that? Why would Terrence Montagner come back to harm you?" Abley shakes his head.

"I'm clutching at straws to make sense of it all." Daisy picks up her glass again, perhaps a little more at ease from Abley's confidence.

"We're still treating both investigations as missing persons, which is why I can still have a picnic with you. Should this change to anything else, I should not be able to fraternise with a suspect."

"What?" If it is possible, Daisy looks even more shocked at this news. "What are you talking about?" Daisy now drinks her drink down in one, forgetting there is no alcoholic kick to it.

"Have you been into College much?" All of a sudden, Abley feels uncertain as to what he is doing here with Daisy. Could it be fuelled by his ex-wife and her brand new marriage?

"No. I find it a bit stifling. All that judgement on my intelligence, or lack of," Daisy replies, looking at Abley staring up at some swifts flying overhead. "Inspector?" Daisy touches his arm.

"Someone has defaced a photograph of Atticus. Given him devil horns," Abley recalls.

"And you think I did it?" Daisy is mildly offended.

"And an angel halo over Logan Lax. And the library was upended."

"Upended?" Daisy shakes her head, biting into a strawberry. "I'm not sure why you're telling me this, Inspector?"

"We're struggling to think who might have defaced the image of Atticus?" Abley asks, staring at Daisy for the first time, not revealing that he knows it was Atticus who turned over the library.

"Wait, his photograph was defaced?" Daisy asks. Why would anyone do that? If I wanted to hurt him, trust me, I would not start by scribbling on his photo." Daisy raises her eyebrows, adamant about her belief in this.

"You knew him better than I," Abley adds.

"Hmm," Daisy replies, looking completely unsure where this conversation is headed, narrowing her eyes for the first time at Abley. "Anyway, if you think I would hurt anyone, which I presume you might or wouldn't be here, then why are you also being so nice? Are you just trying to trick me into saying something?"

"What would I want you to say?" Abley shakes his head and smiles warmly, picking up a strawberry and popping it in his mouth.

"You tell me. The more I think about it, the more I think that's why we're here," Daisy pulls her cutest frown again, still attractive while mildly angry.

"You invited me, remember?" Abley laughs. "You had things to tell me about Atticus." Abley notices a few young men on the path further away in St James's grounds point at them. He suspects it is because of Daisy. "Looks like you have some admirers." Abley watches the young men walk towards them, and one of them plucks up the courage to talk to Daisy.

"Can I have a picture with you?" The young man asks.

"Of course, Darling," Daisy jumps up, swishing her hair and smiling wide, revealing her pearly white teeth.

"What are you doing here?" Another young man asks, surprised to see Daisy sitting out and about.

"Raising money for an animal rescue centre. Taking a break now. But do donate if you can. All the deets on my stream," she beams at them coyly.

"Right," the man leans in, takes a photo, and says, "Thanks, awesome." The young men leave, looking at the photographs they have just taken.

Once the men have gone, Abley observes Daisy's face change as she sits back down beside him. He is a little surprised by how quickly Daisy has switched back from what seemed like a fake influencer mode, masking somehow who she really is. He noticed a little harder, perhaps colder side than she had previously shown, almost unnoticeable to someone not in the habit of studying people for a living.

"Are you okay?"

"I'm fine," Daisy replies, a little distant. They do not say anything for a short while. Abley spots a wasp that has landed on the picnic on the bank and is now eating some of the jam dropped from Daisy's scone. She takes the bottom of her beaker and squishes the wasp dead, then flicks its dead body off her rug and into the river.

"Atticus?" Abley looks at Daisy.

"We have these security rings. Both of us. See?" Daisy shows Abley a plain-looking white-gold colour ring on the first finger of her right hand, a bit thicker than a normal wedding ring. Atticus calls it a health band. It's a smart ring. He hates the idea of wearing a ring, so won't call it that." Daisy smiles. "It captures data, you know, heart-beat, blood pressure, sleep patterns. Atticus set them up. We're on the same programme. It means we can see each other's. His idea is that we will be able to know if something is up, like if one of us collapses on the floor. Like those panic alarms old people wear around their necks."

"Oh," Abley wonders where this is going.

"I don't know why I didn't tell you before," Daisy admits, continuing, "I think I was hoping it would start again, and I'd find him first. You see, his stopped sending data the day we argued.

I mean, he could have taken it off. But when I remove mine, I can still see the historical data. But his just went blank. Nothing."

"That's very interesting," Abley replies. "Please let me know if you have any other evidence or movement on the ring. Let's arrange for a police officer to accompany you to give you peace of mind. Try not to worry, okay? Be more careful about where you go, who you speak to, who you hang out with."

42 BILLIONS DISAPPEAR

After her punt and picnic with Inspector Abley, Daisy decides to catch a cab back to Logan's home. She accepts the Inspector's apology that he must return to the police station as he walks her through the city centre to the taxi rank. She explains that it seems easier than calling for one of Logan's drivers and waiting or bothering Logan while he is working.

As Daisy sits in the back seat of the taxi, she turns and looks through the rear window as it pulls away. She watches Abley push his bike across the road, growing smaller and fading into the crowd. His crinkly face smiling at a pedestrian as they step out in front of him. Was she done with rich billionaires? Should she just find a normal man, the man next door? Well, not next door to where she is now, but somewhere where Abley lives. He told her about his tiny terrace in Grantchester, which sounded so cosy. She wonders whether she should turn up by surprise at his home. Knock for tea. Take crumpets and scones. "Bob," she says quietly to herself.

Her taxi gets stuck in a bit of traffic, and Bob, now on his bike, begins catching up on the road outside. She feels herself getting excited to see him again. She starts to wave in case he spots her. She can feel her heart beating faster as he gets closer. She knows it is silly but cannot put her finger on it. He's right up close now, perhaps ten feet. She finds herself knocking on the window. Finally, his head turns, and his eyes lock with hers. He beams from under his crash helmet, and before she knows it, he is gone again. Daisy can feel her heart sink as she watches Abley cycle past and carry-on down St Andrew's Street towards Parker's Piece. She shakes her head. What is she thinking? But then drifts back into watching his figure grow smaller and smaller. There is something warm about being in his presence. Maybe it is because he is such a good man.

Daisy sighs, thinking about all the men she has mixed with recently. Are they good men? She knows in her heart that something does not sit right with either of them. Something even with Logan. If she hadn't met Bob and had this picnic, she wonders whether she might have even felt her unease, but in the taxi back to his home, she finds herself comparing Logan to Bob. Logan is not the man she thought, wondering if she has made a big mistake going from one wealthy man to another. She takes out her mobile phone and makes a call.

"I can't do this anymore. It has to stop."

*

When Daisy opens the front door to Logan's home, there is no Logan, no staff and no Lady Woof Woof.

43 EX-WIFE

Abley locks up his bike around the back of Parker's Piece Police Station, still thinking about how his punting skills were not as bad as he thought. Looking up, he notices his ex-wife Maureen is sitting on the wall. Abley's heart skips a beat. All thoughts run through his mind. Has she run away from her new groom? The groom probably said or did something stupid, which he would, of course, it would only be a matter of time. Has she seen the error of her ways? Does she miss Abley and cannot keep herself from seeing him? Abley smiles, then notices how Maureen does not smile back. In fact, her arms are folded, and now she looks at the ground, her lips tightly pursed. His heart sinks, as surely if she wanted to get back together, she would be running into his arms or at least smiling right now. Oh, how he had dreamt of things turning out like that. He begins to wonder why she is here if she is not happy. What's happened? His mind races to the children.

"Lemon said you were on your way back," Maureen speaks flatly.

"Are the kids okay?" Abley asks urgently.

"Yes, yes. They're fine. Don't you think I'd phone you if anything like that (happened)? You'd phone me, right?" Maureen replies, her tone mildly irritated.

"It's lovely to see you." Abley breathes a sigh of relief. "Yes, of course, I'd call. I don't know what I was thinking. Forgive me. Just overreacting." Abley smiles at his ex-wife, just happy to see her. For them to be alone together like this. He holds out his arms in front of him, hoping for a hug.

"Yes, well, on that note. What were you thinking?" Maureen stands up from the wall and uncrosses her arms. She puts her hand out to stop Abley from hugging her.

"Well, I was just thinking how well you look. Apart from that, not much really. About to head up to my office," he shrugs, answering her question. "Working on the missing case, you've probably heard on the news." Abley looks at Maureen. He wished she was not frowning back at him. "It's good to see you, Reenie." Abley tries to cover the punch to the stomach that he feels from being blocked from a simple hug with his ex-wife.

"No, I mean, what were you doing turning

up at my wedding?" Maureen raises her eyebrows and dramatically shakes her head, waiting for his answer.

"Why are you not on your honeymoon? Is everything alright?" Abley tries to brush off her hostility with a friendly question.

"We go next week. Please don't turn up to that!" Maureen raises her voice to a stern level.

"Anywhere nice?" Abley cannot believe he just asked that, now wanting the pavement to swallow him whole. Why is he being so nice when she's being so horrid?

"Two weeks in the Maldives. But then you probably know that as you've been stalking my online socials too, haven't you?" Maureen starts to tap her foot on the pavement. Abley notices and, for a second, looks at Maureen like she is a stranger, as the woman he loves would not be so cruel.

"What? No. Of course not. No." Abley lies.

"Well, the data says otherwise," Maureen replies accusingly.

"Data?"

"Yes, data. Someone has checked out my social page over a thousand times who happens to live in Grantchester. And, unless I'm being recruited into some undercover cult, then who do you think that might be?" Maureen asks blankly.

"What are you doing here?" Abley asks Maureen, almost imploring her to stop crucifying him. But Maureen misses the cue. She is too mad and wants things to stop.

"You do remember I was married to a copper who told me how to keep an eye out for stalkers?"

Abley knows he has been caught red-handed and does not even try to defend himself.

"I didn't think you'd go through with it," he finally admits, his own head now sinking, the words painful to say. He leans on the wall himself, the blood now draining from his legs.

"I did. I have, and I'm in love!" Maureen spits at Abley. This cuts him like a thousand knives. Some defence mechanism pulls him off the wall again, preparing to escape this pain.

"I know." Abley starts to walk off.

"Sorry, I didn't mean to (upset you)." Maureen sees she has gone too far. "You just need to leave me alone." Silence hangs in the air as Abley stands still, his back to Maureen, and finally, Maureen breaks it. "Whatever we had, it died years ago."

Abley cannot find the strength to reply, but at the same time has so many questions, so many things he needs to say. He does not even know where to start. He turns back around and stands in front of her, staring, until finally, he finds his voice, frail and broken.

"I still love you, Reenie," Abley looks straight into Maureen's eyes, "I've tried not to. When you told me it was over, when you sent me the divorce papers. I've tried, for your sake. But in here," Abley holds his hand to his heart, "I've loved you for all these years. Two children." Abley takes Maureen's hand, and she lets him. "We were happy. Don't tell me we weren't. We had something better than good. You're the love of my life, the only thing that makes sense. When I wake up, there's that little moment of time when I still think you're lying next to me. It's the best moment of the day. And then, I look over to the empty pillow, the empty side table," Abley uses his sleeve to wipe away tears. "I still make you tea. I still look left on the sofa when I'm watching a film, to laugh or be shocked with you. I only have one coat on the peg, and my slippers have the rein of the hallway. I have a small fridge with hardly anything in it. The shampoo lasts forever, and my toothbrush stands there, pathetically, all alone. Everything is where I left it when I get in. I miss your women's magazines, reading the horoscope together, and laughing with you. I miss sitting in the garden with you and doing the crossword over a morning cuppa. I miss hugging you when it's raining outside the window at night and feeling like I'm home." Abley is exhausted by his own speech. His knees buckle a little, and he shakes his head to compose himself until he takes the biggest breath and looks at Maureen tenderly. "I'm lost without you, Reenie. You didn't just leave. I'm a ghost." Abley's eyes have filled with tears. Maureen pulls her hand out of Abley's, taken aback by her ex-husband's speech and can see how cut up he is, but enough is enough.

"I still love you too, but not in that way anymore," she continues, resolute. "You have to move on, Bobby. You have to move on." Maureen lowers her face and stares at Abley's shoes. Abley looks back at Maureen with all the love in his heart. A heart that is breaking. He feels sick and wobbly. Every ounce of his body wants to hold, kiss, and tell her he's sorry. "Still wearing the moccasins," she adds, trying to change the subject.

"I fucked it up, didn't I," Abley's voice trembles.

"No one fucked it up. We fucked it up. We both did. We were–"

Constable Love walks up the path towards them, unintentionally crashing into the intimate moment.

"Sir, we have found out more on those smart rings, you know, that you phoned in to Lemon just now. Stamp's assistant gave us the logins. Coming in to look?" Love stands close to the pair, breaking whatever field of communication that existed between the ex-couple. Maureen steps back, having recognised the pattern of interruptions countless times before. Abley has to go.

"We could go for a drink?" Abley ignores the Constable, who is now standing at the station door, holding it open so that Abley can join him. Abley implores Maureen to take a moment with him. "Not that I drink alcohol in the day anymore. I stopped. I stopped a while ago. When you left." Abley realises the impact of his words, knowing that they are almost true. "You make me a better person, Reenie." Abley cannot take his eyes off Maureen, but she has already started to step backwards and away from him, no longer making eye contact. He can feel the moment has broken. Then he asks, remembering Lavenham and their walk. "Do you still have that scarf with the tiny blue butterflies?"

"What?" Maureen frowns a little.

"You looked so pretty in it."

"I don't know. Maybe. I have to get to the shops. Take some shoes back to John Lewis. I'd better go." Maureen turns without looking back and heads towards Parker's Piece. Abley glances at Constable Love.

"I'll just be a minute," Abley explains his action, then starts to follow Maureen across the Piece.

44 THE BENCH

Daisy sits on a bench on Jesus Green. After leaving the house, she has walked everywhere to look for Lady Woof Woof. Tears run down her face as she looks out across the Green at those playing tennis and listens to the thwacking back and forth of the small yellow ball. She notices the poppies swaying in the wild meadow that the Council planted around the courts and people lying under the shade of the London Plane trees, which cuts across to Jesus Locke. She watches a man sitting on a petrol lawn mower, making the familiar sounds of summer. Everything feels and looks normal in this picture before her eyes, but everything is upside down in reality. How did she get to be here? Where is Logan? She hopes he has just taken Lady Woof Woof for a walk, but why did neither of his assistants know where he was? Why had he left his phone, keys, and wallet? It was like someone from space had come down and beamed him up. It made no sense as to how he could completely vanish.

She has already posted on social media a plea for their safe return with a reward. Her online profile has lit up with various people announcing sightings that make no sense. One said they'd spotted Lady Woof Woof in New York, another in Malta. Neither place could be reached in time since she had been without her beautiful dog. Daisy is busy doom-scrolling when Elizabeth walks by with Hector, Monty, Clive, and Patty. Clive approaches Daisy to say hello, and then Daisy spots Elizabeth.

"Hello," Daisy says to Clive, the Old English Sheepdog, wiping away her tears.

"Hello," Elizabeth replies.

"I don't suppose you've seen Lady Woof Woof, have you? I don't know where she is."

"Have you contacted the local vets, the dog warden?" Elizabeth replies, not really wanting to stop and talk to Daisy, but concerned about the dog.

"No, should I? I called the police." Daisy says.

"They'll be able to read the chip and locate Lady W. There are also drone companies that will find her. They send their equipment up into the sky. A bird's eye view. Where was Lady Woof Woof when you last saw her?"

"At home. Or, well, at my friend's home," Daisy explains.

"When did they last see her?" Elizabeth asks, remembering Logan running out of the Rescue Me centre, angry at the world, looking for a dog not long ago.

"I don't know. They're also gone. They might have my dog, I suppose. D'you think they might want to take my dog? I thought they liked me?"

"Well, I don't know about that, Dear."

Just as Daisy is about to phone the first vet, Martin turns up with his dog and Lady Woof Woof.

"Oh, Lady!" Daisy shouts, dropping her phone and leaving her bag. You're okay," Daisy bursts into tears, hugging Lady Woof Woof, who is pleased to see her but utterly unaware of the commotion.

"I found her in the city centre, walking down St Edward's Passage. I saw her collar and your name, and I was going to hang onto her until I found someone with your phone number, as it only had some company number on it. Here you are!" Martin replies, a little shocked to find Elizabeth with Daisy.

"Oh, thank you, thank you," Daisy kneels and plants a million kisses on her dog. Lady Woof Woof soon decides a run is in order when she sees Monty and Hector bounding about, and so leaves Daisy to go and play.

Elizabeth tries not to be curious about why Martin has Daisy's dog and is here on the

Green instead of handing the dog into the police station. She really tries not to think about the case at all. She turns away and decides to give Patty a hug. She tries hard to ignore Martin who is telling Daisy he is so glad he could help, and Daisy repeating to Martin that Logan Lax really has disappeared. What does she mean? No, Elizabeth, no!

45 WHERE IS THE POWER?

Abley ignored all the signs of common sense and reason and had chased Maureen across Parker's Piece to the John Lewis department store, where she told him to halt all communication and to stop following her. Things got heated on the pavement outside, and people started to stare. Desperate, Abley lied and said he could still be friends and not break things off completely. To give him a chance to be an adult. This was when he burst into more tears. Everything came out, and he started to sob. He remembers dropping his jacket and sunglasses while making some grand gesture of love with his arms, and he watched as she picked them up for him, unimpressed. How he had then tried to grab Maureen, to stop her from entering the shop, from ending their conversation, had somehow spun around and fallen back into one of the shop windows, which made a clanging noise, and there had been a gasp from the people standing waiting at the bus stop, in case it had smashed. And how there had been a second gasp, as when he stepped back, his nose was bleeding. He shuddered to think that this was not his lowest point, but rather when he, after this, then fell at Maureen's feet and begged her to come back to him, holding on to one of her legs as he wailed that he could not imagine life without her. She was his world, and how he would never be worthy, but he could not stop loving her. He remembered her telling him to be quiet, that everyone was watching and that he was embarrassing himself, and how he looked up and saw a crowd of people staring. Then he remembers how he just sat in the street, dusty and hot, watching Maureen walk through the automatic doors into John Lewis and not look back, and how he had stared at the doors for a while, watching people follow behind. It felt like he was watching time pass and Maureen pull further away. Until that is, a man from the bus stop queue held out a hand to him to stand and said, 'Mate. Plenty more fish in the sea. C'mon. Don't let the side down.' And the man then patted him on the back and half-pushed him on his way. Abley, without direction but feeling the blood trickle down onto his lips, then remembers wiping his face and quickly walking into the University Arms Hotel toilets, on the opposite side of the street, and right past the pretty young lady standing behind reception, who looked concerned. Then, when he was in the toilets, he remembers looking at himself in the mirror—a dishevelled, bloody, blotchy face and eyes that looked broken inside. And then, he remembers a cloud passing over his entire body, covering any chance of happiness ever again.

A short while later, Abley returns to the station. He walks through the reception area without making his usual small talk at the front desk. If he can just get to his office to compose himself, shut the door, and at least have a moment. But he is surprised to see that Constable Jack Love has moved back in. Love's desk is full of food and beside it some exercise equipment. Abley's putting green all folded up in the corner again.

Abley notices Lemon standing by the window and is grateful, as he is sure he cannot handle the Constable alone right now.

"Daisy said she got home, and her dog and Logan Lax were gone. Logan's left his phone, wallet and keys. But that the car and nothing from his wardrobe are missing," Lemon updates Abley.

"He's in the fashion industry. Won't he have a wardrobe in each city?" Constable Jack Love suggests, having wandered over after hearing Lemon's update.

"What?" Abley frowns, still surprised at having just been with Daisy and enjoying the summer's day by the river. "So now we have a missing politician and two missing billionaires," Abley states.

"Maybe they all went missing because someone was trying to steal Daisy's dog in the first place." Constable Jack Love flicks his hair, his muscles rippling, his blue eyes piercing, "It's always been about a dog theft. Daisy said that Atticus Stamp had stolen her dog. But what if he didn't?" Love beams at Lemon.

"What?" Lemon shakes his head.

"Lemon, I know I'm being quick with my thoughts, but stay with me," Love continues kindly. "This is what happened. Atticus Stamp didn't steal Daisy's dog the first time. Someone else did."

"What, and the dog ended up at a rescue centre?" Lemon frowns.

"Could be." Love opens his eyes wide, continuing, "Then, the dog gets stolen again. Only this time, that fashion guy gets in the way. The dog's gone, right? Might be a rare breed, or have a diamond sewn into its skin or something sick, rich people do, eh?" Constable Love pins a photo of the missing dog onto Abley's wall, and for the first time, Abley turns around to see the huge web of photos and string that Love has pinned up. "Hope this is okay? Raynott said I should move back."

"Where did you get all these photos?" Abley asks, noticing the photographs are covering his favourite golfing calendar, which now has pins and tape all over it.

"Internet," Love wipes the corner of the printed photo to lay it flat. "I've only gone and solved the case. Got all the suspects up there. Don't you think?" Love explains confidently.

"You know we have software to do all this now," Lemon tells Love, staring blankly at the wall of photos.

"Yes, but this is much more romantic, don't you think? I saw it on an old '70s cop show. My dad loves 'em," Love replies.

Feeling completely out of it and happy that neither of his colleagues has noticed his change in mood, Abley pulls at a bit of string and follows it where it goes.

"It seems to connect Lady Woof Woof to everyone?" Abley says, letting go of the string and staring at the wall of suspects and a dog in the centre of everything. Still feeling hopeless.

"Everyone is a suspect right now of stealing Lady Woof Woof," Constable Love nods at Abley, "that's why."

Abley stares at all the dogs down one side. Although the wall of string looks insane, it is glaringly apparent that quite a few dogs are attached to the people involved in this case.

"So, you think this whole thing is about

Lady Woof Woof?" Abley asks Love.

"Exactly!" Love smiles, pleased with himself and for helping his boss.

"Not being able to see the murderer for all the dogs," Abley says to himself quietly.

"That's why we need to impound all the dogs right now," Constable Love suggests. "Before another is stolen."

"No. No, we really don't. Cats would love it, but we will be ripped to shreds." Lemon tries to remain calm, using as many of his new leadership skills as possible, then looks at Abley properly for the first time and notices something is off with his boss. Lemon continues, "We have no evidence to back up your theory, Constable. We cannot impound dogs, or we will be headline news for doing so. This is a potentially explosive case in the press," Lemon explains. Love walks out of the room, nodding. Lemon continues to look at Abley, who slowly nods in agreement. Lemon shows Abley his phone and clicks through story after story where the headlines read, 'Three billionaires go missing in Cambridge.'

"Terrence Montagner is not a billionaire, is he?" Abley asks quietly.

"I don't know," Lemon replies, watching Constable Love walk back in with a step ladder and climb up to pin more dogs along the top of his wall of suspects.

"No. Take it out," Abley is

uncharacteristically short with Love, shaking his head at the Constable, who looks forlorn and walks back out with the stepladder. Abley picks off the photographs and pieces of string from his golfing calendar then takes it down and puts it on his desk.

"The link is staring us in the face," Lemon looks again at the wall of photos and string, trying not to ask Abley what has happened but knowing that it is likely to be personal. Against Terrence Montagner, the wall of string has the word 'fishes', and against Atticus Stamp, there is a photograph of him and the lion he shot. "So many faces and so few clues."

"It's only been a few hours since I played golf with Logan this morning. How can he be missing? The news is being hysterical." Abley looks at Lemon. They both know that it is likely that Logan Lax is missing. Who leaves the house with nothing?

"Simon at the Blue Ball Inn just phoned, by the way," Lemon explains. "He has two sets of golf clubs he's keeping for you. He says one set is very fancy. He asked if you stole them."

"Two? I only have one." Abley wonders what that is about, then touches Logan's photograph, which is not far from Mikayla's photograph with the words 'dresses up dogs', the 'rescues animals' against Eadie and Muriel, the 'talks politics' against Martin's, and Daisy's which says 'influences people'. "I think Logan has given me his golf clubs." Abley frowns, knowing that if indeed he now has Logan's clubs, then they are probably the best golf clubs he'll likely ever own in his life. He cannot bring himself to give them up, job or no job. He's never broken a rule before. "Maybe Simon got it wrong," Abley suggests, not needing Lemon's permission. "They might not even be his golf clubs."

"What? Whose?" Lemon pieces things together. "You have Lax's clubs?"

At this moment, Constable Love comes in.

"Did I miss something? Shall we bring in the dogs?" He asks again.

"No," Abley replies, turning to Love. "I'm sorry, lad, take no notice of my temper. You're doing fine work," Abley stares at the wall of string and suspects again.

"I wonder how Daisy is?" Lemon asks Abley.

"Shall we bring her in?" Love asks, listening in.

"No, let's arrange a warrant to search Logan Lax's home, pronto, please, Constable. His staff are unlikely to let us in without one," Abley replies, feeling more like himself for a moment. "If Logan really is missing and not just out on a walk, then let's get ahead of the game. There will be some clues there. Perhaps we can speak to Daisy if she is there. She told me she's living with Logan at the moment." Abley then looks at the Constable. "And Constable, if you can stay here, please. See what else you can find out about the missing dog, and the dogs. Keep up the good work." Abley glances at Lemon and then back at Constable Love. "Oh, and also see what you can find out about Daisy."

"Alright, but I think we should bring in the dogs, too," Love suggests.

"No," Abley replies firmly, walking out of his office, hoping it is not a big ball of string when he returns. He is not sure whether searching Logan Lax's home will turn up anything useful. If it does not, then what will he do?

46 IT'S OFFICIAL

It is the next morning, and the dog parents are out in force in the Mill Road Cemetery. Mikayla is telling everyone who will listen that she has big news and agreed to sell her clothes with Logan Lax. Most have seen the newspaper headlines this morning, talking about the missing billionaires, and Mikayla explains she still hopes his team will honour his agreement.

"It's terrible news about Logan. I hope he comes back soon. We're on first-name terms now," Mikayla beams. "He promises to make me a millionaire with my costume designs. Loves them. Said they are genius. He even suggested setting up a separate clothes store on Regent Street and one on Fifth Avenue in New York, where he said he could see all the women's clothes being replicated for their dogs. And by me! I could not stop him talking about it, you know. He was riffing, bouncing ideas. He told me to keep it top secret for now, but I know I can trust you all about it." Mikayla looks at Elizabeth, Martin, and Eadie, who are all standing in the centre of the graveyard, throwing balls and offering their dogs drinks of water. Eadie and Elizabeth are trying hard to block out Mikayla's bragging. Martin, on the other hand, is smiling proudly.

"You'll be terrific," Martin says supportively. "You're so talented." Then he thinks about the risks attached for someone like Mikayla in getting involved with such a powerful man. "Just be careful. Men like that eat us for breakfast and spit us out by supper, Mika." Martin affectionately pats Mikayla's back. "And, anyway, what if they're plotting to do something sinister? It has to be some kind of plan to all disappear together don't you think?"

"What do you mean?" Eadie asks Martin. Elizabeth says nothing.

"Well, it's just strange they've all gone at the same time. As far as I'm aware, Cambridge does not have a magic portal into a parallel universe. It feels like it is intentional, in some way organised. All I'm saying is that if you have that kind of money, it would not be hard to organise so that when you get back, you can announce something. Let's face it, it has everyone talking."

"Interesting theory," Elizabeth replies, knowing that when they were both alone in her garden, they discussed the likelihood that Terrence Montagner and Atticus Stamp were dead, not missing. She is not sure if Martin knows more than he is letting on. "Maybe worth a second paper?" Elizabeth refers to their earlier conversation about Martin's past academic papers and his infamous interview, in which he talks fiercely about bringing powerful men to their knees.

"I know nothing about it, I really don't – whether you believe me or not, Elizabeth." Martin shrugs. "I can see your beady stare at me," he smiles. Mikayla touches Martin's arm.

"Honey, you couldn't hurt a fly. I love you for it," Mikayla squeezes him.

"I'm not involved, don't want to be involved, am not judging you. I'm here to walk my dogs, believe it or not," Elizabeth replies.

"And steal my fashion designs. What have you done with them?" Mikayla asks Elizabeth, mildly annoyed.

"What did you say?" Eadie asks Martin. But Martin turns to go. Before Martin can leave, however, Elizabeth pulls him back.

"I know what you did on the College lawn," Elizabeth raises her eyebrows. Martin looks back, his eyes caught in the headlights. "'Rip off his skin and see how he likes it'. Emily sent me a photograph. They're having real trouble cutting it out of the lawn. If you are going to write graffiti on grass, then you should really watch how you write your letter ‘t’s. You cross too low.” Elizabeth stares at Martin, but he shakes his head, pretending that he does not know what she is talking about. His cheeks suggest otherwise.

47 THE SEARCH WARRANT

It is still early when Abley and Lemon bring a warrant to search billionaire Logan Lax's luxurious Cambridge residence. They are outside the home, located in a leafy suburb, having both come by bike, waiting for backup to arrive.

"Shall I tell them to put their nee-nahs on?" Lemon smirks, both of them drinking from their water bottles, no police car in sight.

"Why do you insist on calling them that?" Abley shakes his head.

"Because it annoys you," Lemon smirks again. "We'll solve this case, you know. I have a feeling about this place. Something isn't right about a bloke who pulls the fur off animals."

"Not like we have cold winters here," Abley raises his eyebrows, the warmth of the day making him sweat.

"Never seen the point of fashion. Pair of joggers, trainers. What else does a person need?" Lemon gulps his water.

"Golf shoes," Abley replies without thinking, then looks up at Lemon, nodding.

"D'you think that's why he's missing? Because he's starting to sell fur again?" Lemon asks thoughtfully.

"He hadn't launched the line here. It was being produced abroad, but increasing, Love said," Abley explains.

"Daisy is leaking it all over her account. Let me check my notebook." Lemon gets it out of his pocket. "Yes, looks like that's how the press got hold of it, too. Motive?" Lemon ponders.

"Never mind that now. Call them to put on their nee nahs. We don't have all day," Abley replies.

Lemon takes out his phone to call his colleagues. Abley gets off his electric bike, pulls out a handkerchief and starts to polish the frame, much happier with his bike than he thought he'd be, all black and shiny.

"You know you can get these helmets with a radio built-in. I must admit, I do miss listening to Radio 2 and Five Live in the motor."

"I don't think they have a radio built into them. It's just Bluetooth," Lemon replies, hanging up the phone and having instructed his colleagues about the sirens.

"Oh, for goodness sake. That's no use. What if you're in a no-signal area? Then you lose it. I want good old FM radio. When you could hear things?" Abley frowns.

"Can you hear the cars over the music?" Lemon replies, imagining his boss on his bike with Radio 2 in his head, oblivious to oncoming traffic.

"Well, I'm not going to have it cranked up to eleven, am I?" Abley pulls a face, then carries on cleaning the spokes. Lemon gets off his bike, walks it over to the fence, and locks it up.

"Who's going to steal a bike around here? These houses cost ten mill a pop. They don't want your racer," Abley says.

"No, but the thieves who want their stuff might take my bike!" Lemon explains.

"You know, this lock cost almost as much as my bike?" Abley decides to put the lock across his bike, conceding the point.

"I guess you have some expensive golf clubs to make up for that," Lemon comments wryly. Abley coughs with embarrassment, thinking of Logan's gifted golf clubs.

The police car finally turns up on the street, announcing to everyone that it has arrived with its nee nahs.

"They sound more like a wail," Abley tells Lemon. Before they can knock, the doors open, and a member of Logan's staff welcomes them in. There was little need to wave the warrant under the staff's eyes, but Abley does anyway. He and Lemon are followed in by four uniformed police officers, not quite in SOCO but with gloves and bags.

"We saw you on the cameras," Daisy explains as Abley and Lemon make it through to the back of the house. "Let me offer you a drink. What would you like? Tea, coffee, something cold?"

"I'm afraid we've brought our team. We have a search warrant. He has it over there," Abley points to the butler who let them in, who is reading the piece of paper. "It feels a bit soon to be looking through Mr Lax's belongings, but in the circumstances our Super thought it prudent and offer apologies later when he turns up. We're being on the cautious side."

"You just had to ask," Daisy replies, a little confused by the officious nature of the visit. The butler hands Daisy the warrant. Daisy looks at it but has never seen anything like it, so she scrunches up her face. "I really don't know Logan's affairs. Is this to do with his business? I found out about his involvement in the fur trade, I was shocked. It seems I'm not the best at choosing my men. Trophy hunting, fur traders. What next? A baby killer? What will you find here?"

"There's always an element of surprise with a search warrant. It allows us to look about before anyone has had a chance to hide things.

Not you, of course," Lemon lies, still suspicious of Daisy. "But, Mr Lax's staff," Lemon speaks quietly and looks in the direction of a number of Logan's staff now scuttling after the uniformed police officers, picking up things as they go, trying to protect them from getting broken.

"Ah, well, search away. And if you find any clues, please do something. Please find logan. I'm angry at him for his animal cruelty business. Very angry," Daisy looks at the post about Logan and the fur on her phone. "Logan has fur farms in America, Canada and Russia, if my Followers are right, Daisy explains. "What am I going to do here all alone? I'm pulling my hair out, I really am," Daisy explains. "I can't stay here. Not now."

"I'm glad you found Lady Woof Woof. Where?" Abley looks at the dog sniffing in the garden.

"Professor Martin Smith found her in the city centre. He brought her to me on Jesus Green," Daisy explains.

"Did he call you and meet you there?" Lemon asks.

"No, he just turned up," Daisy replies, stroking Lady Woof Woof, who has returned from the garden for some affection.

"How did he know you were there?" Abley asks.

"He said he was looking for me," Daisy shrugs, then frowns. "I guess it was a bit funny. You don't think he stole the dog just to return her to me?"

"Perhaps just a lucky coincidence," Abley is unconvinced.

"And Logan. I would like to find him too. And, although we're no longer together, I would also like Atticus to come back and let us know he's okay," Daisy says, watching a police officer open drawers in the living room.

"So, you're officially moved in here?" Lemon asks.

"Yes, I suppose. But I can't see myself living here. Not now." Daisy still holds her phone and the fur trade story.

"I suppose you'll be finding somewhere else to go?" Lemon asks flatly. "Not being married or anything."

"Look, I can stay here and have other places I can go. I have a new home in Melbourne Place. I picked up the keys yesterday from the estate agents. Yes, I'll probably go there," Daisy says lightly. "It's so tiny, but cosy. Hidden."

"It would be good if you could stick around in Cambridge for a bit longer," Abley says, a little too seriously for Daisy's liking.

"Look, to be honest, I'd just left Logan a message before he disappeared to say that I wanted to end things, that I couldn't do this anymore, and it had to stop."

"What?" Lemon asks, surprised.

"I know. I said the same thing to Atticus. Whenever I say it, the men in my life disappear?"

Daisy looks to Abley for answers. "I'm not exactly feeling safe right now either," Daisy holds Lady Woof Woof tightly as she sits beside her on the sofa.

"Let's get you that police officer to watch over you." Abley looks to Lemon to make the call. Lemon nods and picks up his phone again to organise things.

"Thank you," Daisy turns white. Abley cannot tell if she is white from fear about the gravity of what is happening or perhaps because she hasn't eaten. She looks particularly gaunt.

"Perhaps you should have something to drink or eat?" Abley suggests. Lemon hears his boss's words and raises his eyebrows a little while holding on to speak to the right police department. But he makes sure his boss does not see. He does not share Abley's opinion of Daisy, instead seeing her as someone using her beauty to get what she wants. He knows the type, but now he has had some leadership training and knows that he can never talk about a woman like that again. He will have to find a better way to frame it when he shares his concerns.

"Okay, we have an officer coming over to be with you. There will be two officers who will rotate. You need to confirm where you'll be in the next couple of hours," Lemon explains.

"I'll get my things shortly. Yes, Lady Woof Woof and I will move into Melbourne Place today," Daisy replies, worried by the gravity of the situation.

"That makes things a lot easier. You'll just be a stone's throw away from our offices," Abley says, trying to reassure Daisy that she is safe. Abley, unlike Lemon, wonders if Daisy will disappear next as this case grows more sinister.

"Okay, will you come and check in as well?" Daisy reaches out for Abley's hand. Abley walks closer and takes it. Lemon looks confused.

"Of course. You're going to be fine." Abley lets go of her hand, patting it kindly. "If you will excuse us for now, we must go and see how the search is coming along and if our officers have found anything of significance."

"You might want to check his office. I walked in the other day, and there was a secret door. He was coming back out of it."

"A secret door?" Lemon asks.

"The wall is fake, I think, as you go in. The one facing you."

"Right, we'll tell them now." Lemon walks ahead.

*

When the officers finally figure out how to open the secret door, they walk into a room full of animal trophies all around the room. Stags, boar, a zebra, a lion. Abley and Lemon are horrified. There must be twenty or more shot and stuffed animals.

"Why do billionaires take such pleasure in

killing animals?" Lemon shakes his head. Lemon watches as Abley picks something up from a desk. It is a Will, and it looks new, along with Logan Lax's signature. Lax is leaving everything to Daisy.

As Abley leaves the secret room, a police officer comes down the stairs, shaking his head, as they found nothing.

"It's okay, I think we have found more than enough," Lemon replies.

"Maybe the hunters are being hunted by a very clever influencer after all," Abley says, articulating what Lemon is thinking.

48 AN EX'S PERSPECTIVE

After the fruitless search warrant, Abley has come home for lunch to think. His electric bike is becoming his most favourite thing, allowing him to disappear from the station in minutes. He is looking forward to making a quick burger and checking the golf scores before returning to the office to work out what to do next. When he climbs the steps up to his front door, Maureen is the last person he expects to see waiting for him.

"Your pub landlord delivered these when he saw me waiting," Maureen looks at two bags of golf clubs. Abley immediately recognises his own and the clubs Logan Lax had bought, which cost a large fortune. He was right, he had been gifted them. A note is tucked into the top of the bag, attached with string. Maureen has pulled it out to read while waiting and shows it to Bob now: 'To Bob. Now, when you slice it into water, you can at least do it in style. Logan'. Abley shrugs, trying his best not to focus on the clubs despite how they will raise his game no end and just be present for Maureen. "I presume that is the same Logan that is in the news? Isn't it wrong to accept gifts from missing persons and possible suspects?" Maureen raises an eye, clearly having followed the papers and Logan's disappearance.

"It's lovely to see you," Abley says, ignoring her comments about the clubs and quite taken aback that she is here in front of him at all. He stares at her longingly until he checks himself and says, "Come in, come in." He unlocks the front door and indicates that Maureen should go inside, picking up the clubs and putting them inside the door. Once in, Abley immediately feels embarrassed by the size and the state of his home. "I've not been here long, as you probably know. I've still to decorate and buy stuff and things." Abley, for the first time, sees what she sees, an empty shell. "I've been busy," and as soon as the words fall out of his mouth, he regrets them. "I don't mean work busy or golf busy. I've got a garden. I have a cat," he back peddles, knowing Maureen always complained he was too busy for her. "Can I get you a cup of tea?"

"I'm not staying long," Maureen replies. She looks around the tiny yet almost empty living room, except for a saggy old sofa, the television, a random box, and a solitary dining chair. She spots the photo on the top of the television, with her hair coloured in cartoon red and her eyelashes drawn in comically long. She chooses not to say anything, knowing full well that the cause likely was a fit of pique.

"Tea doesn't take long to drink. You like tea," Abley tries his best to suggest she stay, even if for a short while.

"Tea is never just tea, though, is it," Maureen says quietly.

"Please. For old time's sake," Abley tries to hide his plea but fails spectacularly.

"Okay, just a quick cup." Maureen follows Abley into the kitchen and watches as he fills the kettle and pulls down two mugs from hooks he put up last week.

"Milk, no sugar, right?" Abley says quietly, remembering how Maureen takes her tea.

"Do you have any decaf, actually?" Maureen asks.

"Oh, you're on that now? Yes, somewhere. I think someone brought some." Abley bangs the cupboards, worried he has no decaf, then is relieved to find some at the back of the cupboard. He sniffs them, and they look okay, so he pops one in a mug, walks over to the back door, and opens it for fresh air. "Would you like to sit in the garden?" Abley feels completely stressed now. The tea bags, the unexpected visitor. Maureen.

"Okay," Maureen steps outside and is quite

taken aback at how peaceful and lovely it feels. She glances across the row of preened and manicured terraced gardens, all with low or no fences, the pretty summer flowers, including wild, as the gardens run up to fields at the back. A large oak tree in the closest field casts a shadow under which she notices some horses seeking shade from the blue sky heat of summer. Maureen breathes in deeply, remembering times when she was happy with Abley. At that moment, he steps out into the garden, holding two mugs and some bourbon biscuits. He opens a parasol poised over an old wooden bench, and the two of them perch, looking out across the view.

"This is very peaceful," Maureen says, taking her tea. The two sit in silence for a while, momentarily comfortable in each other's presence.

"Have a bourbon," Abley holds out the packet, and Maureen takes one. They munch for a while and sip their tea. A robin swoops down onto the fence, watching everything. His red breast faded in the summer glow. He jumps down into the borders, and it is so quiet for a moment they can hear him pecking about amongst the shrubbery. That is until Arnold appears out of nowhere and sits in the middle of the tiny patio immediately outside the backdoor, next to the overly large barbecue.

"Who is this?" Maureen is surprised to see

the cat.

"Oh, this is Arnold. Arnold, this is Maureen."

"You hate cats?"

"I've changed," Abley smiles. Maureen does not know what to say. She is pleased Abley is not falling apart but also a little hurt that he seems to be getting on with things better than she thought without her. But then she remembers his tears outside John Lewis.

"So, are you going to stay here for a while?" She asks.

"Yes, I think I like it. The neighbours are friendly." He knows he has broken the moment between them as soon as he says it. "I mean, they are just nice. It's just nice here." But Maureen has already taken the comment as a dig, and he can see her visibly recoil and pull back, sipping down her tea quickly, perhaps looking for an excuse to make this whole thing shorter than it needs to be. "I honestly didn't mean. I wasn't. I want you to be happy, Reenie. That's all I've ever wanted."

Maureen looks at her ex-husband, wanting to believe him. His phone rings in his pocket, and he pulls it out and cuts the call. Sitting closely, his hand almost crosses her lap. She notices that he is still wearing his wedding ring.

"Bob." She looks down at his ring so he can see what she is looking at. He shrugs. Tears spike his eyes, and he tips his neck back to stop them falling.

"I didn't have anywhere safe to put it," Abley replies, his head tilted, his voice somehow smaller. "Don't you still have ours?" He asks. Maureen doesn't answer, so he continues, "I remember buying them together. They're our bond. We wore them on our fingers, never taking them off all those years." Abley finally puts his head down, having only just stopped the tears.

"That's what people do with rings, Bob. They're important." Maureen hides her new wedding ring and engagement ring, which is much more expensive than the one Abley had bought her. But Abley prises open her hand and looks at the huge diamond.

"I still have yours. I have them in a tin at the back of my wardrobe, that tin of sweets you bought me when we went to Mundesley for that weekend and just lay on the beach, eating ice cream." Maureen looks at Abley kindly, admitting her secret. Now, Abley cannot stop the tears. Holding Maureen's hand, he shuts his eyes and slowly breaks down again, the bourbon packet dropping on the floor. "I will always love you. I came to say sorry for being so cold outside John Lewis. We had the best years of our lives. We still have two beautiful adult kids." Maureen smiles. "I want to get along for their sake, for our sake. I don't want to spoil those happy memories by filling the present with sour, mean, nasty words. I appreciate that they have mainly come from me. But, when I think about it, you were my best friend for so long." Maureen rubs Abley's back. "I just need a new adventure, you know." She stops speaking. Unable to find the right words, perhaps. Abley is utterly broken now. So, she continues, perhaps trying to find words to make sense of it all. "I don't know. Maybe we grew apart. Maybe time changes things. I understand it less over time, I think. It all went so fast while we were living it. And, somewhere, well, it went wrong. I don't think it was anyone's fault. I came to tell you that as I don't want you to beat yourself up. But I know that I need to be happy. And we weren't making each other happy at the end."

"You have always made me happy," Abley coughs, the biscuit dry in his mouth.

"It wasn't your fault. I care about you. I just wanted you to know that."

Abley breaks down further, and Maureen continues to rub his back. The two of them sit on the bench, looking out across the fields. Maureen comforts her ex-husband as best she can.

*

After Abley had stopped crying and talked a little bit about Arnold, what he feeds Arnold, how Arnold watches golf with him, small talk, to mask what was really going on, Abley finally could not keep Maureen any longer and had to walk her out. Now alone, Abley feels utterly drained. He sits back down on the bench in the garden and picks up Maureen's mug of now empty tea, her lipstick still on the side. He holds it, looks out across the gardens, and then shuts his eyes for a while, holding onto the moment.

On finally opening his eyes, Abley takes out his phone and calls Lemon.

"Yes, I'll be in shortly. Yes, I know. No." Abley lets Lemon talk, then replies, "Can you get a search warrant for Daisy's new home in Melbourne Place? No, no, don't tell her. Just turn up. I'll meet you there tomorrow morning if you can swing it. Yes, we're looking for a ring."

49 THE ARREST

Abley walks along Melbourne Place, an alley that starts at Parker's Piece and ends at two pubs, The Cricketers and The Elm Tree, within two yards of an exit from Parkside Secondary School. He has often wondered how many teachers are tempted to sneak in at lunchtime. With the Police and Fire Stations less than 200 yards away, as well, it is often noisy for entirely different reasons. Saturday mornings, like today, however, are often quite the respite for this row of Victorian townhouses. And he is finding it a very pleasant stroll as each front garden is teaming with bumble bees and the sweet smell of lavender, roses, and hollyhocks.

When he arrives at Daisy's new home, midway down the lane, a present – by all accounts a flippant purchase – from Atticus Stamp, he is glad that Daisy is not in. Lemon has phoned ahead that her police protection officer has told them that she is currently in the Gonville Hotel, and it is suggested she may be having brunch. She will have no idea that the police are currently rifling through all her belongings that have started to be moved into the property, presumably from Atticus Stamp's, and then from Logan Lax's after their discussion only yesterday with Daisy. It feels strange to Abley that she has decided not to stay at Logan's, as if she already knows he is not returning. He is also a little irked that it took nearly a day to get another search warrant.

As Abley enters the property, putting on the SOCO slippers and gloves, it looks like professional movers have unpacked everything. Abley knows it has only been days since Daisy has owned the place. But with money, anything is possible.

"Nothing so far," Lemon says, greeting Abley in front of the other police officers.

"Hmm. Rings are small. It could be in a keepsake box, or tin or something. Let's leave no stone," Abley points around the room.

"Right you are," Lemon runs up the staircase and disappears. Abley looks out the front window. Ugh, there she is. Daisy. Her police protection following behind has clearly not updated anyone. She sees Abley in her house.

"What are you doing?" Daisy bursts into the house and the drawing room to shout at Abley.

"We have a search warrant," Abley replies, holding out his hands to calm her down.

"So, is he just a spy then?" Daisy points at her police protection officer, who is holding Lady Woof Woof's lead and fluffing up the hair on her head, clearly enjoying his duties.

"No, of course not. He would not make a great spy," Abley replies, looking at the police officer, indicating a heads-up would have been welcome. The officer holding out his hands silently to apologise and indicates that the Gonville Hotel is only a couple of minutes away.

"We are taking every precaution in the case," Abley adds to Daisy while still pulling faces at the police officer.

"So, this mess is just for my safety?" Daisy flaps her arms and swings around, looking at the officers searching through boxes and what has already been unpacked. "I've just moved in. What on earth do you expect to find here that will help you with your disappearance cases?"

"The ring," Abley replies matter of factly, watching Daisy's face for any flicker of guilt.

"The what?" Daisy feigns ignorance.

"You told me that Atticus's ring, the one that you bought him for his health, along with your own – you know, that expensive bit of kit that monitors your heart – you said his had been turned off, and that worried you. That the data was not being sent back to your account anymore. You wondered where he was and what could have happened."

"Oh, the smart ring. Yes, that's right. I was worried. That's why I wanted to tell you," Daisy's face remains blank as she beckons Lady Woof Woof to her.

"You see, the thing is, Daisy, that does seem to check out," Abley replies.

"Exactly, that's what I told you," Daisy replies then kisses Lady Woof Woof and then gives her a big squeeze.

"Yes, it does seem to check out. The data about Atticus's heart stopped being sent. But," and Abley pauses dramatically. Daisy cannot bear to look at him and buries her face in the hair of Lady Woof Woof's neck. "You might not have realised that even when the ring is turned off, it still has a GPS tracker. So, we could still find the ring. We, of course, were very excited about this, as we thought that if we found the ring, we might find Mr Stamp. And, what was even more interesting is that when we asked the company to provide the details of his ring, given that Mr Stamp was missing, and they agreed to show us everything, well, how surprised do you think we were when we found that the ring has been tracked directly to this location? Right here."

"What?" Daisy lifts her face from Lady Woof Woof and looks right into Abley's eyes like butter wouldn't melt. "It's here?" Her face turns pale.

"Yes. The company that produces the rings

allows people who have lost them and are out of battery to find them through this tracker system. They don't need to be turned on, Daisy."

"I don't understand?" Daisy holds her hand out for Abley to see her smart ring on her finger. "Surely, that must be mine. Look. That will be mine that is here. They're synced."

"Hmm, we already have yours. Yes. There are two here, Daisy."

"I think I might still have my old one?" Daisy explains, "Yes, like phones, they bring out better ones every year. I'm sure I still have one of the old ones somewhere." Daisy shakes her head, now dismissing the whole thing as a misunderstanding.

"Old one?" Abley asks, rooted to the spot.

"Yes, this is my second one. I kept my old one of these. Don't know why. It must be somewhere." Daisy gets up. "Let me see if I can find it."

"Daisy, if you can remain here, please." Abley grabs hold of her arm to stop her from passing him. Daisy remains silent and walks towards the window. It is quiet outside, bar from a solitary shopper passing by.

"This really is a lovely place to live," Daisy says. "A secret lane in the middle of a vibrant city. Thousands of people are just three hundred yards away, and all we can hear are the birds and bees. We could be anywhere." Daisy's voice breaks a little. "I just wanted a quiet place to settle down. That's all. No one ever listened to me when I told them. I told them I just wanted to stay here for a while. Everyone wants a piece of me, but they're not actually listening to the words coming out of my mouth. How loud do you have to shout before someone actually hears, Inspector?" Daisy turns around and sighs deeply. As she does, two SOCOs and Sergeant Lemon descend the stairs.

"What have you got?" Abley looks at the sack that one of the officers is carrying. The officer finds a table and unzips the bag on it. Inside is a huge stash of jewellery, including men's watches, bracelets, and cash. Abley puts on a glove so as not to contaminate the contents as he looks in. Inside, he finds a smart ring, just like the one that Atticus wore, which had been missing.

"Where did you find the bag?"

"Under the floorboards, under the bed. Hidden," Lemon replies, looking at Abley. As Abley continues to look inside, he finds an envelope. Inside is what looks like a Will, setting out that Daisy is in his Will. Abley looks at Daisy, waiting for an explanation.

"I was just scared. I didn't know what to do with it. I don't need Atticus's money. I don't want it. I got scared, you have to believe me," Daisy pleads.

"Read her the rights and bring her in," Abley says, saving for now that he knows she is also in Logan Lax's Will too. Lemon follows as a Sergeant reads Daisy her rights.

"I didn't see it. I went punting with her," Abley tells Lemon.

"We had nothing on her. She told you about the ring on the punt. If you hadn't gone, then maybe we would never have known. She could have left the country and thrown it away. You did your job." Lemon tries to reassure his boss.

"No, Maureen did it."

50 THE KISS

"I had no idea you lived so close." Martin has followed Mikayla into an upmarket pub, The Petersfield, on the corner of Hooper and Sturton Street – two Cambridge streets lined with Victorian and Edwardian terraces once built for railway workers by wealthy businessmen. If you look more closely, you might notice that some were old corner shops, perhaps bakers, as they still have large windows and bigger door frontages. The local history group has made blue plaques that new residents post on front windows to remind children passing by which bootmaker, seamstress, or milliner might have lived there long ago. Just memories now, as today they are more likely filled with academics or tech entrepreneurs with young families in what is now a highly sought-after conservation area postcode.

The Petersfield has just opened for

Saturday lunch. Kropotkin, Martin's greyhound and Luna, Mikayla's cockapoo, follow them inside, having finished a long walk together, and all sit beneath the ceiling lined with wine bottles that glow, bouncing green and yellow light around, reflecting the sunny day. This works well with Mikayla and Luna's matching bumblebee outfits, their antennae bobbing ahead of them.

"There is a lot about me you don't know," Mikayla beams. "But I want you to know I'm so glad you asked me out on a date." Mikayla smiles at the waitress, who nods, waiting for their order.

"Is this a date?" Martin laughs.

"Isn't it?" Mikayla raises one eyebrow and waits for an answer.

"Busted," Martin replies, beaming.

After choosing a bottle of wine to share, it isn't long before a barmaid has brought the dogs water and treats, and Martin and Mikayla are tucking into lunch. Conversation flows, Mikayla's laugh grows louder as the second bottle is ordered, and the dogs fall asleep on the floor.

"Can I tell you a secret?" Mikayla says, shaking her head and shutting her eyes.

"I'm all ears," Martin sounds intrigued, finishing his last bite of tangerine sorbet.

"I lied about Logan Lax. There was no deal. He was horrible, actually."

Martin smiles.

"Why are you smiling?" Mikayla asks. "He

was horrible." Mikayla is a little confused and leans back, waiting for Martin to explain himself.

"Nothing surprises me about that man. What an idiot. I have a strong feeling that you dodged a bullet, Mica. You're a wonderful woman. You don't need his patronage. I know you care deeply about animals, which means the world to me. Just keep pushing your creativity on local avenues. One of them is bound to say yes if you ask enough."

"Aww, thank you, Marty," Mikayla grabs Martin's hand. "To be honest, after he was so mean to me when I heard he had disappeared like the others, I was kind of pleased. So I wouldn't have to hear about him anymore. Sod him!"

"Cheers!" Martin lifts his glass to Mikayla in agreement. Then he notices her looking at him funny.

"Did you really write 'Rip off his skin' on your College lawn?" Mikayla asks in disbelief, letting go of Martin's hand.

"I neither confirm nor deny," Martin smirks.

"You did!" Mikayla looks impressed and bangs her fist down on the table.

"Whoever did it did it because he deserved it," Martin opens his jacket to give Kropotkin a treat and one to Luna, as they both wake on hearing Mikayla's noisy gesticulations.

"He totally deserved it. At the very least. What a cruel man." Mikayla nods.

"You know, the more I get to know you, Mikayla, the more I kind of adore you," Martin tops up Mikayla's glass as she holds it.

"Kind of?" Mikayla laughs loudly again. "Thanks, I think."

"No, I'm being serious," Martin hiccups and then is silent for a moment, mortified that Mikayla will think he is drunk when he says what he means. "I'm very fond of you."

"And I'm fond of you," Mikayla replies, feeling happy.

"I'm buzzing," Martin smiles, looking at Mikayla's bumblebee costume as if he is looking for the first time.

"Careful, I have a sting," Mikayla smiles, opening her eyes wide.

A wave of love washes over Martin. Perhaps the alcohol, but more likely the feeling that he has found someone he really likes and doesn't feel so lonely today. Being a bachelor in his mid-fifties is not all it is cracked up to be, and as time has gone by, there has been less and less to live for – no one to care for, apart from Kropotkin. Sometimes, he wonders if Kropotkin is the only thing keeping him going. Perhaps today can be a good day, and the start of his retirement and all those negative thoughts of life stretching out ahead into a void will begin to evaporate – something new, something to hope for, to plan for. Mikayla is so warm, kind, and so funny. Mikayla leans forward and kisses Martin gently on the lips. She feels lucky to have found Martin right under her nose. A kind man, funny and generous. Having come to Cambridge from the States, she has found herself more than she cares to remember feeling a little isolated, sometimes even the butt of peoples' jokes for a country she has no control over. In this moment, she feels different. She feels seen. Maybe she has found someone who understands her and loves her for it. Maybe everything will be okay after all.

"My sting is only used on bad men. For you, only kisses, Marty. Only kisses."

51 SMART RING

Abley is finding this interrogation harder than usual. They have been in the room for two hours now after Daisy's arrest for hiding evidence and perverting the course of justice, going around the houses to see what she knows and what she will willingly admit. It is not an understatement to say that he feels double-crossed and played. Abley cannot forget that Daisy told him about the smart ring when they were punting. For crying out loud, she invited him on the trip along The Backs and dropped her bomb there—her cover.

"But I told you about the smart ring. Why would I do that if I was guilty?" Daisy says again, stretching over the desk, imploring Abley to believe her. All to make herself look innocent. He knows it. But he is finding it hard to prove her guilt, to feel like he has enough to charge her with anything. He has been so preoccupied by Maureen he is just not himself. It has been a week since her new marriage to that window salesman. His heart feels black, like treacle. And yet, it is his ex-wife who is helping him solve the case. His ex-wife. Telling him, admitting to him that despite her love for her new husband, her large diamond ring, and impending honeymoon – he cannot bear to think – she still keeps the engagement and wedding rings that Abley bought her in a tin. Safe. Safe for what? To look at and laugh? To keep him dangling? Keep him thinking that there is still hope. Or, is it just like a trophy, his head on the wall like some deer that she slaughtered? It is all heartbreakingly cold from someone who grew to resent his work. Someone who would dig at him for his late finishes or early starts. Who told him that their marriage was well and truly over. And then, to cap it all, hands him the clue that had been staring him in the face all this time.

It has been unpleasant for Abley's colleagues to watch him so uncharacteristically angry during the interrogation so far, refusing Daisy a comfort break or any let up. At one point, he raised his voice so loudly that Lemon had to step in and request Abley take a break. Now, having had a pep talk from his best buddy at the station over the coffee vending machine, Abley is told by Lemon to take things more slowly and kindly. Kindly? Abley is taken aback. When has he not been kind? He begins to wonder if he should sign himself off work. Looking into

Lemon's eyes and being told to take a breath, he nods and re-enters the room to finish this interview with Daisy.

"Why did you try to stitch me up? I could understand if you'd said nothing. But bold as brass, you sit on the riverbank and tell me how you both, Mr Stamp and yourself, have these smart rings." Abley is back, firing on all cylinders.

"I've told you already. It had not occurred to me about them, about them being important, until it did, and then I thought I should tell you about it. Be open and honest. They're just rings," Daisy replies flatly, exhausted by the repeated questions.

"I ask you again, if they were just rings, why did you hide his ring in your new house under the floorboards?" Abley frowns. "All the time, you had already found Atticus's smart ring, yet suggesting he might have it, wherever he is."

"No, no, that's not true. I was scared when I found his ring, I admit it. I didn't tell you that. But I was as freaked out as you that I had found it. If I was guilty of anything, would it not have made more sense for me to throw the ring away? I always hide my valuables. I don't think I'm any different to the rest of the population on that. I hope Atticus's okay and he returns soon." Daisy is close to tears.

Abley pauses for a moment and looks at the police officer standing by the door. Then he glances at the two-way mirror on the wall, knowing Lemon is listening to everything.

"So why not tell us that you found it?" Abley asks again. From behind the glass, Lemon sighs. This is going nowhere fast.

"I spotted it on the driveway. It glinted. I don't know. Maybe I thought he'd dropped it the day we had a row, and you'd think I was guilty of something because we were arguing. I don't know. I don't know what." Daisy pulls her hair and drops her head into her hands. "I know it makes me look guilty of something. I know it. But I'm not. I don't know where he is," she whispers.

Abley stops for a moment. It really does not make sense. Why did she hide it? Why didn't she throw it away? Perhaps it's just poor judgment on her part.

"What did you even have these smart rings for? Were you planning his 'disappearance' all along and using the smart ring to deflect us away, saying his data was wiped as if by someone else?" Abley asks, now banging his hand on the table. He has been briefed on what these rings can and cannot do and is quite convinced that Daisy just had them for health purposes, but he wants to find ways to provoke her, to make her say something.

"They're just expensive pieces of kit to monitor your heart, you know this," Daisy shakes her head. "They're not spyware."

"But you could track where he was using it? You were tracking him, weren't you? Planning the best location and time to do the deed, weren't you?!" Abley shouts. He can hear himself. This is not him. He does not recognise his own voice. "Weren't you!?" He continues.

"What deed? Honestly, I've done nothing. I'm as in the dark as you are." Daisy looks up blankly at Abley despite his shouting. "I'm not hiding any evidence."

"And, let's go back over what we already know. You were overheard saying that Mr Stamp 'would not be around for much longer'. What did you mean by that?" Abley asks.

"I've told you already, I don't even remember saying that?" Daisy shakes her head.

"We have more than one witness who heard you say it while you were walking your dog," Abley replies bluntly.

"Atticus travels all the time. I feel sick with worry. I've no idea where he is," Daisy is turning pale. She shuts her eyes, tired from the barrage of questions.

"Everyone you date seems to disappear? Where is Logan Lax?" Abley stares at her, worried that Daisy is beginning to look ill, yet he cannot stop. He knows he is taking out his anger at Maureen's wedding on this suspect and knows just how wrong that is.

"I have no idea."

"When were you going to tell us that his

Will leaves everything to you?"

"What?" Daisy looks visibly shocked. "First I've heard. I told you. I've left him. We didn't even start dating. It was just a few days. That's insane." Daisy screws up her face, completely taken aback.

"Hmm," Abley observes Daisy, almost believing her. He turns to Terrence Montagner, "You said you didn't know the MP, but you did."

"I don't know the MP in case you had forgotten?" Daisy is completely broken.

"We have a photograph of you and Terrence Montagner MP looking cosy at a dinner. So, you obviously did know him," Abley continues to have an answer to all of Daisy's excuses.

"Atticus told me he had that photograph and knew everything about me. That gave me the creeps. Why does a man like Atticus have all the photographs?" Daisy wonders about her ex's and looks at the anger of this man in front of her, who she knows has just split from his wife. Does all the anger come from women leaving men? "It was Atticus who had a thing for that MP, not me. He had the beef."

"He runs the world's media," Abley replies, irked. "Of course, he has all the photos." He cannot let her get away with it, and he cannot let Maureen get away with it! "And when we checked St Andrew's College Hall dinner records, we can only find them eating together once."

"Can I get a cup of tea? Or some water?" Daisy looks frail. She is flagging under the interrogation.

*

Abley pauses the recording and then storms out of the interview. He cannot seem to compose himself. Outside, Sergeant Lemon is waiting.

"You okay?" Lemon grabs Abley's arm to get him to slow down and pause a moment for a water. Lemon runs the water cooler and passes Abley a cup.

"Of course," Abley, red in the face, looks anything but okay, gulping down the water.

"Maybe we can give Daisy some time in the cells to think? She'll come round," Lemon suggests, more to give his Inspector time to compose himself. "We can talk about what to ask her next, maybe later? We can keep her for hours yet."

"Are you managing me, Sergeant?" Abley replies wryly, knowing full well that Lemon is just trying to look after him.

"I don't know what I'm doing, to be honest." Lemon scratches his head, having not known his Inspector to be so out of control like this before.

"Nonsense, your leadership skills have always been there, and now, well, you're just terrific. I couldn't ask for a better Sergeant,"

Abley looks at Lemon, knowing that without Lemon having his back, this week would have gone much worse than it has. The two men stand, not knowing what to say next or how to tell each other how much respect they have for one another.

"I do have a message from your friend, to meet you at the Tea Orchards in Grantchester." Lemon shares a note. "Apparently, she has some information," Lemon hands the note over to Abley, who reads the message 'I think you might be barking up the wrong tree', it reads.

52 TEA IN GRANTCHESTER

Elizabeth Green pushes her cycle down the grassy track into the Grantchester Tea Orchards. Her black bicycle with a wicker basket is typical of many of the older-fashioned cycles in the city. She opens her eyes wide when she spots her friend, Bob, with his electric bike on its stand right next to his deck chair, looking entirely out of place in a frazzled state in this dreamy field in the middle of the village, which could be a painting on the wall with its cherry and apple trees and tables full of scones and jam, and people sitting reading the paper or dozing under a hat. The clash of centuries makes her frown for a moment.

"You could have left that modern contraption out on the street," Elizabeth frowns at the electric monstrosity.

"It'd get nicked," Abley explains, looking a little irked at Elizabeth rather than pleased to see her.

"You're a policeman. No one is going to steal your bicycle," Elizabeth states, quick as a flash.

"I can't exactly write that on it, can I?" Abley pulls up his sleeve and wipes a smudge off the frame. "Anyway, I thought you'd approve? I'm doing my bit to save the planet."

"I most certainly approve that you're out of that beast of a car. But I can't say I care for the widespread replacement with these heavy death traps, which, let's face it, travel faster than any car in this city, without number plates or any liability for the injuries they cause to others in their wake. And, hadn't you noticed that we live in a flat county? What's wrong with your legs?"

"I need something to chase the bad guys," Abley says, sounding upset and in a low mood. He removes his jacket, as even the shade cast by the apple bows cannot shield him from the afternoon's heat.

"These bad guys you mention are either stuck in traffic or doing ninety down the M11. Either way, they can burn more rubber or simply lock their doors," Elizabeth reminds him.

"I must say, I'm mildly disappointed in your attitude," Abley says unhappily.

"Yes, well, me too. But that doesn't change the facts." Elizabeth adds, "Also, you live five minutes away? What a waste of electricity."

"Anyhoo," Abley lifts the teapot and pours. "I got peppermint tea and a flapjack, just for you. I'm barking up the wrong tree, am I?"

"Hmm, what do you want?" Elizabeth asks.

"What do you mean what do I want? Lemon said you wanted to see me?" Abley questions. Elizabeth says nothing, and Abley puts two and two together. "Lemon, he set you up to this, didn't he." The penny drops for Abley, that his newly trained Sergeant with fresh leadership skills has sent him off to decompress with Elizabeth.

"Can't a friend see a friend over a pot of tea in an orchard in summer? Then I don't know when a friend can see a friend." Elizabeth stares at Abley, but she can see he is having none of this. "Oh, alright, yes. Lemon might have said that you could benefit from a bit of time out. That the case is 'insane', his word. Thought I'd pop over to your neck of the woods. See what all the fuss is about."

"So, he thinks I'm failing at my job. Well, that's just great!" Abley's face turns red.

"Calm down. It's just tea," Elizabeth pushes a cup of tea across the table towards Abley.

"It's never just tea, though, is it," Abley sips the tea and burns his lip.

*

Elizabeth and Abley sit in silence for a while. Around them, people in deck chairs clink cups against saucers, their knives clanging on plates, and there are gentle ripples of laughter from children playing under the boughs. The sun spills through the leaves, leaving dappled shapes on the lawn. Occasionally, a member of staff can be seen carrying trays filled with empties back up to the hut. But the overriding sound is of peace. Like a huge garden has been opened to the public and filled with goodies just for a chosen few to enjoy the afternoon. Everyone here seems to have nowhere to go and is in a hurry to do nothing – Niksen. Something Elizabeth has been trying to enjoy since her return from Italy.

"How is Godric, that lovely grandson of yours?" Abley asks, wondering what to discuss, knowing Elizabeth has made it clear she will not talk about the case.

"He's good. In Florence until late September. He's found art. Apparently now a painter, or so he tells me."

"I thought he was studying natural sciences?" Abley tries to remember some details about Godric to show that he cares.

"I'm all for him being creative, but I do fear that he will give up his studies and never come home. His mother, I'm afraid, couldn't stick at anything," Elizabeth replies disparagingly about her own daughter without any seeming guilt.

"And, how are you?" Abley asks, searching for light chat topics.

"Bob, you really are terrible at small talk,"

Elizabeth replies, screwing up her eyes at Abley.

"Pot, kettle!" Abley laughs.

"I can do small talk. I'm trying it. Albeit a new thing, but I think I excel at it," Elizabeth defends her reputation.

"Go on then," Abley raises his eyebrows, taking a sip of peppermint tea and screwing up his face, wondering why he decided to drink what Elizabeth was drinking.

"You want me to do it now?" Elizabeth feels put on the spot.

"Yes. Right now," Abley replies, wanting to get his own back for this horrid beverage he always buys her when they meet.

"Alright. Alright, I will." Elizabeth pauses, then turns to Abley, lifts her sunglasses and glares at him. "How is your golf going? Apparently, you were at professional level, but according to Cuthbert, you've had a bad week or two, and your handicap has slipped a bit?"

"Call that small talk?" Bob Abley laughs. "My handicap is actually lower, thank you. It's improving! About the only thing that is. And now I have a set of clubs from a missing man, which is just the butter, and I cannot use them if he remains missing, which I fear he will. And I know I'm breaking the small talk, but you should see these clubs." Abley shuts his eyes, picturing the expensive metal, sublime grips and polished heads of the set of clubs.

"I didn't mean to hit a nerve. It's

your pastime, a non-controversial topic, no?" Elizabeth replies. "And I think you are the one that is bleeding into non-small talk topics."

"I don't think you're supposed to look so stern during small talk," Abley smirks at Elizabeth's impish frown.

"I wasn't," Elizabeth raises her voice in consternation.

"The glasses, the glare. You have to remain easy and relaxed. Make the other person feel warm and comfortable," Abley sips his tea and frowns again. Bleugh!

"Oh, this is too painful. Tell me about the case, for crying out loud. And pass that piece of cake, it looks nice."

"That's my cherry cake!" Abley is mock angry when Elizabeth moves the cake to her side of the table.

"It's vegan. It's mine," Elizabeth picks up a fork and pops in a bit of gooey sponge.

"I yearn for the days when you couldn't just steal my... Okay, okay. The case. Three men missing. All billionaires, or one multi-millionaire and two billionaires."

"You know, if you compare time with money, one million seconds equals eleven and a bit days, but one billion seconds equals just over thirty-one and a half years. Imagine that difference in money," Elizabeth licks her fork.

"Why are you telling me this? You're putting me off my train of thought?" Abley huffs.

"And I presume you will only allow me a window of conversation on this, so hush for now. My turn." Abley watches Elizabeth eat his cherry cake.

"You can't lump them all in together, that's all I'm saying. There is a big difference between a millionaire and two billionaires." Elizabeth shakes her head and takes another bite of cherry cake.

"Well, they're all missing, okay?" Abley raises his eyebrows. "And, it would have been amazing if you would have taken an interest in this case days ago," Abley scolds.

"Dead. They're all dead. Let's be clear," Elizabeth chews cake.

"You seem so sure?" Abley checks.

"Aren't you?" Elizabeth tilts her head to the side as if to say, 'Really?'

"I don't know. We had police protection on potentially the next victim, and now I've got her in the cells for hiding evidence," Abley explains. "Is she a killer? She's tiny. If she poisoned them, where are they?"

"Who?" Elizabeth is intrigued.

"Daisy–"

"No, she didn't do it." Elizabeth shakes her head, convinced.

"What? How do you know?" Abley asks, frowning.

"She's a nice person," Elizabeth shrugs. "She likes dogs."

Abley and Elizabeth watch as a small child runs past them, stops, stares at them and then runs off. This small child is followed by a larger child, perhaps an older sister, shouting after them to come back. Followed soon after, a mother carrying a drink, possibly the small child's. Elizabeth notices the wasps above her head, sniffing at early fruits, perhaps looking for one with broken skin.

"The Super's driving me mad. He's calling me night and day." Abley finally decides to eat the flapjack and pulls the plate closer to him, still upset that his cake is being demolished.

"Didn't Terrence Montagner like fish?" Elizabeth asks.

"To catch yes," Abley agrees. "Why?"

"And, wasn't Atticus Stamp a trophy hunter?" Elizabeth checks.

"Apparently, according to reports," Abley takes a bite of the flapjack and is pleasantly surprised.

"And Logan Lax, as we know, was putting a lot of money behind redeveloping the fur trade," Elizabeth replies.

"I believe so, yes. Not the best bunch of human beings," Abley munches.

"Maybe you've been looking in the wrong direction. Can't you see the pattern?" Elizabeth cuts another morsel of cake ready to pop into her mouth, lifts her cup of peppermint tea, and takes a sip. "Hmm, delicious."

"What do you mean? Barking up the wrong tree?" Abley asks.

"I mean, maybe it's not about the money. It's not the money. None of them were nice people for reasons other than their being super wealthy," Elizabeth looks across the tea orchard, happy to see that a dog has entered and seems so bouncy. "You know, not everyone cares about being rich. It's not the be-all and end-all. Cliches abound, but it does not bring health or happiness."

"What do you mean? What are you thinking?" Abley takes another bite of flapjack and makes a mental note to order it again next time, secretly now pleased he was left with it.

"Oh, I don't know. They all have other things in common than money. Maybe Daisy murdered Atticus not to inherit his wealth but because he stole and tried to dispose of her dog. Maybe Mikayla was upset when discovered Logan's fur trade cruelty, and Martin did something about it? Maybe Eadie bumped off Terrence Montagner because he wanted to kill their fish."

"I don't understand. Did he? I mean Montagner?" Abley is confused.

"He said he wanted to adopt some fish, but he was a fisherman. That makes no sense." Elizabeth replies, popping more cake into her mouth. "I have to go to the Rescue Me rescue centre after this and talk to Eadie."

"About fish?"

"About a hedgehog," Elizabeth replies.

Abley is confused and looks at his cup of peppermint tea, wishing it was a beer. He does not want to know about hedgehogs. "You know, Atticus Stamp ransacked his own College library, and the only thing he stole were books that MP Terrence Montagner had donated about fishing. We're also pretty sure that he had someone ransack Montagner's constituency offices too."

"Maybe the vandalism has nothing to do with the disappeared dead bodies, and more to do with coincidence of hatred amongst egotistical wealthy men. It could have been the perfect unplanned cover for whoever has been doing the deathly deeds." Elizabeth shrugs, then changing the subject adds, "Talking of small talk. Why didn't you buy any scones? We're in the Tea Orchard. They're compulsory purchases."

"I thought we'd dispensed with the small talk?" Abley breathes in, now aware that he is beginning to unwind from all the chaos. Just half an hour in Elizabeth's company was all he needed.

"Okay, I'll go and get some. One? Two?" He asks.

"I'm not greedy. One is fine." Elizabeth watches Abley walk towards the food hut to buy some scones, then sips her tea and looks up at the sky. It is clear blue all the way, and the heat is making her thirsty. She shouts at Abley.

"And ginger beer, too!" He turns around, hears, then nods, and continues his walk to the kiosk. Elizabeth smells the summer air full of wild rose scents, climbing jasmines, and ripening apples. Bumble bees pass her nose as she finishes the cake slice and sips the last of her tea. Things could not be better unless, of course, Godric were here. Elizabeth watches Abley walk back towards her with a plate of four scones and two bottles of ginger beer.

"I said just one," She scorns.

"What, and I don't get to choose how many I eat?" He scoffs. Abley sits down and immediately cuts into a scone, passing another to Elizabeth. "They said the trick is to eat them quickly before the wasps discover the jam." He dollops a huge amount of clotted cream onto his scone and then puts the same spoon in a pot of jam and dollops it on top. It seems to Elizabeth that he puts half a scone into his mouth at once, as there is not much left.

"Look what you've done to the jam. You've contaminated it." Elizabeth wipes the dairy cream to the side of the jam, then spreads her vegan cream onto her scone and chooses a different spoon to place it into the jam. Much more measured, she takes a bite and shuts her eyes. "I supposed I might have space for two," she looks at Abley, who smiles and nods and says nothing, munching and leaning back into his deckchair. "I do miss you, you know."

"I miss you more," he replies, looking up at the clear sky and feeling glad to be alive again.

"I think you will find someone new," Elizabeth refers to the wedding and Maureen.

"You mean like you have?" Abley replies without thinking.

"I'm not (looking)," Elizabeth sighs.

"Maybe we don't need to find anyone new. Maybe we just need to be happy with ourselves?" Abley replies, unconvinced.

"D'you think we can?" Elizabeth asks Abley seriously.

"I don't know," Abley sighs again. Elizabeth spreads vegan cream on her scone. She is much hungrier than she thought.

*

After a while, Elizabeth leaves, explaining that it will take her twice as long to get back into the city as she has to use her own legs and not cheat using an electric bike. Abley orders a beer and is glad that no one knows where he is. Raynott cannot find him. Even Lemon has not called. He looks at his phone and puts it on the table. Elizabeth may have the right idea of not having a wretched mobile. He turns it over. He ponders on Elizabeth's words about looking in the wrong place on the case. That it was not about money. Not about money. He starts to think about hedgehogs, whether he likes it or not.

53 RESCUE ME

Having left Abley in the Grantchester Tea Orchard, there was something on Elizabeth's mind. She had a niggling feeling about what she had said to Bob. She had fought so hard not to get involved in this missing persons' case, at the very least, because those missing, in her opinion, were truly awful, and the whole world was better off that they stayed missing. But also, perhaps that her gut instincts were telling her something too horrible to want to believe. Her feeling of unrest started when she realised that too many missing were likely last seen in the same place, and then there was the hedgehog. They were looking the wrong way. Saying out loud to Bob that this was not about money or jealousy had only made it clearer in her mind. Sometimes, things are staring you in the face, right under your nose, too terrible to be true that you just, well, it is as if the truth blinds you.

Elizabeth walks up the driveway of the

Rescue Me rescue centre. No children are skipping away with rescue puppies, nor are rabbits being brought to see the weekly free vet. There is no smell of sweets from the foyer and no escaped balls rolling down the drive, having just been thrown for happy-looking dogs being taken away to their forever homes. The centre says 'closed' on the entrance sign. The lights are off. Elizabeth wonders if she has had a wasted journey and is almost ready to turn back and try again tomorrow. But something makes her continue, just in case. It is Saturday afternoon, after all. Why is it shut when it is usually wide open for adoptions at the weekend?

No one is around as she peers through the double doors, which display a sign, 'All Animals Welcome, and Well-Behaved Humans.' Elizabeth stares at the sign for a little longer than perhaps most would. She hesitates before pushing the door to enter. To her surprise, it is not locked. She takes a deep breath, a little nervous about what she might find this time. Elizabeth walks in and quietly says 'hello', but there is no answer. She peers into a back office behind the reception and says 'hello' again, this time even more quietly. Nothing. She continues along the main corridor. On one side, she peers through open doors into offices, vet rooms, cloakrooms, and a kitchen. On the other side, floor-to-ceiling windows overlook a green and lush courtyard. She watches a solitary robin splash in a bird bath. No one sits outside on the patio furniture.

"Hello?" Elizabeth speaks more loudly this time. In the distance, from the kennels on the other side of the outside space, a dog is barking, and she can hear the radio playing, which she knows Eadie puts on for the dogs to make them feel less lonely.

Elizabeth continues around a bend in the corridor, where there are fewer windows, and the paint is a more muted, darker colour. She feels like she is now alone in an empty building, apart from dozens of sleeping animals. There is something both beautiful and eerie about it. She stands still for a moment, uncertain if she heard something. There it is again. A groaning?

Elizabeth remains standing for a while as the noise repeats. She hears someone say, 'Shut the door,' and it is almost certainly a woman's voice. Then Elizabeth hears footsteps. Coming around the corner is Muriel, who seems to already know it is Elizabeth before she can see her, having identified her shouts. 'Elizabeth,' she hears. Then Muriel arrives, looking a little dishevelled.

"I've just come to see how the hedgehog is doing," Elizabeth lies, then asks, "Who's that groaning?" She cocks her head to indicate that she is listening and can hear something, or someone.

"Oh, that's Eadie. She's not feeling very well. I'm sorry, but we're closed. I need to lock up. Busy day." Muriel holds her arms out wide in an attempt to usher Elizabeth back the way she came. But Elizabeth refuses to budge, curious whether Muriel is telling the truth. "Is it anything urgent? Or can we speak tomorrow?" Muriel leans her head to one side, smiling, hoping Elizabeth will answer that it can wait.

"The noise doesn't sound like Eadie?" Elizabeth remains stationary, refusing to move, observing Muriel's reaction.

"I really need to lock up, Elizabeth. Please, let's catch up tomorrow about the hedgehog," Muriel insists. "I've had such a long day. The last thing I want to do is debate the sound you heard. We're in a rescue centre. Actually, it is probably one of the cats. I'd better go and check, so I need to ask you to leave, please, so I can do my rounds."

"Can I look?" Elizabeth asks, knowing that this will probably annoy Muriel but worried perhaps someone needs help. "It sounds distressing. Perhaps someone has fallen?"

"Look at what?" Muriel starts to frown. "We fixed the crooked step. No one has fallen." Muriel points down to what clearly looks like a repaired part of the flooring. A section of wood finely sanded to fit a hole in the concrete. And continues to explain, "Yes, no one will fall over here again. No one is hurt today."

Elizabeth watches Muriel glance down at the floor. Something about it seems odd. Suddenly, it begins to make sense to Elizabeth.

"I'll just–" but Elizabeth doesn't finish her sentence as things seem to have turned a little strange. Instead, she walks past Muriel, wanting to get a head start on whatever is going on, and rushes around the hallway corner. She opens closed doors one by one on either side of the corridor. The contents reveal a broom cupboard, an office with a desk, another medical examination room, and a room with cages to hold short-term rescues for observation and recovery. Then Muriel starts chasing behind.

"Hang on. Wait. Don't go in there!" Muriel shouts.

Elizabeth ignores Muriel's pleas and continues to try to find the source of the groaning. She is guided by the sound of another moan. She looks back at Muriel, whose face is blank.

"Who is that?" Elizabeth asks.

"That's the cats. I told you they do that when things go quiet." Muriel says, knowing no one in their right mind would mistake the cries for a cat.

"That was no cat." Elizabeth continues to the end of the corridor and a dead end. There is just one last door facing her. She opens it slowly, Muriel now right behind her. Elizabeth is not expecting what she sees. Mikayla, her hands and feet tied to a chair in the middle of a room, Eadie standing beside her. "Mikayla!" Elizabeth rushes over to untie her feet. "Are you okay? What happened?" Elizabeth watches as Mikayla's chin drops onto her chest. It is clear that Mikayla is not able to speak. Leaning down on the cold floor, fiddling with the rope as Eadie shakes her head, Elizabeth feels a pain in her right shoulder. She looks back and can see Muriel standing over her with a long needle.

Almost immediately, Elizabeth feels like she is floating and starts to see everything in different colours. "What?" Elizabeth twists her body around to face Muriel. But in doing so, she trips over Mikayla's legs and falls on the room floor. "Did you just drug me?" Elizabeth tries to keep her eyes open. Then, it all starts to fall into place. "You fixed the step?" Elizabeth is mumbling. "You fixed the step. Did he trip and die? What did you do with his body?" Elizabeth is struggling to speak, her words beginning to slur. She shuts her eyes and shakes her head, trying to get her bearings. She makes her best effort to stand, but her body feels like the weight of a hundred horses.

"What have you done?" Eadie's voice is grave, looking at Muriel, who is still holding the syringe.

"She knows," Muriel spits back at Eadie. Muriel takes a couple of steps until she is standing over Elizabeth. Watching Elizabeth's best efforts to stand up and seeing that she is no longer a risk, she looks back at Eadie. "We can't let them go now."

"Oh, what have we done? What have we

done?" Eadie is half crying, half pleading with Muriel for it all to stop.

"Are you going to hurt Mikayla?" Elizabeth asks, slurring quite badly now. "She's very annoying but doesn't deserve that." She tries to pat Mikayla on the head, but misses and gets her foot instead. Mikayla, at that moment, perhaps feeling Elizabeth's hand on her, groans and moans, her chin still resting on her chest, completely out of it, unable to focus on what is happening in the room. "Help! Help!" Elizabeth shouts, but still slurring. "Ooh, rainbows," Elizabeth holds out her hands to touch the distracting hallucination. She then notices her own reflection in a floor-to-ceiling mirror and starts speaking to herself. "Your curls are like Curly Wurlys." Elizabeth is in shock, as if her hair is doing strange things. She raises a hand to try to hold her curls but can't touch them as her spatial coordination is off-kilter. She then opens her eyes wide at Muriel and stares. "What have you given me? I can hear colours. It's amazing." Elizabeth smiles at Muriel. "Don't do anything bad, will you."

"We can't harm Elizabeth," Eadie urges Muriel. "She's done nothing wrong. She has animals of her own. What will happen to them?" Eadie pulls the syringe out of Muriel's hand.

"What choice do we have? She's seen we have Mikayla. She knows about the step." Muriel is stressed, sweating, and not happy with her choices. Elizabeth tries to stand up again. She feels some strength in her legs and gets halfway up but falls back down again. Muriel bends down to shout in Elizabeth's face, "Stay there! Don't move!"

"Maybe we can tell Elizabeth it was all just a dream?" Eadie begs Muriel. "And Mikayla, too. They're hallucinating. Mikayla was drunk when she was screaming at us earlier. We could take them to their homes and deny everything?" Eadie suggests. "Tell them that maybe we accidentally put something in the tea. Anything. You may be too ill to go to prison, but they'll lock me up. Then what will happen to the animals?" Eadie says.

"Muriel," Elizabeth slurs.

"Shut up, shut up. I'm thinking!" Muriel shouts at Elizabeth.

"I'm thinking too," Elizabeth continues to slur her words. "You bumped off three nasty men. They were horrid. You killed two of them," Elizabeth tries not to laugh, but the drugs are beating her, and she lets out an enormous, manic giggle. Then she opens her eyes wide, confused, wondering if the laugh was coming from her or someone else. She looks around more carefully at the room, which appears to be pulsating. It is not an office but a food preparation room. There are rows of fridge freezers and a metal table with sharp knives hanging above a large industrial sink and waste disposal unit. "Chop, chop, chop,"

Elizabeth slurs, realising they are probably going to cut her into small pieces. She tries to twist her neck to look at the table but can't see what is on it. She stretches further, but it is no use as the drug Muriel administered is taking effect. Elizabeth hears Muriel walking over to the sink and lifting a knife off the wall. Elizabeth looks down and notices the tiled floor sloping into a drain, much like a butcher's shop. Elizabeth tries to lift her arm, but it has gone floppy. She does the only thing she can, try to speak again, understanding the gravity of what is coming next.

"I'm a good person. I love dogs. You know, I have four dogs and three cats," Elizabeth counts with her fingers. "Spare me. I'll," Elizabeth manages to lift a finger, hold it to her mouth, and slur a 'shh'. "I won't say a thing." Elizabeth laughs manically again.

"Oh, Muriel. See? See?" Eadie pleads, but Muriel continues to sharpen the knife using an electric knife sharpener attached to a preparation table. The metal-on-metal screeching louder than Eadie's pleading. Muriel has finally sharpened the knife enough. Eadie knows what Muriel is about to do and cannot watch.

"Go. I'll finish it," Muriel looks at Eadie. Eadie walks out. Muriel waits for Eadie to shut the door. Elizabeth watches the blade Muriel is holding. It glints and reflects the light.

"It's like one of those films my grandson watches with the superheroes." Elizabeth falls back onto the floor, her back completely on the tiles. She can now only look up at the lighting and ceiling and cannot move her limbs. "They have knives like that. Have you seen it?" Elizabeth asks, mumbling, "What are they called? They fight crime, kill the baddies, and make the streets safer for the goodies. Goodies and baddies. Goodies and baddies. There's too much action, I say. Not enough tea drinking. You know, if they drank tea instead of fought, they'd all be friends," Elizabeth is now babbling.

"Stop talking, will you? Stop it!" Muriel holds her head, torn and angst-ridden. Muriel walks across to Mikayla, who has gone silent. She wonders who to kill first. How much mess is this going to make?

"Goodies and baddies. Fish, lions and mink. Fish, lions and mink. Ooh, they are swimming. I can hear and see them. Fish are swimming on your ceiling. You'd better get a tank. They might fall." Elizabeth's words grow more faint. She wonders if she has any words left in her, but her mouth seems unable to open. The only word she can think of to say is 'rescue', but nothing comes out. She can hear Muriels's feet moving on the tiles and things growing darker.

*

Abley stays for a short while longer in The Tea Orchard, thinking about his friend. He misses working with Elizabeth. Maybe it is the female company, definitely her genius, but it is something else. Being inspired by her sideways view of things. The lack of ordinary about her. More than that, it is her friendship. She knows him, how he thinks, acts, feels, dreams, and more than anything, knows his darkest fears. Abley wonders what is going on with Elizabeth. She hasn't really shared much today or the other day, come to think of it. Since she had returned from Italy, it's like she's been keeping him at arm's length.

Abley leans back in his deckchair, his eyes drifting to the apple boughs above his head, leaves shimmering in the sunshine. Through them, the sky gleams in quilt-like patches, part blue, part puffy cloud, warm rays spilling back onto ripening apples. Can there be a more idyllic, more peaceful spot? So, is he not feeling happy? It's all about work, sleep, eating, and golf. Will his life be like this from now on? Make no mistake, he would not remove the golf, but was that the only thing he had in his life? Is he more happy than sad or sad than happy? A sharp pain of loneliness creeps into his being, like it has entered his fingers and toes and worked its way up to his heart. Abley's thoughts are broken when his phone starts to ring. He looks at the caller, it is Constable Love. Abley thinks there will be more ideas to arrest all the dogs and tie them up in string. Something makes him accept the call, perhaps out of guilt.

"Inspector, is that you?"

"Yes, Love," Abley replies.

"A pub landlord called you. Said you gave him your card?" Love waits for a reply, but when none comes, the Constable continues, "Er, well. He said he remembered something." Love notices another silence. "Inspector, are you still there?"

"I'm waiting for you to tell me what he said." Abley tries his best to be kind but feels his afternoon being interrupted.

"Yes, yes, of course. Well, he said that you told him to call you and left your card, and he said, hang on, let me see my notes. Yes, yes, here it is. He said, 'Tell your Inspector that Terrence Montagner MP did talk to me that day.' That it had completely slipped his mind. It was such a short conversation as the MP was ordering his drink. Apparently, Mr Montagner had said that he had to go to an animal rescue centre that day and that he was dreading it because the whole thing was a waste of time and they should just 'put the puppies down, and that he was of half a mind to tell them when he got there.' Did you get that, Inspector?" Love is about to repeat the whole thing, so Abley cuts the call. At that moment, a dog starts to bark, perhaps in the far corner of the orchard. It will not stop. He can hear the owner shouting at the dog. Maybe the dog has seen all the clotted cream teas piled high on low tables, just out of reach, so close he is salivating. The flavours causing that dog, like nothing before, to be as anxious as Abley. Abley sits upright and thinks of Elizabeth. Was she serious about paying a visit to the Rescue Me rescue centre? Could she be back on the case again? Hang on. If she is back on the case, why is she going there?

Abley's mind starts to race. He pictures Constable Jack Love's wall of photos and the mess of string between all the people. He can see the photograph of Eadie and Muriel standing outside the Rescue Me centre, in the middle of the wall of suspects and string. With big words against it, 'rescue's animals', and right next to it against Terrence Montagner's, Atticus Stamp's and Logan Lax's, fishes, hunts animals, and skins animals. It is black and white, staring him in the face. It was where Lady Woof Woof first turned up after Atticus let her loose, so Daisy told him. It was even the last place Terrence Montagner was seen after his TV interview. Abley has a bad feeling. He jumps out of his deckchair and pulls out his phone, dialling Love back. As he waits, he sees the dog has stopped barking. They have managed to grab a scone off the table from a distracted child.

"Get a car round to the Rescue Me rescue

centre now. Yes, sirens, I don't care. Just get it there. Tell Lemon I'm on my way and to meet me there. Tell him to go in and don't wait. Just find Elizabeth. Tell him it's important. I think she might be in trouble." Abley hangs up the phone to Constable Love and unlocks his bike.

54 GONE TO THE DOGS

Noticing Elizabeth's bicycle leaning against the railings, Abley wastes no time locking up his bike and races through the entrance of the Rescue Me rescue centre, checking the reception and behind, pulling doors open in a frenzy. Then he stands stock still. He hears a crash. He cannot be sure but runs down a corridor where he thinks the noise is coming from. All the doors are open but one at the end. Eadie is standing outside, staring back at him in horror. He can hear screams. Abley barges in and sees Muriel bending over Elizabeth with a large chopping knife. His feet seem to fly the last ten yards, and before he can take a breath, he pulls Muriel back and grabs the knife. In total shock, he sees Elizabeth on the floor. She has been moved onto some plastic bin liners. She is moaning, her eyes half shut. Abley catches his breath, his heart racing. He can see Mikayla still tied to a chair in the corner. He looks around, and it is clear that it is a meat preparation room. He is acutely aware that he has just stopped Elizabeth from being chopped up. "Elizabeth! Elizabeth! Are you okay?" Abley frantically looks at Elizabeth's body for entry wounds. "What have you done?" He screams at Muriel. Abley lifts Elizabeth, looking frantically, but finds no injuries. He looks up at the heavens and lets out a scream of fear. He turns around to catch Muriel's eyes, but she has already left the room and is walking down the corridor towards reception, followed by Eadie, so he turns back to Elizabeth.

"It's over. Whatever this was, it's over." Abley drops to the floor to sit beside Elizabeth, then lifts her into his arms, her body resting against his as he wraps his arms around her protectively, then dials the station front desk. "We're going to need two ambulances. Rescue Me rescue centre, and pronto."

*

Abley watches as Elizabeth sits up in the ambulance, a drip in her arm, a paramedic taking her pulse. The paramedic nods at Abley to indicate that she will be okay, as Abley perches on the end of the stretcher.

"Thank you," Elizabeth replies to the

paramedic, feeling woozy but not so out of it that she is not aware of the gravity of what just happened. She turns to Abley. "What took you so long? I was nearly chop suey." She looks at him, vulnerable, grateful.

"I thought you were going to take it easy? You said it so often." Abley narrows his eyes. "You were clearly right about me barking up the wrong tree. Atticus Stamp did not murder Terrence Montagner, Logan Lax did not murder Atticus Stamp, and Daisy did not murder all of them."

"They've been feeding them to the dogs," Elizabeth says quietly. Abley nods silently. Neither of them speak for a moment, the paramedic's eyes widen as he checks the bag of fluids is going into Elizabeth's arm, then nods that he will give them a moment and steps out of the ambulance to head to the other ambulance across the drive.

"It had nothing to do with blackmail or squabbling egos, did it?" Abley sighs. "All that rampaging in libraries and constituency offices was just anger about press laws, fears of losing girlfriends, and not being taken seriously."

"Atticus certainly had an ego. In the end, not taking no for an answer could have been the reason for his downfall."

"We'll take a close look at the evidence," Abley glances back at the mass of SOCOs going into the rescue centre, less sure about the moral compass of the two old women who Lemon is handcuffing and putting into separate police cars. "But how did you know?"

"You know, I believe Terrence Montagner actually died of natural causes here, and that's how the whole thing started," Elizabeth says. "They filled in a bit of the corridor recently. Muriel made a point of telling me that it had been fixed and no one had hurt themselves today. It was odd of her to mention that. I hadn't asked. They were even talking about the floor before Muriel tried to kill me. Maybe Montagner tripped, fell on his head or something, and died. He never left. I guess you will be able to check forensics on the location," Elizabeth shrugs a little in her seat.

"I tripped in that corridor. Twice! When I was carrying some food for them and when I picked up Arnold in his basket. I nearly dropped him. They looked at me strangely. I thought they were worried I'd make a bad cat parent, but they were concerned about me remembering the wonky flooring!" Abley replies, shocked.

"They must have been scared about being shut down from health and safety failings. What would happen to all the animals if they had to close? I think they fed Terrance Montagner to the dogs to dispose of the body to cover things up, and that's how it started," Elizabeth looks at Abley grimly. Not even being able to comprehend the horror. "Poor dogs. Bet they tasted awful."

"We're going to have to check all the

waste from the centre," Abley replies, not looking forward to having to analyse dog excrement.

"What will you do with all the dogs, cats, rabbits? There are so many animals in there?" Elizabeth looks worried.

"There are a lot of animals in that centre," Abley replies, admitting the problem Eadie and Muriel have left behind.

"You're not going to harm them. They must stay here. I will find people to feed them, until they can be rehomed," Elizabeth whispers. "Give me your phone. I'll do it now."

"They'll be staying here for now. And you're too poorly right now. Stop worrying. Please," Abley replies.

"Give me your word that no animal will come to any harm," Elizabeth tries to sit up.

"I give you my word. Please, stay calm, sit back." Abley looks at the paramedic who has stepped back inside and has picked up the blood pressure sleeve to wrap around Elizabeth's arm. "We will keep you posted about all the evidence. The animals will be okay." Abley squeezes Elizabeth's hand for her to calm down.

The two friends sit in silence for a moment, hearing the air leave the blood pressure monitor, relieved to have escaped the drama in one piece. The paramedic explains that they are nearly ready to leave, and begins to write up Elizabeth's notes and lean in to speak to the other paramedic in the front seat. Abley finally continues quietly, out of earshot of the ambulance staff, "So, if Terrence Montagner was an accident, what happened to the others?" interested in Elizabeth's deductions, knowing she likely has already solved the whole case.

"Eadie told me in the cemetery that she had watched their security CCTV at the front and saw Atticus Stamp dump Lady Woof Woof outside where they found her, tied up to the railings. But when I came to bring in a hedgehog, there was no CCTV. If it had been there, it would have shown that Terrence, Atticus and Logan had all gone separately into Rescue Me and never come out. So, either it was never there, or they have taken it down. Either way, it made me suspicious. Maybe they led Stamp into a room with Lady Woof Woof, and Muriel did her stabby thing with a syringe in his neck. Presume their motive was his trophy hunting? In for a penny. He fell into their lap. Or should I say Muriel's? With her stage 4, she thought she could remove these men from the face of the earth, thereby saving all the animals from torture and cruelty that might have crossed their paths."

"Why didn't you tell me about your hunch?" Abley asks.

"I wasn't entirely sure. I was coming here today to double check on the CCTV. I would have told you if I was right," Elizabeth replies.

"So, Atticus was wandering in, trying to give Daisy's dog away," Abley says, adding, "I bet they dropped his mobile in the cemetery and took off his smart ring after he was dead and threw it in his driveway so as not to have any evidence left. That's when Daisy found it. Atticus's car was in his driveway though. Daisy said Atticus had driven off with Lady Woof Woof?" Abley buries his head in his hands for a moment, feeling guilty for putting Daisy through an arrest and interrogation.

"Maybe you need to check for Eadie and Muriel's fingerprints in Atticus's car. If they dumped the ring, maybe they dumped the car back to his house? This centre is only minutes away," Elizabeth suggests.

Abley looks up and continues, "Of course, Atticus's car keys were still in his car. I thought it was odd." He shakes his head, then continues, almost not wanting to hear any more of the grim details. "Then Logan Lax, what happened to him? I suppose when he came looking for Lady Woof Woof, they did the same thing?"

"Maybe Muriel thought she was taking out powerful, horrid men to make the world a better place. Ultimately, they were trying to protect the centre from the first tragic accident of Terrence's fall. That's my hunch. Maybe Logan Lax demanded he check everywhere in his frantic search for Lady Woof Woof and stumbled on Atticus Stamp's freshly dismembered body and any remains of Terrance Montagner. Muriel had nothing to lose. She is in stage 4. She knew she probably wouldn't make it through trial and delays in court," Elizabeth explains. The two take a moment to let what Elizabeth is voicing sink in. It is too awful to contemplate, but they both know that Elizabeth is never wrong.

"What about never working alone?" Abley reminds her, shaking his head with worry about what could have happened. Elizabeth says nothing. Abley continues, "This will certainly create headlines. Two old ladies bring down three billionaires who dominate our politics, our news, and how we look."

"I am pleased to say that I've never bought any Logan Lax fast fashion! Speaking of designers, how is Mikayla?" Elizabeth asks.

"They've taken her to hospital. She is going to be fine. When I saw her just now she was talking to a paramedic about her doggy outfits, and trying to sell them her banana design," Abley smiles.

"What will happen to Eadie and Muriel?" Elizabeth can't help but feel sorry for the old ladies.

"What d'you think? Arrested. Charged. Prison."

"How did it all go so wrong for them?" Elizabeth knows the answer to her own question and does not really seek an answer from Abley.

"They broke the law, Elizabeth. That's all I know. That's all I do. But, I do it better with you."

"You saved me this time," Elizabeth looks

at Abley gratefully.

"You laid the breadcrumbs, you always do," Abley smiles, squeezes her hand again, and then lets it go. You know I would not have got here in time if I'd only had a bicycle. It was the motor on my bike that got me here quickly. And now someone has stolen it while I was inside rescuing you."

"You should have locked it up?" Elizabeth replies flatly.

55 RESCUE REVOLUTION

One month later, Elizabeth walks up the drive to the animal rescue centre. She is wearing clothes like she means to clean out the kennels. She looks at the new sign, 'Rescue Revolution', which makes her smile from ear to ear. The doors swish open to find Abley walking back out, carrying a bike helmet and a basket with a cat in it."

"What are the chances?" Abley beams at Elizabeth.

"I told you I was coming to volunteer today. Are you stalking me?"

"You won't return my calls. A little dickie bird told me you might be here."

"Yes, well, now I'm feeling up to it, so I thought I'd support my local animal shelter. Looks like you are, too." Elizabeth looks down at the basket, quite bemused that her friend Bob is carrying a cat.

"Arnold looks a bit lonely sometimes. I wanted to get him a companion." Abley lifts the basket to show Elizabeth a closer look at the kitten. "Little female tabby."

"I see a new side to you, Inspector. A side that I quite like," Elizabeth replies, putting a finger into the wicker carrier for the cat to sniff.

"And they found my bike helmet. So, win, win," he holds up his bike helmet. "Dumped around the back field after thieves stole my bike." Then Abley looks a little more serious, adding, "Muriel confessed last week, after her vow of silence, to the murder of Atticus Stamp and Logan Lax. High dose of ketamine. Fed them to the dogs. You were right about the motive. They were concerned at first that Terrence Montagner's accidental death would lead to the closure of the rescue centre. Terrence had stormed off, Eadie explained, after having been refused a cat, but then marched back in and was heading towards the cattery when he fell and tripped. Atticus wanted to dump Lady Woof Woof with them, but they refused. He marched in to leave the Saluki in a room and stumbled into the preparation room where you were, and most probably saw something left of Terrence, so they murdered him to keep quiet. And quite a similar thing happened to Logan Lax, only he managed to get as far as the dog kennels looking for Lady Woof Woof and apparently saw some of the meat, smelled it, and worked out it was no ordinary dinner. Muriel explained they were cruel to animals, so were getting their 'just desserts'. Her exact words." Abley sighs heavily in disbelief. "When you think you've policed everything." Abley looks at Elizabeth, who says nothing. "Are you ready to come back to work?" He asks.

"I'm helping out here today."

"What about tomorrow?" Abley persists.

"D'you think you will ever stop asking?" Elizabeth rolls her eyes.

"Let me tell you a story. I was gifted the best set of golf clubs I have ever seen by Logan Lax, and I declared them as a gift, as it was a potential conflict of interest. Now, they're sitting in the holding room until Raynott feels I have solved enough crimes to release them. He could give them to me tomorrow if he wanted."

"So, you want me so that you can get your hands on a set of golf clubs?" Elizabeth raises her eyebrows.

"I just adopted a kitten. I'd say we're even," Abley smiles. "See you tomorrow then?"

*

After chit-chatting outside with her friend, Elizabeth enters the swish of the doors in reception, pleased to feel no chills from what happened before, instead, smelling fresh cut flowers arranged on the reception desk, and seeing the walls have been painted yellow and inviting. Behind the counter is Martin Smith, with a hair clip holding back his fringe and wearing a pinny. This makes Elizabeth glad. To see her retired peer looking happier than she has ever seen him.

"Hello, Elizabeth! Welcome. Thank you for volunteering like this. We have been inundated with people wanting to ensure the animals are saved and safe. It's been tremendous," he beams. "You know Daisy is one of our biggest donors. We don't actually need to fundraise at all, and we're meeting with architects and her next week to look at expanding our footprint here and opening a second rescue centre further out, in Histon. She said she's using different architects than Logan's 'white monstrosity' at St Andrew's and is just happy to use their money for good. She's invested a lot of money into charities trying to end the fur trade. I really did not like Lax starting that up again. It made me so mad! Oh, and Daisy is also supporting charities to campaign to end boar hunting. When she found out about that man shot and injured by Terrence Montagner, after Inspector Abley confirmed it in that police press statement about the case, even though it wasn't anything to do with her, she's helping him to get back on his feet. She's one of the wealthiest women in the world now, apparently, what with being in Atticus Stamp's

Will and getting some inheritance, split with his ex-wives, and Logan Lax's too, given he had no relatives alive."

"Goodness, let's hope she does not hold a grudge against Bob." Elizabeth wonders whether he will get any fallback from arresting Daisy.

"Nah," Martin replies, "She said she forgave him because she heard about how cut up he is about his wife. Ex-wife, and how out of sorts he was that day. Love does strange things to people, I told her," Martin explains.

"Look at all those outfits," Elizabeth says despairingly, distracted by the colours.

"The soon-to-be missus gets what she wants," Martin replies, waving his engagement ring. As he finishes speaking, Mikayla walks in from the reception back room carrying packets of dog treats in a small box to put up on hooks. Martin stares lovingly at Mikayla like she is an angel on earth.

"You haven't wasted any time," Elizabeth looks at the newly engaged couple.

"When you know, you know," Mikayla beams at Elizabeth and then gazes lovingly at her new fiancé. "We both care about animals, so when we heard about this place, we wanted to fight for it. When Marty cares, he gets things done."

"Yes, we all saw the letters writ large in white paint across the front court lawn of St Andrew's College!" Elizabeth replies.

"Not sure what you are talking about," Mikayla tilts her head to the side, refusing to acknowledge anything so as to protect her husband and his enjoyment of College privileges in his retirement.

"Well, I think you're both heroes," Elizabeth is about to say other nice things until her eyes meet the fancy dress costumes again, hanging up in reception. "I still don't think these are a good idea," Elizabeth pulls at the clothing line for dogs, "But I do think you've done a wonderful thing here. Saving the rescue centre from closure. More than that, to turn it around. Who would have thought?" Elizabeth watches a smiling family enter the rescue centre and head towards the cattery.

"Retirement was the push that I needed. Mikayla has me sorted out now," Martin replies. Then he pauses. "You know, engagement to this lady saved me from years of loneliness and turned this old codger around." Then Martin realises what he has said. "But it has to be right, doesn't it." Martin acknowledges what Elizabeth had with Gerald was special.

"No more egging people, graffitiing lawns or slashing tyres, then?" Elizabeth says under her breath, not welcoming the advice about marriage making people happy. Martin isn't sure he heard her but decides nothing will get in the way of his happiness right now.

"You want the tour? Give Liz a tour,"

Mikayla pushes Martin towards the centre corridor.

"Elizabeth might not want to remember. We have you down for rabbits along the other way," Martin replies sheepishly, having planned for her voluntary work to be nowhere near the area where the attack happened, but Elizabeth starts to walk along the corridor, not waiting for Martin. "Oh, okay," Martin looks back at Mikayla, then quickly follows Elizabeth down the corridor.

Elizabeth opens the first security door into the kennels, then closes it behind her. Then she opens the second. Her heart sinks and soars at the same time. So many beautiful animals needing homes. A tiny dog cowers in the corner of his bed at the very back of his kennel.

"A micro chihuahua. Been here for a long time. Nine months, maybe? Problems with his jaw and teeth. He needs a lot of vet bills and continuing treatment. He was here when, you know," Martin huffs, having caught up with Elizabeth. Elizabeth looks at the bars for the name and details.

"Walter, you're coming home. Right now." Elizabeth holds out her hand for the keys. Martin looks at her blankly.

"We have paperwork you need to complete. We need to come to your home and check that Walter will fit in with your, well, your menagerie. Do you have time to look after him properly?"

"Keys, now." Elizabeth is not listening to this from a man who has been to her house, watched her with her own dogs, and walked his dog with hers on Jesus Green many times. Finally, Martin hands over his master key for all the kennels.

"Give me that straight back. I don't trust you with it," Martin demands. Elizabeth unlocks the door and picks up Walter, leaving the key in the kennel door and ignoring Martin. She is so gentle with Walter, who is cowering in her hands. Elizabeth softly strokes his head, then kisses him and adds, "The food is much better at Foxes' Haven. No tasteless billionaires for tea at home. Come on." Walter stares into Elizabeth's eyes, and she can feel him trembling. "It's okay. It's all going to be okay now. It's all going to be okay." Elizabeth kisses Walter's head again, then pops him into the inside of her jacket, where there is a pocket where he sit and also poke out his head to look at what is coming next. "We're going home, Walter. Martin will have to find someone else to clean out the bunny litter trays today!" Elizabeth starts to stride out towards the centre's exit.

"I didn't know you wanted a dog. Are you sure you don't want to look around first? This is literally the first cage right by the door." Martin realises as soon as the words escape his mouth that if she went any further inside the kennels she would have to adopt them all. He hurriedly locks the kennel, then the gates behind them and follows Elizabeth to the exit.

"I think you made the right move in retirement," Elizabeth tells Martin, then leans in to kiss him. Martin is taken aback. In all the years he has known Elizabeth, she has not even hugged him. "You are an angel in disguise."

"Well, um, thank you." Martin is about to go on and say something, but Elizabeth is already walking away towards her bicycle.

*

Abley gets back to his small terraced home in Grantchester, this time with his kitten, having ridden on his replacement electric bike he just picked up after his other new bike was stolen. It is an upgraded version, with even more space for his golfing equipment and cat baskets, because he has realised that he deserves it, deserves to be happy.

As he locks up, he glances up the steps to his front door, remembering how Maureen had visited him here not so long ago, and how she told him that she kept their wedding rings. He can picture her standing outside, knowing that now she is likely on her honeymoon, with her new husband. He sighs, then picks up the basket with the kitten inside and climbs the steps. He wonders if his eyes are playing tricks with him. There is no Maureen. But to his surprise, lying flat, wrapped in brown paper, are the very expensive golf clubs that Superintendent Raynott was keeping in the holding evidence room out of spite. He pulls the brown paper away and sees the beautiful clubs glinting in the sun in an old golf bag. Not the bag they were originally in. He cannot believe his eyes. In the top is a note.

'I did a switcheroo. He'll never know, Sir. Constable Love.' The Constable's last act before returning to London. Speechless, Abley picks up a club, putting the cat basket on the step for a moment. "Well, I'll be damned. I knew that boy would go places." Abley swings a club, then turns to the basket and the kitten. "Now then, Tiger. Come and meet the rest of your golfing family and discover the joys of watching The Open on the box while eating sardines." Abley walks inside the front door, with golf bag and kitten, closing it behind.

THE END

Thank you very much for reading *Dog Eat Dog*, Book 7 of the series The Cambridge Murder Mysteries.

Titles available in The Cambridge Murder Mystery Series:

Book 1: Poison

Book 2: Cursed

Book 3: Blood Moon

Book 4: A Christmas Mystery

Book 5: Valentine's Day – Kiss of Death

Book 6: Holiday Mystery

Book 7: Dog Eat Dog

Book 8: Coming soon

Short Stories and Novellas in the Cambridge Murder Mystery Series:

Christmas Eve in Grantchester

Green *(available by subscribing to my newsletter)*

Other titles by Charlot King:

Animal Tales: Woof

Animal Tales: Pup

For more information on the other books in the series please do visit www.charlotking.com where you can also subscribe to Charlot King's VIP Club newsletter. If you'd like to follow what Charlot King is up to you can find her on X: @queencharlot or Instagram: @charlot_king_cambridge. And, if you enjoyed this book, Charlot would be so very grateful for a review on Amazon and Goodreads as well as telling all your friends. Much appreciated! Thanks again, and very happy reading.

Printed in Dunstable, United Kingdom

67998725R00240